Readers love
WADE KELLY

My Roommate's a Jock? Well, Crap!

"…a very character driven book… with well drawn characters who made me smile or want to shake them (*ahem, ELLIS) but who made me want to keep reading."

—Hearts on Fire

"Thanks, Wade, for creating this uplifting, although angsty at times, story; it will always have a special place in my heart."

—Rainbow Book Reviews

"…an entertaining story and I can't wait to see what future stories the author has planned."

—Top 2 Bottom Reviews

No! Jocks Don't Date Guys

"Wade took us on a roller coaster of emotions, from comedy, sadness, erotica and elation."

—GGR Reviews

"…a nice story about family, friendships, loyalty, and finding the strength within oneself to push forward."

—Gay Book Reviews

Names Can Never Hurt Me

"Wade Kelly did a fabulous job with this story… I would highly recommend this book, and I double dare you not to love it!"

—The Novel Approach

"It is a beautiful trip that carries the reader along and shatters us with its breathtaking truth. I highly recommend this novel to you."

—Joyfully Jay

By WADE KELLY

Bankers' Hours
Names Can Never Hurt Me

<u>The JOCK Series</u>
My Roommate's a Jock? Well, Crap!
No! Jocks Don't Date Guys

<u>Unconditional Love</u>
When Love Is Not Enough
The Cost of Loving

Published by DREAMSPINNER PRESS
www.dreamspinnerpress.com

Bankers' Hours

Wade Kelly

Published by

DREAMSPINNER PRESS

5032 Capital Circle SW, Suite 2, PMB# 279, Tallahassee, FL 32305-7886 USA
www.dreamspinnerpress.com

Bankers' Hours
© 2016 Wade Kelly.

Cover Art
© 2016 Anne Cain.
annecain.art@gmail.com
Cover content is for illustrative purposes only and any person depicted on the cover is a model.

ISBN: 978-1-63476-973-0
Digital ISBN: 978-1-63476-974-7
Library of Congress Control Number: 2015918431
Published March 2016
v. 1.0

Printed in the United States of America
∞
This paper meets the requirements of
ANSI/NISO Z39.48-1992 (Permanence of Paper).

I would like to dedicate this novel to all my readers who continue to support and encourage me. Some days have not been so easy and your constant outpouring of love really means a lot to me. Chad, Lynn, Kayla, Simon, Jason M., Z., and so many more, you will never know how much I appreciate your kindness.

To beta readers, whom I will refer to as "my pack." (Like in *Teen Wolf*, ha ha.) Taryn, Will, Jeff, Beth, and Mandy, you guys rock!

To Poppy, thank you for believing in me.

And to that random bank guy, Josh, who unwittingly inspired an entire book simply by being adorable. Thank you!

Chapter One

Same Job, New Location, And Starting My Life Over

"WHO'S THE hottie?" a female customer asked my colleague Jessica. She "whispered" her question in a none too hushed voice, as if it wouldn't be overheard four feet away in the adjacent teller cubicle. I kept my back turned, pretending to tidy my work area, because I wasn't sure how to respond. I didn't really know Jessica, since I'd only worked in this branch of the bank for a week. I certainly didn't know the customer who asked the question. I hadn't seen her in the bank before. I did, however, know enough to understand I was the object of the question.

It wasn't the first time I'd been referred to as hot, although I wasn't sure why. I didn't have the muscle I normally associated with hotties. I guess I was okay looking, and I was kind of tall, but after people got to know me, my looks never mattered. I was pedantic, persnickety, and on some days positively puerile. But even though I knew myself pretty well, that didn't mean I knew how to change. I guess I was a little too much for most people. I had very few friends, and I rarely got asked out twice by the same man. Actually, I couldn't remember *ever* being asked out twice.

I almost threw a pity party for myself in my cubicle, but knocked over my pens instead. When they went rolling everywhere, I stopped stewing over being twenty-six and never-been-kissed. It was more rational to think of my virginity as "saving myself," but truth be told, I was a loser and no one had ever liked me enough to kiss me. I picked up my pens, set them back in the container, and moved it to a different location.

"That's Grant," Jessica answered her customer. "He transferred from another branch when it closed."

I made the mistake of glancing over and caught Jessica and the woman staring at me. Was this what penguins felt like? No, they probably didn't notice the humans staring through the glass as they swam at the zoo. Monkeys were more intelligent. Maybe monkeys understood the uneasiness associated with being gawked at. It wasn't merely the staring, or the compliment she'd given me; my problem was in knowing the remarks never stayed on the complimentary level. Once they got past my dark blond hair and blue eyes, people eventually laughed at me for something.

I turned away from Jessica and headed toward the restroom. Once I locked the door, I took out my phone and texted my mother. I didn't live with her—I wasn't completely pathetic—but we texted often.

How are you, Mom?

She texted back quickly, as usual. *I'm fine, Grant, but you're supposed to be working. Stop texting me.*

I'm on a five-minute break.

Stop ducking into the bathroom every time something stresses you out.

Nothing stressed me out.

Did you pee, or did you lock the door and take out your phone?

"Shit," I mumbled. I glanced at my reflection over the sink. "I *am* pathetic." I texted my reply: *I peed.*

Liar. Go back to work. You'll settle in fine. Talk to people, make friends, and then the new branch won't seem so scary.

But it took me a year to make friends with Laura, and then she moved across the country and left me two months before they decided to close my branch. I feel like my life is in turmoil.

Grant, go back to work. Talk to people. Talk to the ones you work with AND the customers. Maybe one of them lives near you and will turn out to be a good friend. You need friends. It isn't healthy to text your mother for every little thing. I need to go. I have a massage in ten minutes.

Fine. I'll try.

Good. You know I love you.

I love you too. Bye. Have fun.

She didn't text back. She probably thought I was ridiculous. I pocketed my phone and washed my hands. I liked clean hands. I also enjoyed the smell of the grapefruit-scented foaming hand soap. Sometimes I washed my hands just so I could smell my fingers while I worked. People may have thought I had an unusually itchy nose, but I only rubbed the tip of it so I could smell the soap scent. I had a thing for smells. Or maybe I had a thing for grapefruit. Either way, I washed my hands repeatedly at work, and it wasn't always to get them clean. I had an antibacterial pump in my cubical, but the alcohol scent made me sneeze. I should probably look for grapefruit-scented antibacterial gel. *Oooh.*

When I got out of the bathroom, I returned to my cubicle to discover a line had formed. Banking customers often came in waves. One minute I could be straightening my deposit slips and reorganizing my ink pad and teller stamp, and the next minute fifty people would show up in the lobby at the same time. I put on a bright smile and called a woman over.

"Good morning," I said to the older lady.

"It's the afternoon," she replied gruffly.

I glanced at my computer screen. "Technically, it's morning until after noon."

She glared and shoved a check my way. "Cash this. I want it all in twenties."

I took the check and flipped it over. "Can you please sign the back, and may I see your driver's license?"

She snatched up a pen and proceeded to scribble her name. "My license is in the car. Surely you can ask one of the other tellers to vouch for me?"

"I could, but then how am I to learn your name for the next time?"

"By memorizing the name on the check," she huffed.

"Well, I'm new here, and it's procedure to ask for a driver's license for all transactions. Even with customers I know, I'm supposed to write the number on the check or at the very least double-check the name."

She ignored me and fussed at my coworker. "Jessica, can you tell this boy who I am, please? I don't have time to follow his—" She paused. "—procedures."

"You can cash Mrs. Caldwell's check, Grant. I know who she is," Jessica said. She didn't seem smug or condescending, but I felt snubbed all the same. I had protocol to follow, and my first customer of the day had sidestepped it.

Rules were rules. Why have them if they could be shirked off willy-nilly? I grinned and nodded politely, but I counted out the twenties begrudgingly. "Will that be all, Mrs. Caldwell?"

"Yes, thank you." The terse woman put the wad of bills in an envelope before I even had the chance to ask if she wanted one and then stormed away.

The next person to walk up to my window made my breath hitch. I swallowed hard. "Ca-can I help you?"

The man grinned, but only with the left side of his mouth. "Yes. I'd like to deposit this in the account at the bottom, and I'd like to withdraw money from a different account. I've written down how I want it back on this slip of paper." He slid a piece of paper to me across the counter. His hands were soiled and greasy. I suddenly wanted to wash mine.

"Oh, okay. I can do that. I'll just need to see—"

"My driver's license," he said, sliding it across the counter. He lifted the corner of his mouth again.

"Oh, thank you," I replied. I was slightly startled by his compliance, and half-nervous over his grin. I took his license and wrote the number on the business check for Carr's Automotive. Tristan Carr. "Is this your company?" I asked.

"Yes. My father started the business, and I took it over before he died. If you ever need an auto mechanic, I'm only fifteen minutes north of here." He winked.

My mouth went dry. Was he flirting or just being friendly? "Um, okay. I bet you often hear jokes about the name."

"Sometimes."

I punched in his account number and clicked the corresponding options on my screen. I ran his checks through the scanning machine and then set them in the correct bin—facing the same direction as the check from Mrs. Caldwell. I handed him the receipt for his deposit. "How did you want that back?" I asked. He glanced down and tapped the counter. "Oh, right, you gave me a list." After I counted out the appropriate amount and zipped it up in his money pouch, I asked, "Is there anything else I can do to—*for*, do *for* you?"

I expected a smirk or a facial tick to reveal he'd heard my slip, but he only paused before answering, "No. Thank you." He glanced at my name placard. "Grant, I'm sure I'll see you again. Perhaps the next time you won't need to ask for my license."

Why would he say that? He couldn't know I was checking him out. I'd barely made eye contact. Maybe he was repeating what the previous woman had said. "Perhaps," I replied. "It was nice to meet Mr. Carr of Carr's Automotive."

He grinned again and stuck out his hand. As I went to shake it, I bumped the container of pens, which I'd set next to the window after I'd knocked it over in its previous location, and sent the pens rolling across the counter and through the window onto the floor at his feet. I was so embarrassed. "Oh God. I'm so sorry." I gathered them up and set them in the container I uprighted.

Mr. Carr bent down, retrieved the pens from the floor, reached through my teller window, and put them into my container. Three were upside down, so I took them out and flipped them over. This time he smirked the smirk I was expecting and said, "Until next time." He picked up one of my business cards from the stack next to my name placard and read it. "Grant Adams," he repeated my name. "It was a pleasure to meet you." He pocketed the card and stuck out his hand again. I *didn't* knock over the pens when I shook it.

His hand was dirty and rough and completely swallowed my tiny palm. "Likewise."

He nodded and walked away, and I glanced at my hands. They felt gritty.

I looked to the next customer and smiled as she stepped up, but I couldn't stop thinking about the feel of his skin touching mine. I rubbed the tip of my nose. My hand had an oddly earthy aroma, which repulsed me almost as much as it intrigued me. I glanced at the unappealing bottle of hand sanitizer and considered it for a second. Which would it be—nauseating alcohol smell that made me sneeze or earthy mechanic smell? The woman set her money and checks on the counter, but I had to excuse myself. "I'm sorry. I need to wash my hands." I took a step backward. "I'll only be a second."

She gave me a questioning look but warily conceded, "Okay."

I dashed to the bathroom, pumped three squirts of foam onto my hands, and lathered thoroughly for twenty seconds. Mr. Carr's hands had appeared greasy, and even though there was no evidence of grease or dirt on mine after he shook it, I still had to wash. I rinsed and dried my hands. I looked down at my open palms, fresh and clean. Sniff. The earthy scent was gone, and for some odd reason, a tiny part of me regretted it. He'd touched me. A man I'd just met had held my hand briefly. I'd introduced myself to countless people before, some of them male, yet Mr. Carr's warmth still lingered inexplicably.

I heard a knock on the door and I jumped. "Grant? How long are you going to be in there?" Lucinda, another teller, asked. I opened the door and she said, "There's a line. I don't want to call Tracy over to help."

Tracy was the bitchy branch manager I'd come to loathe from day one. She was not friendly by any means, but did her job well enough to garner the customers' adoration. Lucinda had been kind enough to warn me about her before I got myself fired over nothing. Tracy was all business, and as long as I did my job to her satisfaction, Lucinda had assured me Tracy would leave me alone. Only I hadn't been here long enough to earn a reputation for excellence. Tracy hadn't worked with me at the other branch, and apparently word of mouth wasn't good enough.

"No," I replied. "I'm coming." I shut the door and returned to my station. The same woman was waiting there. I greeted her with a smile. "Good morning."

"It's 12:10, therefore afternoon," she corrected, handing me her deposit.

"Oh, I'm sorry. Time flies when you're having fun," I joked, hoping she would let my inattention slide.

"Or chatting up a customer," Jessica commented as she walked past me on her way over to the drive-thru window.

I blanched and hoped my customer didn't notice as I entered her account number into the computer. I couldn't believe Jessica would say such a thing with a customer right there. Was this the type of person she was? How was I supposed to make friends with someone who embarrassed me in front of customers?

"That man *did* look dirty," the customer said, oblivious to Jessica's comment or at least ignoring it. "I don't blame you for washing your hands." She slid her license toward me without a prompt.

"Thank you. Although it's not necessary for a deposit."

She smiled. "I come in here several days a week. You're new, so I wanted to make sure you got familiar with my name… and face. It will make it easier the next time."

"True." I read the name. "Ms. Gina Snyder." I chuckled, finding her name ironic. "I have Snyder's pretzels in my lunch today. I don't suppose you own the pretzel company, do you?" Her deposit *was* large, but there had to be hundreds of Snyders in the greater tristate area. Snyder's was a Pennsylvania company.

"*Mrs.*," she stressed. "And not directly, no," she replied, grinning rather mischievously. Her eyes lingered on me, and my face flushed. "I'll see you another day, my dear boy." She winked and turned away.

Two winks in one day. If this was any indication of the type of town Westminster was, I wasn't sure I could handle it. I was used to attention, but this was silly. I wasn't sure I'd last in this branch if every customer flirted with me, although perhaps I was assuming too much. Mr. Carr couldn't possibly have known I was gay, and Mrs. Snyder wouldn't flirt with a guy my age, would she? I was young enough to be her son.

Jessica stepped up behind me and whispered, "Be careful with her. She's a cougar."

I turned around sharply. "What?"

Jessica glanced at the lobby before saying, "She's an aggressive older woman who likes to prey on hot young guys."

There was one person filling out a slip and another waiting to see the manager about opening an account, so I had a minute or two to fuss. I protested, "I'm not hot."

She snorted. "Oh, please. You're hot. I wouldn't normally admit it to your face, but since you're gay, my opinion won't get misconstrued."

"Gay? I'm not…," I started to protest, but the look she gave me screamed, "Stop before I smack you." I glanced around and whispered, "How did you know?"

She snorted again, louder this time. If she'd been drinking something, it would have come out her nose for sure. "I know this is going to sound awful, but you *drip* gay. From your pink shirts—"

"Straight guys wear pink," I blurted.

"To your perfect hair—"

"Straight guys comb their hair."

"And your obsession with cleanliness—"

"Straight guys can be clean."

"There isn't a single thing about you I've seen this week to convince me you're straight. Maybe Mrs. Snyder can overlook your less-than-straight qualities because she wants to bag you, but I pegged you from day one. I'm just saying… be careful and stop flirting with the customers."

"I'm not." Besides the fact her assessment of me was offensive, I didn't flirt. *Did I?*

"Oh, right," she laughed. "Then you better control your blushing, because women like Mrs. Snyder will eat you alive, and guys like Mr. Carr will punch the shit out of you. I saw him at a Papa Joe's once. He got off his motorcycle and walked across the parking lot like he owned the place. It scared the crap out of me. He could be a police officer, or a general of an army. Believe me, you don't want to mess with him."

I couldn't imagine Mr. Carr punching me. He'd seemed very nice. His half smile intrigued me—it made me think of trouble brewing under the surface. He certainly had that bad-boy quality I'd always appreciated from afar. "I don't know what you're talking about. He didn't seem dangerous to me. Besides, I'm not flirting with anyone, and I don't blush easily."

"The hell you don't. Just watch yourself, or Tracy will haul you into her office and rip you a new one. She's all about policy, and dating customers is frowned upon."

We were only standing in my cubicle, but as she hissed at me so intensely, she might as well have yelled, I felt as though she'd shoved me into a corner with her finger pointed in my face. "Okay, okay. Jeez. I haven't done anything."

Her expression changed. "I'm sorry, Grant. I like you. I don't want to see you get fired or hurt. You seem very sweet, albeit a bit naive."

She had me there. My cheeks heated from embarrassment.

"See, you're blushing again." She reached up and touched my arm as I clapped my hands over my cheeks. "I'm sorry I commented about chatting up the customers. I think it was my way of challenging what I'd seen. Part of me hoped it wasn't true. You're seriously cute, Grant. Being gay would ruin my chances."

I sighed. "You're right, I'm gay."

"Then why be so defensive about it?"

"I guess because you deconstructed my sexuality based on stereotypes. I don't like labels and definitions. I think there are too many people out there who don't fit into a category. Some get offended."

"But yours are obvious." She looked over my shoulder. "Sorry. Customers. I gotta go." Jessica patted my arm and waved the customer in line to head over to her window.

I waved one over as well. I greeted the older man, saying, "Good afternoon."

I WENT home after my shift and gazed at myself in the mirror of my dresser. Was I really stereotypical? I liked pastel shirts, and I didn't see a reason to wear white or black just to blend in. I undid my pink-and-white striped tie and pulled it from around my neck. I hung it on the tie organizer in my closet and unbuttoned my shirt. My pasty white skin sagged in my reflection. I flexed. The lack of muscle made my self-image worse. I was scrawny and awkward, and my body wasn't one guys like Tristan Carr desired, or any guy for that matter. Even with the .02 percent chance Tristan was gay, I highly doubted I had anything he'd find attractive once he took his eyes off my okay-I-admit-it's-pretty face. In my suit and tie,

I had the hot-young-executive appearance in my favor. Out of the suit, I was a pathetic twenty-six-year-old virgin with zero appeal.

I took off my trousers and hung them up, then pushed my underwear down and reassessed. My sad little penis hung to the left. "Negative twenty appeal." I rubbed my crotch and scratched my patch of blond hair. "This poor thing will shrivel and fall off before I find a guy to suck it."

Heavyhearted, I took a shower and put on my pajamas before heating up leftovers.

After I had washed my plate and put it away, my phone rang. I could tell it was my best friend, Mel, by the ringtone. His jingle was different from my mother's.

"Hello," I answered.

"Hey. How's your first week been?" he asked.

I met Mel Tersiguel on my first day of work right out of college. I had graduated with an accounting degree, but I felt the need to ease my way into the work world after so many years in school. Some guys couldn't wait to break free of their parents, but I hadn't been one of them. In fact, it had taken me three years after college simply to move into my own place. Mel had applauded me for my independence, although I still waffled about the decision a year later.

"Fine, I guess," I answered.

"Hmm, you don't sound fine. What happened?"

"Nothing, I guess. Do you think I'm flamboyant?" I asked.

"Wow. Where did that question come from?"

I stretched out on the sofa and pulled the afghan off the back of it to cover my legs. It was the middle of September and I wasn't very warm natured to begin with, so any slight drop in temperature had me covering up. I sighed into the receiver. "I don't know. A girl at work said she knew I was gay from the first day. I've only been there five days."

"So? You've never denied it, have you?"

"No."

"You were as up-front with me as I was with you. Remember our first lunch?" he asked, his voice conveying his happiness so well I could almost picture the smile on his face.

"Yeah, I remember. But it was the way she said it and based her assumption on my clothes and mannerisms."

"Ah! Stereotyping. You've always hated that, haven't you?" Mel asked, but I knew it was rhetorical.

"Mostly since meeting you. I guess I don't want to admit my appearance isn't more neutral. But you didn't answer my question: am I flamboyantly gay?"

"Of course not. But it's more than your Easter egg colored wardrobe, Grant. When a guy… for example, you… ogles another guy's ass as often as I've seen you do, then that guy's gay, and it doesn't matter what color his shirts are or how much his hips sway when he walks."

"My hips do not sway!" I protested.

Mel snickered. "Okay, they don't sway… *much*, but the way you openly check guys out is obvious."

"I haven't done that at the bank, I don't think."

"Just be careful, Grant. Carroll County is a way more conservative part of Maryland than Howard County. You don't want to piss off some old-school farmer, or a Harley-Davidson–loving auto mechanic." I choked and pulled the phone away from my mouth to clear my throat. When I brought the phone back up to my ear, I heard Mel laughing. "Oh, wow. Did you ogle a farmer? You slut!"

"Oh my God, Mel. Don't make this harder than it already is," I whined.

His tone changed right away. "I'm sorry. I know relationships are hard for you. I didn't mean to poke fun."

"I'd almost prefer being a slut to being alone. I hate it. Every night I come home to an empty house. Maybe I should move back in with my mother."

"Grant," he warned.

"She's all alone. She's got that stupid cat I'm allergic to, but I could take shots."

"Grant, don't."

"But, Mel!"

"No buts. Moving out last year was the best thing you've done for yourself. And if you *do* meet a hot farmer, then at least you don't have to explain why you're still living with your mother."

"I could tell him she's sick," I countered.

"But she's not. Your mother is perfectly healthy and active. There is no reason that doesn't make you sound pitiful. You're a big boy. You can take care of yourself."

"You're right. So do you think I'm attractive?" I asked, even though we'd covered the answer before.

"Yes, you know you are. But I've told you before, I'm attracted to girls, so your looks don't matter to me either way."

"I know. But do you think my looks would be enough for an auto mechanic?"

"You know I was only joking about the auto mechanic, right? There *are* other professions in Carroll County."

"Oh, I know. I'm asking because there was a guy who came in today who's an auto mechanic."

"And?"

"And he's hot," I whined.

"Oooh, do tell." I appreciated his interest. Mel had egged me on for details about all three guys I'd been interested in since we'd met. And he'd been there to support me after all three had bombed after one date. He was used to my crushes and hadn't discouraged me from dreaming.

I drew my knees up and tucked my afghan under my feet, positioning myself for the juicy details I was about to spill. "Okay, he's built like a tank. Taller than me, and he has more muscle than the bodybuilder guy we used to make up stories about last year."

"Mr. Goodwin?"

"Yeah."

His voice went up two octaves. "Oh my gosh! How do you know? Was this guy wearing a tank top or something?"

"No. He had on a uniform and coveralls, but his sleeves were rolled up to his elbows, and his forearms were bigger than my biceps."

"Niiice. What else? Hair, eyes, height, name?"

"His name's Tristan Carr."

Mel giggled. "And he's an auto mechanic? I bet that's a drag."

"Yeah. I guess. I thought it was amusing. Anyway, I didn't look directly into his eyes long enough to notice the color." I had wanted to look, but I'd been too nervous.

"And you say he's taller than you? *Jeez.* You're six foot, Grant."

"I know, right? This guy has to be six four, and I've never seen shoulders that wide."

"Wow. I'll seem like a midget."

"You aren't a midget."

"I said *seeeem.* I know other guys shorter than me, but compared to six foot four, my five five is going to *seeeem* like I'm a midget."

"*Okaaaay*," I mocked his mocking tone for mocking me, and then we both laughed.

"What color's his hair?"

"Don't know. His head's shaved."

"Fair enough. I've seen some hot bald guys. So what's your opinion? Do you wish he had hair, or is he fine without it?"

"Oh, absolutely fine without it. He's very tan and sexy. Possibly cover-model material for a biker magazine."

"Good, but I've got a question for you. How clean are his hands? I know how you are."

My heart sank. I had been fine talking about how nice Mr. Carr looked until Mel brought up his hands. "Well, they looked like they were covered in grease. He shook my hand and they didn't feel greasy, but I still had to wash my hands after he left. His hands were rough and huge, and stained black around his fingernails."

"That's typical. When I work on my car, I get oil and grease on my hands, and sometimes it takes days to come off. Imagine working on cars every day. I bet his hands were clean, but you couldn't tell."

"You're probably right, although my hand *did* have an odd scent on it after he shook it."

"Odd good or odd bad?"

I knew why he'd asked. Mel was one of the few people in my life who understood where my hand-washing fetish came from. I said, "The jury is still holding session over that one. The scent was new to me, and I paused before I bolted for the bathroom."

"Interesting. Usually you react right away."

"I know."

"Maybe it was because the smell came off a really hot guy?" Mel goaded.

"Stop. He's probably straight anyway, so speculating over things that would unnerve me is unnecessary—good and bad smells included. I think he was just being nice because I'm the new guy."

"Maybe. But you better promise to call me if he turns out to be gay. I want to know if this *odd scent* is particular to his hands or found on other parts of his body."

I chuckled. "You're so incorrigible." Mel was a great friend, but I needed to change the subject. "So, how about you? Are things progressing with you and that girl you saw working at the chicken place?"

"Boston Market," he corrected. "And nah, I'm still hesitant about saying hello, let alone anything else. What if she doesn't accept me? I think I'll wait."

"Really? You're not even going to take a chance? You could start with going there to eat every week and see if she notices."

"Maybe, but you know I want to wait to date until my scars heal and I figure out my next step in the process. I want to feel more secure about myself before I face my fear of rejection, especially from a girl as pretty as Cindy."

"Mel, you know I love you, but just like you pushed me toward independence, I need to push you a little toward dating."

"I know. Just… can you keep your fingers crossed for me? I'll try going in for lunch and see if she looks at me. Okay?"

I nodded, but then realized he couldn't see me. "Yes, of course. I'm here for you."

"Thanks. I'm here for you too. And if Mr. Carr, the auto mechanic, turns out to be gay, I'll be here for advice on how *not* to screw it up. The next guy you go out with will be *the one*, I'm sure of it!"

"I hope so. My internal clock is ticking."

"Grant, you're twenty-six, not fifty-six. You'll find the right guy to marry and settle down with. I promise."

I sighed.

We said our good-byes, and I set my phone on the end table. I hoped Mel was right. I was tired of being alone. There had to be a guy out there who would tolerate my need to iron my boxers and group my shirts according to color. Other people *had* to despise it when their food touched on their plate, right? Or when restrooms only had air-drying machines instead of paper towels? I was not a freak. I was a somewhat nice-looking gay man cursed with an unusual personality that repelled men. I was special. I would find someone eventually who appreciated my quirks.

I went to bed thinking about what my second week of work would be like. This weekend I would do laundry and clean my three-room house. On Monday I could worry about the cougar woman Jessica had warned me about, and the auto mechanic who'd winked at me for no apparent reason. Because even if he *was* gay, he'd never want to take me to bed, so I was better off playing it cool and being his friend.

Friends. My mother had told me I needed to make some.

Chapter Two

Making Friends, Moving On, And That Squishy Feeling In Your Belly When A Guy Says Your Name

HIS SWEATY body pressed me against the wall. I felt a sting as he sucked on my neck. He lifted me off my feet and helped me wrap my legs around his waist. His long, hard shaft ran under my balls and pulsed with need. I gasped and cried out….

"Tristan!" I cried, bolting upright in bed. I looked around at my empty, dark room. "Oh, jeez." I flopped back down on my pillow and panted in my residual dream euphoria. That was the most vivid dream I'd ever had.

AT WORK on Monday, I decided it was time to get to know the people around me. Sure, I knew most of their names, but I didn't know them like I had known the people at the other branch. I had worked there for four years. It wasn't like making friends was difficult, but as I'd gotten older it seemed more tedious. I guess in high school, making friends was a given. When you saw the same people day after day, it made sense. In college, the group of people I hung with had gradually diminished. At the bank, those people in my daily life had shrunk to a smaller group that still fed my relational needs. And then my workplace sanctuary had closed.

When forced to relocate, it puts relationships to the test. Were they really my friends, or was it a nominal thing because we worked together every day? Well, so far it appeared to have been nominal, because the only person I talked to consistently was Mel. I rang Jenny and Mary, but they sounded busy making new friends and getting settled in their new positions.

I needed to move on like my friend Laura had the day she left. I hadn't heard from her in months. Again, our friendship must have only been nominal. When would I make friends with someone who wanted to brush our dentures together or play chess in the park after we retired? I didn't want that permanent fixture in my life to be my mother. How depressing.

Jessica handed a receipt to her customer, and when that woman left, I attempted a conversation over the little half wall that separated our cubicles, as I referred to them. "So, Jessica, how long have you worked at this branch?"

"Two years. I was at a different bank in Baltimore, and when this bank bought them out, they relocated me. I like Westminster, so it's been good. I had another friend, though, who got transferred to an area she hated and ended up quitting the bank. She works at Safeway now."

"I guess banks taking over other banks is typical."

"Yeah, it seems so."

"All my friends got relocated when a branch closed in Columbia," I explained. I noticed bits of masking tape stuck to the top of my cubicle and scraped at it with my nail.

"How did you end up here? Columbia is like an hour south. Did they give you a choice?" she asked.

I was happy Monday started out slow, because last week had been a challenge to keep up. During this lull I could chat briefly without interruptions. "There were twenty employees who needed to find jobs, and twelve positions at other branches. Some bigwig sat us down individually and gave us a choice. Mine was here or Bethesda."

"Oh, I like here better than Bethesda." Jessica had one of those lilting soprano voices I liked. I could picture her singing "Whistle While You Work" alongside Snow White while dancing around the bank in an effort to help me see how much fun working here could be.

"I've never been there, but my mother lives closer to Westminster, so it made the choice obvious."

"Did you have to move, or are you still living in Howard County?" Jessica glanced up when a person walked through the front doors and headed over to the side table to fill out a slip.

"I moved. I was renting a room from someone, and I really didn't like it anyway. When I told my mother I was considering moving to

Westminster to be close to work, she found me a house for rent. She knows the woman who owns it. It's small, but I have it all to myself for less rent than I paid at my old place."

"That's cool. Are you close to your mother?" she asked innocently.

"Yeah," I said, not wanting to divulge the fact that I had lived with my mother until last year.

"What about your dad?"

"He died in a car accident six years ago." It was not a memory I enjoyed, but it was less painful to talk about as time went on.

She frowned. "I'm sorry. Are you an only child?"

"Yes. Probably why I'm close to my mother. It's only the two of us. She had me later in life, and most of my relatives are dead."

"How depressing," Jessica commented before turning to the man who had finished filling out his slip. She changed her tone immediately. "Good morning. Can I help you?" I supposed it was like that for customer service employees. You could be all serious and deep one second, but in the next you had to flip the switch back to "pleasant and cheerful." It was exhausting.

Two more people came in, and I knew our brief chat session would have to wait for a while. Maybe I hadn't found out much about Jessica, but I felt comfortable answering her questions about me. I did a deposit for one gentleman and cashed a check for someone else, but when I glanced up to call over the next person in line, my breath hitched the same as it had the first time I'd seen him. Tristan Carr was walking through the front door. His eyes caught mine, but I couldn't stare when I had someone else to take care of.

"Good morning sir," I greeted an older man with a smile. The whole time I was talking to him about IRAs, I was peripherally aware of the auto mechanic in line. Would I be finished in time to help Mr. Carr? As soon as I said, "I hope you have a nice day," to my customer, I heard Jessica call Mr. Carr over to *her* window.

Our eyes met again briefly as he moved from the front of the line to her window and my customer walked away. It was a huge disappointment, but if he'd been in on Friday and was back again today, then there was a good chance he did business here often. Maybe the next time I would be able to service his needs.

I giggled to myself as I punched in the account number for my next customer. I was glad when she didn't comment, because I could not explain my internal fantasies about servicing the auto mechanic. If he needed a lube job, I was more than happy to assist. I giggled again.

"Thank you, Mrs. Smith. Have a nice day," I said. She walked away, and the next customer walked up.

It was the cougar from Friday. "You look chipper this morning," she commented.

I guess she had seen me snickering to myself. "Yes, I suppose I am. How about you, Mrs. Snyder?" I asked politely, taking her deposit.

"I'm well, thank you. Did you have a good weekend?" Her eyes on me felt strange. I think it was the way she *didn't* blink.

"Yes. I painted part of my kitchen." Not that she needed to know the details of my life, but that wasn't revealing. Painting was a task, not personal.

"What color?" she asked.

"It's called Salmon Sunset. I thought it seemed cheery."

She smirked. "You know, the color of one's kitchen says a lot about a person. It's the room we spend most of our lives in, other than the bedroom."

I handed her the receipt. "Oh? Then what does that color say about me?" I was slightly afraid to ask, but I couldn't stop the question from slipping out.

She smirked again. "I think it says you're… *happy* and carefree." She put her receipt in her purse and winked as she walked away.

The hair stood up on the back of my neck. Happy and carefree sounded like code words for "gay." Did she know, or was she toying with me? Or both?

I straightened my deposit slips and aligned my container of pens with the edge of the window, took a deep breath to cleanse me of Mrs. Snyder's icky vibes, and then called over the next customer.

My breath hitched… *again*. It was Tristan Carr. Good God, I'd never had such trouble breathing normally before, and my tongue was plastered to the roof of my mouth. Where was a glass of water when I needed one?

I had to clear my throat. "C-can I help you, Mr. Carr?" I asked as steadily as I could. This time I kept eye contact as long as my jittering nerves could stand. His eyes were blue. Dark blue compared to my sky blue.

"You remembered my name," he commented.

"You were just here on Friday. Remembering for a couple days isn't a challenge."

He nodded slightly.

"Weren't you just in here? Jessica helped you." I pointed out. "Did you forget something?"

"As a matter of fact, I did. I need change for my cash box." He took a check out of his pocket and put it on the counter. "May I borrow your pen?"

"By all means," I said, gesturing to the container full at his left.

"I find it interesting that you have a plethora of pens when other tellers have one pen lying in their windows." He filled out the slip and signed it.

"I found a single pen seems to walk off. If I have a bunch, they tend to stick together longer."

"Then I guess he needs to join his friends," Mr. Carr said, smirking. Only, his smirk lacked Mrs. Snyder's smugness. His was more of a whimsical grin. He slid the check to me and deposited the pen into the container… *upside down.*

I was not about to right the situation in front of him. It could wait. I might seem anal, and not in the way I liked to think about that term. "Did you want this back any certain way?"

"Four rolls of quarters, a roll of dimes, a roll of pennies, and the rest in ones."

"Okay," I said. I punched in the numbers and opened my drawer. "I only have one roll of quarters for some strange reason. If you'll excuse me, I'll just go grab a few more." I locked my drawer and went to the vault, got my quarters and logged the exchange properly, and returned to Mr. Carr.

After I put the quarters in the drawer and left four rolls out for Mr. Carr, I noticed *three* pens were upside down. That couldn't be right. I blinked and shook off my confusion when Mr. Carr asked, "Is there something wrong?"

I cleared my throat one more time. "What? Um, no. Nothing wrong. Why do you ask?"

"You spaced out for a second as if you were thinking about something."

I couldn't very well explain that my pens weren't nestled correctly. I could fix it after he'd gone. "No. Everything's fine. Do you need anything else?" My hands were shaking, and I wasn't certain whether it was because of the pens or the guy. Mr. Carr made me self-conscious, but those pens wouldn't write properly if the ink ran to the top and not the tip. I could not keep my eyes from darting to the container as I strained to pay attention to my customer.

"I suppose not," he said.

"Then I hope you have a nice day, Mr. Carr," I commented, thinking it was the end of our exchange and I could remedy the situation.

"Tristan," he said.

I blinked. His voice was gentle and his gaze soft. Unexpected heat rolled down my chest and swirled in the pit of my stomach, and suddenly the pens weren't as important as his attention. "Tristan," I affirmed.

He nodded slightly and smiled as he walked away.

My legs nearly gave out, and I steadied myself. I swallowed hard and grabbed a few deposit slips to fan my face. Jessica turned to look at me and asked, "What's wrong with you?"

"Oh, nothing," I said, setting the deposit slips down and flipping the three pens back over. If I was supposed to act businesslike at work, then the customers needed to stop turning me on with a glance.

I HAD an hour for lunch, so I sat in the break room and removed my peanut butter and jelly sandwich from my paper bag. It seemed like a lunch for ten-year-olds, but I didn't exactly make a load of money, and I preferred spending it on redecorating my new place and then maybe on clothes. I could handle cheap lunches.

Mel and I used to eat lunch together, so sometimes we'd go out, but since I'd been eating alone this past week, my pathetic sandwich choices would have to suffice. Maybe I could splurge once a week and eat at a local restaurant, if I could find someone to go with me. I didn't want to be one of those sad guys who dined alone.

My phone buzzed. *How are you, dear?*

I had done well over the weekend. I'd only texted my mother twice. *Fine,* I replied. *Working here has been seamless so far. It's the same computer system and setup, so I've been happy with it. And I like Westminster, btw. :)*

Good. Have you made any new friends?

Sort of. I'm working up to personal information with a girl named Jessica. She thinks I'm cute, knows I'm gay, and told me to stop flirting with the customers.

Flirting? That doesn't sound like you. Unless you've learned to loosen up since I last saw you.

Mother! How many times do I have to tell you I'm not uptight?

Oh, really?

I huffed. No one was in the break room to sympathize with me. Seconds ticked. Was I really uptight? I texted back: *Fine. You win. I'm uptight and repressed.*

Just remember you were the one to use the word repressed—not me.

I made a face, fake-laughed, and stuck out my tongue at my phone as if I was making fun of her behind her back. It irked me how well she knew me. *I'll admit I blushed, but I swear it was only because of this one guy that came in.* I probably shouldn't have mentioned him, but I never had learned how to keep my mouth shut when talking to my mother. It was just her and me, so I guess normal filters had gotten overlooked.

Oh? What guy?

An auto mechanic who owns his own shop. He is very... nice looking. I downplayed my assessment. I thought he was fucking hot, but I didn't feel the need to say it like that to her. I suppose I did filter things with my mom… sometimes.

Hmm. A business owner sounds promising. Only, be careful not to make the same mistake as last time. Remember what happened with that flower shop owner. Best to find out if he's married first.

She had to remind me! *I will. Next time I'll check for a wedding ring. TTYL.*

I ended the conversation before she brought up all the gory details. The shop owner, Raymond, was probably the closest I'd gotten to an actual boyfriend, even though we'd never kissed and one date had been enough. We'd flirted at the bank for several weeks, and when he finally asked me out, I'd jumped at the chance. But then, while on our date, his wife showed up and made a scene. On top of the obvious reasons she'd caused a scene, she hadn't known he was gay. I'd felt extremely small, sitting at the candlelit table while they yelled at one another.

You'd think I would have been the one to end it, but he beat me to the punch, saying, "I just don't think I'm ready for a relationship yet." Understatement of the year! At least with Raymond, the reason had been legitimate given the display over dinner. That had been eight months ago.

Westminster, though, was a clean slate. I could start over. People in this town didn't know me. I could be as outgoing and congenial as I wanted. I could like sports or skydiving. I could flirt and ask a guy out and have wild sex in the parking lot. I could be or do anything!

My mother texted again: *Be careful.*

My high hopes came crashing to the ground. I wasn't all those things I thought I could be. I was Grant Adams, magnet for sob stories and losers.

My special guy was out there—he had to be. I believed there was someone perfect for everyone. Sometimes people went their entire lives never finding their soul mate, but I was not losing hope I'd find mine. My Prince Charming was out there!

Maybe he'd like fixing cars and have dark blue eyes.

I shivered. It was too idealistic to be real. My fantasies always promoted heartache. If I never indulged myself, I wouldn't be so let down.

I cleaned up from lunch and headed back out to my window.

THE REST of the day went rather slow, so the manager, Tracy, showed me how to search customer accounts for fraudulent activity. I'd done it before, yet she insisted she show me her way. I found it interesting how certain types of transactions could be indicators of money laundering and other illegal activities, as well as fraud, so her reiteration of instructions I already knew didn't bother me. I let her talk.

I checked my watch. Twenty minutes to go. Working in the other branch hadn't been this boring. It was always busy from open to close. Columbia had more than five times the population of Westminster, and it showed.

"Do you have any hobbies?" Jessica asked. I guessed she was bored too.

"Not much. I'm not that interesting."

"Oh, I bet you are. I like to bake. I make cinnamon toffee cookies that are so good."

I grinned. "They sound amazing. I don't bake very often. I guess I could, and I do like cupcakes, but I live alone so I'd have to eat all of whatever I made."

"Sounds lonely."

"Sometimes. I've only lived in Westminster since the end of August. I'm sure as I make friends with people I'll bake things and have dinner parties." I suggested it, but it had never happened while I lived alone in Columbia. I had had friends, but the four of us had never sat around eating filet mignon and drinking red wine. We played video games and ate Cheetos. I probably wasn't sophisticated enough to throw a dinner party.

"I'll be your friend," she suggested with a smile, sitting up straight and proud. "Maybe we could plan a party for the bank employees around Christmas time."

I smiled back. She seemed nice. Jessica had pretty blonde hair and a bright smile. Sure, she'd made that comment about me flirting and stuff, but maybe it was true. Maybe Jessica wasn't being mean, only helpful. I replied, "That would be nice."

OUR CONVERSATIONS continued all week. I found out she liked chick flicks and sushi, while divulging my penchant for knitting and baseball. I'd never play baseball professionally, but after playing in high school, I still enjoyed watching it. Moreover, the tight baseball pants showed off the players' asses. Yup, I liked baseball.

Friday was busy again, just how I liked it. A busy day went by faster. Some tellers liked breaks in between to catch a breath, but constant work had never bothered me. This was a nine-to-five job, for the most part. I could rest after work. I remembered my dad working from five in the morning to six thirty in the evening every day of the week and some Saturdays, and he had never complained. Work was work. I certainly had no room to complain about bankers' hours when my days were normally eight hours long.

When Tristan Carr appeared in the line, my heart sped up, but at least I hadn't gasped for breath this time. His presence was becoming familiar. Lucinda and I were free at the same time, and we both waved him over. He glanced from me to her and then back again. He chose me, and I jumped for joy inside my unemotional facade.

I smiled and played it casual. "How are you today, Tristan?" He *had* given me permission to call him by his first name. I'd never done that with a customer before. For years I had known my customers' first names yet only called them by their surnames because it had been proper and businesslike. With Tristan Carr, I liked the way his eyes softened when I said his name.

"I'm well, Grant. How about you?"

My insides quivered. He said my name so naturally, so pleasantly. He'd used it before, but this time my ears sent a signal straight to my groin. His voice made me weak and warm. "I'm good." I kept my answer short and grabbed his stack of checks and deposit slips. I punched in the numbers and ran the checks through the check-scanning machine to the right of my window.

"Are you all right?" he asked, giving me a concerned look.

"What? Yes, of course. Everything's fine." His stack of money, however, needed sorting. The bills were upside-down and backward. It looked as though he'd dropped the stack on the way in and only scooped it up before making it over to my window. What a mess.

"You just looked, I don't know, bothered about something."

How could he read me that easily? Was I transparent, or was he psychic? "No," I told him. I picked up a check that didn't seem to go with the rest. "Do you want to cash this, or did you miss it on the deposit slip?"

"Cash it, please."

I did and counted it back. I struggled to make eye contact, as I had that very first day. His eyes and voice certainly did something to me, and I wouldn't be able to stand it if he continued to gaze at me so attentively. Was he studying me? Did he like taking in details, or was he amused by how nervous I got? Did he feel the same sexual tension, stretching the air between us so thin I could hardly breathe? He'd only been in a few times, but I could have sworn there was something unspoken going on between us.

"You're wearing glasses," he stated, picking up on a detail only Jessica had noticed today.

"Yes. Sometimes I like wearing my glasses. They go with my tie."

Tristan took the bills and opened his wallet. "Yes. I'd say the black frames pick up the black in your tie very nicely. I like them." As he stuffed his money in, a few business cards fell out and flew over to me.

I picked them up. One wasn't a card, but a picture. "Aww, who's this?" I asked, handing back the cards.

He smiled at the picture. "My daughter, Claire. She hates this picture," he chuckled. "She's probably eight here."

Daughter? Oh fuck me, he's straight. I'd never been so disappointed, but the info was probably for the best. If I had gotten this worked up over him in a week, then it was better than finding out he was gay and destroying our friendship with a date. The first date always spelled doomsday for me. *Tristan Carr is straight,* I told myself. Maybe he'd turn out to be a really good friend. My hormones could calm down. Although I'd probably cry about it a little after I got home, for now I could relax and enjoy the conversation.

"How old is she now?"

"Fifteen. It's a challenge having a teenager, but I like our relationship. She's old enough to have a semiadult conversation and young enough that she doesn't feel embarrassed to talk to me. I know our relationship will change soon, and she'll stop walking next to me in the mall and start wanting to pretend I'm not there when her friends are around, but for now it's great."

Tristan seemed so happy talking about his daughter. I think his voice was even more soothing now than when he made small talk. Saying my name had given me chills, but his relaxed tone made my anxiety lessen. I bet I could plop down on my stool and listen to him go on for hours about Claire. He had such a lovely voice. I sighed to myself.

"She sounds great." No ring—he was probably a single dad. That had to be tough, but at least he liked his kid.

He looked at me. "I'm sorry. I don't mean to bore you."

"You're not. I like kids. Maybe one day I'll have my own." *If I adopt or find a surrogate.* "Feel free to talk about her anytime. I like how relaxed you are right now."

His eye twitched. He regarded me softly, and slowly lifted the corner of his mouth. "I will. I'll have to find a current picture and show you. If Claire knew I'd shown you this one, she'd probably die."

I snickered. "That sounds like a teenage girl." I didn't know that much about teenage girls, but the comment fit the topic. I went with it. "Don't forget these." I handed him his deposit receipts. "I guess I'll see you another day."

He nodded. "I guess so. Do you have big plans for the weekend?"

"I'm going to finish painting my kitchen, and I was thinking of joining a gym." I replied so casually I almost didn't recognize myself. Knowing he was straight made me loosen up, I guessed. Why be tense and awkward when there was no prospect of something beyond friendship? He was just a guy I could talk to. *I can. I can really talk to this guy.* The revelation was freeing.

His expression brightened. "A gym, really?"

His question irked me for no reason. "Yes, I can join a gym. I might not be built like you, but I can lift weights the same as any guy."

He was taken aback. "I didn't mean anything by it, Grant. I was merely surprised, but in a good way, I assure you. We have that in common. I go to a gym myself. I find it relaxing. It's nice not having to think about anything. A good hard sweat is cleansing for the body."

I'd upset him, and that didn't go over well with my need to hear his soothing voice. His apologetic voice made me feel bad for jumping to conclusions. "I'm sorry. I guess I'm used to people giving me a hard time about everything. Ever since I came out, it's felt like an uphill battle."

His eye twitched again. "Came out? As in… out of the closet?"

My synapses misfired. "Huh, what?" I blinked.

"You just said 'since you came out,' and I wondered if you meant you're gay."

Panic, shock, nerves frazzling. He'd made me feel so comfortable chitchatting that I'd come out inadvertently. *Oh, shit.* I glanced over at Jessica, only she wasn't at her station. She was twenty feet away talking to Tracy by her office door.

I looked the other way, and Tristan said, "No one heard you, Grant. You're fine."

I heaved a sigh. "Oh, good." I swallowed. Two more breaths and I felt calmer. "It's not like I've hidden being gay, but saying it out loud to someone I barely know—no offense—freaked me out a little."

"A little?" he chuckled. "You all but panicked. You turned white as a sheet."

I should have gotten angry with him for making fun of me, but I just couldn't. Something in his tone and his smile overrode that option. "Thanks," I said sarcastically. Then I chuckled. Tristan really did make me feel calm. I liked him, and not just in a wet dream sort of way. He was nice. It was better that he was straight and we only saw each other for ten minutes a week at the bank. In time, maybe he'd be as good a friend as Mel. Most likely he lived close, and it was healthy for me to have more friends who weren't my mother.

"Anytime," he said, grinning. "Have a good weekend, Grant. I'll probably see you Monday." This time when he winked as he walked off, I didn't take it to mean anything untoward. He was simply a friendly guy who apparently had no qualms about my sexuality.

Yeah, he'd make a nice friend.

Chapter Three

The Gym, My Fears, And Making Friends With A Straight Guy

I'D CHECKED out a few gyms in my area, but none of them had suited me. I was looking for a family environment: A place where I could display my weaknesses. A place where I would not be judged. I wanted machines and free weights, but not the commercialized chain gym that advertised bodybuilders and muscle-bound freak shows. My body didn't need assistance to feel inadequate. If I could find a place where overweight housewives and scrawny guys like me went, then I'd be happy.

The Westminster Family Center was my next stop of the day.

As soon as I walked up to the counter, a mother and her teenage daughter came out with gym bags on their shoulders and freshly washed hair. I assumed the relation because they looked very similar, and their hair was too wet to be from sweat. Their presence in this gym, though, made me think I'd found the right place. I inquired at the counter about membership details and asked for a tour. The tour did the trick.

All the same equipment as those bigger gyms, but only a few of each machine—not twelve treadmills lined up next to sixteen stationary bikes. The walls weren't even lined with mirrors. Only one wall had mirrors, so if I didn't want to see how bad my form was I didn't have to look. This place was heaven.

I filled out the paperwork, scanned my nifty card, and entered my new gym.

Of course, I didn't actually know how to use most of the machines. I felt slightly stupid looking at the pins and weights and levers, but not stupid enough to ask for help. I thought I'd give it a little time. Maybe by watching other people I'd be able to suss it out. I managed the treadmill for twenty minutes. That wasn't bad. I figured the next time I'd bring my iPod so I'd be entertained while I walked.

When I moved over to the ab machine and took too long studying the diagram on how to adjust the weights, I heard a familiar voice ask if I needed help. I turned and got the shock of my life. "Tristan?"

"Grant! Wow, what a surprise." He lost his brief elation when I didn't answer back. "Grant? Did you hear me?" he asked, waving his hands in front of my face.

I was having one of those out-of-body experiences where I could see myself immobile and blankly catatonic. I knew I was staring, but no matter how much I wanted to, I couldn't blink for several seconds.

When I found my ability to respond, I apologized, "I'm sorry."

"I didn't mean to creep on you or anything. I saw you fiddling with the machine, and I thought I could help. I didn't realize it was you until you turned around. I swear."

"W-what are you doing here?" Because I couldn't manage a hello. I'd had another supersexy dream about him again last night and figured it would take a while for my brain to catch up to the notion we were just friends. Mere friends didn't daydream and jack off in the shower thinking about their other friends. That was probably frowned upon. Friends also didn't drool over what *could* be under their friend's coveralls during the day, and then practically groan aloud when they could see their imagination had greatly underestimated. Unfortunately, I *was* that friend, as the object of my fantasies stood in front of me wearing shorts and a loose tank top.

Oh, holy fuck. How do I look him in the eyes now, when I can see the hair on his chest and all I want to do is touch him?

He smirked. Apparently he thought I was amusing and not at all rude. *Good.* He explained, "I told you I go to a gym. I go to *this* gym."

"Oh."

He squinted his eyes slightly. "Grant, if my being here bothers you, I can go back to doing flies and pretend I didn't see you. I know it's weird running into people you're used to seeing in a different context. The first time I saw my accountant here with some friends playing basketball, I swear my chin hit the floor. I'd never seen him in anything but a suit. I promise you, this is a coincidence. I'm not stalking you. You can ask the front desk. I'm here every Saturday at nine, and usually two mornings a week."

"But… w-why don't you go to Gold's Gym or something? Why here?" I was still in shock. I *should* have stood and politely shaken his hand or something. I *should* have at least said hello and thanked him for asking to help me. But nooo. My mouth went dry, and I felt trapped. If Tristan went to this gym, then I'd have to go on different days or reconsider my membership. I wasn't ready to see him dressed so casually and *not* get hard. All the muscles I could see were huge, and my natural inclination to run my fingers over them was stronger than my willpower to make my hard-on stand down. I didn't know how to be polite in the face of someone who fit all my criteria for the perfect man. Life was so fucking unfair!

His expression darkened. "Wow. You aren't at all like I thought. You seemed cool at the bank, but…." Tristan took a step back.

He's straight. He's straight. He's straight. Will the attraction away. Little Adams, go stand in time-out! He's only a friend. I repeated this to myself and cleared my throat as I stood up. "I'm sorry," I said. He stopped moving away and eyed me skeptically. I explained, "Seeing you threw me."

"No shit."

"I don't know many people in Westminster, and I didn't expect to see you here, dressed differently and asking to help me. It's bizarre."

His eyes still held a hard edge, telling me I'd offended him. I would have to try harder at being nice. I was normally nice. I had to blame my rudeness on the situation. I'd never had to try to reroute my hormones to be friends with someone, let alone a straight guy. My friends had mostly been women. I didn't make male friends often. In fact, I think Mel was my only one.

"Okay," he said. "Start over?" He held out his rough and slightly dirty-looking hand, which last time had sent me to the bathroom to scrub mine after shaking it, and waited for me to clasp it.

I hesitated but shook the hand that basically swallowed mine. When he let go, I looked at my palm, and then I sniffed it.

"What's wrong?"

"Well, your hands look dirty, and I expected some would come off."

He chuckled with a mocking pitch and shook his head. "Wow. You're rather impertinent, aren't you?" He held out his hands. "They're stained, Grant. I've worked on cars every day, of every week, for the last ten years. I get more oil and grease on my hands in a week than you'll have on yours in a lifetime. I wash my hands all the time. I promise. Go ahead, touch me. My hands are as clean as they're gonna get."

Yes, this was the strangest exchange I've had with a guy, but I was not without curiosity. I *had* wondered about his hands. I ran my fingers over one palm. "It feels sweaty."

He laughed. "Yeah, I guess so. I've been working out for thirty minutes. Other than sweat, my hands are clean."

I wiped my palm down my sweatpants, and Tristan smirked again.

"All right, let's try something else," he instructed. "Sit down at the machine like you were, but in the other direction."

I did as asked, and he pointed out which pegs to move in order to adjust the weights. When he leaned over to explain something else, I could see down his loose shirt. *Oh shit, his nipples are pebbled.* I was glad I wasn't lying on my back for this exercise. Things were getting *harder* to control.

He's my friend. He's my friend.

The effort it took to move the weights helped relax my semierection. I couldn't exert this much effort and think sexual thoughts. I did three repetitions, and Tristan stopped me. "Let me change this. It shouldn't be this hard for you to lift."

He changed the weight, and I tried it again.

"There. That's better. Do twenty of those, and then I'll help you figure out the next machine." He smiled at me and went to the bench to resume flies.

I indulged my unhealthy desire and watched him. Tristan sat on the bench, picked up his weights, and lay back with one foot on the floor on either side. He held his arms straight out to the side, holding free weights in each hand. His chest flexed. I could see a slight mound in his shorts and looked away. Lusting over someone I'd never have would only serve to kill the friendship.

I sighed and concentrated on my own issues. I had a terribly underdeveloped body. My abs weren't used to exercise. I should have been glad he hadn't laughed when he changed the weight I was using. It was pathetically little.

The more I thought about it, the more I was actually glad Tristan was only a friend. If he were gay and we got along this well, I would never have been able to work out in the same gym with him. I'd have been too embarrassed. It would have murdered my pride to allow him to see how little weight I used and how stupid I was in my inability to figure out the diagram for the machine. It was sad. I was sad.

Tristan, on the other hand, was nice and patient. He didn't have to be. I'd been really rude. He had every right to go to this gym. I finished and walked over to another machine. It was easier to figure out, so Tristan didn't need to help. He glanced over at me and winked as I counted reps. After I finished and moved to a different one, Tristan walked over.

"I'm all done here, so I guess I'll see you around."

"Okay."

He nodded but hesitated to leave. "Just to warn you, since you kind of freaked about seeing me here, next week I have my daughter. We normally come here together every other Saturday morning. She likes the elliptical and some of the classes."

Daughter? "Oh, yeah, sure." The idea of a kid laughing at my efforts scared me.

"We normally come at nine for a couple of hours. If you show up around then, we'll be here. I just thought I should warn you."

"Thank you."

"Okay. See you later. Have fun painting your kitchen."

He walked away, and I watched him go. He was so nice.

DURING THE week, Tristan came in on Monday, but I'd missed him on Friday. I wasn't sure how, assuming he'd come in as he had the other Fridays, but I'd been talking to the manager about selling IRAs and two hours of the afternoon had disappeared before I knew it.

Saturday morning, I had a choice to make. Did I go to the gym when I knew Tristan would be there with his daughter, or go after they'd left? I showed up at 8:45 a.m.

I was hiding on the treadmill in the back when I spotted them entering: Tristan, looking as sexy as ever in shorts and a loose blue tank top, and his daughter, a short, thin, blonde teenage girl with similar features and a bright smile. She was laughing as he poked her side. They seemed so happy. I looked away. Their family time didn't need prying eyes.

I moved to the leg press. I thought I'd start with a hundred pounds. That was a lot, right? I glanced over at Tristan before lying back. He smiled softly before turning his attention back to his daughter, who'd come up and was pointing at something on the other side of the room. I sighed. He was a dad, and I was just a guy who worked at his bank.

After using two other machines in my rotation around the gym, I assessed my decision to come this morning when I knew Tristan would be here. Why had I come? I wanted to see him. I enjoyed seeing him. We'd made small talk at the bank, and his smile surely did things to me that weren't healthy in a friendship like ours, but being around him in a nonprofessional way also conflicted with my sensibilities. Avoiding him until I could move past my attraction was probably best, but if I avoided the gym when I knew he'd be there and he noticed, then I might as well kiss our friendship good-bye. He'd probably get mad. He would know I was avoiding him.

Today, though, he'd come in and spent a good thirty minutes working one machine and then the next, stopping to help his daughter, but hadn't come over to talk to me. I thought it might have been because of the way I'd acted last week, but it also could have been having his daughter with him. Maybe he didn't want me to meet her. Maybe he thought she'd annoy me. Maybe he wanted to keep her away from a gay man.

"No," I mumbled. "I doubt that." He hadn't seemed bothered about my sexuality and hadn't treated me differently. "He got angry when I was rude," I mumbled some more.

I finished chest presses and glanced over at him again. It had become a habit for the last five stations. I couldn't go about my routine without knowing where he was. Tristan was looking my way this time. I smiled softly, much like he'd done to me last week. I thought he'd walk over, but he didn't. I took a deep breath and realized I wouldn't be happy sitting across the room, so I walked over.

"Hey," I said. "I worked the machines on my own this week."

He grinned. "I noticed."

I gave him my guilty look. "I have a confession. I came in Wednesday night and asked an employee to show me how to do everything."

Tristan chuckled. "That's great. I was wondering because you seemed more at ease."

"I am. It's all new, though. I never really worked out before. I'm more of a couch potato."

It seemed like he was about to comment, but his daughter interrupted. "Dad, that class I wanted to do is starting upstairs."

"Claire, this is my friend Grant. Grant, this is my daughter." He gestured to me and then back to her, treating this like any other introduction. No hesitance or strangeness.

"Hello," she said, rocking on her heels. "It's nice to know you have friends, Dad."

"Hey! I have friends. Jeff and Will are my friends."

"Jeff and Will work for you. That doesn't count. Can I go do the class?"

I enjoyed the way she ribbed him. They seemed comfortable with each other.

"Sure," he said. "I'll be down here when you're done."

Claire looked at me and said, "Watch out for my dad, will you? He's a mess without me."

Tristan moaned quietly, and I chuckled as Claire took off down a hallway. "She's funny."

"Very," he commented drolly. "I'm doing leg presses next. Where are you off to?"

I shrugged. I'd made my round, and I was tired. How did I tell the workout master I was done? "Um, I thought I'd finish with the treadmill for twenty minutes."

"Weren't you on that when we got here?"

He'd seen me? "Oh, yeah. I guess I'll… I might do…." I glanced around, trying to figure out which machines to name.

"You're done for the day, aren't you?" How did he know? Tristan sensed my shock and explained, "You're sweaty, and your last rep over there was a struggle, wasn't it?"

I nodded. He'd been watching me as I had been watching him. I'm not sure how I felt about that, considering we were only supposed to be friends. "Yeah. I'm really tired. I guess I'll see you around. It was nice meeting your daughter. She's cute." I felt odd standing next to him as he sat on a weight bench. If someone wanted to use the equipment, then we'd be in the way.

He smiled wider than I'd seen before. "Thanks. I think she's awesome, but I'm very biased."

"You're allowed to be." I wasn't good at small talk, but I couldn't leave quite yet. I was still conflicted. I was attracted to him, yet I knew I shouldn't be. We were friends, pals, buddies. Nothing more. "So, is it true you don't have many friends?" Kids could exaggerate. I wouldn't be surprised if Tristan had loads of friends. He seemed nice and friendly.

Another guy came over to the machine next to us. It felt like he was invading our conversation, although he didn't even look at us.

"Yes and no. I have friends, but I rarely see them anymore."

"Oh?"

"I'm married to my work, and they're stationed overseas."

"Stationed?" That was an odd way of describing it.

"Did I not mention it before? I was in the military."

"Which explains the muscles," I mumbled, my eyes going wide immediately. "Oh gosh, did I say that out loud?"

Tristan chuckled. "Yes, but you're fine. I've heard it all before. I was a workout buff before I joined the Navy, and I continued after I got out."

"Ah! Now the tattoo on your bicep makes sense."

Tristan pulled his arm forward and touched the tattoo. It was the Navy insignia. "Yeah. My buddy Josh and I got them together."

The drop in his tone told me something was wrong. I asked, "Do you still see him?"

He shook his head. "No. He died a year after we got them. We were on a boat somewhere between the Arabian Sea and the Indian Ocean, and Josh got sick. He thought it was influenza but ignored it way too long. He died a week later."

I almost got tears in my eyes. Josh's death sounded so tragically avoidable.

"Are you using this?" a different man asked, gesturing to the equipment we were standing next to.

The man's question seemed to snap both of us out of our momentary funk. "Oh, no, sorry," Tristan said, getting up and motioning for the other man to use it.

We stepped to the side, and suddenly I felt awkward. There were more people in the place than I had realized, and having a conversation in the middle of the room made me self-conscious.

Tristan gestured over to the wall, and I followed him to the side of the room. "You're tired, and this place is too crowded to talk. I'm sorry to drop Josh's death on you like that, but it just came out. It's been twelve years, but sometimes thinking about him takes me back to the times we laughed." He shook his head and blinked, as if shaking off the bad memories. "Anyway... maybe we can grab a beer sometime, and I'll give you the rundown of my military history. Josh and I did have some fun times together." He grinned. Was he joking? How much military history could he have?

His question threw me. "I, um... I guess."

"I'd really like to hang out with you. Claire wasn't kidding about my lack of friends. I don't take time out of working long enough to make any."

A too-damn-irresistible smile graced his perfect lips. Our friendship wasn't going to work if he kept smiling at me like that. My groin didn't know the difference between a straight guy and an interested guy, especially after he licked his lips. I coughed into my fist and then said casually, "Why make an exception for me? I'm not all that interesting."

He frowned his disapproval at me. "I like you, Grant. You're... *simple*."

Lust jumped the track in favor of irritation. "Simple?" I snapped. I didn't like the word, and I didn't veil my reaction.

Tristan explained, "Not simple as in 'simpleton.' What I mean is that you're straightforward. You say what you mean, and I don't have to guess what you're thinking. Your intent is written on your face."

I didn't see that as a plus when I'd been thinking nonfriendship thoughts for a couple of weeks. Every time he walked into the bank, I felt heat swirling in areas that had been neglected all my life. I couldn't think of a response for being called "simple."

He touched my arm, and I glanced to his hand and back up to his eyes.

"Grant, don't be mad. I didn't mean to offend you. I like you. Can we go for a beer and get to know each other? You said yourself you're new to the area. If I don't have many friends, and you don't have many friends, then why don't we give this a shot?"

He let go of my arm, and I swallowed. Friends with a straight guy whose touch made me shiver and whose lips made me salivate? Oh, holy hell, I was in for a rough ride.

"Okay," I said.

He smiled again, glad I had agreed. "Wait here one second." He disappeared up the steps toward the front desk and returned with a slip of paper. "I don't have a card on me, but here's my phone number. Call or text me a time you're free. I'm busy with my daughter this weekend, but I can certainly meet up with you during the week, or next weekend."

I looked down at the slip of paper. He'd really given me his number. *Huh*. I'd made a friend. I'd have to tell my mom. "Thanks. Yeah, I guess I could have a beer, but I'm telling you I'm not all that interesting."

His face lit up. "That's fine. I have plenty of stories if you run out of things to talk about."

"Okay." I didn't know what else to say. I mean, the whole exchange felt rather odd already, but if he had as few friends as I had, then I supposed this was one way of making some. "I'm gonna go. I'll talk to you next week."

He stuck out his hand. This time when I shook it, it didn't feel dirty. It was either because of my own sweat and grime, or because he didn't seem as filthy.

"I MADE a friend," I told Mel. I'd already called my mother. She hadn't seemed as impressed as I thought she might. "A straight male friend."

"Oh, wow! Good for you. I thought you had way too many girl friends. It isn't healthy."

"I know what you mean. It's not like I mind chick flicks or pedicures, but I think it'll be fun watching a football game for a change, better yet a baseball game. He asked if I wanted to get a beer sometime and talk."

"Do you even like beer? I thought you said you've never had a drink."

Mel knew me too well. I answered, "I haven't, but there's a first time for everything. I'm sure I could have something light."

"If I were you, I'd go to a local liquor store and talk to someone."

"You think so?" I walked from the stove, where I was cooking beef stew, to the table, where I set my bowl and arranged my spoon and napkin. Mel and I normally chatted for a few minutes several times a week as I made dinner, or shortly after I'd finished.

"For sure. If you needed to know about wine, I'm your guy, but I don't like beer."

"Okay. Maybe I will. Did you talk to Cindy yet?" I had to change the subject. We'd been talking about me in every conversation for a week. I needed to let Mel know I cared about his life too.

"Yes."

"What? When? Why didn't you text me?" I was so excited I almost dropped my spoon right into the pot.

"I talked to her today. I ordered some cornbread to go."

"That's great!"

I was so happy, but Mel's voice said the exact opposite. "No. It's pathetic. I didn't want cornbread. I only ordered it because no one was around and she was the only employee out front. I felt like a doofus."

"I'm sure you didn't look like one. Did she smile, or say anything to give you an indication she thought you were cute?"

I was glad to hear Mel's snicker. "Yeah, sort of. I'm not sure what to make of it."

"Then I think you need to go back again and find out."

"I don't know. Can we talk about something else? I haven't…." He huffed into the receiver as he paused. "I haven't dated anyone in over four years. I've spent all my time with you, because you've always accepted me for who I am. What if I've gone through all this only to find out no one wants to be with me? What if I'm alone the rest of my life?" I could hear his emotion, and it stirred my own. Mel was not a crier by nature.

"Mel, don't. We always said we can't dwell on what-ifs. I've been alone for twenty-six years."

"At least you've had dates."

"Dates with losers who found my personality repulsive! You and I have to keep trying. My soul mate is out there, somewhere, and so is yours. I have to believe that!"

He took in a long shaky breath and said, "Look, my dinner's done. I gotta go."

"Okay. Bye."

"Later."

I hung up and set my phone on the table. His situation bothered me because it wasn't so much different than mine, but scarier. Yet I worried more over the hurt I heard in his voice. Hope was something I had to give him, but what if he finally gave up on it? I didn't have answers for myself, let alone for Mel. I picked my phone back up and texted: *I'm sorry, Mel. I'm sure things will work out for you. Go see Cindy at work one more time. Just try.*

Don't apologize, you're right. I know I need to approach her, but I'm scared.

I know. I love you like a brother.

:) Thank you, Grant.

This time when I put the phone down, at least I didn't feel like there was unfinished business. I never wanted to go to sleep knowing one of my friends was mad at me, let alone my best friend. Mel would be okay.

I ate dinner alone and contemplated painting my bedroom next.

I VENTURED to The Home Depot to pick out paint colors. I figured there had to be one in the area, so I pulled it up on Google. I might not know my new town, but how different could it be from other towns? I mean, really. I found it, and an hour later I came home with twenty-seven different color cards because I couldn't decide on a shade while I was there. I liked blue, but did I want a blue bedroom? I taped three different blues in one spot to stare at and other colors on different spots on the wall: beige, green, yellow, and even purple. If the color I painted my kitchen said a lot about me as a person, as Mrs. Snyder had suggested, then what did the color in my bedroom suggest? I guess if I painted my bedroom black or bloodred people might mistake me for a vampire, but would green suggest one aspect of my personality and blue another? I wasn't sure, so I thought I would mull it over for a while.

Right now, the entire house was painted white, except for the kitchen. I didn't care for white. My mother's house was all white. Having a different color was my mind's subconscious way of declaring separation. It wasn't like I'd thought, when I had painted my kitchen, "I'm going to paint this salmon so I am completely different from my mom!" No, I didn't think about that at all. I liked the salmon. Mel had given me some dishes for my first new place, and they had salmon-colored flecks in the design along the edge. I'd been in an apartment before, but since I'd spent most of my time over at Mel's, I just hadn't expended the effort to paint it.

This newest new place felt different. It was small, with only a kitchen, bedroom, and dining/living room combination. No basement. No porch. No real storage. I had described it as a three-room house, but I did have a bathroom and a closet. It had come with a couch, which I hated, and a dining room table, which was okay. I wanted to furnish it myself as soon as I saved up some money. I used to have some, but two years ago Mel and I had gone on a trip to Ireland and spent quite a lot traveling around and staying in different counties. It had been worth it, but I had to save up again.

All day Sunday I must have taken out my phone a hundred times wondering if I should text Tristan. He'd given me his phone number, but should I call him the very next day? I didn't want to appear desperate. I didn't have to call him. I had other friends.

My other friends lived an hour away, but I could still do things with them.

BY MONDAY afternoon, I still hadn't texted, and I felt strange when Tristan came in with a deposit. He was as pleasant as ever, his half smile cajoling me into an uncomfortable semierect state that made me regret wearing the tight trousers I'd chosen. Luckily, if I stood at the counter, no one could see the front of my pants until things had settled down.

BY FRIDAY, Tristan must have waited long enough. After handing me his stack of disorganized bills and checks, he asked again about the beer. "I waited for that text. Either you don't want to have a beer with me, or you lost my number. Either way is fine, but you could have said you weren't interested. I'll still talk to you, even if you don't want to hang out."

How should I word my answer? It wasn't as if I didn't like him. It was the thought of spending time with him outside the bank that made me nervous. I had difficulty controlling my anatomy. What if, while we were chatting, I popped one? His voice *did* wash over me in the way a hot cup of tea does on a snowy January Sunday. It soothed. How could I go out with him for a beer, which I had never drunk, and talk, when I still could not think of him solely as a friend?

"I'm sorry. I do want to have that beer. I was going to text you… but then I didn't." It wasn't a lie. I had punched his numbers in my phone and saved them, I just hadn't used them.

"Oh. Okay. Well, what are you doing Saturday night?" Tristan asked, tucking his receipts into his wallet.

"I work until noon. Then I'm helping my mother hang some shelves on her wall. It'll probably take all day, and she offered to make me dinner."

His lips moved but could not quite make that half smile I was used to. He was disappointed, and I felt bad for allowing it to happen. He was trying, but I had not. "I'm free Sunday," I offered.

There's that dangerous smile I sooo *should not love!*

"Okay. Sunday."

I took out my phone after glancing around for anyone who could fuss at me for texting during work. "Just so there's no doubt"—I pressed Send—"I sent you a text."

"You saved my number," he marveled.

"Of course I did."

I heard his phone chime. He took it out and smiled. "Thanks. I was convinced you threw it away after I gave it to you at the gym, thinking I was a deranged stalker."

"Nope. I intended to text. But time slipped away, and here we are on Friday." Time, and the fact I didn't know how to be friends with a straight guy who turned me on with his smile. I was so screwed.

"I know how it is. I get very busy myself. Well, I guess I'll see you on Sunday, since you'll be working while I'm at the gym." Did he really sound disappointed, or was that me?

"Yup. Sunday."

Tristan walked away, and another customer walked up to my window before I had a second to run over our conversation in my head. He had seemed different this time. Happier. I waved off the notion and punched in the account numbers. I couldn't think about Tristan. It was dangerous to think about Tristan. It was wrong to think about Tristan. He was my friend. I could handle one beer without crying myself to sleep over the irony of finding the perfect guy only for him to be straight. No, I would amend that. All the perfect-looking guys I'd ever met had happened to be straight. The only ones who'd been interested in me were the imperfect ones with more flaws than I had.

Just once, I'd like to find a perfect gay man!

Chapter Four

Wet Dreams, Anticipation, And Completely Blowing The Date That Wasn't A Date But Was

He climbed over my body, sweaty and nervous, separating my thighs with his knee. He pulled my leg up and over one shoulder as he positioned his throbbing cock at my entrance. I felt him waiting, pressing slightly yet not enough to breach. Then suddenly, he thrust hard and filled me with....

My body convulsed as I panted myself awake. I blinked uncomprehendingly as my eyes adjusted to the moonlight streaming in through the bedroom window. I was in my bed. Alone. Tristan wasn't here. The tingling in my groin alerted me to what had happened, and I slapped myself on the forehead.

"Crap," I mumbled, reaching down under the covers to confirm. "I just shot my wad." I lay there a second, but as the moments ticked I became more aware of the wetness in my underwear. "Shit!" I grumbled, throwing the blankets back and storming to the bathroom.

I washed up and changed my underwear, returning to my bed.

"Why can't I find a nice gay guy to dream about?"

I rolled over and closed my eyes. Going out for a beer with Tristan was a bad idea. I liked him too much. I should probably suggest waiting a week or two so my body could calm down. How could I casually hang out with a guy who was the object of way too many fantasies? He had been the main character in my subconscious for about seven wet dreams thus far, and I'd only met him two weeks ago.

I curled my legs up toward my chest and readjusted my feather pillow as I hugged it. A rebellious tear slipped out of my eye, and I felt it roll over my nose and drop onto my hand where it lay on the pillow. I just knew I was going to screw up the friendship before it started. Tristan would end up hating me. I couldn't make friends with a guy I lusted over. Sunday was doomed.

SATURDAY PASSED as any other Saturday when I worked and helped my mother. We'd done plenty of things together on Saturdays because it never interfered with her mah-jongg tournaments on Sundays. I liked mah-jongg and used to take part in the tournaments until Mel had pointed out that no twenty-something guy played mah-jongg with his mother and her friends.

I'd given it up some time before I'd moved out.

SUNDAY MORNING, while sipping my tea, I got a text from Tristan.

Hey, Grant. I wanted to check in. What time and where do you want to meet? O'Lordans Irish Pub is a nice place. They have good food as well as good beer. You know, in case you want to eat too. We could meet there, or I could pick you up.

Food? He couldn't have been asking me to dinner. *Meet there?* I thought about that option, but realized my potential for drunkenness and texted: *Can you pick me up?*

I didn't want to explain that I'd never drunk before. I might sound pathetic. He replied and asked for my address, so I happily gave it over. Not having to drive home after would be a good thing.

SUNDAY EVENING I stood in front of the mirror trying to figure out what to wear. Every shirt I owned looked like I was going to work. What was the appropriate attire for a pub? "T-shirt and jeans, probably," I told myself. I owned one pair of jeans and zero T-shirts. I had seven white undershirts, so I figured if I unbuttoned the front of one of my dress shirts and rolled up the sleeves, it could pass for casual. But which color?

I opened my closet and peered down the line of pressed dress shirts organized by color. Mel was right when he said they were very Easter-eggy. Pastel purple, which was technically lavender, baby blue, sage green, butter, salmon, and three shades of pink—holy crap, I realized I had the entire Easter rainbow lined up in my closet.

I dropped my head back and groaned. No wonder I was undateable.

"I could rearrange them," I mused, lifting a handful of hangers off the rod and rehanging them in a different order.

I stood there for a full sixty seconds before the chaos overwhelmed me. "Now it looks like Easter threw up," I said, correcting my mistake. Once they were back in the appropriate spots, I chose a blue one. Blue was good and manly even if it was *baby* blue. Besides, Tristan had seen this shirt before, and I wasn't out to impress him. It was a casual beer, much like grabbing lunch with Mel.

I heard a knock and took one last look in the mirror before heading to answer it. I looked fine.

"Hey," I greeted Tristan as I opened the door and stepped out onto the cement landing. My stomach did a little jig, but my nerves were much less active than when I'd been on dates. *This is a beer with my buddy*, I reminded myself.

"You look nice," he commented as he opened the passenger door of his truck.

I glanced down as if I'd forgotten what I was wearing. His compliment threw me. "Um, thanks," I said. Did straight men compliment their buddies? I'd never had straight male friends, other than Mel, so I shrugged it off as a possible maybe. Tristan had always been pleasant at the bank, so this was probably his nature.

Ironically, he was also wearing blue—a blue T-shirt that said something about a Dogfish Head. I would have to look that one up when I got home, because I wasn't sure why heads of dogfish were appealing, or even if dogfish were real fish. For all I knew they could be mythical creatures like jackalopes.

"Are you hungry? I know I mainly suggested beer, but they do have good food." Tristan turned onto Route 27 and glanced at me as he watched the road in front of us.

"Not really. I ate some leftover stew an hour ago."

"Oh."

"Yeah. My sink decided to clog, and it took a few hours to take it apart and clean it. Then I had to put it all back together and make sure it didn't leak. It was a whole ordeal, and by the time I was finished and showered, I was hungry. Besides, you said we were going out for a beer."

"Yes, you're right. That's what I said."

I didn't understand why he sounded disappointed. I'd eaten because I'd been hungry an hour ago. This wasn't a date, so I didn't see the big deal.

"I noticed you're wearing your glasses."

"Um, yeah. My eyes were red this morning so I opted for the glasses. I probably look nerdy, but I hope that's okay for a pub. I've never been to one."

He chuckled. "Guys wear glasses in pubs, Grant. It's not a parochial school with a dress code. You're fine."

Was he laughing *at* me or *with* me? I ignored it.

After parking in a garage next to a stone building, he said, "So you've never been to a pub before?"

"No."

He locked the truck, and we walked side by side to the entrance and down a sidewalk next to the building. "Then I'm glad I picked this one. It's nice. I've never seen drunken disorder or rowdiness except maybe on Saint Patrick's Day." He opened the door for me and I went inside.

THE EVENING went better than I expected. We talked about some of his adventures in the Navy. He'd enlisted and been deployed shortly after his daughter had been born, and went to college for four years after he'd gotten out. Tristan said he didn't regret being in the Navy, but he'd been grateful his father had asked him to take over the family business while he went to college because it had given him a valid excuse to change careers. He said, "Being away on a ship so often right after Claire was born just about killed me. I missed her a lot."

He didn't talk about his daughter's mother, and I wasn't sure why they weren't together, but he did tell me he had Claire with him every other weekend and two weeks in the summer. He sounded pleased.

I also learned that he *loved* craft beers, and Dogfish Head was a brewery. I made a mental note.

"So, this was fun," Tristan said as we walked out of the pub and headed to his truck. I was glad he'd picked me up, because I was feeling lightheaded even after the one beer.

"Yeah. I can't say I've ever gone out drinking before."

"I'd hardly call one beer drinking. It's more like sampling." We walked up the sidewalk toward the parking garage. I stumbled on an uneven part of the pavement, and Tristan grabbed my arm. "Whoa," he said. "You okay? I guess one really is your limit, if you're walking sideways."

I snorted. "No. I'm fine. It's that bit of sidewalk," I said as I turned around and pointed.

"Okay there, soldier, anything you say," he mocked. I don't think he believed me.

We entered the lower level of the garage, and I glanced around. Nothing looked familiar. "Where'd you park?"

"Second level."

"What'd you drive?"

"Blue Dodge Dakota. It's this way." He waved me to follow. "I can't believe you're this tipsy after one drink. I think next time we need to eat first."

"I'm f-fiiine," I slurred, exaggerating my speech on purpose.

He stopped, regarding me seriously. "You're kidding, right?"

I smiled. "Of course I am. My head might feel a little woozy, but I'm not drunk." I scoffed at the notion.

Tristan smiled. "Come on, you." He rolled his eyes and pinched my sleeve, bidding me to follow. I'd probably follow him anywhere—he had a nice ass. We got in his truck, and Tristan backed out of the parking space.

I commented, "I had a great time. I kind of wish it didn't have to end, but we both work tomorrow."

He stopped at the light, looked my way, and smiled. I think he'd smiled the entire night. "Me too. But hey, we can do it again another time. I'd like to take you out on a *real* date. We could have dinner and maybe catch a movie."

Maybe I *was* drunk, because it had sounded like he said date. "Wait… what?" I screwed up my eyes and stared at him across the seat.

"*What*, what? Do you not want to go?" he asked.

I was still confused. "Did you say you wanted to take me out to dinner?" Because that didn't make any sense. My mind was all kinds of confuzzled.

Tristan turned onto Route 140 and answered, "Yes. I hardly call one drink and a calamari appetizer a date, so yeah, I want to take you out to dinner."

I dropped my eyes to my clasped hands in my lap and mulled over what was happening. Tristan had asked me out. *On a date*. Another thought occurred to me, so I turned my attention back to him. "Was *this* a date?"

He gave me a weird look, then slowly pulled his truck to the side of the road and came to a stop. It wasn't abrupt, but it did make me a little worried. I leaned closer to the door. When the truck was in park, he turned on the seat. "What did you think this was, Grant?"

I shrugged. "I don't know. Two buddies having a beer." My heart was racing. I squeezed my hands together as my only form of security. I didn't understand what was going on. It was dark, and sitting on the side of the road made me a little scared. I estimated we were over eight miles from my house, so if he made me get out and walk, I'd have a long trek back.

His shoulders sagged, and he leaned against the door, resting one arm over the steering wheel. "Grant, I've been flirting with you for two weeks."

"You have? When?" Rewinding our interactions, doing a mental assessment of everything we'd said to one another, I couldn't remember where I'd gone off track.

Tristan said, "Well, for one, I've turned the pens upside down every time you weren't looking."

My mouth dropped open. "That was you?"

He chuckled. "Yes." He seemed so pleased with himself.

His posture didn't suggest anger, so I eased away from the door and relaxed my hands. I still fussed at him. "I couldn't for the life of me figure out how they ended up like that. It drove me nuts."

He grinned. "I know. I thought it was adorable."

"My pain was adorable?" I bristled. I had to admit, now that I knew it was Tristan who'd flipped the pens, it made more sense. "Did you shuffle the bills in your deposits on purpose too? Because that was ridiculous."

Tristan nodded.

"Oh my gosh! I didn't say anything because I didn't want to be rude, but you were the only customer who didn't arrange his deposits and stack the bills all facing in the same direction, lumped by denomination."

"It was the only thing I could think of to extend my visits. I knew it would take you longer to count it," he explained. "I've never been in the bank so many times, Grant. I used to send one of the guys in on Fridays. I only went to the bank that first Friday, the day I met you, because Will was in the middle of a job and I'd finished rotating a set of tires on a Pilot sooner than expected. But I have to say, I've never been happier rearranging my schedule. As soon as I saw you, I knew I had to find reasons to go to the bank. I even took money out of the ATM over the weekend so I could go on Monday and redeposit it on the off chance you'd be there."

How did I miss all this? Sure, I knew he came in at least twice a week, and some of his transactions had seemed redundant, but I wasn't a business owner. I wasn't going to tell him how to run things. Every time he came in had given me another chance to look into his blue eyes and enjoy his smile, even if I knew there wasn't a chance to go beyond friendship. No, wait....

"I thought you were straight," I said. How could I have been so wrong?

"I don't see how, unless I wasn't as obvious as I thought. I even winked at you. How many straight guys wink that often?"

He had me there. "I *was* confused about that, but then you showed me a picture of your daughter. I thought, 'Damn! He's straight.' How was I supposed to know you're gay *and* you have a daughter?"

He sighed, and his shoulders sagged as if I'd deflated him completely. "I am so sorry, Grant. Had I known you'd misunderstand my intentions, I'd have spelled them out. I swear, I thought you knew I liked you."

However we'd gotten to this point, it didn't really matter after he said he liked me. They were words I rarely heard but longed for. Someone liked me and wanted to date me, and that someone was gorgeous and nice. There had to be a catch. Guys this awesome didn't happen my way or simply show up at my teller window. There were always horrific complications that destroyed the relationship before it even progressed to kissing. Just once, I hoped I'd met a guy who would actually take a chance and kiss me.

I apologized this time, quiet and sincere. "I'm sorry too, Tristan. I guess I couldn't see your gestures because guys like you have never been interested in me before."

"I can't imagine why. You're so... pretty, but in a manly sort of way." He grinned, but I felt emasculated.

"Thanks, I think I'll be putting my tutu on for the next date. And maybe some eyeliner and lipstick." Perhaps my sarcasm wasn't necessary, but it was a knee-jerk reaction. One other guy I'd gone out with had made a similar comment about me being "too pretty." I wasn't fucking pretty. Nice looking? Sure. Cute? Maybe. But I was damned if I was going to be called pretty. I'd seen pretty guys, the ones who could be models or actors. I'd met a "pretty" guy once in Columbia near the bank where I used to work. He was absolutely beautiful... and straight. I knew

I was not one of those guys. Backhanded compliments made me angry. Don't pay me lip service; just tell me the truth.

Tristan was quiet for a long time. He was studying me, or trying to figure out what to say. Maybe his tactics worked on other guys, but I wasn't going to be so duped. He'd tricked me, and I wasn't going to fall into his trap. *Dinner? Why would he want to take me to dinner?* Nothing good could come of it.

He finally turned back to the steering wheel and put it in drive, pulling out onto the road in silence. We turned down a few more streets and before long ended up in front of my house. He parked. "Good night, Grant," he said, not even bothering to look at me.

I hesitated to open the door. What was happening? We had argued over this being a date or not, him calling me pretty, and now… what? It was over? I was to get out and go into my house without another word? I glanced at him and then at the door. "Um, bye," I said feebly. I shut the door and walked to my front landing in a daze. This was not how I pictured a date would end, even if I hadn't realized we were on one. Ten minutes ago I'd said I hadn't wanted it to end, and now I was going inside with this creeping notion I'd killed my best chance for an actual date. A torrent of emotion swelled. I'd been so stupid.

I fumbled for my keys and dropped them. "Damn it." I bent to pick them up.

"Grant."

Tristan's voice behind me caused me to bobble my keys and drop them again. I turned around. "What are you doing?"

"Grant, I… shit, are you crying?"

I stiffened and shrunk back. "No, that's absurd."

"Look, this isn't how I planned it. I wanted to—"

"Humiliate me?" I countered. I was up against my front door, so I didn't have anywhere to hide.

His eyes twitched again. I was coming to recognize that those ticks were signs of irritation or confusion. He didn't understand me. Tristan shook his head and squinted. "No, Grant. I wanted to—"

He kissed me. He just dove in and kissed me soundly on the lips. I'd never felt another person's mouth on mine, and it took a second to react. Even though I'd seen chick flicks galore, I was still surprised when Tristan moved his mouth on mine. I'd thought once two lips were pressed together they remained that way, but I was wrong. He kissed with a grabbing motion, his lips grasping mine before releasing them for another position. His lips nibbled at my mouth as our noses rubbed and our breath mingled.

I felt his hands holding my face on either side, capturing me. I reached up and held his ribs, but as the kissing continued, I encircled his waist in order to hold myself up. I was suddenly lightheaded and woozier than from the beer. I couldn't breathe. His mouth kept suckling at my lips as if determined to torture me with the new sensations that traveled down my body and filled me with tingling flushes of heat.

I groaned, pulling his body tightly against mine. Something hard pressed against my crotch, and I felt a primal need to thrust. I fisted the back of his shirt and tilted my hips, but he drew back, releasing my mouth.

"Please don't stop," I pleaded.

He ran his eyes over my face and touched my hair. "No, I think that's good for one night."

"But… please? I'm sorry I got sarcastic. You can call me pretty if you want to. You can call me anything as long as you kiss me again. I'll do anything," I pleaded. I could hardly keep my eyes open. I still held him around the waist because I feared slipping to the ground if I let go. He made my head spin.

Tristan's eye twitched again. "Grant, I don't think that's a good idea. You were angry before. Don't tell me you're so easy one kiss can get me into your pants. I thought you were better than that." He stepped back, pulling out of my embrace.

I reached for him. "Tristan, wait. I'm sorry. I'm not sure how I'm supposed to act." I slid my hands up his chest, and he took hold of them and squeezed. He sighed and wet his lips. I continued, "You're the first guy who's stuck around long enough to kiss me. You're right, I hate being called pretty, but that's because there was a guy who called me pretty as a joke. It hurt being toyed with, so when you said it I guess I was shocked you of all people would toy with me. I didn't understand you liked me, and I'm sorry I assumed you were straight, but I don't want you to walk away without giving me a chance."

"Will you tell me one thing?"

I nodded. "Anything."

"Do you even like me? Or are you throwing yourself at me because I kissed you?"

"I like you. I swear I do. I've been dreaming about you for weeks and struggling to think about you *purely* as a friend, because I get hard every time you're around. I think you're the hottest guy I've ever seen, and I can't believe you'd look at me twice."

"Grant, that can't be true. You're adorable, and yes, pretty even. You've got a hotness all your own going on, and I can't believe you're shocked I'd think so. I also can't believe I'm the first guy to kiss you." His eye wasn't twitching, but he was definitely confused.

I was on the verge of tears again, but I hoped I wouldn't cry. "It's true. I've been on twelve first dates, and not one guy's walked me to the door and kissed me. A few even left in the middle of the date. I repulse people that much." I dropped my head. I couldn't admit how pathetic I was and look him in the eyes at the same time.

Tristan let go of my left hand and pulled my chin up. "Let me clarify a few things. I like you, a lot. You don't need to doubt that. I do intend to give you a chance, and I *will* kiss you again." I gasped and hedged forward, but he stopped me with a finger to my lips. "Not tonight." He smiled softly. "I don't know how you managed to make it twenty-five years—"

"Twenty-six," I corrected.

"Twenty-*six* years without a real boyfriend, but it *does* explain a lot about you. I'm going to take you out again next Friday—"

"But I work Friday until eight. And then I have to count out my drawer, and—"

"Stop interrupting." He shook his head. "You're certainly argumentative, aren't you?"

"I'm sorry."

"Grant, you're not the only one that's new at this. I haven't dated anyone in fifteen years. I'm willing to take a chance on you because your compulsive need to flip those pens made my heart yearn for the first time in my life."

"The pens?"

"Yes. I've never taken the time to see people before, really see them. My life has been consumed with work and my daughter. No guy has ever snagged my attention so strongly that I was willing to alter my nondating, workaholic lifestyle for a chance at something good. This isn't a one-night stand deal for me. I want to plan a future with someone special. You got my attention, Grant, and despite your belligerence and your eccentricities, I can't walk away without trying."

I'd never heard anything so beautiful before. I mattered to him—me! This seriously sexy man felt that I was worth not only his time, but worth altering his lifestyle. My internal clock took notice of the phrase "plan a future," and I couldn't breathe.

As my emotions surged again, I lunged into his arms. When he put his arms around me and squeezed me tight, I pressed my face into his neck and whispered, "Thank you."

"I want us to start over, okay?" he whispered back.

"Okay."

"I'm not coming in to the bank this week."

I pulled back so I could look him in the eyes. "But…?" I thought he'd said he'd give me another chance. "Why?" My pathetic whiney voice came out. If he really liked me like he said he did, maybe he'd overlook it.

He explained, "To give you some space. Think about whether or not you really want to date me with intent."

"I *do* want to date you!"

"Grant, calm down. I don't believe you're thinking clearly. In the morning, when the alcohol is out of your system and you can process everything I said, then text me. We can talk during the week, but I think you need to consider what you want in our potential relationship. We'll talk about it on Friday."

All I could do was nod. I felt awful, but hopeful at the same time. He could have easily driven away without explaining himself, or without kissing me. *Tristan kissed me.* I could have sighed, cried, and died.

"Good night, Grant." He kissed my forehead and got back in his truck.

As SOON as he drove away, I dashed inside and called Mel.

"How'd that beer go? What kind did you order?" he asked.

"He's gay!" I blurted. I plopped on the couch and kicked off my shoes.

"Who's gay?"

"Tristan!"

"No way."

"Yes, way. Totally gay. And get this, he told me he's been flirting with me all week. I don't know how I missed it!" I unbuttoned my shirt and pulled it out of my jeans.

Mel mumbled, "Because you never admit when guys come on to you."

"What?" I sat up straight.

"Nothing."

"No, I heard what you said, and it isn't true."

"Yes, it is, Grant. I've watched you."

"When?"

"All the time. You're oblivious to any kind of flirtation or advance if the guy's hot. But suddenly it's like your extrasensory perception is turned on high when the losers bat their eyes."

"I've never done that," I protested.

"Yes, you have. It's because you have an unrealistic self-image."

"My self-image is perfectly reasonable. It's yours that needs help!" Mel had no idea what he was talking about.

He ignored my comment and kept at me. "On a scale of one to ten, where one is Mr. Bean and ten is Charlie Hunnam or Darren Criss— depending on your taste—where would you place *you*?"

Easy. "Four."

Mel laughed so hard it hurt my ears. "Match point and proven."

"That doesn't make any sense."

"You proved my point. You think you're a four? Grant, you're at least an eight when pitted against Darren Criss. He's got the talent and the voice, but you're just as good-looking."

It was my turn to laugh—at his absurdity. "Right! I'm hanging up now." I pressed End and tossed my phone on the couch cushion as I headed into the bedroom. I removed my shirt and placed it into the hamper. I had laid my wallet on the dresser and folded my jeans by the time Mel called back. I answered the phone in my boxers and undershirt.

"Took you long enough."

"Another call came through before I could dial you back. Grant, you can hang up on me every time if you want, but the fact still remains that you don't think you're good enough to catch the hot ones. Stop thinking like that and believe me when I say *you are*."

I held the phone to my ear a few more seconds but couldn't think of a response. *Could Mel be right?* I heaved a sigh and said, "I'll talk to you later."

Mel was used to my abrupt good-byes. Sometimes I marveled over how easily he forgave me for being rude. I glanced at the picture of the two of us on my end table. Mel was such a great friend. I put the phone in its cradle and turned off the lights.

As I lay there staring at the ceiling, I thought about calling my mom. Should I? I was confused over Mel's comments. Did I really need my mother adding more drama to my situation? I didn't know what to do. Maybe I did need to think about everything Tristan had suggested. I had wanted a relationship for many years—a committed, long-term relationship. Should I jump in with both feet? It was all so sudden.

I needed sleep.

DURING THE week, I contemplated my situation. Mel had called me out on my self-doubt, and if I was honest he'd been right. During a slow moment at work, I flipped through the pictures of all the guys I'd ever dated. I had fourteen hundred pictures on my phone. I never deleted anything.

Spring of 2007: Donald Baker. He had been a year ahead of me in high school. We'd both been out since middle school and joined the photography club in ninth grade. By the time he was a senior, he'd built a reputation for being a slut. There had only been a few other gay guys at our school, so I wasn't sure where the rumors of his prowess had come from until he asked me to go to prom. I was nervous, because I wasn't sure the school would let us go together, but I was thrilled he asked. We went on one date two weeks before prom, and he told a few people the next day we'd done it. It wasn't true. He hadn't even kissed me, yet he started rumors of a sexual encounter. Needless to say, I didn't go to the prom with Donald.

I flipped several years to the fall of 2010: Vincent Granger. He'd been in my sociology class at college. He was fine to look at until he smiled, revealing a missing tooth. One missing tooth would have been okay because anyone could get that fixed, but when you took a closer look it was obvious there was a bigger problem. All his teeth were rotting. I had agreed to go on a date, but once we were sitting at a table for two and he smiled, I couldn't bear to look him in the face. He'd gotten offended and stormed out before dessert. I felt bad, but I thought he should take better care of his teeth if he got that upset over it. Later on, he'd gotten arrested for meth production or something. I was truly glad I'd screwed up our date.

Spring 2011: Kenny Dillenger. Good old Kenny. We had barely ordered dinner when I spilled my soda across the table and into his lap.

He jumped up, threw some expletives my way, and stormed out. Come to think of it, storming out had been a habit for my dates four times in a row. I didn't know why I kept saying yes when a guy asked me out.

I put my phone away and stared at the front door of the bank, hoping that Tristan would walk through it. If my self-loathing had been the impetus of failed relationships, then I needed to refocus and change my outlook. Tristan was willing to give me a chance, so I needed to be willing to give myself the same chance. He was so nice looking. Why couldn't I believe he liked me?

The next customer was a balding man with good taste in clothes. He smiled and handed me his transactions. He kept smiling as I punched in his numbers, and I knew right away he was into me. It was the way his eyes undressed me as I worked. I counted out twenties and a ten, counting back his money as I would any other customer. When I was done, he winked and said, "Until next time."

I cringed.

"Why couldn't I see Tristan's interest so easily?" I whined aloud to myself.

My phone buzzed. Tristan. I sighed. His text said: *Because I have more respect for you than Mr. Palmer. I'd never stare at you in pubic like you were a piece of meat.*

How could he…? I glanced around the lobby and spotted Tristan way over in the corner by the table with the pens and deposit slips. I gave him a confused look, and he sauntered over.

"How did you know what I was thinking?" I asked when he stepped up to my window. Luckily Jessica was getting change from the vault, so she wouldn't be able to eavesdrop.

"Because he's been in my shop. He looks the same way at any younger man, gay or straight. Ask Wes. You felt cornered, didn't you?" He spoke so confidently. It was weird, because our previous conversations at the bank had been so businesslike. I felt the shift in our relationship. I didn't know who Wes was, but it didn't matter. Suddenly I knew that Tristan knew me in ways I wasn't prepared for. Not details of my life like a stalker or anything like that, but Tristan did have an uncanny bead on me no one ever had before.

"Yeah. I felt queasy when he was watching me. Did you hear me just now, or do you have cameras in the building?" I glanced up and around the ceiling.

He grinned. "No. I noticed last year that if you stand in that corner by the fake plant when no one else is in the lobby, the sound carries all the way over there." He pointed to a spot by the drive-thru windows.

"Really?"

He nodded. "When a friend of mine had a crush on a girl who no longer works here, he said he'd stand in that corner and listen to everything she said."

I gaped at him and made a face. "Oh, that's terrible. It sounds worse than stalking. Why were you doing it to me?"

"I didn't intend to. I walked in when he did, but I wasn't comfortable standing in line because I thought I'd be called over to a different window and I wanted to talk to you. So I waited over there and watched."

Tristan's eyes on me felt different, and I grew more self-conscious as the seconds ticked. Had I wiped my mouth off after lunch? Was my hair okay? Would he find fault with something and comment? "Why did you come in? You told me you were staying away for a while. It's only Thursday."

"Pull my account up on your screen. Here's the number." He handed me a piece of paper.

I did what he asked. "Here it is." Why wasn't he answering me? Was he going to give me a hard time for being an idiot? And why did he have such a devilish expression on his face? *Oh my God, I'm going to die if he keeps watching me like that.*

"Okay. Now, point at the screen and pretend you're talking about my transactions. If someone gets close enough to hear, randomly throw in a comment about a deposit. Got it?"

"But why?"

"Because I want to talk to you, and I'm not getting you fired for personal conversation on the bank's time. Just pretend, and you'll be fine." His voice was so smooth and sexy.

Why had it taken me this long to notice how he spoke to me? "Okay," I agreed, not knowing what I'd agreed to. I was too distracted by the memory of his kiss.

His self-satisfied grin grew wider. "You have to be the most adorable person on the planet."

I didn't see what that had to do with his account. "Huh?"

"You. I've never seen someone blush so deeply before."

"Oh God," I cried, covering my cheeks with my hands. I could hardly catch my breath, and now he sent my heart racing from embarrassment. I could feel a panic attack coming on. *Oh God.* I wanted to believe I could give myself a chance, and yet here I stood flipping out on the inside because he was gazing intently at my outside. Why me? I was nobody.

His blue eyes seemed darker than usual and his smile too alluring. "Especially when I haven't said anything suggestive," he added. "What are you going to do when I start describing the things I want to do to you with my tongue?"

"Oh!" I covered my mouth in shock. I lowered my hand slowly and whispered, "Oh my God. You're a porn star, aren't you? You're going to lure me into your sex club and videotape me being whipped and chained, aren't you? No wonder you're into me. You probably see me as this helpless, gullible little virgin who's so repressed he'd do anything with a guy like you." My heart was beating a thousand miles an hour, and I thought I was about to puke.

Tristan's expression changed immediately. He no longer had the demeanor of a swaggering stallion. His eyes grew huge, and he held up his hands and apologized right away. "What? No! Grant, I was joking. Do you really think I'm a skeezy, whip-wielding masochist?"

"Sadist," I corrected automatically.

"What?"

"You mean you're not a *sadist*. A masochist derives pleasure from pain, whereas a sadist is the one who enjoys inflicting the pain."

"Why…. What…. How do you even know that?" I wasn't sure if he was impressed or disturbed by my knowledge.

"I have the Internet. I may not *do* any of the things I know about, but I get bored watching cat videos and Netflix streaming. I poke around at stuff." It seemed logical to me. The illogical thing was our conversation. Where the heck was this going, and why? "Is there a point to your visit? This conversation is getting really weird and uncomfortable. Besides being at work, you're making me feel worse than that other man did. I sort of know you, but I don't think I know you at all, and I'm thinking I'm a little scared." I had to get all my thoughts out at once, because I heard the vault door shut. It was close to closing. Soon I'd have to count out my drawer and settle my deposits. I needed Tristan to tell me what was going on, or leave.

He took a deep breath, closing his eyes, and placed both hands on the counter. Was he meditating? He took a cash envelope and a pen and wrote on it. As I watched him scribble his note, I couldn't help but think, *they aren't supposed to be used that way!* Then he slid it over to me and pointed at my screen. "Will you tell me the amount that check number sixty-two fifty was written for?"

Dumbfounded, I stared at the screen. "Ah…." He tapped the paper, and I glanced down. It said:

> *I'm sorry. You're not used to my sense of humor.*
> *I was making a joke about doing things to you with my*
> *tongue, but I didn't mean to scare you. I'm not a sadist. I*
> *don't own a whip. I came in tonight because I missed you*
> *and I wanted to say hi. That's all. I promise. I might have*
> *some ideas of things I'd like to do to you, but any and all*
> *sexual inclinations are on hold. I want to get to know you*
> *first. Sex is not my priority. I'm not going to use you, and*
> *I'm not going to hurt you. I'm not even sure why you would*
> *jump to that conclusion. I'm sorry I freaked you out.*

Well, his note, printed in perfectly legible sentences, left me speechless. I knew I had plunged headlong into that assumption, but it made his interest in me seem more logical in my mind. I glanced up after reading it and gazed into his eyes. They didn't seem like the eyes of a serial killer, a con artist, *or* a whip-wielding sadist. He looked 100 percent sincere, and I was beguiled. Plus, he'd mentioned sex. I might actually get to have sex.

"The check is for eleven dollars even," I said, continuing with the charade. My voice had no strength.

"What? Oh, um, yes, thank you."

I wrote a reply of my own on a sticky note and stuck it to the counter in front of Tristan. Very casual, no one would know I wasn't actually working unless they took the note.

He read it.

> *I'm sorry. I had a bad date experience in college.*
> *I met a guy on Facebook. We had agreed to meet at the*
> *mall since it was a public setting. He was decent looking,*
> *but I couldn't go through with the date after he handed me*
> *a list of things he wanted to do to me.*

Tristan looked up with sadness in his eyes. He whispered, "Oh, Grant. I'm sorry."

Jessica moved around the half wall and went into the break room. We were alone. There were five minutes before closing, so most employees on Thursday night were ready to leave.

"Do you mean it?" I asked.

"Mean what? Everything in the note is true."

"That you missed me?"

I must have finally said the right thing, because he smiled the softest, most amazing smile. "Yes, Grant, I missed you. That kiss was… well… it wasn't enough. I want to kiss you again."

"Okay." I melted.

"But I was serious about sex. I'm not taking you to bed, not yet. I've had way too many relationships that skipped over every pleasantry and headed straight to sex. Not with you."

"Not even a little sex?" I couldn't help but beg with my tone. I wasn't keen on him having lots of sexual partners, and we *would* be discussing that, but the prospect of no sex was depressing.

He smirked and shook his head. "Not even a little, until I know where this relationship is heading. I'm thirty-two years old, Grant. I've had a wild youth. I'm ready to settle down and live my life committed to someone special. Tomorrow, we can talk about what *you* want. Okay?"

I nodded. He knew how to say all the romantic things. It sounded to me like he was seeking a husband type. Did he mean me? Was I really husband material? I had to admit growing old with someone, *one* someone, sounded super wonderful. My mom had told me that was what she and my dad had planned. It probably would have happened too.

Tristan tapped the counter in front of him as if contemplating his next move. He said, "Good night," and headed to the front door. Tracy locked it after he left.

Chapter Five

Misconceptions, Misunderstandings, And Getting A Taste Of Full-On Lust For The First Time

WE HAD agreed to meet at his house this time. After I plugged the address into my GPS, I realized how familiar it sounded. Sure enough, I passed this street every day on my way to work. We only lived about five minutes apart. His auto shop was on the corner, but I hadn't read the sign until now.

"How unobservant am I?" I asked myself as I parked. I checked my hair in the visor mirror and then got out and locked the door.

It was a small farmhouse, but much larger than the one I rented. Half the flowers in the beds were brown. A tailpipe jutted out from one bed to obstruct mowing, so the grass growing around it was five inches taller than the rest of the lawn. "That would drive me nuts if I lived here," I mumbled, ringing the doorbell.

Tristan opened the door and smiled through the screen. "Hey. Come on in," he offered, opening the screen door for me.

It was an older, two-story farmhouse with creaky wooden floors and decor from the seventies. I cringed at the duck wallpaper border in the kitchen and the psychedelic orange-and-brown throw rug in the living room. "Um, there's an engine on your dining room table," I pointed out, literally pointing at it.

"Ah, yeah," he said, glancing at the engine and then back to me as if thinking of a reason but finding none. "I've lived alone for a long time. Claire and I normally eat at the breakfast bar." He motioned to the area over by the kitchen, but the "bar" was stacked with magazines.

"There's no room there either."

Tristan walked over and started moving them to the side, but there wasn't space. He gave up. "Yeah, I was looking for a specific one. They were my dad's. I found them in the attic when I was clearing out some old boxes. I got to looking through them and just haven't put them away yet."

Tristan's house was the exact opposite of mine. His things were in disarray all over the place. Stacks of books, CDs, DVDs, a few coffee cups, and…. "There's a muffler under the coffee table," I said, observing yet another oddity for one's living room.

"I know this looks bad," Tristan said, stepping in front of me and pressing his hands together as if to pray or beg for forgiveness.

"I guess you aren't worried about grease stains. That carpet looks like it's been soiled for decades."

"Like I said, I've lived alone for a long time. The muffler's been under there for two years. I'm married to my work, and I tend to carry car parts home all the time."

"I noticed you live behind the shop. That must be convenient." Tristan was wearing another beer shirt. This one was gray and said something about imperial stout.

"It is handy. This was my parents' house. After my dad died, my mom gave it to me since I was already in charge of the family business. My sister lives in Baltimore, and my mom lives with my brother in Leesburg, Virginia. I see Claire every other weekend. You're the first person outside my family and the guys I work with to step inside this house."

"What about dates?" I asked.

"I don't date, Grant. My life's been on hold ever since my daughter was born. Look, let's go eat. It's getting late fast, and we can talk more on the way and over dinner." He gestured to the door, and I nodded.

We walked around the house and to his truck, got in, and started on our way.

I thought about what he'd said in the house, and it was similar to something he'd mentioned before. "You said something yesterday about skipping over pleasantries and going straight for sex." I heard him heave a sigh as I framed my question. "What did you mean? Are you one of those guys who hooks up in gay bars and strip clubs?" The idea bothered me. He could have AIDS or another STD. Having no guy almost seemed better than dating a sex pig. I didn't want to catch a disease. I wanted sex, but after thinking about his earlier comment I had realized sex meant something to me. If it hadn't, I could have done exactly what he'd done. I truly was saving myself for my soul mate, Mr. Right.

"Yes and no." He paused a long time after his ambiguous answer. I'd been argumentative enough, so I waited this time. He finally continued. "I *have* done those types of things. In my twenties, I hooked up much more often with guys I met in bars. I got out of the service when I was still young, and I think repressing how I felt all that time got the best of me, because for several years after that I couldn't get enough. I had a different guy practically every weekend."

I couldn't look at him as he said those things, so I watched the passing trees out my window. It made me ill to think of him with so many men. I couldn't understand that lifestyle, even if I was aware it happened all the time. It wasn't me. I had never wanted meaningless sex just to satisfy a need to fuck. But he did. I was in a truck, going to dinner, with a man who had needed to fuck so badly that he'd hooked up with guys he didn't know just to satisfy his lust… every weekend.

A tear rolled down my cheek.

"Why did you stop?" I asked quietly, still watching the passing trees and road signs.

"A guy I knew died."

I sucked in a quick breath. "That's horrible." I glanced over at Tristan. He wasn't looking at me. "Was it AIDS?"

"Everyone jumps to that conclusion since he was gay, but no, not AIDS. He was jumped in an alley by a group of guys, raped and beaten, and left for dead. He died in a hospital three days later of hemorrhaging in his brain."

My stomach almost emptied itself on the truck seat. I held my mouth and willed away the quaking in my gut. I wanted to cry, I wanted to vomit, but somehow I was shocked into stillness. My brain couldn't even comprehend that kind of crime. I'd never seen one, even on television. I tended to stay away from news because it was all depressing. This was a class A example. I hated that people in the world I lived in did things like this to others. I had been picked on throughout my life, even before I came out, but it was normal harassment of a scrawny kid who didn't know how to fight back. I'd never been hurt physically, and even the jibes and name-calling hadn't affected me all that much. I'd been a normal kid growing up, before and after I'd come out. Things like this man's death never happened in my sphere of experience.

Tristan parked the truck. He must have noticed how quiet I'd become and realized why. He reached across the console. "Come here."

I turned into him as best I could with the console pressing into my ribs and cried softly into his shirt. I felt like an idiot, but the tears wouldn't stop.

He rubbed my back. "I cried too, Grant. His death was why I stopped. He had put himself into too many precarious situations with guys he didn't know. Someone saw the men leaving the alley, but no one was arrested. I've been with two guys since then. One I met at a car show, and we had sex a couple times. Another I met at the airport. Neither of them filled any kind of need other than sexual gratification. We fucked, and we were done. I haven't been with anyone in two years."

I pulled out of his arms so I could look into his face. "Why?"

He shrugged. "Maybe because I wanted my thirties to be different. I went to my daughter's thirteenth birthday party and watched her with her friends. No guy I'd ever been with was worth the time necessary to bring him into my life. I saw how I'd kept everything separate. My daughter's mother didn't know I was gay. My daughter would have to be told eventually. I watched the guests and thought about what it would be like to sit at a party like that with a guy I cared about." He gazed deeply into my eyes as he spoke. "I'm done being a stupid kid, Grant. I want to build a life with someone—someone like you. I want to go to birthday parties with a man who'll appreciate how incredible my daughter is, not just the size of my dick. Does that make sense?"

I felt my heart melting again. "That's the most romantic thing anyone's ever said to me."

He chuckled. "Then you don't get out much." He ran his fingers through my hair and caressed my cheek. "Oh, Grant. You're such a beautiful person. I've just dumped a lot of information on you, and your reaction is to tell me how romantic I am?" He chuckled harder. "I knew taking a chance on you was the right decision."

"But you hardly know me." I had to point that out, because most people who tried to get to know me found out they didn't like me.

"I will. Let's go eat." I thought he'd pull away to open the door, but he only stared into my eyes. Then his gaze dropped to my lips. He looked up as if to make sure it was okay and then leaned in and kissed me softly. One kiss, but it was enough to calm my nerves.

I mewled.

"Now we can eat," he said with a wink.

I wiped my eyes as I closed the truck door and followed Tristan into Olive Garden. I wasn't sure how he knew this was my favorite restaurant, but he scored some points as far as first "real" dates were concerned. And, he'd kissed me already. The evening was starting off on the right foot.

After the hostess seated us in a booth, the waitress walked up and took our drink orders. "Can I have a raspberry iced tea?" I asked.

Tristan settled on water, no lemon.

As I contemplated my choice, I noticed how Tristan observed the people at other tables and the pictures on the walls, but not the menu. "Aren't you going to look at the menu?"

He shook his head. "No. I already know what I want. I come here all the time."

I smiled. "I used to go to Olive Garden with Mel for lunch back where I used to work."

"Hmm." He nodded. "Who's Mel?"

"My best friend. He lives in Ellicott City. When our branch closed, he was one of twelve who were offered positions at other branches."

"Like you?"

"Yeah. He works in Montgomery County now."

"Where all the money is," he commented.

"I guess. I moved to Westminster, so we haven't seen each other in a few weeks, but we talk almost every day."

"Is he gay?"

I wasn't sure if it was a casual question or jealousy, but I said, "No. He's interested in this girl who works at a local eatery named Cindy."

His smile seemed thankful. I think he *was* jealous.

"Here are your drinks," the waitress—although in my head, I thought the term "server" was probably more appropriate—said. "May I take your order?"

He ordered Chicken Parmigiana and I got the Ravioli di Portobello. After she'd taken our menus and walked away, I proceeded to move my drink from the right side to my left. Only the moisture on the outside made the cup slippery, and I dropped it. The cup dumped its contents all over the table and into Tristan's lap. I was horrified.

"Oh my God!" I gasped. "I'm so sorry." I flashed back to my memory of Kenny as Tristan jumped out of his seat, tea dripping down his leg, crotch soaked through. "I don't know why I get so clumsy. Please don't leave."

He held up an urgent finger as if to silence me. "Stop. I'm going to the bathroom. You get us another seat while I'm drying my pants under the hand dryer."

"I'm so sorry."

"Grant…," he warned.

I covered my face with my hands as soon as he'd walked away. "This is a nightmare," I moaned. I composed myself and waved the waitress over. "Can we please have another table? I spilled my drink and it's all over the seat."

She checked the seat and under the table. "Oh, wow! Of course. Let me check with the hostess." She returned and gestured to the booth next to ours. "You can hop right over to this table, and I'll get someone to mop that up."

I was grateful but also thankful we'd come at five fifteen and not six, because by then the tables would have been full. I'd switched my schedule with Lucinda, and I owed her one. Tristan returned, and I hung my head in shame.

"Grant, look at me," he insisted, taking his seat across from me.

I did, but barely. I was so ashamed.

"Did you do it on purpose?" he asked.

My eyes popped open. "No! Why would you think—"

"Then stop beating yourself up over it. Accidents happen. Just let it go."

"You're not mad?" I couldn't believe it.

"I'm not happy about it, but how can I get angry over an accident?"

"I don't know." I felt so insignificant under his forgiveness. He gave it so readily. *Why?*

"Grant, can I ask you a question?"

I nodded.

"Have you done that before? Have people given you shit over spilling a drink?" It was like he could see into my mind and watch the reruns of Kenny and our failed date.

I hesitated but nodded again.

He marveled, "You certainly have had terrible dating experiences, haven't you?"

I confessed, "Once, my date and I went to this fancy French restaurant, and he told me I could order for us, since I know French and he liked hearing me speak it. Well, I ordered something with chopped scallops and shrimp folded into a crepe with a wine sauce. It was the special of the day and I like shrimp."

"That sounds good so far."

"He was allergic to seafood," I said. "He took one bite and went into anaphylactic shock. Luckily a doctor was dining two tables over and knew what to do while someone called an ambulance. I never saw him again." I hung my head.

"Grant?" he urged.

I looked up. He was reaching across the table, palm open. I took the hint and placed my hand in his.

"I will never treat you like that. I promise. It was an accident, and if he was allergic to seafood, then he was the stupid one who ate it. I've never had a seafood dish that didn't smell like seafood. He could have smelled it *before* he put it in his mouth, or made you aware of his allergies before you ordered." He squeezed my hand reassuringly, and I felt like I wanted to cry again. He helped me see that horrible date in a different way than ever before. I had always blamed myself for ordering the wrong thing, but Tristan was right, that guy should have been more careful. It wasn't my fault.

"Thank you," I said, feeling too choked up to elaborate.

Our food arrived, and he let go of my hand and sat up. I wasn't sure if it was to make room for our plates, or because he was embarrassed to hold my hand in public.

"Oh, don't let go of his hand on my account," the *server* said.

He held my gaze briefly and grinned before telling her, "Nah, too hard to use a fork with my left hand."

"All right," she replied. She moved her attention to me and said, "I tried."

I giggled. I hadn't known when I moved here that it would be so easy to live out. Folks in Columbia were generally accepting of homosexuals, but I hadn't thought the same about Westminster. So far, I felt pretty good about living here.

We ate and talked about his Navy years. His daughter. He told me he was never married. He explained, "It was one of those stupid teenage moments where you think, 'Oh, I don't need to wear a condom,' and then she's pregnant." Apparently it had been a rebellious decision on her part, and he had only been there for the ride—literally. Tristan hadn't been completely sure of his sexuality until he enlisted. "Then I was surrounded by gorgeous men in uniform and with an unequivocal desire to fuck each and every one of them. I think that's why I went overboard after I got out," he said.

I didn't talk a whole lot about myself. I liked how his voice caressed me. It was the best date I'd ever been on. He even paid!

WHEN WE got back to his house, he suggested a movie after giving me a brief tour of the ground level. "You can pick anything you want. I have a stack of DVDs, and I have Netflix." He walked into the kitchen and pointed to the living room.

"You're not going to lock your door?" It's not that I didn't feel safe in his house, but I always locked my door after I got home.

"No. I never lock it. I don't think I've locked the door in eight years. My shop is practically in my yard. I come home every day for lunch, and the only people that visit me either work for me or are related to me, so I've never felt the need. Do you want anything to drink? A beer or something?" He stood by the fridge, waiting for me to answer from the living room.

"I don't think I want a beer. The last time, I was really sleepy as soon as I walked in the door." I started to kneel down in front of the stack of DVDs, but reconsidered. I squatted instead. The carpet looked grimy, and I didn't want the knees of my pants stained. His DVDs were in disarray, upside down and in no particular order. One was out of its case and covered in dust. If they'd been mine, they would have been alphabetized and lined up on a shelf. One title caught my eye, and I slipped it out of the stack. "How about *Gone in 60 Seconds*?" I asked, waving the case around to draw his attention.

He cocked his head and walked over to me with two bottles of water in his hand. "Why did you pick that one?" he inquired curiously.

"I don't know. I've seen it twenty times, and if I get distracted while we watch it, I won't miss anything important. Why? Don't you like this one?"

His soft smiles were becoming sappier every time. "It's my favorite movie. I guess I'm surprised you picked it."

I glanced down at the case in my hands and then back at Tristan and smiled. "Yeah, well, I almost picked *Pitch Black*, but I have a hard time resisting this one." I winked, and he chuckled.

He said, "I'm fond of *Pitch Black* too. Either one would have been fine. I'm glad you like some of the same movies." Tristan placed the water bottles on the coffee table and sat on the sofa. He grabbed the universal remote and turned on the television.

I opened the case. "It's empty."

He smirked. "It's already in the player."

I put the case on the top of the stack and sat next to Tristan. "By the way, I've seen probably 90 percent of the movies in that stack, and I liked most of them."

The look on his face was priceless.

Tristan started the movie, and I opened my water and kicked off my shoes. I was really thirsty, and I knew it was from nervousness. Would he kiss me again? Would we mess around, and how far would he go? He said he wanted to take things slow, but I'd been sitting on idle for so many years I wasn't sure how slow I could go without getting blue balls. I was tired of doing the one-fisted tango alone or coming in my sleep.

Tristan had his arm across my shoulders, and I leaned onto his chest; however, the position was awkward and not very comfortable on my neck. *And what should I do with my hands?* I had them folded on my lap, but the prospect of rubbing his thigh was very enticing. I moved my right arm so my elbow sat on top of his thigh and my hand comfortably rested over his knee. As soon as I slid my palm around to the inside of his leg, Tristan made a little noise. I continued caressing his knee area, because I didn't want to push my luck. He'd never said how far he would go, which wasn't my fault, but I feared his disapproval if I ventured too far up the inside of his leg.

I kept my fingers in check, but I was dying to rub his crotch.

Imagining what his body might look like, I licked my lips. He'd worn shorts to the gym, so I knew he had solid calf muscles and his brown leg hair wasn't too thick. He had cords of muscle above his kneecap, which I could feel through his jeans. I bet his thighs were amazing.

At that point I forgot the movie. I heard the dialogue in the background, but Nicolas Cage was not my focus. Tristan's breathing had changed to heavier, more rapid puffs. My head was against his collarbone, and he nuzzled my hair with his cheek as I caressed his knee. As I grew bolder and moved my hand north, he placed his hand over mine and squeezed.

"What are you doing?" he asked, but his voice was far from steady.

I lifted my head off his shoulder and gave him a droopy-eyed expression. I all but stuck my lip out and pouted. "Nothing."

He made a guttural noise, like a growl, but deep in the back of his throat. He was two seconds from either shoving me away or eating me. "Grant," he rasped. "We can't do this."

"Just one kiss?" I suggested, looking as fake-sad as I could.

He grunted but brought his mouth down on mine. He was trying to maneuver on the couch as he kissed, but I was quicker and turned where I sat so I was practically kneeling on the couch as I worked my way into his lap. I wound my arms around his neck and kissed him like we'd done before, only I wanted to use my tongue. I hoped he was into that.

It wasn't like I knew all that many gay men personally, but I had heard there were men who didn't like kissing, and some who didn't mind kissing as long as there was no tongue involved because they had a thing against saliva getting all over their face. I couldn't say I disagreed with that, but since I'd never experienced the messiness first hand, I figured I was still open to the option.

I had one leg bent on either side of his thighs as I sat in his lap, kissing him aggressively and working up my nerve to lick. When I did, Tristan groaned as he grabbed the back of my head and held me in place while thrusting his tongue into my mouth and kissing me wildly. He lifted me off the couch in his arms and turned us around so he could place me onto the cushions, then leaned down, still kissing me, and knelt between my legs.

It probably would have been wiser to stop kissing, because as he groped for the pillow wedged between me and the back of the couch, his other knee slipped off the side and he tumbled to the floor, nearly dragging me with him.

I giggled as I peeked over the edge.

"It's not funny," he said, staring up at me.

"Yes, it is," I replied, giggling louder.

Tristan wasn't laughing, but he also wasn't upset. He reached out. "Come here."

"But the floor is dirty," I said, wrinkling my nose. His carpet was soiled from grease stains and ground-in mud. It was disgusting.

"You can use my shower later. I promise the shower is very clean." He shoved the table out of the way, muffler and all.

I climbed off the couch and onto his outstretched torso. Once I was lying on him, Tristan held me around my back and rolled, switching our positions so he was lying on top. He smiled into my eyes, proud of himself, as he descended, kissing me again just as deeply as he had before he had fallen off the couch.

I enjoyed his weight on me. He wasn't as heavy as I thought he'd be, or maybe he was holding some of his weight up by his elbows and knees. I didn't know. What I knew was that being in that position made me realize the ache and need I had inside to be fucked. I'd pondered for years how people knew if they were tops or bottoms. Was it experimentation or dumb luck? In this moment, at least for me, it was an undeniable yearning for Tristan to sink inside of me.

I wasn't a kid. This was the age of the Internet. My naïveté was long gone. I'd gone years not knowing anything about what two men could do with each other, but one year I typed in "porn" and lost my intellectual virginity. I'd watched videos, I understood the mechanics; it was practical experience I lacked. As I lay on the floor under Tristan, I burned for him to rip my clothes off and give it to me good.

My one leg sprawled open, so I easily bent it at the knee and pressed against Tristan's hip. I found the hem of his shirt and rubbed the smooth skin of his lower back. Tristan was between my legs, and when he ran his hand down my side to my thigh and pulled, I felt his ample package nudging my crotch. I grabbed the back of his shaven head and kissed him fervently as I lifted my hips off the ground. I felt him press against my erection for a few seconds before releasing my mouth and sitting up.

"We need to stop, Grant." He was breathing hard, and his face was red and slightly sweaty. "I wasn't going to push this far."

I sat up next to him and tentatively reached out. I needed to touch him, but I was afraid he'd pull away. "It's okay. You're not pushing. I don't want you to stop."

He rubbed his head as if frustrated and then looked at me with this weird suffering expression. "I think you should go home." He moved from the floor to the couch but kept his eyes averted. "I'll call you tomorrow."

"Okay." I wasn't sure what I'd done wrong. I sat quietly and put my shoes back on, then walked over to the other chair and picked up my coat. I hesitated by the door. "Can I ask you one thing?" He did at least look at me as I asked the question. "Was my kissing okay? I don't have any experience to know, and I hope I didn't disappoint you."

Tristan dropped his head forward and mumbled, "Oh, Grant." He stood up and gestured to the crotch of his jeans. "This is what your kissing did to me."

I saw the wet spot near his zipper. "You came?"

He grinned and shook his head. "No. It's precome. I don't wear underwear, so it looks worse than it really is. My point is that your kissing is just fine. I didn't want to stop."

"Then... why did you?" I hated asking, but I had thought the date was going so well.

Tristan joined me by the door and caressed my cheek. He explained, "Because I wanted to prove to myself I could have a relationship with a man *not* based on sex."

"Even if I want the sex?" I did sound pitiful, and I hoped he wouldn't think me terribly immature for whining.

He smirked. "Even if you want the sex. I told you at dinner that I'm looking to settle down. Maybe not tomorrow, but dating you—for me— isn't casual. Deep down in my gut I can tell there's something special about you, and I want to spend time with you. If you're not looking for a long-term relationship, then this won't work."

"No—yeah, I get that. I've never wanted to play the field or date loads of guys. I've wanted someone special too. Ask Mel! All I talk about is meeting Mr. Right and settling down. I've been hoping that waiting so long to have sex would be worth it. Ya know? Like maybe it was fate telling me my first time needed to be special."

"Precisely. I think you're special. So I didn't want to rush things between us sexually, because I thought there would be plenty of time later."

I pointed to the couch. "And that's why you stopped whatever was going to happen just now."

"Yeah. Go home. I'll call you tomorrow, and we can talk." He kissed me softly. "I care about you, Grant."

I didn't know how to respond, so I didn't say anything. I slipped through the door without more confusion. Tristan liked me a whole lot more than I expected. He wasn't kicking me out for good, and he most definitely wanted to see me again. Hands down, it was the best date ever!

I got in my car and turned the key. The engine made a strained sound. I tried again. It groaned. One more turn of the key and the engine made a click and then nothing. I slumped forward on the steering wheel. "Tristan's never going to believe me," I groaned. I got out of my car and knocked on the door. No answer. I knocked again. I remembered he said he never locked the door, so I turned the knob.

I peeked into the house. All the lights were still on, but Tristan was nowhere to be seen. "Tristan?" I called, but he didn't reply. I walked slowly through the living room and entered the bedroom, unsure of how he'd react. "Tristan?" I saw a light from the bathroom door. I stepped closer and heard a grunt and a heavy sigh. It was probably the sound I thought it was, so I gulped, steadied my nerves, and knocked on the door. "Tristan?"

He yanked the door open. "Grant?" He seemed surprised and then squinted his eyes. "What are you doing?" he asked suspiciously.

I felt so foolish I hung my head. "Um, my car won't start."

There was a pause, and then Tristan snickered under his breath. "You're kidding."

I lifted my eyes to meet his. "No!" I exclaimed. "I don't know anything about cars, but mine won't turn over."

The mirth faded, and he asked, "Does it click? Or does it sound like the engine won't quite start?"

"When I got in, it sounded strained. Then it clicked. Now I got nothing." I apologized, "I'm sorry. I tried a few times, but it won't do anything. I didn't want to bother you, but...."

I guess he could tell I wasn't lying. He placed his hand on my shoulder and squeezed. "Calm down, Grant. It's all right. As much as I'd love to go out at midnight and use a flashlight to figure out what's wrong, I think I'm going to pass. You can stay here tonight."

"Are you sure?" I asked, thinly veiling my excitement.

"Yeah, it's fine. I'll just find you a blanket for the couch." He walked over to a closet and took out a fuzzy blue blanket.

"Couch?" I asked, letting my shoulders slump.

He lifted his eyebrow and smirked. "You didn't think you'd get to sleep in my bed, did you?"

I shrugged. My disdain for sleeping on couches dated back to when I was ten and used to go to my grandmother's house. Her couch was awful. Even as a little kid, my back would end up sore by morning. I'd avoided sleeping on couches ever since, even my own. "I don't know. I hadn't thought about sleeping arrangements when I walked in here. This situation just sort of happened, but your couch seems awfully short for me to sleep on."

He opened his mouth, probably to counter my argument, and then decided against it. "Fine. You're right, it's small. It's actually a loveseat, but I never call it that when people come over."

"I thought you didn't have much company here."

"I don't. Look, you can sleep here, but we're *not* having sex. Remember that." He pointed at me for emphasis and then put the fuzzy blanket back in the closet. "Do you want something to sleep in? My shirts might be too big, but I have a pair of shorts with a drawstring I think will fit you." Tristan walked over to the bed and turned down the comforter.

"No. I'm fine. I have a white T-shirt under my dress shirt, and I normally sleep in boxers." I stood on the opposite side of the bed, unsure when to disrobe. The situation grew more uncomfortable as time ticked. Did I jump right in? Should I ask for a toothbrush? I'd never slept with anyone, except one night when Mel and I were playing video games years ago and had fallen asleep on his floor in front of the television.

"Grant? Hello?" Tristan waved a hand as if they were in front of my eyes, even though he was across the room. "Do you need anything? You can have one of the new toothbrushes under the sink. There was a sale, and I tend to go through them." I gave him a look, and he explained, "They're really good for cleaning small parts and detailing."

"Oh. Um, okay, thanks." I awkwardly remained planted in my spot next to the bed. Initially, I had been charged with energy. The prospect of sleeping with him exhilarated me. But now I realized I barely knew him. I was about to sleep next to a strange man who might live alone because he strangled his lovers in their sleep. *What if I wake up and I'm tied to the bed? What if he has a closet full of sex toys and really does own a whip?*

"Grant?" I turned toward his voice, right next to me, and swallowed hard. "Shhh," Tristan soothed, gliding his fingers down my cheek. He leaned in and kissed me softly. "You don't need to be terrified—unless you had a weird dating experience involving a slumber party."

I giggled. "No."

He kissed my forehead. "Okay. Just checking. I promise I'm not a serial killer, I'm not a drug dealer, and I'm not a sex-club Dom. I'm an auto mechanic." He gazed into my eyes and continued to rub my cheek with his thumb very softly. "We're only sleeping."

Sleeping. I could handle that. "Could I get a drink of water?" My throat was dry from nerves.

"Sure." He grinned. "And if you want to take a shower like I promised, feel free. I'll go get you a bottle of water."

I'd showered twice today, so I wasn't motivated to do it again now. His carpet had been awfully dirty, but I'd also been fully clothed. My hair might need washing, but I was fine until morning. I unbuttoned my shirt and hung it over the back of a chair that had a stack of folded towels on it. As I undid my belt and kicked off my shoes, Tristan came back in the room.

"Here ya go." He held up the water bottle. He came around to my side of the bed and set it on the nightstand. "I'm going to brush my teeth."

He went into the bathroom, and I undressed the rest of the way. I felt so very unsexy in my boxers and T-shirt. I crossed my arm over my chest and squeezed my opposite shoulder while I crossed my other arm over my midsection. It was a posture I'd adopted when I was a gangly teen at a swimming pool, trying to cover my body with my two scrawny arms. I might not be as scrawny now, but the pose was a comfort thing, like embracing myself would protect me from being laughed at.

I slunk over to the bathroom and asked for a toothbrush.

Tristan spit into the sink. "There's a bag under there." He pointed. "I'll be done in a second."

"Do you have any more pillows? I usually sleep with three."

He wiped his mouth. "Three?"

"Yes. Two under my head, and I cuddle one." Admitting it made me open to criticism, but I really did like my pillows.

"No, sorry. I only have two. But you can have mine if you want."

"It's okay. I'll be fine." I almost accepted the offer, but it seemed selfish because he wouldn't have any. He left, and I brushed my teeth, washed my hands, and splashed cold water over my face to try and calm my nerves. I dried my face and hung the hand towel back on the towel holder. After smelling my fingers, I glanced at the soap bottle. *Orange ginger.* Sniffing my fingers again, I sighed. This scent was even more pleasant than the grapefruit one at work.

When I returned to his room, he was rummaging through a drawer and explained, "I'm looking for underwear. I normally don't wear any, and I sleep naked, but since you're here I thought I'd throw on a pair. Except I can't find any underwear in my drawer. Oh, wait," he said, pulling out some tighty-whities. "These'll work."

I walked over to the bed and slipped under the covers as he sat on the other side and removed his shoes and socks. When he stood and undid his belt and zipper, I looked away. Tristan chuckled. A second later he commented, "You can look now. Happy Harry is undercover."

I turned back, but one thin layer of white underwear wasn't enough to hide what was underneath. I could tell he was stimulated by our situation, as was I. His bulge seemed large, and my desire made itself known in my extremities, burying my fear of sleeping with him. When he removed his shirt and I got to see his tightly muscled chest, covered in a sheen of light brown hairs, in all its fine detail, I gasped and my jaw dropped open.

He smirked. "Like what you see?"

"As if any man in his right mind wouldn't? You're built like a god." All that muscle, close enough to touch, gave me a full-on boner in seconds. *Oh, jeez, how am I supposed to get any sleep now?*

Tristan climbed into his queen-size bed next to me. There was room for two, but I could feel his heat under the covers. Before turning out the light he asked, "You gonna be okay?"

I nervously nodded and surreptitiously squeezed my penis. *I will not jerk off next to him. I refuse to be this horny. I will go to sleep.* Silently talking to myself wasn't helping.

"Good night," Tristan said. He smiled and turned off the light. He rolled onto his side, facing away from me.

If I could sleep at all while lying next to such a gorgeous, virtually naked man, it would be a miracle.

Chapter Six

Arguments, Rash Decisions, And Jumping Into The Deep End Without My Swimmies

LIGHT WAS streaming through the bedroom window when I opened my eyes. I felt very warm and safe. Tristan's body was pressed up against me. Wait! Tristan's body was pressed up against me! *Oh, shit.* Yes, my dick knew it. Apparently his did as well, because as I mentally took note of where our bodies touched, I felt a very stiff object jammed against my ass. I doubted very seriously that it was a fire extinguisher.

I shivered with desire. Feeling him pressed *there* made me want it so much more.

His left arm was under my neck, and his right firmly held me across my chest. I could feel his head close to mine, so I dared not move and clock him in the nose. Instead, I rubbed his arm and squeezed his hand where it held me. Waking up in someone's arms was a wonderful experience. My body was humming with desire but also quiet contentment. I really, really liked being in his arms.

Tristan sighed and tightened his hold on me. He rocked his hips into my ass and groaned. He nuzzled my hair with his nose and then kissed me behind my ear. "Morning," he whispered.

"Good morning," I whispered back.

I felt him nuzzling again. "You smell really good. Mmm," he sighed, moving down far enough to kiss the back of my neck. He released his hold on me and continued kissing until his lips had inventoried my neck, my throat, my chin, and over to my opposite ear as he rolled me onto my back. Tristan slid his arms under my back and inserted one knee between my thighs. His erection rubbed against mine, and I thought he meant to dry hump me.

"Um, Tristan?" I panted. "What about waiting? Didn't you… oh… yes… oh…." Talking was impossible while he sucked on my collarbone. I had woken up wanting this, but somewhere in my guilt-riddled brain, I knew sex wasn't what Tristan wanted. Not yet. "Tristan?" I pleaded again. "I'm gonna come if you don't stop rubbing against me. Please, stop." I whimpered, and he froze.

"Grant?" he asked, lifting his head and shifting his weight so he slid to the side and off my unbearably hard cock.

I didn't like his tone, especially when I had been thinking of *him* when I asked him to stop. "Who'd you think I was?" I snapped.

"You!" he answered. "But I thought it was a dream you, not the real you."

I pulled the covers up protectively, as if covering my T-shirted chest was safer than exposing my undergarments. "How could you not know?" Because that pissed me off.

"I didn't… exactly. I've dreamed about you for weeks, Grant. Sometimes I wake up to find I'm humping a pillow and I only dreamed it was your ass. I'm sorry."

He did appear sorry, and dream-humping my pillowy ass seemed sort of… sweet. "You dream about me?" I asked, giving him an approving smile.

Tristan reached over and cupped my cheek. "Yes, I dream about you. I was groggy when I woke up, and I guess my brain hadn't kicked in yet. But you're right, I do intend on taking things slower. I nearly shot my load."

I pulled him in and kissed him. "Then I forgive you."

He smiled. "Thanks. Can I offer you pancakes as a peace offering?"

I pursed my lips. "Hmm, frozen or box mix?" I asked.

"Neither. For you, I'll make them from scratch. I use my mother's recipe." He lifted his eyebrows twice. I was about to gush over it, but he jumped up. "I'll get breakfast going, and if you want to take a shower, the pile of towels is on that chair. Somehow they never make it into the linen closet." Tristan grabbed a pair of shorts off the floor and slipped them on before leaving the room.

I sat up and glanced around his bedroom. Drab paint, which had probably been white at some point in its history, covered the parts of the wall I could see, but it had seen too many years to be white now, or even cream. It was awful. The pictures were worse, as they could have belonged to my grandmother—strike that—my great-grandmother. Prints of ships, six different ones, hung cockeyed around the room. I normally liked ships, but these were so old and faded they'd lost their appeal.

The only recent picture was a photograph. I got out of bed to inspect it. As I moved past one print on the wall, I straightened it before I looked at the picture of Tristan and his daughter. It was obviously at a concert, and Claire looked just about the same as when I'd met her. Tristan hadn't changed either.

"When was this picture on the wall taken of you and Claire?" I called to him in the adjacent room.

"May 24. I took her to an All Time Low concert at Pier Six in Baltimore. It was awesome!"

I straightened two more of the ship prints, but they tilted askew as soon as I took my fingers off the frames. I sighed and left them be. I wandered out to where Tristan was in the kitchen. "I've never heard of All Time Low," I confessed, taking in the horrific scene in the kitchen. Flour dusted every surface. Counter, floor, cabinets, and even the handle on the refrigerator had flour sprinkles or flour fingerprints. I closed my eyes and took a deep breath. *This is his house. I will be fine.*

Tristan didn't notice my agitation. As he stirred his batter, he said, "They're an alt-rock/pop-rock type of band, I guess. They're a local Baltimore band, which I think is cool. Claire really likes them. She used to play their music so much, one day I started singing along and didn't even realize I knew all the words." He laughed. "Their sound is unlike anything I normally listen to, yet I think they're a great band. The lyrics are solid, their sound is clean, and the drummer's hot. What's not to like?" He moved over to the stove and turned on the skillet.

I liked pop music, but I couldn't think of talking about bands when the kitchen was atrocious. I wet the dishrag, which hung over the spigot, with hot water and rung it out. I couldn't help myself. The counter and such needed to be wiped clean of flour. I started with the fingerprints on the fridge.

Tristan said, "Thanks. Sometimes I forget to clean it off for days."

I flinched at the notion, but again, this was his house.

"I thought you'd take a shower. I swear it's clean."

"I know. I was going to, but I don't have any clean clothes. I couldn't bear the thought of showering and then putting my dirty clothes back on." I rinsed the towel and wiped another section of flour-covered counter. Tristan left the pancakes and came up behind me.

He wrapped his arms around my waist and kissed the back of my neck. "How about you stay until after we're done with breakfast, and then you take my truck and drive home for a shower and a change of clothes. In the meantime I'll see what's wrong with your car, and maybe later we can have dinner or go bowling or something?"

I turned in his arms. "You bowl?" I hardly knew anyone who did that anymore.

"It's been a long time since I was on a league, but Claire and I go every now and then. She likes ten pins, but I prefer ducks."

I ran my hands up his chest, thankful he hadn't donned a shirt when he pulled on the shorts. "I do too! I'm not very good, but I love the challenge of duck pins." His pecs were tight and hard under my fingertips and touching his chest hair piqued my desire to rub my face over it.

"Then we'll go tonight. Loser buys dinner next weekend."

I snorted. "Thanks. I'll take you out for hot dogs."

"Don't underestimate your chances. Besides, I like hot dogs," he said with a wink, right before he kissed me. We both smelled the pancakes burning, and he rushed over to scoop them off.

I got the full view of his tattooed back and nearly drooled on the floor, but then I glanced at the pancakes and made a face. "Eww, they're black."

He shrugged. "Doesn't matter. If you smear peanut butter on them, they make a great sandwich. I'll eat them on Monday."

"Really? I wouldn't."

"I eat pancakes all the time. They're a great snack. I usually make a big batch on Sunday and eat them all week. If you put blueberries or strawberries in them, then you get fruit in each bite."

"I love blueberries."

"Then tomorrow morning, I'll make blueberry. That is… if you want to stay again tonight." That damnable grin was difficult to resist.

"No sex?"

He frowned. "No sex."

I considered it for all of two seconds, but waking up in his arms had felt really nice, despite not having sex the night before. "Okay."

WE ATE breakfast in silence and flirted with our eyes. He made me giddy without any conversation. After the dishes were in the dishwasher,

I went into the bedroom to get dressed. As soon as I entered his room, I heard a door slam.

A woman yelled, "I can't believe you told Claire you're gay!"

I stopped in the middle of bending down for my pants and crept over to the door to peek around the frame.

"You had no right to inflict your perversion on our daughter like that!"

The woman yelling must have been Tristan's ex. Claire resembled her a great deal, except Claire had been nice to me. This woman had just offended me by calling homosexuality a perversion, and one to be *inflicted* on others. I waited, but I was ready to jump out and give her a piece of my mind if she kept going. This was his house; she had no right!

"I'm not perverted, Teresa!" he yelled back. "Why do you think I've never told you?"

"Because you're ashamed?" she spat.

Her exclamations sent my mind whirling back to last December and Raymond's ex-wife. *Shit! I hope Tristan doesn't reconsider dating me because of her.*

"Because you're a hateful person!" Tristan countered. "All I've ever done is work my ass off to take care of Claire, but nothing's ever good enough for you. So yes, I told our daughter I'm gay; excuse me for wanting to be happy for once in my life!"

"Happy?" she questioned. "You're *happy* taking it up the ass, spreading diseases, and perverting everything God intended for marriage?" Teresa stood opposite Tristan with her hand on her hip and her attitude puffed up like a cobra's hood. But if she spat venom like those accusations much longer, I'd have to join the fray myself. She pissed me off.

"I'm perfectly healthy, Teresa. I know how to be safe. I get tested regularly, which is something *you* should think of doing with the number of men you sleep with." His reply made me feel better, but his ex was not easily placated.

She gasped and glared. "I do not!"

"That's not what I heard. I've heard a rumor you've had three boyfriends this year alone, and all of them have lived…. In. Your. House." Tristan growled the words he wanted to emphasize. "Who are these guys, Teresa, who you let live with you and our fifteen-year-old daughter? What if they hurt Claire?"

"They wouldn't."

"How do you know? Rumor has it you can't keep a man long enough to remember his last name."

Her teeth were clenched—I could tell from across the room. Tristan was getting to her, and she was formulating her counterargument. "Like you're any different. All men are whores," she argued, her words stabbing my very sensible and virtuous heart. "Gay men are no different. Is that what the Navy did to you? All those nights on a ship at sea, you had to find a way to get off so you decided to be gay?" She was laughing in her hatred. "I should have known. You always were a pussy."

"I've always been gay, Teresa. The Navy had nothing to do with it. Sleeping with you was the only mistake I made, but I would never take it back because I love my daughter."

"So you say."

"I do!"

"So how many men have you been with, if you're so high and mighty about my affairs? Tell me. Fifty? A hundred? Two hundred? All men think with their dicks. I bet you'll fuck anything that moves."

I could have jumped out of my secluded spot and argued her points, but I was curious about what Tristan would say. How many guys had he been with? I kind of wanted to know.

"Thirty-eight. Two before I was deployed, three while I was in the Navy, and thirty-three after I got out."

"And you think you're so much better than me!" she spat.

"I am. I have *never* brought a man to my house. I kept my sex life separate, because I didn't want to hurt Claire. Until now, she was too young to understand anyway."

"She's still too young!"

"She's fifteen and in high school, Teresa. How naive are you? She knows exactly what you do as an adult, because you don't hide it."

"That's a whole lot better than sneaking around fucking in bathrooms," she argued.

At this point, I lost my restraint and jumped into view. "We do not!" I shouted.

Both of them turned their attention my way. Teresa questioned, "Who's this?" while Tristan mumbled, "Grant," lowering his head and clenching his jaw. Maybe my entrance wasn't the best idea.

Teresa argued, "I thought you said you've never brought a man home, Tristan? Or did you find him abandoned on your doorstep, so you brought the stray puppy in?"

Tristan threw his hands out in shock. "What?"

"You're half-dressed and he's in his underwear! How the hell do you explain that?"

"I...." Poor Tristan was tongue-tied, and it was probably my fault.

I explained, "My car broke down after our date. He let me stay. But there was no sex, least of all in the bathroom, and I'll have you know not all gay men have lots of sex. Your insinuations are offensive."

"Insinuations?" she questioned, drawing her shoulders back, probably readying a strike. "I insinuated nothing. I'll flat out tell you men are nothing but shiftless lowlifes who fuck around. They can't commit long-term, because they lack the staying power. Gay men, straight men, you're all the same. But I can see the appeal of being gay. You go in knowing neither one of you will commit, so it's easier to fuck and run."

"That's not true!" I yelled as she mocked me. "I'll have you know there are hundreds of historically documented same-sex couples who committed themselves to one another, even before marriage equality." This was an issue I felt strongly about, for obvious reasons. "Gays have all the commitment resilience of anybody else."

She sneered. "Doubtful because you're men."

This woman, in my mind, represented all the hostile people who had mouthed off about homosexuality without knowing any of the facts. She was ranting about her beliefs without basing them on truth or experience. She was the worst kind of antagonist. I had to stand my ground. I stepped closer to engage her instead of yelling across the room. "It's true," I said, holding my head up high. "If Tristan hid his true self all these years, it's because of people like you who are ill informed and bigoted. Men can love each other and live their lives committed to one another, the same as hetero couples. Just because you can't hold on to a man, doesn't mean Tristan can't!"

I couldn't say I'd ever argued so emphatically about it before, but this was a topic I had contemplated myself. Because I'd been single for so long, I needed to believe that it wasn't for nothing. I had to hold on to the hope that my soul mate was out there—or possibly standing next to me—and I wasn't going to let this stupid woman crush my dreams.

She turned to Tristan. "Are you going to let him talk to me like that? Who the fuck is this guy?" She gestured at me with a flip of her wrist.

Tristan calmly regarded me and then turned to her and said, "He's my boyfriend." He lifted his arm as if to beckon me under it. I happily complied, and he hugged me to his side.

Teresa made a gagging face. "Oh, that's just peachy. I suppose he's moving in next. If he does, you can kiss seeing Claire good-bye. I'm not letting her come here every other weekend to see you flaunting your perversion in front of her, or hear you fucking in the next room. That's sick!"

"Stop calling us perverted!" I growled. If she were a guy, I might have considered punching her.

"Well, you are."

Tristan replied, "No, we're not, Teresa. Besides, you can't say anything. You've got men moving in and out all the time. Grant means a lot to me. He's not going anywhere. At least Claire won't have trouble remembering his last name."

I added, "I met Claire. She seems nice."

I shouldn't have said that. Her face resembled a roiling volcano, and I thought if she had the ability to narrow her pupils to a slit like a snake, she would have. "You let this random guy into your house and introduced him to Claire?" She hissed her question, making my previous comparison to a cobra even more plausible.

"No, they met at the gym, and he's not random!" Tristan held me tighter. I think he needed to reassure himself, or me, that his words were true.

Teresa put her hands on her hips and tossed her head like I've seen women do when they're about step a fight up to the next level. "Oh yeah? How long have you known him, Tristan? Two minutes? He walks into the room in his underwear, and you expect me to believe this is something more than a one-night stand?" She paused and changed her expression. "You know what? I wasn't sold on the whole gay thing, but I was wrong. This is exactly what two men would do. You play 'daddy' every other weekend, and then fuck the rest of the time. It's pathetic."

She turned to leave. Just as she got to the door, Tristan grabbed her arm and whirled her around.

"Let go of me, you faggot!" she yelled, ripping her arm free of his grasp.

"I resent the things you accuse me of. They're unfair, and untrue." Tristan was angry, I could tell, but he reined in his rage. "We are committed to each other, unlike the relationships you have, and unlike your father."

She snarled, "How dare you mention my father."

"I'm saying, I think Claire would be better off living with me than she is watching her mother drinking every night and sleeping with strangers."

"You dare challenge me? I'll sue your ass for everything."

"We were never married, Teresa. You have no rights to my property. I pay you child support voluntarily for Claire's sake, but maybe I want more time with my daughter. Maybe I want to take you to court and file for joint custody, or better yet, file for full custody and give *you* every other weekend."

Tristan's challenge only made Teresa seethe. "Oh really? What court is going to grant you rights? You and your transient lover?"

"We're getting married," I blurted, stepping up to Tristan and looping my hands around his arm. He blinked at me in surprise. I wasn't sure why I said it, but the heat of the argument had gotten to me.

She threw her head back and laughed uncontrollably. "Married?" More laughing. "That's rich!" Still more laughing. It was bordering on ridiculous.

"Yes, married," Tristan interrupted her self-satisfaction. She was way too pleased with what she presumed was outlandish. "Just because you don't agree with it, doesn't make it less true." Although the fact that I had blurted the solution out in defense of Tristan's fatherly honor *might* be an indication of fabrication. I couldn't believe he was going along with it.

Teresa stopped laughing. She eyed him and then glared at me. "You're kidding."

"No, we're not," Tristan asserted. "We're getting married. We're committing ourselves to one another until death do us part, just like so many others in the country who've been given the legal right to do so."

"When?" she scoffed.

Tristan hastily said, "Tomorrow!"

I quickly came to his rescue with logic. "Tristan, honey, we discussed this." I patted his chest, and he looked at me curiously. "Tomorrow isn't the seventeenth." I moved my attention to the dumbstruck ex, whose gaping mouth could catch flies. "Tristan's been so excited to tie the knot that every day feels like the eve of our wedding day. I've reminded him several times that it's still a week off. He's just so excited." I giggled to play up the story.

"Oh, how wonderful. Two fags exchanging vows? Please. It won't last. Tristan is too selfish, and you...." She paused. "You're too young to understand what marriage is about. He's got a kid, you know? What guy jumps into a marriage with a workaholic weekend father and doesn't realize his mistake two weeks later? I give you three weeks, and this little farce will dissolve on its own. Marriage between men?" I heard her hysterical laughter long after she slammed the door on her exit.

Tristan released me, and we faced each other by the door. "What have I done?" he asked.

"What have *we* done," I corrected.

He blinked. "Why did you say that? Why did you jump in and validate it? I could have called her later and told her I was angry and said things I didn't mean. She'd laugh at me, but I could have handled it."

I slouched, feeling rejected for my support. "I didn't like the things she said. They weren't true. She made me angry."

"Angry enough to say you're marrying me?" His voice contained an edge I didn't like or expect.

"A long-term relationship was your idea! I just went along with it."

"Out of anger."

"No!" I protested. "Out of haste. Yes, I rashly jumped into an argument I knew nothing about, but it wasn't completely blind. You said yourself you wanted this relationship to deepen into something permanent. *You* said I should think about what I wanted in life because *you* wanted to grow old with someone. *You* said I meant more to you than a one-night stand and that's why you wouldn't fuck me on the first date. *You* said all those things, Tristan, so excuse me if I got caught up in the moment and agreed to marry you on a whim. People do it all the time, don't they? Couples get drunk in Vegas and end up in an all-night chapel or something, don't they? We'll just be another one of those couples. But if you really don't want to marry me, then we can just do what you said and call Teresa. We can say it was a mistake. We can admit to being sexaholics who fuck in bathrooms."

I was on the verge of tears. Maybe I *had* been reckless, but after citing my own points for marrying him I felt so emotional I needed to cry. I tried to dash away, to hide in the bedroom until my emotions settled, but he grabbed my arm and spun me to face him.

I think he was going to yell, but his expression softened, and he loosened his grip on my arms. "You're shaking."

"Duh! I'm freaking out!"

"Oh, Grant," he sighed. Tristan took me into his arms and held me tightly. He rubbed my back and kissed my temple. "I'm so sorry. I should never have argued with Teresa in front of you. It wasn't fair. She's not a nice person. I knew she'd react like this when she found out about me, but I didn't think it would escalate the way it did. I'm so sorry."

I sniffled and buried my face in his neck. He smelled like pancakes.

"What was the comment you made about her father?"

"Oh. Her father left when she was a kid."

I asked, "That's it? Then why is she so mean toward us?"

"Ever since I met her, Teresa has had a chip on her shoulder about her father and has talked down about men for years. She's never been out-and-out hateful toward homosexuals, but hearing I'm gay probably added gay men to her list." Tristan looked up at the ceiling as if to heaven or God and said, "I apologize to all gay men everywhere. I didn't intend to incur her wrath."

"We forgive you," I said.

Tristan smiled at me. "Thanks. I make no excuses for Teresa, but I know she's never forgiven her father for leaving, and she's never forgiven me for not marrying her."

"Oh. Why didn't you?"

"Because I don't love her. I didn't know she was pregnant until I was out of boot camp. I mentioned marriage out of guilt, but she turned me down, relating me to her father in some sort of twisted way. Her father had cheated on her mother multiple times; Teresa told me she wasn't about to shackle herself to a potential cheater. I let it go because I knew I was gay by that point and would never be happy if I married her. Her mother started drinking years ago, which explains Teresa's drinking problem. The whole situation is a clusterfuck. By the time I was out of the military, coming out as gay seemed to be self-serving. It wouldn't have helped Teresa, and Claire was too young to understand. Teresa and I were never truly together, so I let it go. I figured I'd tell her on a need-to-know basis."

I snuggled my face into his neck. "But why didn't you explain all that in the argument? You aren't like her father, and it sounds like you were trying to save her feelings." He smelled so yummy it was increasingly difficult to focus on the conversation.

"I'm not, and I was, but I'm also not vengeful like her. She has always had to one-up people. I thought it best not to stir up more trouble. Claire knows I'm gay, and I have you. There isn't much more I need."

"Then I'm glad." I couldn't help but kiss his skin—he smelled so good.

Tristan snickered and released me, pulling back far enough to look in my eyes but not letting go of my waist. "You are amazing. I can't believe, after all that, you'd still find the desire to kiss me. Aren't you pissed? You said you're freaking out, but still you kiss me?"

I shrugged, settling my hands on his chest and brushing my fingers lightly over his chest hairs. "What can I say? I'm still attracted to you. You're shirtless and you smell like food, so I kissed you. Arguing with your baby momma doesn't change how I feel about you. I'm not running away, especially now."

"So you're willing to marry me after one date?" He sounded bewildered.

"Yes. I know it's stupid. We hardly know each other. We live vastly different lives and we've only been on one real date. But if this was where our relationship was heading eventually, then why wait? Reneging now proves Teresa right."

"No, it doesn't. She's wrong, no matter what we do next. Getting married on a whim isn't logical or smart."

I ran my fingers across his collarbone. Debating half-clothed was now my favorite way of discussing things. His skin was so warm. "But neither is allowing her to feel self-righteous. I'm not going to stand for her insults. We can make this work. I know we can."

Tristan's eyes danced over my face. He smiled softly, as he often did while gazing at me, and agreed, "Okay. We'll get married. But why did you pick the seventeenth?"

"I knew it would take a few days to get a license, so we couldn't possibly get married tomorrow. We need to buy rings and find an officiator for the ceremony. Most people don't get married during the week, so it had to be a Saturday. I'm off on the seventeenth. I'm not even sure if a week will be enough time, but we can try. We should probably invite people, don't you think? At least close friends, and maybe your daughter."

He tilted his head back. "Oh God, I'm getting married." He looked me in the eyes and squeezed my shoulders. "You and I are getting married. Holy shit!" He laughed and pulled me into a hug. "Well, I guess you better go home, shower, and get your ass back here, because we've got some planning to do."

I laughed until I cried. It was all so much, so fast, and yet I didn't want to get off the ride. I knew I simply needed to hang on tight.

Chapter Seven

Daughters, Diamonds, And Divas Who Materialize Out Of Nowhere

I SHOWERED and returned to his place to find my car running.

"You fixed it!"

"It was the battery," Tristan explained, shutting my hood and wiping his hands on a rag. It was already dirty, so I wasn't sure how much good it would do him to wipe his fingers on it. "When I got in to turn the key I noticed the visor mirror was open. A small light *could* have drained the battery if you hadn't replaced it in a while, but then I noticed the headlights weren't fully shut off. You left the running lights on. I gave you a jump—no problem."

I remembered checking my hair in the mirror, but not leaving the lights on. How embarrassing. "My mom told me driving with the running lights on was safer. Newer cars have lights that come on automatically, but mine don't. Thanks," I said, feeling a little guilty for my mistake. I spotted a hammer sitting on my fender. "Then what's the hammer for?"

"Sometimes a car won't start when the starter sticks. I brought my hammer just in case I needed to tap it."

I smirked and joked, "A hammer? Is that why you make the big bucks? You can fix things with hammers? How very male of you."

Tristan grunted like Tim "The Tool Man" Taylor and I giggled. He waved me to follow him inside. I kept a safe distance from Tristan and his rag, since I wouldn't appreciate getting grease on my dress khakis. "It's two o'clock. Do you want some lunch?"

"I don't know. I guess?" I felt guilty eating all his food. He had already made me breakfast.

He tossed the oily rag onto the dining room table next to the engine and furrowed his eyebrows. "Are you not hungry, or is there another reason? Because, to tell you the truth, I wasn't really sure you'd come back today." He walked to the kitchen sink to wash his hands. I couldn't help thinking hands like that should be washed in a slop sink or at the very least the bathroom, not in the kitchen.

I squirmed when he picked up the dishtowel to dry them, but I responded calmly, "You have my car."

"And you took my truck."

I plopped down on one of the swivel chairs at his cluttered breakfast bar and pushed aside some trash so I could rest my elbows. His house, in the daylight, was more distressing than when we had been making out on his couch. It was in need of some serious organization. "I don't know what I want, Tristan. My stomach's queasy."

Tristan walked around behind me and slid his arm around my waist. He whispered in my ear, "I'm sorry. I wouldn't blame you if you wanted to back out."

I laid my head back on his shoulder and rested my arms on top of his. "No. It's not that. There's just so much to think about, and I guess the last few hours have given me a headache."

He kissed my temple and nuzzled my hair with his nose. "I know. If it makes you feel any better, we could go shopping?"

"For what?" I asked, turning my head to look at him.

He grinned. "Rings."

I smiled. "Oh yeah, we need those."

"I also need something to wear. You always look dashing in your dress shirts, but I don't own anything nice. My wardrobe consists of T-shirts and jeans."

"And one pair of underwear," I pointed out, holding up my index finger.

"Ha-ha, yes, one lonely pair of underwear. I think I need to go shopping. Will you help me?"

He let go of me as I rotated my chair around to face him. I took his hands and said, "Yes, Mr. Carr, I'll help you find nicer clothes and a ring for your betrothed."

Tristan smiled wider, squeezed my hands, and kissed me before saying, "I'll go grab my wallet, and I'll meet you at the truck." He dashed to the bedroom with a skip in his step as if shopping for wedding rings was exciting. Maybe this whole situation *would* turn out well and my unease was unnecessary. Tristan did seem happy, which gave me a warm feeling inside.

I smiled to myself and walked toward the door. "I don't mind driving," I called after him.

"Okay," he called back. "I'll be out in one minute."

I DROVE us down to Columbia Mall. I hadn't been there for a while, but it was familiar, and it was one of the largest malls around. Tristan needed lots of stores to choose from, so I made a decision and drove there. He did ask why we passed the Westminster Town Mall, and I gave him a look.

"I walked through there once two weeks ago. There are very few stores, and we'd be done in twenty minutes. We're going to a place where we can check out lots of selections, have some ice cream, and not feel like we ran out of stores before we're done."

He seemed amused by my answer and leaned his head back. I caught movement out of the corner of my eye, so I glanced down. Tristan held his hand open, his arm stretched across the console, waiting. I looked back to the road. I felt giddy and nervous. He wanted to hold my hand. He had held it before briefly, but the mall was an hour away. We'd be holding hands for potentially an hour. Although I could drive one-handed during straightaways, I wasn't confident that turning could be done well without the use of two hands.

I took in a shaky breath and placed my hand in his. When he closed his fingers around mine, I thought for sure I spurted just a little. My body hadn't felt this collectively happy since I'd woken up in his bed. I didn't know what was going to happen between us if and when we went through with this marriage, but I certainly knew I liked him. We could make it work, right?

WE MADE it to the mall, and I parked near Nordstrom. I always parked near there because then I'd never lose my car. And I knew where all the stores were, relative to where I entered. Tristan said he'd never been in a mall that large. He rarely shopped, and Walmart normally did the trick. I cringed.

I picked out some dress shirts in Macy's, and he was measured for a suit in Lord & Taylor, which did their own alterations and would have the suit ready for pickup by Tuesday. I found him multicolored boxer briefs, and he agreed to get them, but he pointed out that he would most likely slip them off when he got into bed. He said sleeping with clothes on had felt too weird for him. After we bought a number of items for Tristan, he took me to Hot Topic and told me it was my turn.

"Why?" I asked, skeptically glancing around at the displays of fan gear for *Doctor Who*, Harry Potter, and *The Walking Dead*. You could get a T-shirt, necklace, and action figure all at once! I did like *Doctor Who*, but why would I want an action figure?

Tristan replied, "Because you need some clothes to chill in. Do you even own a T-shirt?"

"I...." I opened my mouth, but there weren't any script answers forthcoming. He had me. I had white undershirts, but that wasn't the same. Then I remembered something and snapped my fingers. "I have an Aerosmith T-shirt!"

He gave me an incredulous snorty giggle, which was actually sort of cute. "You? You listen to Aerosmith?"

Guilty posture: toothy grin, wide eyes, hunched shoulders. "No," I confessed. "It was my cousin's. I was at a birthday party four years ago, and my shirt got trashed by Silly String–wielding maniacs."

Tristan gave me a disbelieving frown. "Silly String doesn't stain." He turned and walked on, weaving around the display racks, so I followed him through the store.

I explained, "It does when they corner me and I bump into the tie-dye table and suddenly I'm the one being unwillingly tie-dyed."

Tristan chuckled again, shaking his head at me. He had been laughing at me ever since I'd met him, but not in a mean way. He snickered often, as if he truly enjoyed being around me. He hadn't rolled his eyes or anything mean, only smiled and snickered.

"Here," he said, stopping by the wall of T-shirts. "How about this one?" Tristan held a medium T-shirt against my chest.

"Who's Lynyrd Skynyrd?"

He widened his eyes. "What? You don't know?"

I shook my head. "Should I?"

"What kind of music do you listen to?" He folded the tee and put it back on the pile.

"Meghan Trainor and Taylor Swift, and whatever Pandora plays when I turn it on."

"No way."

"It's true. Why do you look so shocked?"

"I don't know. You seem like a nerdy type to me, no offense. You wear your dress shirts all buttoned up, and your hair is never out of place. When you wear your glasses, you carry a certain air about you."

"Stuck up?" I'd been told that before. I'd had people think I was snooty.

Tristan disagreed. "No. That sounds harsh. How about 'refined'? I figured you go for classical or maybe jazz, not chick pop."

The way he said it sounded better than others who had teased me for my fastidiousness. "I like what I like. I also have a few soundtrack CDs." I was afraid to admit my addictions, but if we were getting married, then he'd find out soon enough.

Tristan held another T-shirt up to my chest. "Yeah, I like this one." He threw it over his shoulder and looked for more. He held the next one up.

I shook my head. "I'm not wearing a giant tongue on my chest."

"Okay. No Rolling Stones." He rummaged through another stack and held up a shirt for All Time Low. I nodded approval because I liked the graphic design on the front. I only hoped I liked the band, since I was consenting to wear their shirt. "Which soundtracks do you have?" he asked.

I paused before answering. Would he be amused by my behavior as before? I stopped following him, and he turned around. Tristan gave me a look. I hung my head in preparation for this next tidbit. "I have all the music from *Glee*."

"*Glee*?"

"The TV show."

"Never heard of it," he commented while bending down to look through a stack of T-shirts on a lower shelf.

I clutched my chest for my impending heart attack. "What?"

He glanced back at me. "Nope. I don't watch television, because I'm usually working. I'll pop in a DVD if I have time to chill, but mostly I read in my spare time."

Reading? Hmm. Definitely something I'd have to ask him about later. "The final season ended last spring, but I loved it. I went to a concert in 2011 when they were in DC. I'd never gotten into show choir or singing or theater in high school or college, so this was different for me, but I watched every episode and then downloaded all the music. Okay, not *all* the music, because there are probably a thousand songs, but I have over two hundred. So when I say I like Meghan Trainor, I do, but I listen to *Glee* music most of the time." I spotted a T-shirt I recognized and grabbed it. "Oooh, Journey! I like them."

Tristan was laughing again, and he shook his head in amusement or amazement, I wasn't sure. He stepped closer, and before I could react, he kissed me right there in the store. I felt self-conscious at first, but as he kissed longer and slower, I simply melted into him. He squeezed my hips and pulled me tight against him. No tongue, but his kiss was pretty darn knee buckling without it.

Then I heard a word that chilled my growing lust and forced it into hiding. "Dad?" a female voice asked.

Tristan pulled back, peeling himself away from me in slow motion. I would have thought being caught by his daughter, kissing a man, would have jolted him into jumping away from my body, but it hadn't. Maybe it was akin to the police yelling, "Freeze!"

Claire wasn't as relaxed and preoccupied as I remembered from the gym. Her jaw was two inches from the floor, eyes bugged out, and she was mirrored by her two friends.

Tristan swallowed so loud I could hear it. "Hi, Claire," he said, probably because there wasn't anything else he *could* say.

"I don't believe it," she said, still gaping. "I mean, you called and told me you were gay, but I didn't think you were *actually* gay. You don't even look gay. But now… you're… holy shit, that's the guy from the gym!" Her eyes bugged out even further as she pointed at me and dropped her bags.

Tristan said, "His name is Grant."

I weakly lifted my hand. "Hi."

"Whatever." She rolled her eyes.

"Claire!" her male friend chastised. "Don't be rude. Besides, that guy's cute."

I knew I blushed. I blushed at everything, so a compliment from a kid wasn't going to escape the list.

Tristan grinned at me and then addressed the kid. "Thanks. What's your name?"

"Danny," the boy answered, batting his eyes and smiling way too sweetly at my man. He was wearing a tight sweater with a blue scarf. I liked the scarf. My shirts didn't accommodate scarves, and therefore I mainly wore ties. Still, I appreciated his style even if I could do without his flirtation.

Tristan then asked the girl, "And you?"

She answered, "I'm Kirsty. I think it's cool you're gay."

Claire nudged her. "Shhh. Don't encourage him." She glared at Tristan. "What are you doing here?" she demanded.

Tristan cocked his head to the side. "I should ask you the same thing, young lady. Where's your mom?"

A pain shot through my stomach. I couldn't bear to see that woman twice in one day.

She shrugged. "I don't know. I spent the night at Kirsty's, and her mom dropped us off while she bought some birthday presents."

"Does she know about Danny?" Tristan asked. I sort of knew why, but I didn't want to hear Claire's answer.

She grimaced. "No. Are you kidding me? She hates men. She's a freak when it comes to…." Then I saw her expression open up. Her shoulders relaxed and her tone completely changed. "Oh, God. That's why you've never said."

Tristan nodded.

She cupped her mouth briefly, then said, "I'm so sorry, Dad." Tears formed in her eyes right before Tristan hugged her. I heard her sniffle. "I never realized, until recently, how mean Mom is." Claire pulled out of the hug and took the tissue Kirsty offered. She wiped her eyes carefully to avoid smearing her makeup and continued, "As soon as high school started, everything changed. She started getting strict, like she never had been before. She's been checking my grades online every week to see if all my assignments are in. She e-mails my teachers. I don't understand why, when I've had almost all As since fifth grade. The worst was when I met Danny in Honors Government last year. He came over to research a paper with me, and Mom got really rude toward his father when he came to pick him up. Then she went into this twenty-minute rant about how I'm not allowed to date—ever! I couldn't believe the things she said. She criticized Danny and she doesn't even know him. She just assumed from his hairstyle he was gay and went off about gay men having sex in bathrooms!"

I recoiled. Hearing Teresa's bathroom example again made me never want to do it on principle alone.

"True story," Danny added, holding his hand as if swearing in court. "I heard the whole argument and did my best to act straight and deepen my voice when I said good-bye. I haven't been over there since."

"It's so dumb," Kirsty said. "Besides, Danny has great hair."

I would agree. His hair was very well coifed, but I would hardly call it "gay."

"He's my best friend, Dad, and he can't come over to my house because he's a guy and his dad is single. I don't understand her deal. I thought it was bad enough when she bashed men in general, but she's worse now. It's like she doesn't want me to have friends at all."

It all came together for Tristan as he summarized, "Which is why you're at the mall with your friends when your mother isn't around. I get it. She dropped by to see me this morning, right after breakfast, and denigrated me in front of Grant."

"It was awful," I added.

"Wait, breakfast?" Claire questioned, only to drop her jaw a second time. "How early was she there?"

"It isn't what you think," I defended.

"I think you spent the night and my mom caught you," she said.

Tristan sighed. "Okay, that *is* what happened, but nothing was going on. His car broke down in my driveway."

Danny snickered behind his hand. "Likely story."

"It did!" I exclaimed. I caught sight of the clerk watching us from afar. It was odd, I had to admit, having this type of discussion in the middle of Hot Topic, but at least there weren't loads of other patrons. The store was empty besides us.

"Look, Grant and I are in a relationship. I told you about my sexuality because how I feel about him isn't casual. In fact—" He glanced at me before he said it. "—we're getting married."

"What!" she cried.

Danny clapped while hopping up and down. "Yay!"

Kirsty said, "Aww, that's so sweet."

Claire didn't share her sentiment. "Sweet?" she questioned. She glared at Tristan, and suddenly I felt bad for him. It must be tough being a dad. "When were you planning on telling me, Dad? And don't even say it's because I'm too young to understand. I'm fifteen; I understand plenty. My best friend is gay, I take Health—which is much more detailed than back when you were in school—and I know a girl who gave birth in eighth grade and posted pictures of the delivery on Instagram. Trust me, I know way more than most."

Birthing photos? Good Lord! Yes, I believed being a father was way harder than it looked, and it looked pretty rough. I just waited to see where this was going. It wasn't my place to divulge information to his daughter. Plus, the Instagram thing made me throw up just a little in my mouth.

Tristan explained slowly, "The marriage part of it fell together suddenly… this morning… while your mom was visiting. I promise I did not intentionally hold back information. I was hoping Grant would become a permanent fixture in my life, which is why I told you I'm gay. It never mattered until now."

I touched his back. "Oh," I gushed. Knowing he cared enough to say something to his daughter made me feel really special.

Tristan gave me a soft smile and said, "I knew when I met you, Grant."

I got choked up and covered my mouth. What could I say to that? Yes, this was moving very fast, but it was also romantic. Tristan was practically sweeping me off my feet.

I sank into his arms as he slipped his arm around my back. I needed the security of his embrace when his words made me feel vulnerable.

"That is just too cute," Kirsty commented.

"I have to admit, Dad, seeing you kissing was kind of gross, but this…." She gestured. "It's sweet." She exhaled and added, as if reluctantly, "And I guess you kinda look cute together."

"Totally," Kirsty agreed, Danny nodding right along with her.

Tristan snickered. I think the guy was easily amused. He held me around my back and rubbed my arm with his other hand. I wanted to bury my face against his neck, but then I'd be rude to the rest of them. I turned my body to continue the conversation, but I refused to let go.

Tristan said, "I'm glad you approve. I know the wedding plans are last minute, but if you want to, you can come. It's your weekend anyway."

Claire was pleased. "Really? I'd love to! I've never seen a real-life gay wedding before."

"It's not going to be much more than standing in front of a clerk. We haven't planned a big thing with a reception. I figured we could come back to the house and have hamburgers."

Not what I would have planned, but it *was* last minute. I told him, "Hamburgers sound good."

Claire said, "It doesn't matter if it's a big thing or not; I've only seen gay weddings on television shows like *Glee*."

"*Glee*?" I asked quietly, my eyes locking on hers. "You've seen *Glee*?" I relaxed away from Tristan's chest, turning slightly more toward the others.

"Heck, yeah."

Danny said, "We've watched it at my house. Blaine is my favorite character."

I let go of Tristan. "Mine too!" I cried. This day was getting better and better. Now I'd found out I had something in common with Tristan's daughter and her friends. "Look," I insisted, holding out my phone to show Danny the lock screen.

He gasped and placed his hand over his mouth before lowering it to ask, "Did you take that picture?"

I smiled proudly. "Yup. I went to see *Hedwig and the Angry Inch* on Broadway in June before his run ran out. I about died!"

"What are you talking about?" Tristan asked.

Kirsty, who was also eye-poppingly shocked, answered, "Darren Criss. He's the guy who played Blaine Anderson on *Glee*. Grant has a picture of him. Do you have more?" she asked me.

"Um, yeah, I think so. I'm not the best at taking pictures. They always turn out blurry. I snapped about fifty, and only six are clear. Of course, none of them have him smiling. The one where I know he was smiling has a guy's playbill in front of his face. I have horrible luck."

"You were that close to him?" Danny asked.

"Yup. About four feet with people in between me and the barricade thingy. He was the nicest guy. I swear. He talked to every fan who said something to him, and signed every piece of paper shoved in his face. Classy guy, gracious and patient. I walked away with an autograph, some photos, but also a deep respect for him as a person. I hope he's always like that. Some actors get rude over time. I hope Darren Criss retains his genuine niceness." I knew I was rambling, but it was how I felt. It was the first time I'd been close to someone famous, and I'd gotten a really great vibe off of him. It made me like his music and acting all the more, knowing he was a nice guy in real life.

Danny put his hand over his heart in a dramatic fashion and said, "I believe an all-night *Glee* marathon is in order."

I smiled. "Sounds good to me. Although I might be tempted to sing along." Suddenly I was as comfortable as ever in Tristan's world, because I didn't have to stop being myself.

Kirsty waved her hand at me. "Danny sings too. You'll fit in just fine." She turned to Claire and said, "I really like your dad's boyfriend."

I thought Tristan would make another comment, but he didn't.

Kirsty and Danny started talking to me, but I caught sight of the expression Claire gave her father. Not anger. Not disappointment. Not frustration. Not embarrassment. Claire exuded contentment. I think she was truly pleased with her dad.

"I love you, Dad," she said finally, hugging him tight.

"I love you too, sweetness."

If I hadn't been caught up in the moment talking plot issues and character flaws with Danny and Kirsty, I might have cried.

THE MANAGER of Hot Topic kept watching us, and eventually I suggested we leave because he made me feel uncomfortable. Tristan bought me a few shirts, and we added another bag to our load. His daughter and her friends joined us for ice cream but decided to scamper off when everyone was finished. Kirsty had commented, "Hanging with your dad, Claire, isn't as cool as I thought it would be, even if he is gay." We went our separate ways, but in good spirits.

Tristan stopped strolling and pointed to a jewelry store. "Well, are you ready for this?"

I nodded slowly. "I think so."

"Just remember, if you don't see something in this store, there are plenty of other places to try. Don't settle for something you don't want."

"Okay."

As soon as we walked through the door, several sales associates made eye contact. The sudden lust for a sale filled the room, and I grabbed on to Tristan's arm instinctively. I didn't want them descending on me all at once. I felt like the only duck in the sky on the opening day of hunting season.

Tristan must have sensed my unease, because he whispered, "I'll handle it."

He walked toward the display case at the back of the store, but a woman stepped up and asked, "May I help you?"

"No, thanks. We're just looking," he said curtly.

"We have a few sales if you're interested in—"

He stopped and spoke more sternly. "We're fine, thank you."

She looked flustered and shrunk back. "Okay."

Tristan continued toward the back of the store, and I increased my grip on his arm. Tristan patted my hand. "Trust me."

"I am."

He drifted past a few cases of rings and stopped by the wedding bands. As he perused the selections, my eyes wandered over to the case next to us. *Diamond solitaire rings.* I sighed. I would not have described myself as a queen, and I had never been interested in planning out my wedding or imagining what my "gown" would look like as a typical bride would do, but as soon as my eyes lit upon those sparkling gems, something inside woke up.

"What about this one?" Tristan asked, pointing at a gold band with filigree around the edges.

"It's nice, but it seems a little fancy for you."

"Too fancy?" he questioned. "You don't think I could be fancy?" Tristan lifted an eyebrow, challenging my assumption. I couldn't tell if he was upset about what I'd said, or curious as to why.

I shrugged. "I don't know. Maybe. I was just thinking about all the dirt and grime that might get lodged in the grooves of the design. It would be hard to keep clean."

He lifted the corner of his mouth. "I wouldn't have thought of that, but you're right. I guess I should get a plain band. I thought matching bands would be nice, but I didn't think you'd want something simple."

How did he know that? "I don't know. I might be okay with a simple band, if…." I paused, reluctant to say what I was thinking.

"If what? Is there something you're interested in over there?" he asked, pointing to the other case.

I dropped my gaze and answered quietly, "Maybe."

Tristan snickered, stepped closer, and lifted my chin. I straightened my shoulders and looked him in the eyes, readying myself for whatever he was about to say. Tristan touched my chest with the back of his knuckles and slid his hand down a few inches. "You're adorable."

I felt my cheeks get hot.

He pointed out, "Those are engagement rings, Grant, but I suppose I owe you one, if that's what you want."

My heart fluttered. I ran my eyes over them again. "They're really pretty," I mused.

Tristan slid his arm behind my back and leaned closer. We peered at the rings together. "Which one do you like?"

"I like that one," I said, tapping my finger on the glass over a square diamond set in a silver-colored band—which I assumed was white gold or platinum. Silver wasn't very expensive. It was outlined in smaller diamonds, which ran down the sides of the band as well. It reminded me of something my grandmother had worn. It was more old-fashioned compared to the other ones, but I could not tear my eyes from it.

"Yeah?"

I nodded, trying to contain my delight—although he could probably hear my pounding heart, it was beating so loud in my ears.

Tristan patted my back and walked over to a sales associate. Not the first woman who had addressed us, but a man who was rearranging some necklaces in a case. "My fiancé would like to look at a ring when you have a moment."

"I can help you with that," the other woman said, stepping away from her area.

Tristan objected, "No. I'm sure this man can do it." Tristan turned back to the guy, and he smiled.

"I'll be right there," he said.

Tristan strolled back over and waited until the guy locked the case he'd been working in.

I whispered, "Why that guy? What's wrong with that other woman?"

He whispered in my ear, "I don't like pushy salespeople. That other guy is young and probably doesn't get as many sales as the older woman. When I buy something, I don't like to feel pressured. If that woman helped us, I get the feeling she'd say all the right things to convince us what we should buy. I can't explain it, but I just don't like her."

The young guy walked over but did glance at the woman behind us. He smiled and asked, "What can I show you?"

I tapped on the glass again. "That one. The second from the top row on your left."

"Ah! The Rosemont. Good choice. It's new." He unlocked the case and plucked the ring from the display. "It might be a little small for you, but we can size it for free." He shined it up with a piece of cloth and then handed it to me.

I was so excited that it surprised me how steady my hands were when I took the ring from *Jim*—I read his nametag. Jim handed me the ring, and I held it like my most prized possession.

Jim explained, "This is a princess-cut, three-quarter karat diamond set in white gold, surrounded by micro diamonds, with three others on each side, totaling 0.3 karats, for a total weight of 1.05. Notice the hand engraved, scrolling filigree around the top of the tapered band and along the sides, which elevates the setting. It's quite stunning; I can see why you chose it."

"Can I put it on?" I asked.

Jim replied, "Of course. Remember, if it's too small we can size it."

I glanced at Tristan nervously.

"Go ahead, Grant. If that's the one you like."

I stared at the beautiful ring in my hand. I was afraid to put it on. It wasn't because it might not fit. I had long slim fingers, so my chances we good. I was afraid that this was all really happening. I was going to get married to a man I hardly knew, and this ring was a symbol of the commitment I'd leaped into. I started breathing faster.

I paused too long, and Tristan took the ring from my grasp. He took my left hand and held the ring steadily at the tip. Before I knew what was happening, he dropped to one knee. "Grant Adams, will you marry me?"

My breath hitched. What could I say? I had agreed before under duress, but now I had the freedom to back out. Only... Tristan seemed so sincere, and his eyes regarded me so tenderly. I panted, but even my near panic couldn't stop my mouth from saying, "Yes."

He slid the ring up my finger and over the knuckle.

"I can't believe that fit," Jim commented.

I stared at my hand and absently explained, "I play piano. My mother always told me I have musician's fingers." The diamond sparkled like nothing I'd ever seen. A tear rolled down my cheek. *I'm getting married.*

Tristan got off his knee and took me into his arms, kissing me soundly before hugging me and lifting me off my feet. He sighed heavily in my ear when he set me back down as I gazed over his shoulder, inspecting my ring. Then he whispered, "I love you."

I forgot the ring and jumped back. "What?" Surely I'd heard him wrong. I wiped the tear off my cheek and stared at him.

"I love you," he said again, reaching out and taking my hands in his. "I know I'm crazy, but I've been all over the world, Grant. I've been sick, sad, scared, happy, hungry, and hurt, but nothing compares to how I feel about you right now. I love you."

I didn't know what to say. I'd never been in love, so I couldn't disprove his feelings, though they seemed sudden. "Tristan, I...."

"I know. I'm okay waiting until you know for sure, but I had to say how I felt. Teresa might have prompted the situation, but I would have asked within the year."

By God, he was romantic. How could I get upset? I started shaking, and another tear rolled down my cheek. Tristan hugged me again, and I heard the clerk sigh.

Tristan released me, took my face in his hands, and kissed me. "Now take the ring off." I did and handed it reluctantly to Jim. Tristan said, "Go wait for me by Starbucks. Have a pastry thing or a Frappuccino if I take too long."

"What are you going to do?"

"Pay for the rings."

I felt stupid. "Oh. But what about matching bands? Can't I help pick?"

"Okay. But after we decide on the band, then you go wait while I pay."

He glanced at the clerk. "Can you show us some plain bands that might go well with this ring?"

"Absolutely," he said, standing up straight, preparing himself for the task.

After checking out the selection, we agreed on matching white gold bands with a tiny bit of design around the edge. Nothing Tristan would get grease caked in, yet enough design to look appropriate next to my fancy schmancy ring.

I walked out slowly, watching Tristan and the clerk talking as I left the store. It felt weird letting him pay, but I didn't feel right arguing either.

I knew where Starbucks was. I liked their Morning Bun. I could get one while I waited. I walked along the upper floor of the mall feeling more lost than ever. I knew where I was, but this mall—the one I'd been to hundreds of times—felt strange. My life was strange. Who was I? Everything about me had entered a state of transformation, and I felt as though I was trapped in a chrysalis. Who would I become once my metamorphosis was complete? I sat at a table outside Starbucks and watched people walking by. Mel and I used to get frappés and pastries and watch the people all the time. Why did I feel so unfamiliar with my surroundings?

"Grant? Grant, is that you?" I heard my name and turned toward the woman who'd said it. Kyra. I hadn't seen her in weeks, but her commanding presence electrified the air around her. "Oh my God, it is you!" She descended upon me, and I had no choice but to stand and hug her. I liked Kyra. She was one of the many women friends I'd had at the bank where I used to work.

"Hello, Kyra. It's nice to see you."

She smiled and waved at some women across the food court. "Debra, Janis, look who I found!"

The other women squealed and came rushing over. Soon we were all hugging and catching up on teller gossip. Debra had found a job working for Wells Fargo, and Janis was working at Giant Food. Both were happy and asked how my transfer had gone. Everything was fine, smooth, and normal until Tristan showed up, reminding me that my life was not smooth or normal. It had been uprooted and was currently undergoing transformations into something I couldn't imagine.

I stuttered as I introduced him. "Um, who's this, you ask? Ah... this... is... Tristan. My... fian... fiancé."

All three women dropped their jaws and gaped at me, eyes bugging out just like Claire's had. "No... *way*," Kyra finally said, flipping her hair to the side.

Tristan was as casual as ever, responding, "It's nice to meet you all. How do you know Grant?"

"We worked with him at the bank," Janis answered. "Um, did Grant just say you two were getting married? Because I don't remember getting an invitation."

I had to think fast. These were people I considered to be my friends. "Um, yeah, we were... um, considering a formal wedding in the spring for all our friends as a way of celebrating the civil ceremony we're having next week. We were going to plan a big wedding but decided we couldn't wait that long to make it official."

Kyra looked right at Tristan. "Did you get him pregnant?"

I laughed hysterically, but Tristan eyed me oddly. "Are you okay?" he asked.

I kept laughing. "Me? Why? Of course I'm fine." I waved him off.

Kyra gave me a hard stare and then looked at Tristan.

Debra spoke for the group. "Okay. Well, as fun as this is *not*, I think we need to go. You make sure you send that invitation, because I *am* going to go to y'all's gay wedding and cry my ass off. You hear me, Grant?"

"Of course, of course," I agreed, unable to get my fake laughter under control. I didn't know what was happening to me. I felt intoxicated, and not in a good way. *Swish, swish, swish, swish,* my ears thrummed with rushing blood, pounding a staccato rhythm to remind me I was far from fine. My sanity was unraveling and dangling me over a dark abyss. If I fell, where would I land—if at all?

Tristan shook each lady's hand and said good-bye. Then he grabbed my elbow, pulled me into a corner where no one would overhear him, and barked, "What is wrong with you? That lie was the worst I've ever heard. What's gotten into you?"

I began hyperventilating. "I don't know." I heaved. "I panicked." I clutched my chest. "They know everyone I know." I dropped my bags and grasped my forehead on both sides. The floor was spinning. "They're going to tell everyone."

"We came to the mall you grew up near. Didn't you realize we'd probably see people you knew?" When I didn't answer and couldn't catch my breath, Tristan picked up the bags and led me to a chair. "Seeing Claire was a surprise, but your friends shouldn't have shocked you." He asked the person behind the counter at Starbucks for a cup of water, but I was breathing too hard to sip it. "Breathe, Grant, breathe. You're having a panic attack." Tristan squeezed my hand and instructed, "Look at me." I did. "Good. Breathe with me. In. Out. In. Out. Good. Slower. Good. Try drinking again."

I did. Then I told him, "I want to go home."

Chapter Eight

Apprehension, Desperation, And The Need To Have Another Person In My Bed

"DO YOU still want to stay at my place tonight?" Tristan asked as he drove.

I felt better after he'd gotten me out of the mall. Shopping had started out fun, but I hadn't processed the possibility of seeing my friends. I had wanted the familiarity, but seeing Kyra and Janis made everything that had happened over the weekend crash into the compartmented walls I'd constructed around it. It was all real. I was getting married. I had never expected my life to change so drastically just because I'd changed jobs. My overwhelming reality was catching up with my brain, and I couldn't deal.

What had Tristan asked? His house? Another overwhelming issue.

How did I explain my aversion to the mess in his house without offending him? Maybe I should save that thought for another day. I suggested, "Maybe you could spend the night at my house? At least we know your ex won't show up in the morning while I'm making waffles."

"Waffles? That sounds great. I'll just stop at my place on the way and grab some clothes."

He did.

I closed and locked the door when we entered my house. "I need a shower," I said, setting my bags next to the sofa and leaving him in my living room. I stumbled into my bedroom and started unbuttoning my shirt. The room seemed hazy, as if I were peering at it through a milky window. Then the glazed room tilted, and everything went black.

I OPENED my eyes and saw Tristan sitting next to me, bare chested, leaning against the headboard of my bed. I was in bed? How had I gotten there?

"Tristan?" I rasped. My throat was dry.

He turned his head and looked at me. "Grant. You're awake." He leaned down and kissed my head. "I'm glad. I was worried I'd have to call an ambulance, and I didn't know any of your insurance information." He repositioned himself so he was lying on his side right next to me, his arm across my stomach.

"How did I get in bed?" I asked weakly.

"You fainted. Don't you remember?"

"No."

"I heard you hit the floor. I rushed in and helped you up. You were dazed, but you spoke just fine." He seemed concerned. "You don't remember, do you?"

"No."

"Hmm. Maybe you *should* see a doctor to make sure you don't have a concussion."

"I'll be fine. I'm sure it will come back." I touched my chest and fingered my T-shirt. "Did I undress myself?" I didn't remember that either.

"I picked you up, Grant, and tucked you in bed after removing your top layer. I knew you'd be upset if I took everything off."

I gave him a tiny smile. "Very true." My throat was scratchy, so I asked, "Can I get a drink?"

He jumped up. "Of course." Tristan returned with a glass of water and helped me sit up. After I drank half of it, he set the glass on the coaster on my nightstand. "You had me worried." Tristan ran his fingers through my hair and caressed my cheek.

"I'm sorry."

"I know it's a lot to take in."

I rolled my eyes. "Understatement of the year."

"We don't have to do this," he said.

"But you said you loved me," I reminded him.

Tristan reclined on the bed as before, very close, gazing deeply into my eyes. "Yes. I think I do. Every time you look at me something invisible takes a hold of my heart, but that doesn't mean we need to go through with this wedding next week. We can do it in the spring, like you suggested. That makes more sense. By then, maybe you won't faint from stressing about it."

I took a deep breath, held it, and released it. Logic had no seat in my house anymore, or at my dining room table. I had invited chaos in when I had blurted imaginary wedding plans at Teresa. I'd done this. Me. Yes, I could back out and resume my boring, predictable life, where everything had to line up at right angles and zero out at the end of each day, but was the safe bet wise? I closed my eyes and meditated on it. Tristan was kind, romantic, sweet, considerate, attentive, and honorable. Why would I pass that up just because it didn't make sense logically? Life wasn't always logical.

I opened my eyes and took another deep breath.

"No," I said. "I'm not backing out. I want to go through with it. I want to marry you. It's overwhelming, and I'm sorry I fainted, but it was the stress. I didn't freak out and panic because I'm being forced against my will." I held his eyes so he could see my honesty. "I can't tell you I love you, because I've never been in love. I won't lie; I'm scared. But even with the insanity surrounding us, I can't deny I feel *something* when I look at you. No one has ever treated me half as well as you. I believe you when you say you love me. I promise, when I know for sure, I'll say it back."

One tear spilled from the corner of Tristan's eye as he took me into his arms against his chest. He held me in silence for the longest time, rubbing my back and kissing my hair. I wondered what he was thinking. I hoped I'd said the right thing and he wasn't mad, but I couldn't say those words without knowing for sure.

Then he whispered, "You are such a beautiful person, Grant."

BASICALLY WE repeated Saturday morning on Sunday, only at my house and without the insane ex yelling at us. We didn't talk about the craziness of Saturday or my poorly executed reactions. We laughed and made waffles without flour strewn across every surface. We snuggled on my couch and watched *Pitch Black*. We also made out on my bed for two hours before Tristan suggested he leave. This time we controlled ourselves—no dry humping or groping—but I had to relieve the pressure after he'd gone. My balls were aching, and my dick was harder than I'd ever felt in my life. If we didn't have sex soon, I feared something inside might rupture.

Before I turned off my light, I texted my mom. *Are you still awake?*

She texted back: *This is rather late, don't you think? Is everything all right?*

Yes. Remember how I said I met a guy?

Yes. The shop owner?

The auto mechanic shop, yes. Well… we sort of… we're getting married.

My phone rang. "Hello?"

My mother wasn't so polite. "Grant, if this is some sort of joke…."

"No, Mom, it's not. We went out, and it sort of just happened. We're getting married on Saturday. He bought me a ring and everything."

I heard her exhale heavily into the receiver. "I've wondered for years if you'd ever settle down. Although I hoped it would be soon, and possibly with the shop owner, I'll admit I'm shocked. It's a bit abrupt, don't you think, dear? You hardly know this man. What's his name?"

"Tristan Carr." Her arguments were sound and nothing I could dispute.

"And you're sure this is what you want?" she asked.

I breathed a sigh of relief, and then answered, "Yes."

"You hesitated."

"No, I didn't. I was sighing because I thought you'd yell."

"Grant, you're twenty-six years old. At some point you need to make your own decisions and stick by them. I thought it was a miracle when you moved out."

I was flabbergasted. "What? I thought you wanted me living with you all that time. I thought you were lonely after Dad died."

"I do miss your father, but I have friends. Many friends. Since you've been out of the house, I haven't had to worry about them staying over too late. I can have dinner parties and go to the theater without having to worry about you. I even have several bus trips coming up. I'm very busy."

"Oh," I mumbled. Somehow, I felt deflated. All these years I thought I'd been doing her a favor by being so attentive to her. "So you're not bothered that I haven't texted all weekend?"

"Sweetheart, I hoped you were out having sex all weekend."

I sat up and squawked, "Ah! I did not just hear you say that!"

"Grant, honey, you need to loosen up. If this man is patient enough to see the kindness behind your quirks, then I'm glad you two are getting married. Let me know when and where, and I'll attend. For now, I'd like to get some rest. One of my bus trips is tomorrow. A group of us are going to see the Natural Bridge in Virginia."

"Oh, that sounds nice."

"It should be. Now go to sleep, Grant. I know how cranky you get when you don't get enough sleep before work."

"Good night, Mom. I love you."

"I love you too dear. Good night."

I hung up and set my phone on my nightstand. The one call I'd dreaded making and it had totally flipped my assumptions all around. I'd gotten the impression my mother was more relieved about my wedding than upset. *Wow.* I flopped back down on my pillow. This new town was beginning to feel like the Twilight Zone. All this change, and now my mom—I didn't know what to think. I closed my eyes and hoped for sleep.

MONDAY MORNING, Tristan met me at the courthouse and we filed the necessary paperwork for a marriage license. I hadn't expected them to issue the license right then. When we walked out with an official document in hand—that would be valid basically two days later—it frightened me how real it was getting. We had up to six months to get hitched, but Tristan wanted to do it Saturday when he had Claire.

"Are you stopping by the bank later?" I asked as we stood in the parking lot next to my car.

"No. I have way too much work. I've been putting things off so I could come see you during the week, but I need to spend time catching up. I have some bills due." Tristan had his hands on my hips, and I could feel him rubbing his thumbs against my shirt.

"Okay. When will I see you?" I asked, worried it would be a couple of days. Our weekend might have been intense, but I wasn't ready to go back to sleeping alone every night.

"Maybe Wednesday?"

I swallowed the lump in my throat. It wasn't like we were married *yet*; I didn't *need* to see him all the time. "Okay." I glided my hands up his chest and took ahold of the lapels of his work shirt. "Promise to think about me?" Yes, I sounded pathetic, but he was probably used to it by now. He'd had a crash course.

Tristan grinned. Apparently my gloom amused him. "Every minute of every hour until I see you again." He kissed me before I could answer.

"Really?" I asked, less dour than a second before. "You think about me that much?"

"You bet I do. That's why I kept coming to the bank. I'll make time again once I get some things squared away."

I nodded. It was unfair to guilt him into visiting since his reasons were very mature. Of course he had bills to pay and things to take care of. This was not like the other guys I'd dated who never returned after one date. I could trust Tristan to come back to me.

"Hey, look at me."

When I brought my chin up, he paused and then kissed me again, slow and deep. I wrapped my arms around his neck and mewled into his mouth. When he released me, I was good and relaxed. I needed the feeling to carry me through until he kissed me again.

"I'll see you Wednesday. If you need anything, you can drop by anytime. My door's always open."

"Open." The word prompted me to remember something I had for him. "Oh, wait," I said, fumbling to reach into my pants pocket. "I have a key for you. I made it for my mother, but I forgot to give it to her the last time we had dinner together. I want you to have it. I don't leave my door open, but you're welcome to drop by anytime."

He took the key and smiled. "Thank you, Grant." He kissed me one more time. "I really have to go. I have a brake job I'm supposed to get done before lunch, and the day is already disappearing. Take care of that document."

I held it up. "Sure thing. I'm very responsible, I promise."

"I'll see ya." Another chaste kiss, and he was gone.

I had to go to work and put on a happy face. Could I? I set the manila folder that protected our marriage license on the seat next to me as I drove to work.

THE ANSWER was yes. I acted normal on Monday and all day on Tuesday. Luckily the two hickeys Tristan had given me were below my collar, so when I wore a tie, no one at work noticed. My life seemed normal and fine, except for the seventeen trips I took to the bathroom. I wasn't sick, and I hadn't drunk gallons of water like I'd told Jessica; I'd gone into the bathroom so I could text Tristan. He didn't always respond right away, but after several texts he had gotten more responsive. It's like he knew I needed just a little something. Anything. Even a smiley face was better than hours of silence.

Mel called Tuesday night.

"Hey, stranger. What've you been up to all weekend? It's not like us to go four days without talking, or at the very least texting." He sounded chipper, not upset or anything. I also noticed how much deeper his voice was. I had been used to hearing it every day. Now, with some time in between, he sounded huskier.

"I thought you'd let me know how your date went, since I live vicariously through you. You did go out with that guy, right? Tristan?"

I dried my hands after I finished washing the last of my dinner dishes. I had the phone perched between my ear and my shoulder. Not comfortable, but the position was doable until I'd finished washing. "Yeah. We went out."

"Uh-oh. That's a short answer. Don't tell me this guy bombed too. I was hoping this would be it for you." He sounded so sad for me. "One of us has to score."

How could I tell Mel everything? I knew I had to, but how? "Um, no. He was fine." I knew the short answer would prompt more questions.

"Whoa, whoa, whoa. You don't get to abbreviate. Tell me everything."

I strolled over to the couch and sat. I touched the cushion Tristan had sat on just a couple of days before. We'd snuggled there. Tristan had stretched out on my couch and held me against his chest. He'd played with my hair and drawn lazy circles on my arm while we watched *Pitch Black*.

I miss him.

"Grant? Are you crying?"

"What? No, of course not." I sniffled and wiped my nose. Not crying, but certainly working myself close to it by reminiscing. "No, I was just thinking about the weekend. It was fun… and different."

"How so? I need details."

I grabbed the small sofa pillow and held it in my lap as I talked. I liked fingering the silky fringe around the edges. "First we went to dinner, which started out rough because I spilled my drink across the table and it ended up in his lap."

"Oh, no. Like Kenny," he gasped.

"Yes. Exactly what I thought. I tried begging for forgiveness, but Tristan was totally cool about it. He asked if I'd done it on purpose, and after I'd told him no, he said to forget about it because accidents happen."

"Wow. That's terrific. Sounds like he's leagues beyond those other guys already."

I agreed, "He is. After dinner, we watched a movie at his house and ended up making out on his living room floor."

"And?"

"And nothing. He told me I needed to go. Tristan doesn't want our relationship to be about sex. He's really into me and wants this to be long-term." I had to work up to telling Mel I was about to get married to the guy.

"Really? He can tell that about you already? You've been on one date. Unless… unless more happened over the weekend that you're not telling me? Did you see him again on Sunday? I ran into your mother at Starbucks in Ellicott City, and she said she hadn't heard from you."

"My mom? I texted her late Sunday night."

"Ah! That explains it. But get back to Tristan. What happened next?"

I removed my glasses and set them on the side table, then rubbed my face, thinking of where to begin and how to explain everything. I ran my hand over my hair, appreciating the fact it was soft, slightly wavy, and easily managed. It rarely got messed up, even on windy days, because I kept it cut fairly short. All I had to do was rake my fingers through it, and it all fell back into place. Jessica was right: I had perfect hair.

I gathered my thoughts and answered Mel before he asked the same question again, as was normal. I had a habit of taking too long. "To answer the question you're thinking, no, we didn't have sex."

"Bummer."

"No, it's fine. Well, sort of. Okay, I'm hard as hell most of the time, but I understand his reasons. Tristan pretty much described himself as a sex pig in his twenties."

"Twenties? How old is he now?"

"Thirty-two."

"Hmm, not bad."

"No. It's perfect, actually. I think he needed to mature past that stage. Now he's looking to settle down. He wants a husband."

"Whoa. Talk about pressure? I hope you told him this was your first relationship ever, and that marriage was way down the road." That tinge of skepticism in his voice pained me. How could I explain I was engaged?

"Well, it's all a part of his desire to go slow with me. He said I'm worth waiting for. Even when I spent the night in his bed, we—"

"Hold up! You what?"

"I spent the night."

"And you didn't have sex?" Yes, that was the shrillest shriek of disbelief I'd ever heard from Mel, and I pulled the phone away from my ear.

When my head stopped ringing, I answered him. "No. We didn't. But gosh, waking up in his arms was… wonderful. I didn't know it could feel like that. Last night the bed felt empty."

"I can do the math, Grant. You just implied that you've slept together three nights."

"I know. We did. Once at his place, and twice at mine. He's so sweet, Mel. I almost fell asleep watching the movie when he was playing with my hair."

"No shit. I know you like that. You probably haven't had a head massage since you moved to Westminster."

"No. You live too far away to drop by four times a week."

Mel laughed. "Yeah, but my visits dwindled after we made those special brownies and didn't show up for work the next day."

"Oh, my God. You had to remind me. We are never doing that again! So…," I broached. "Have you talked to her?"

"And now we go back to the conversation about you," he suggested. "What else did you do? I assume there was at least some kissing."

I laughed. Normally I wouldn't let him off the hook like that, but he'd been super sensitive the last time I mentioned talking to Cindy. I knew he needed time, but I felt it was my job to encourage him with gentle nudges to get out of his dateless funk. I had faith that the universe would bring Mel happiness; I only wished he had the same hope. "Ok. Yes. Lots of kissing. I think my lips were numb and swollen Sunday night. I've got two hickeys on my neck the size of Rhode Island. Luckily my collar comes up just high enough to cover them at work."

"Good for you. It's been a long wait for you."

"I dreamed about him before we started dating, and I've woken up at least six times with cum all over my crotch. If I don't have sex soon, I think my balls might explode."

This time Mel laughed. "I don't think that's possible."

I sighed. I knew sex would happen soon. Tristan was the king of restraint, but I could tell by the lust in his eyes that I was winning. He'd give in shortly, hopefully by our wedding night. *He wouldn't leave me a virgin then, would he?* The notion made me drift off somewhere in my head.

"Grant?" Mel prompted.

"Oh, sorry. I have something else to say. I don't know how to tell you, so I'm just going to say it. We're getting married."

"Huh? What?"

"Tristan asked me to marry him. He bought me a ring and everything."

"Grant, are you sure that's wise? You barely know him. I realize that you haven't had much luck with men, but are you really ready to marry the first one who comes along?" He didn't sound happy. All I wanted was his happy voice. Why did he have to sound skeptical?

"It's rash, I know. It all sort of fell together that way. I even have a marriage license sitting on my dresser reminding me every time I walk in the bedroom." I couldn't tell him about the ex, Teresa; it would trivialize my engagement. No. Best to stick with a more romantic feel. Best to tell the people I knew Tristan had swept me off my feet. It was mostly true.

I heard Mel breathing on the other end. "Grant, I'm… happy for you." He sounded disappointed, but I thanked him anyway. Then he asked, "Am I invited?"

"Of course. We're planning to get married on Saturday."

"This Saturday? I have to work. I'll see if I can switch with someone. Did you tell your mother?"

"Yeah."

"What did she say?"

"She was skeptical about the timing, but I think overall she was pleased. I think my mom was worried I'd never find a man and I'd move back home."

"I think we all were," he muttered.

"What?"

"Nothing. So you're getting married!"

I heard his fake excitement, but I wasn't going to argue. "Yes. We're going to have a formal ceremony in the spring."

"If you were a woman, I would assume you were pregnant. I don't understand why you have to get hitched right away if you're planning to get married again in the spring. Why not wait until then?"

"You know how I told you he has a daughter?"

"Yes."

At that point, I explained everything about the baby momma and how Tristan was considering filing for full custody of Claire. Tristan had hoped our marriage would look good on paper for attorneys, as it suggested a stable home environment, especially when compared to Teresa's. Mel said it made sense but told me not to place all my bets on a gay marriage holding weight. Some judges didn't care because they viewed marriage equality much the way Teresa had described it. The idea made me feel ill. If it was legally binding, then a marriage was a marriage in my mind. Judges should treat them all the same. It was a nationwide law!

We chatted a bit longer, but I had a headache by the time I hung up. I was frightened by all the roadblocks we had to consider.

IN THE middle of the night—because everything happens in the middle of the night, not the end or the beginning, but the middle—after I'd switched positions twelve times and gone to get a drink twice and peed twice, I heard the floor creak. Someone was in my room at two thirty in the morning. I gripped my sheet and pulled it protectively up to my chin. "Tristan?" I asked warily, scared it wouldn't be him and I'd just informed a burglar I was awake.

"Yeah, it's me. I didn't mean to wake you."

I reached for my light and turned it on. When I rolled over, I found Tristan, shirt in hand, standing next to the bed. "What are you doing?"

"I couldn't sleep. I've missed you." He set his shirt on the dresser. "I was going to slip in quietly and sleep here. I didn't expect you to wake up."

"I'm a light sleeper."

He grinned. "Not the last time I was in this bed. I watched you for twenty minutes Monday morning as I touched your face and kissed your jaw. You were so deeply asleep I hated waking you up to go to the courthouse before work."

It was true. I'd never slept as soundly as I had Saturday and Sunday night. I conceded his point with a half smile. "Are you getting in?" It was comforting to know I wasn't the only one who couldn't sleep alone.

He smiled brightly, showing me his pearly whites. For a guy whom Jessica described as nothing short of terrifyingly badass, he had the prettiest teeth. I guess I always associated smoking with badasses. Smoking, drinking, motorcycle-riding, leather jacket–wearing badasses with nicotine stains and leathery skin. His skin was tanned, but smooth and healthy looking. I guess I was judging people and stereotyping in my own ways. I was guilty too, and it made me feel bad.

Tristan sat on the bed and removed his pants. I caught a glimpse of his bare ass as he pushed his jeans down. I turned away, and Tristan chuckled deep in his throat. The bed moved as he lifted the blankets. "You can look now, Grant. I'm under the covers."

I rolled over and blushed. "I'm sorry. I'm not used to seeing bare asses in my room."

"Which is a bonus for me. I'd rather you *never* see another bare ass except for mine."

I reached out and squeezed his hand. "Don't worry. I plan on being a one-ass guy the rest of my life."

Tristan leaned in and kissed me until I gasped, and he pulled back. "What?" he asked.

I swallowed hard. "I just felt your penis poke my leg." I closed my eyes and struggled to keep my breathing steady. "You know I want to touch you."

Tristan cupped the side of my face and kissed me hard. After a few seconds, he pulled back and said, "Okay. But I'm not touching you... yet. I need time. This restraint is good for me, believe it or not. I'm practicing self-control. I want to prove to myself I have the ability to *not* have sex. I'm used to fucking long and hard. When I finally make love to you, I want it to be slow. I don't want to scare you."

"Scare me? You said you were kidding about the whip."

"I am. I mean scare you because of how rough I like to get. You're green. I'm not pounding your ass like a jackhammer until I know you're ready." He must have seen my eyes grow wide, because he tried soothing me. "Shhh, Grant, I promise not to hurt you." He caressed my face, and I swear I knew he wasn't lying, even if his statement intimidated me. He was right; I was green as ever a virgin could be.

Although…. "You know I'm not a kid, right, Tristan? I've watched porn. I know basically what to do, and I understand the mechanics. I'm not that scared to try things." I had to make sure he understood me, because if he kept treating me like a fragile teenager, I'd be forced to buy rope, tie him to the bed, and create a little BDSM scene of my own. Although I hoped it wouldn't come to that, because I wasn't a take-charge kind of guy, even if I was pushy and opinionated.

"Point taken. You may do whatever you wish," he said, rolling onto his back and folding his arms behind his head.

I sat up and paused in my worry. *Oh, wow. I get to do whatever I want, and I don't know where to start.* I took ahold of the blanket and sheet and slowly pulled them back together so I could take a gander at his naked body. Slowly I revealed his cut chest, chiseled abs, and flat stomach just to his navel. So much hair, it enticed me to rub it, which I did. I ran my hand all over his stomach and up the center of his chest. My chest hair was patchy and sparse, so touching his coarse, dark hair—over his pecs, down his chest, and across his stomach—made me grateful I was still wearing my white undershirt. He'd see my patheticness later, after it was too late to bail.

Tristan closed his eyes and breathed deeper.

I licked my lips and readied myself for what came next: revealing his cock. I was apprehensive about it because I'd seen him in his underwear, and the shaft he had under that little bit of cotton had seemed huge. What if it really *was* huge? What if I gagged on him during my first try at a blowjob and puked, or choked to death? I had a strong gag reflex; anything was possible.

I gripped the blanket again and then pulled it back carefully. I knew it wasn't going to leap out, but I didn't want to be the one guy who injured him because I yanked the covers back too swiftly. I knew what it was like to zip my fly too fast; this needn't be compared to that.

I gasped again. Of course I did. I could not imagine anyone seeing something that large and not being surprised by it. Straight and long, the thing reached his navel. He could beat baby seals to death with it. I gulped air, wishing I had a drink of water to wet my throat. I was even more nervous now, looking at it. I stretched my fingers wide and held my hand above it, measuring. My long piano-player fingers measured about ten inches from the tip of my pinkie to the end of my thumb. He had to be that long!

"What are you doing?"

I snapped my face in his direction as I snatched my hand back. "Nothing."

He chuckled. "It's nine and a half inches long, five and a half around."

I gaped. "That's huge! How is that supposed to fit inside of me? Because I tried a cucumber once, and that didn't work."

I thought he'd have some witty comeback, especially about the cucumber, but instead he closed his eyes and groaned. I saw his dick twitch out of the corner of my eye. It pulsed on its own, precome dripping from the tip. I whispered, "Maybe I shouldn't have said that."

He took a deep breath and exhaled. "Grant, if you don't do something… soon… I'm going to need to take care of it myself."

He got my attention. "Oh. I'm sorry." I pulled the covers off the rest of the way and then situated myself between his legs. Tristan bent his knees and spread them wider for me to have room. Before I even touched him, I had to ask, "Um, are you clean? I could get a wet towel and wipe—"

"I took a shower at five and then again before I came over here. I knew you'd appreciate it if I smelled like soap and not sweat since your sheets are so fresh."

I sat up, looked at him, and sighed. "Aww, thank you. I do like to have fresh sheets. I change them once a week."

"I'm lucky if I remember once a month."

"Eww. Remind me to wash your sheets the next time I'm there." I crouched back down and eyed his assets. He was well groomed; I'd give him that. Big balls, drawn up tight. I ran my palm over his sac. His testicles shifted, and I grinned.

I stuck my face between his legs and sniffed his balls. *Soap. He wasn't kidding.* I figured licking straight up his scrotum was the easiest way to ease into something I'd never done. I kind of liked the feel of his wrinkled skin on my tongue. It didn't taste like anything. I wiggled my tongue over his sensitive skin, and Tristan groaned. When I opened wide and drew his sac into my mouth, gently sucking on one nut, I tingled listening to him moan my name.

I pulled my knees under me, crouching as I grabbed the base of his javelin. I snickered, thinking it could definitely skewer someone— hopefully not me. There was no way I'd get it all in my mouth, but for him I would do my best to stimulate its head. I licked across his frenulum and around the ridge of his mushroom head. The skin was surprisingly smooth. I lapped a long lick up the vein that ran up the center of his penis, and then dared to pop him into my mouth.

Tristan slapped the bed and twisted the sheet in his fist. "Grant, baby… oh, fuck yes!" Tristan rasped as he laid his hand on my head. I lowered my mouth until his dick hit the back of my throat.

I choked and pulled off right away, causing him to whimper. I had to make sure I wasn't going to puke before I went down again, but I was fine. No bile. I opened wide and slipped my lips around his oozing head, holding his cock erect at the base. I licked and bobbed but didn't go down as far as the first time. I didn't want to gag again.

I was really getting into it, and I enjoyed his little grunts and gasps and how he fingered my hair. I stroked his inner thigh with my free hand as well as fondling his balls. I loved the feel of his silky smooth shaft against my lips and even the ache in my jaw as I stretched my mouth wide enough to take him in. I could feel his vein with my tongue as I licked him, and I tasted the drops of precome that seeped from his slit.

He groaned and held the back of my head but didn't force me to swallow him deeper. For him I tried one more time, but I came up for air before I gagged. I knew with practice I'd be able to suck on more of him at once, but for now the first few inches would have to do. His cockhead was too wide for my inexperienced throat.

"Use your hand," he suggested.

I released his heavy rod from my mouth and used my hand, sliding it up and down with my saliva as lube. I could tell it was drying up too quickly, so I spit on him. It seemed so undignified. If he liked me sucking and pumping my fist at the same time, I'd have to find flavored lube or something. Making him chafe would be horrible. It was still too dry, and I was the one rubbing, so I lowered my mouth over him and timed my fist pumps with the bobbing of my head. After a few up and down motions and lots of saliva all over my hand and his dick, Tristan gripped my hair and started panting.

"Grant... oh... I'm gonna... Grant...," he hissed between clenched teeth.

I knew what was about to happen. Hearing him moan for it turned me on. I reached inside my boxers and jerked. I needed to come too. I thought I'd be brave enough to swallow his load, but I chickened out at the last second. I was afraid I'd gag. I kept pumping my hand as he erupted, wave after wave of sticky ropes. Seeing him shoot prompted me, and I emptied in my underwear. At least my seed was contained. Tristan's splooge got all over his chest and my hand, down his balls, and even a splotch on my cheek.

"Damn!" I marveled. "I didn't know there was that much in there."

He laughed and leaned forward to kiss me. "It's been pent up." He winked and wiped the gunk off my cheek. "Did you come?" he asked, noticing my hand inside my waistband.

I nodded.

That pleased him. "Nice. Then I guess we *both* need to get cleaned up." Tristan cupped his junk and slid off the side of the bed. I think he was trying to keep his semen from getting on my sheets, but there were still a few obvious spots. His cock seriously *had* exploded like a volcano.

I scrambled off, keeping my hand in my boxers with all the mess. I met him in the bathroom, where he turned on the shower and hopped in. He explained, "It's easier. That shit's all over me."

I shrugged. "Feel free." When he closed the curtain, I inspected my face. I needed to wash it even if I didn't see any of Tristan's evidence. Actually, I needed to wash all of me just like Tristan was doing, but I didn't want to undress in front of him. I wanted his fantasy of a pretty guy to last a little longer. My body wasn't pretty. It was undefined and pale as a sheet, with a little pudge from eating too many cupcakes last year. I still hadn't lost the weight I'd gained.

"Are you getting in?" Tristan asked, poking his head out.

I shook my head nervously.

That damn eye of his twitched. His face disappeared, and seconds later he turned the water off. He grabbed a towel off the rack and dried behind the curtain. When he pushed it back and stepped out, he had the towel securely wrapped around his waist. He came up to me and gently traced my jaw. "Are you okay?"

I nodded.

"Are you afraid to let me see you naked?"

I hated how transparent I was to him. I looked down.

Tristan brought my chin back up. "You don't have anything to worry about, Grant."

I stepped back and scoffed. "Yes, I do. Look at you!" I gestured at his gorgeous body, tanned and dripping wet like a surfer model on the cover of *Men's Health*. All he needed was a surfboard under his arm and a palm tree in the background. "You're perfect. And then there's me," I stated, sweeping my hand down my length. "Your exact opposite."

"Grant, I don't care what you look like."

I cried out and covered my mouth, shrinking back toward the door.

Tristan reached out and clarified. "That's not what I mean, and you know it. I think you're beautiful, Grant. How many times have I told you?"

"You haven't seen me naked."

"Then enlighten me. What's wrong with you?"

"I'm hideous!"

"Why? Do you have a reconstructed chest?" he asked, probably making fun of me even though he sounded sincere.

"No." I rolled my eyes.

"A third eye where your nipple should be?"

I almost laughed but held it in. "No."

"A donkey's ass tattooed around your belly button?"

I snorted but recovered quickly. This was serious. "No. I just don't look like you." I turned and bolted from the bathroom. The quarters were too close to argue about something he obviously didn't get.

Tristan followed me, still wrapped in the towel. "Why do you think you have to look like me?"

I whipped around to face him and huffed, "Because I do!" I knew that wasn't a reason, but it was the one that came out first.

He stared at me, slowly licked his lips, and then nodded ever so slightly. "Okay. Then prove it."

I froze. "Prove what?"

"Take off your shirt and show me how hideous you are, and I'll never ask you to do it again." His challenge was firm.

I swallowed hard. "No."

He took a step closer. "Take it off." His intent stare unnerved me.

I stepped back, but my legs hit the bed. "No."

Tristan was not a guy to take no for an answer, and I learned it the hard way. He stepped right up to me and grabbed the hem of my shirt. I held it down as he tried to remove it. He pulled upward, and I shoved down. "Stop," he instructed, unblinking.

He made my heart race and my breath hitch when he took the bottom of the shirt and slowly pulled it up over my stomach and told me to lift my arms. I started shaking as soon as I was bare chested in front of another human being. I didn't even do that at the doctor's office. "Lie on the bed."

Never mind that I had sticky, almost dried cum on my hand and all over my crotch, never mind that he'd just forced me to bare my chest when I was extremely uncomfortable doing so, and never mind that I was seconds away from either crying or running out of my house in the middle of the night. I did as he asked, because I didn't know what he would do if I didn't.

Tristan straddled me, towel and all, across my hips. He took my hands, which I had crossed over my chest with my fingers tucked in my armpits, and moved them above my head. "Leave them there, or I'll hold them down." I couldn't answer. I could barely breathe. He had to know how scared I was, didn't he? Why would he do this?

As soon as his eyes left mine and he dropped them to my chest, he groaned, deep and guttural. He grabbed my nonexistent pecs in both hands and squeezed, massaging the area as if sizing up how little muscle there was under the surface. He grunted again. Then he circled both nipples with his thumbs. I shivered. I still couldn't breathe, but it was becoming increasingly difficult to remember the original reason. When he bent forward and licked one nipple, I inhaled sharply and panted the air back out. His tongue swirled around my nipple as he cupped my soft flesh.

He adjusted his position, and I felt his hard shaft rubbing against mine through my boxers as he rocked gently. He moved his mouth over to the other side and suckled me, continuing to squeeze and fondle my chest. He pinched one nipple as he sucked on the other, rousing me to tilt my hips a teeny bit because something deep inside needed more.

He let out a heady groan and moved his mouth to my neck. He latched on, sucking hard. I was very familiar with the sting that followed, but I was not prepared to feel him pinching both nipples at the same time. Not hard, but causing just enough pain to make me writhe beneath him and whimper.

I knew he had told me to keep my hands above my head, but I couldn't. I grabbed the back of his smooth head with one hand and gripped his shoulder with the other. I lifted my hips again into his rocking motion. "Tristan," I gasped, becoming unglued by his talented tongue.

He didn't say anything. He went back to suckling one nipple—but harder this time, painful this time. I felt teeth and cried out as I came.

Tristan lifted up, one hand planted on either side of my body, his face flushed. "If you didn't enjoy any of that," he said smugly, "then you may wear a T-shirt every single night to bed. But if you think you *might* want me to do that again, then you need to think long and hard about *why* you want to cover yourself up. Because, baby, I just came sucking on your tits. I'd call that a pretty damn good reason to let me see your body. I think you're beautiful."

He ran his palm all the way down my chest to my stomach as he got off of me. He rubbed his crotch as he stood, watching me, then removed the towel and dried the underside of his semilimp dick. After tossing the towel into the bathroom, he walked around to the far side of the bed, genitals bouncing with each step, and slipped under the sheet again.

I stood up and looked down. Yup, same body as I'd had before, only now one nipple was red and aching. My groin felt gross, so I went back to the bathroom. I shut the door and looked at my reflection. He'd marked me really good this time. I didn't think I'd be able to hide the huge purple mark beneath my shirt collar.

I showered and felt much better after I was clean. I'd forgotten to bring another pair of underwear in with me, so I had to hope he'd turned the light off while I was busy. He hadn't. I peeked out and asked, "Will you close your eyes and promise not to look?"

He huffed loudly and flipped over in the bed, burying his face under the pillow.

I scurried across the floor to grab another set of boxers. I slipped them on and stared at my T-shirts sitting in the drawer. *Should I?* I glanced at Tristan, still hiding his face. I inspected myself in the dresser mirror. *That* is the body that made him orgasm? Why? I had nothing to offer. Maybe it was just the heat of the moment and not liking me telling him no. He had gotten excited and came because he was overly stimulated. My brain then reminded me, whispering, "Overly stimulated from licking your nipples!"

I rubbed the sore one, the one he'd bitten. I shivered again. Tristan had used his teeth and I'd liked it, even though it really hurt. He'd basically ravaged my man-breasts—tits, he'd called them—and I'd come because of it. They weren't actually pudgy like man-breasts; I knew I only saw them that way because they weren't made of solid muscle. I was flat chested, pathetically weak looking. I could wear the T-shirt, he'd said, unless I wanted him to do that again. I turned around.

Tristan was still under the pillow. I took a deep breath, and for the first time since I was nine I went to bed *without* a shirt on.

Chapter Nine

PDA, OCD, And Seeing Change As An Addition Problem Instead Of A Homogeneous Linear Differential Equation

IN THE morning, while we were still spooning in bed, I stroked the arm that held me across my bare chest. Tristan sighed and snuggled closer. He kissed his way to the back of my ear and whispered, "I'm sorry."

"For what?" I asked, knowing exactly what he meant but being afraid to talk about it.

"For forcing you to take off your shirt. For making you shake in fear. For pushing you to the verge of tears."

I felt the emotion rising, quickly followed by accelerated breathing and a thudding heart rate.

Tristan moved swiftly, rolling me onto my back and repositioning himself right up against me. "Baby, I'm sorry. I will never do that again." Leaning on one elbow, he ran his other hand over my hair and wiped away the tear that rolled down my cheek. "I got angry with you because I just don't see you the same way as you see yourself, and I took it out on you the wrong way. I don't want you to fear me."

"I don't," I squeaked.

"You did. I saw it in your eyes, and yet I kept pushing." He kept his eyes locked with mine, and I felt as though I was caught in his headlights. I couldn't look away. Luckily he broke eye contact first, moving his gaze to follow his hand as he touched my hair again, rubbed my neck, and trailed his fingers across my collarbone. Tristan slid the backs of his fingers down the center of my chest and openly scrutinized my nakedness in the bright light of day. I thought he'd cringe or recoil as I watched him looking me over. He didn't. He breathed more rapidly, openmouthed, eyes dancing over my chest. Tristan seemed dazed. Then he dipped down and kissed my breastbone as he squeezed the side of my chest, his thumb putting pressure on the sorest part.

I winced.

Tristan jerked his head back, his gaze connecting with mine and then dropping back down to my nipple. "I bit you too hard." He gently ran the tips of his fingers over that area. "It's swollen."

"It hurts," I admitted. I wanted to cover it with my hand, but my arm was pinned to the bed under his side.

Tristan leaned in and licked me, flat-tongued, all over the reddened area; then he blew on it. The chill shocked me, yet it felt really nice. He did it again, licking me and swirling his tongue over my nipple before blowing on the wetness. "How's that?"

I smiled faintly. "Feels nice."

He cupped my pec, only gentler this time, and kissed me there. He moved over to the other nipple and licked it until the nub hardened. He nuzzled my erect right nipple with his nose, and I giggled. It seemed silly. "You like that?" he asked, continuing to nuzzle and lick alternately. He'd shifted his position, which allowed me to move my arm, but now I didn't feel like covering myself. I caressed his shoulder as he licked me.

I nodded, but he wasn't looking at me so I answered, "Yes." The desperation in my voice surprised me. I really *did* like it. He grazed me with his teeth and I cried out, but this time more from surprise than pain. He went easier on me, playfully nipping instead of aggressively biting. I mewled my approval as he kissed his way down my stomach and swirled his tongue around my navel.

When he moved his hand lower and gripped my hardening cock through my boxers, I convulsed and gasped. If I had been standing in the room, I would have leaped back three feet, but in the bed with his body leaning on my chest and his leg looped over mine, I had nowhere to go. Still, Tristan understood my reaction and let me go immediately.

His hand in the air, he said, "I stopped."

I felt guilty for reacting so strongly. "I'm sorry. No one's ever touched me there. I didn't mean to freak out."

Tristan lowered his hand and placed it on my upper thigh. Not exactly better, in my assessment. I jumped again, only less convulsively.

Tristan said my name calmly, soothingly. "Grant. Do you want me to touch you or not?" His fingers almost tickled as he caressed my thigh.

I swallowed again, really needing a glass of water. "Yes?"

He narrowed his eyes. "You don't sound convinced."

I cleared my throat. "Yes. Go ahead. I won't scream."

He gave me a weird look, almost a scowl mixed with partial amusement, then turned his attention back to my tented boxers, touching me again and gripping me firmly yet gently through my underwear. He moved his hand down to massage my balls and then back up my shaft. I heard him groan and huff out a hard breath. Waves of heat rolled through my stomach, and I started quivering with need. It felt so good, but as soon as he lifted the waistband of my boxers to reveal the part of me that lay hidden, I shrieked and scrambled up the bed as far as I could go with the headboard behind me.

"I can't," I cried, my heart racing faster than ever before, last night's orgasm included. "I'm sorry." If what had happened in the mall over the weekend was a panic attack, then I knew I was on the verge of another one. I grabbed the pillow next to me and clutched it protectively to my chest.

In my haste to escape his touch, I had pulled my knees up and connected with Tristan's jaw in the process. He sat up and rubbed it, swiveling his jaw right and left. "Okay. I'm backing away." He got off the bed and walked into the bathroom.

I glanced at the clock. I had an hour to get to work. I searched the room: my shirts lined up in my open closet, his shirt sitting on my dresser, my shoes resting next to my desk chair, his shoes located haphazardly in the middle of the floor where he'd removed them. I shifted my attention to the bathroom door. Tristan was haphazard, entering my life on a whim and a chance. He was wild and dominating, yet I had the feeling he could be tamed if I spoke up and told him what I liked and didn't like.

I glanced down and moved the pillow off my chest. I touched it, tracing my fingers over the same areas that Tristan had suckled. I pinched my own nipple, but not the sore one, of course. The tinge of pain didn't feel the same. I got off the bed and walked over to my dresser mirror—the place where I often examined my inadequacies and imagined a different body to go with my nice face. My bleached white skin in the reflection made me think of a shimmery apparition in a horror movie. My skinny, bony chest wasn't anything noteworthy, yet Tristan had enjoyed kissing me there, licking me there, and dare I say—making love to me there. He seemed to like what he saw, and had called me beautiful several times.

Why couldn't I believe him?

The bathroom door opened, and he walked out, in the nude because his pants were lying on my floor and he never wore underwear. The new ones were probably still in the packaging. He stopped three feet from me and waited, probably unsure of what he could say when he'd done nothing wrong this time.

"I'm sorry," I said feebly. "I did like what you were doing this morning. I do like it when you… lick my nipples." Declaring it openly made my face hot. I knew I was blushing.

Tristan smiled softly. I knew he liked my blushing. He held his arms open. "Come here."

I stepped into his embrace, and he held me tight, rubbing up and down my bare back as he was fond of doing.

"I should have known it was too much, too soon. We've known each other, what, three weeks?"

"A little more," I corrected him.

"Okay. Point is that isn't very long. I knew when I met you, you were different than anyone I'd ever known, and I was certain you were worth waiting for. I want to know you so well that I'll be able to predict your reactions and avoid making you panic." He kissed my neck up to my ear and suckled on my earlobe. He whispered, "You are a delicacy, Grant, and I will work my way up to tasting every part of you… at your speed… when you allow." He kissed my neck again and let me go.

I watched him retrieve his pants from the floor and slip them on. His soft penis was less intimidating and more pleasant to look at.

"I *will* let you do things. I promise."

He chuckled. "Oh, I know you will. The sounds you make say a lot about what you feel. You might be nervous, but your body likes my touch. The anticipation of making love has me hard for you practically all day. That's a good thing, Grant." He winked and seductively licked his teeth. He zipped his pants and grabbed his shirt. After he pulled it over his head, he came over to me again. Gripping my upper arms, he grinned at me. "You make me crazy. I want you so much, and it doesn't bother me if you need to wait." He kissed me and then walked away. Stopping at the doorframe, he turned and added, "Just so you know, I think you're fucking sexy." He cupped his crotch and rubbed it suggestively. "Really. Fucking. Sexy."

When Tristan left, I rushed to the bathroom and jacked off in the shower. He was right about my body liking his touch.

AT WORK, Jessica noticed my hickey right away. Her work area was on the opposite side, but I guess she noticed when I turned her way and bent down to get some hundreds out of my station vault, which was located in a cabinet under my teller drawer. I bent down, and her eye spied the huge purple mark Tristan had left, just high enough to peek out of my collar. I'd worn purple, hoping it would blend in, but it was darker than my lavender shirt.

As soon as her customer left, she exclaimed, "Holy shit, Grant! Is that a hickey?"

I couldn't lie, since it was obvious, but I tried anyway. "No. It's a bug bite."

"No, it's not!" She walked around the cubicle wall and manhandled me to face the direction that gave her the best angle. She even pulled the collar away from my neck to glimpse the whole thing and then whistled. "Wow, someone did a number on you! I didn't even know you were seeing anyone. How come you didn't say?"

She didn't seem offended, just very curious. I shrugged. "I don't know."

"You could have, you know? When we were talking the other week and you admitted you're gay. You could have said something, and I wouldn't have judged you. I know we haven't been friends long, but I consider myself an ally. I wouldn't have said anything rude."

"I know."

"Then why didn't you tell me you had a boyfriend?" I was glad there was no one around, but I was also appreciative that she spoke quietly. I got the impression she just wanted to get to know me, and it felt nice, especially since I hadn't seen my other friends in quite a while. Seeing some of them at the mall really didn't count in my book since I'd been on the verge of a panic attack and we hadn't had the time to sit and chat properly over a cup of coffee. I missed real interaction.

I said, "Because I didn't have one at the time. This is all new."

Her eyes grew wide. "Ooh, where'd you meet him?"

Her first question, and I knew it was going to prompt even more after I told her. Chances were that no matter what her first question, they would all come back to "my guy is Tristan Carr," the same guy she'd suggested would punch me out if I flirted with him. How wrong could she be? He'd been flirting with *me* the whole time. I opened my mouth to say something but noticed a customer staring at us. He'd snuck in and was waiting in line. Customers here were nice that way; instead of walking up to a window right away, I did note most stood in the roped lane that designated where the line should form. He was the only one, yet he still waited. How polite.

I cleared my throat and called him over, and Jessica went back to her cubicle.

I steered clear of shock, disbelief, and other inquiries, but only temporarily. After my customer left, Jessica had a customer, so I slipped off to the bathroom to text Tristan.

Hi. I have a question. I hit Send. As I stood next to the door, I reconsidered such a random and ambiguous text, so I clarified. *This is Grant, BTW. My question has to do with our relationship and if it is okay for me to tell people because the hickey you gave me is hard to hide and now my coworker is pressuring me to tell her who my boyfriend is and I wasn't sure what I should say because you never told me if you were out in the community and I didn't want to say anything rude or invasive or presumptuous.* I hit Send again and waited.

My phone vibrated. "Hello?" I whispered.

"Grant? Why are you whispering?" Tristan asked.

"Because I'm in the bathroom."

"Okay, then just listen. I got your long-winded, rambling, run-on text with no punctuation." He chuckled. "You're one of a kind, Grant. Anyway, tell whomever you wish. I'm not worried about what anyone might think or do. I was in the Navy; I can handle myself. I want *you* to feel comfortable."

"Okay. Thank you."

"Grant?"

"Yeah?"

"How's your nipple?"

I don't know why hearing that word gave me a little wiggle in my gut, but it did, in a good, I-want-to-hear-it-again sort of way. I supposed that was why some people liked dirty talk—because it fired them up for when those things actually happened. Maybe I could try that sometime with Tristan. Would he like dirty talk, or dirty text? I grinned at the possibilities. I told him, "It's okay. My shirt keeps rubbing against it and it doesn't feel good, but I'll live."

"Do you want me to come over tonight? I could take an ice cube and run it all over those sore spots."

I sucked in a breath. "Don't some people use ice cubes for erotic foreplay?"

He snickered loudly. "Yes, I think they do, but you don't need to refer to it as 'erotic,' since that's implied. Foreplay by definition is for erotic stimulation before sex. As far as the ice is concerned, the cold is shocking and stimulating at the same time. But in your case, it might make your nipples feel better."

"Okay." There wasn't much more I could say to his proposal. It sounded intriguing.

"Listen, I gotta go. I'll be over around nine. I have to work late. I'm really behind. I might have to hire someone to help with the books. I'm normally on top of invoices and billing, but after meeting you, I can't seem to get it all done."

My heart sank. I was keeping him from doing his job. What if his business went under because of me? What if the IRS showed up for unpaid taxes? What if he couldn't pay his employees because he didn't bill the customers who owed him money?

"Grant," he said sternly. "I can hear your gears turning. Stop thinking it's your fault. I've been working twelve- to fourteen-hour days for as many years as I can remember. I told you I'm married to my work. That isn't healthy. Meeting you, and soon marrying you, made me think about my priorities. I don't want to work myself into an early grave. I want to spend some of my time enjoying life while I'm still young enough. I do have to go, I wasn't kidding, but we can talk about this another time. It's not your fault. The only thing you did was flip those pens over and blush at me. You had no control over my falling in love with you."

I sighed. He said the most beautiful things.

"Grant?" Jessica called from the other side of the door before she knocked insistently.

"I'll be right out," I called back to Jessica. I told Tristan, "I have to go."

"Go. I'll see you after nine."

"Okay. Bye." I hung up the phone and slipped it into my pocket before opening the door.

Jessica asked, "Are you all right? You've been in there a long time. Are you sick?"

"No. I'll be fine." I walked back to my window with Jessica on my heels. She grabbed the drive-thru window and left me be, but it was only a matter of time before I had to answer all her questions. Tristan seemed fine with it.

When I went to lunch, Jessica cornered me. "Let's go to Buffalo Wild Wings to eat lunch," she said.

"You're not on lunch."

"No, I'm off. I had a dentist appointment, but they changed it, so I decided to keep my half day and go shopping, but shopping isn't as interesting as talking to you. So let's go to lunch."

I put away my peanut butter and jelly sandwich and followed her out of the bank. Luckily the restaurant was just across the parking lot, so we didn't have to drive. They were also slow this afternoon, so we got seated right away. After we ordered, Jessica pounced. "So? Details."

I took a cleansing breath and readied myself for her reaction. "Okay. Do you want the slow buildup, or an info dump?"

"Just tell me. Is it someone I know? Did you meet him at the bank? It's not that skeezy Mr. Palmer, is it? Because that's all kinds of wrong."

"Eww, no, I'm dating Tristan Carr."

She narrowed her eyes and stared at me. Then her confusion morphed into astonishment. "What?" She paused. "When? How?"

I lifted my shoulders. "We went out for a beer, and things sort of progressed from there."

"Holy Moses. I don't believe it. He doesn't even look gay."

"Not all gay men wear signs," I declared. The argument was getting old. I'd heard waaay too many times how someone or other "didn't act gay" or "didn't look gay." Those assumptions irked me. Some guys were not obvious. Jeez. When would people get it through their heads that some gay men looked and acted just like straight men? Not every one of us was flamboyant. Not all gay men spoke with a lisp. Not every one of us ogled men's asses to the point of getting caught. Yes, I mentally cleared my throat. Guilty as charged.

The waitress brought our drinks, and Jessica unwrapped her straw. "I know, Grant. I didn't mean to offend you. I guess I'm shocked, is all. He seemed straight, and doesn't he have a daughter? I thought she came in with him before." Jessica sipped her soda and listened.

"He does. She's fifteen. It happened back when he was still figuring himself out. The baby momma is kind of mean, so I'm glad he never married her." I hadn't seen Claire in the bank, but that didn't mean Tristan hadn't brought her with him before I started working there.

"Baby momma?" she repeated and then started laughing.

"I know, that came out wrong. I'm not sure what else to call her. She's not very nice." The waitress brought some chips and salsa for us to munch. "Thank you," I said.

Jessica dipped a chip and asked, "You've met her?"

"Yeah. Last Saturday morning she showed up at Tristan's while I was still in my underwear. Talk about embarrassing."

Her jaw dropped. "Whoa. You spent the night? How long have you known him?"

"Four weeks on Friday. But it's not what you think; we didn't have sex." I don't know why I felt the need to clarify. It wasn't as if I was a minor or anything. I was an adult. Tristan was an adult. What we did together as consenting adults was no one's business but ours, even if we'd only known each other four weeks. Yet even if I didn't need to spill details, I kept going and said, "In fact, we're getting married Saturday."

Her chin nearly hit the table this time. "What? That's incredible. I don't believe you."

"It's true. I know it's fast, but part of the reason has to do with the baby momma and her insinuation that all gay men hump like rabbits and never commit. I got pissed. And Tristan's visitation agreement was challenged. It was a whole big ordeal. In short, we're getting married, and he plans to file for full custody. Claire's mother apparently drinks often and has revolving affairs. She accused Tristan of the same thing and said she'd never let Claire come over if he brought guys home."

Jessica reasoned, "And it won't happen if you're married."

"No. It will be me and Tristan."

She patted the back of my hand and corrected, "You and Tristan, the two gay dads."

I sat back, realizing she was right. Not only was I jumping into marrying a guy I hardly knew, I was agreeing to be a stepdad... of a teenager. "Oh, shit. I'll be a stepdad."

"Sorry, Grant, but I think this is moving too quickly. You two may have had noble reasons, but getting married is huge for most people. Getting married with older children is colossal."

The food came, thank God. I needed to eat and think. Jessica was kind enough to let me eat in peace, but after my last bite, before the check arrived, she asked more questions. "Where are you getting married on Saturday? Is it a church wedding? I know receptions can be expensive, but do you think I could watch the ceremony? I really do consider you a friend."

"Um, yeah, but we haven't planned anything. It was very sudden, and we were just going to ask the clerk on staff to perform a civil ceremony on Saturday since we both have it off. This Saturday is Tristan's weekend with his daughter anyway. She wanted to be there. Claire wants to plan a spring wedding. We thought we'd invite all our friends and family to that one."

"Oh? I didn't think county offices were open on Saturdays."

"What?" I didn't want to believe her. I took out my phone and googled the Carroll County Circuit Court. "Oh my gosh, you're right. It says appointments preferred, but they're only open Monday through Friday. I'd better call."

"You should," she agreed.

We paid the check, and I returned to work. Outside, before I walked back in, I told Jessica, "Thanks for not getting upset with me. This has been a crazy couple of days."

"Sounds like it."

I sighed. "I know I'm going to take heat for this, especially when I show up at work with a ring on my finger, but can you do me a favor?"

"Sure. Anything."

"Don't tell people we've only known each other a few weeks, please? No one needs to know how sudden this was."

Jessica took my hand and squeezed it. "Your secret is safe with me. I hope everything works out."

"Me too."

I STOPPED by Tristan's auto shop on my way home. I'd called the circuit court after work, five minutes before they closed, and found out they only had two options open this week. I had to tell Tristan I'd picked a time and I hoped he'd be okay with it.

I parked in front of the door marked "office." A younger guy, probably close to my age, made eye contact and asked, "May I help you?" I liked that he asked "may I" instead of "can I."

I said, "Hi. I wanted to know if Tristan was around. I need to talk to him."

The guy came up to the counter and said, "Okay, I'll go find him. May I get your name?"

"Um, my name's Grant." It seemed so formal, and I felt stupid for no reason, but then his face lit up.

"Oh! You're Grant. Tristan told us about you. Have you gone home yet?"

"What?" I asked, confused by the non sequitur. "No, why? I stopped here on my way home."

He smiled. "No reason. My name's Wes, by the way. I run the office and order parts and stuff." He held out his hand.

Suddenly I felt so much better. I smiled and shook his hand. "Hi. It's nice to meet you."

"Likewise. I'll go get Tristan." He headed for the door that led into the garage, but stopped at the door. "I'm glad to finally meet you. I've never seen Tristan so happy."

He left and walked up to another guy I could see through a large glass window that allowed people in the office to see into the shop. Maybe it was called a hangar, like for planes. I didn't know, but I rationalized calling it that in my head. The space in there looked big from where I stood. When Wes turned and pointed at me and then walked on, the other guy came into the office.

He held out his hand to me. "Hey, I'm Jeff. I've worked for Tristan the past ten years, and five years for his father before that. Tristan's a good guy. I'm happy for you both. Let me tell you, Tristan can be a little rough around the edges, but he's got a good heart."

"Yeah, I kinda figured that one out."

"Have you gone home yet?" Jeff asked.

It felt odd. Why would he ask me that, especially after Wes had done the same? "Um, no," I said. "Why?"

He shrugged. "No reason. Tristan said you lived close."

"Oh, yeah, I do. It's like five minutes."

"Convenient," he commented, nodding his head in that way people do when they can't think of anything interesting to say. Was he always like this, or did I make him nervous? And if he was nervous, I wanted to know why—because I didn't tend to make people nervous.

"Yeah," I agreed, nodding back in the same uncomfortable manner.

Tristan came through the door and smiled at me right away. "Hey, baby. I didn't expect to see you until later. Have you been home yet?"

"No. Why does everyone keep asking me that?" I asked, slightly irritated. I couldn't dwell on the weirdness. I needed to get to my point for showing up at his work. "Look, Tristan, can I talk to you? Privately?"

He glanced at the guys, and they left the room, closing the door. Tristan lifted the part of the counter that was attached with hinges and folded it over so he could cross to my side. He pulled me to him and hugged me. I felt his lips on my neck, and he nuzzled my ear. "It's so nice to see you. I've missed you. I've been obsessing over last night and hoped you weren't mad with me."

He released me, and I looked him in the eyes. He had such lovely eyes. "No. I'm not mad. You were right about me being scared, but I have to admit I liked most of it. I want you to ravage me like that again, only with less teeth."

He grinned. "I can do that."

"I also like the idea of ice cubes." I blushed and looked away, but I couldn't not look at him—no matter how embarrassed I was to admit it—so I brought my gaze back up before he could do it for me.

"I'll see what I can do later." He kissed me softly several times, but it progressed quickly. In moments, he kissed me deeply and moved one hand up to the back of my head so he could keep me there.

I had my arms around his neck, and I can't say I minded his relentless tongue, but we were in his office—the office with a huge glass window. As soon as he reached down and cupped my ass with his other hand, I jumped.

He apologized, "I'm sorry. You're hard to resist. I want you so bad."

"It's okay. I think it's the large window that's making me skittish." I pointed. He turned to look with me at the three guys on the other side, laughing and making obscene gestures and kissy-faces and touching themselves in ways that made me blush again.

I hid my face against his chest as Tristan laughed and waved them away, encircling my waist with one arm and refusing to let me go even though we were being watched.

"Who's that other guy?"

"Will, my other mechanic. Will, Jeff, and I do the labor, while Wes takes care of the office. We've all worked together a long time. I went to school with Jeff. Will and Jeff met at a hockey game, and Jeff suggested I give him a job because he was looking for work. He's been here six years."

"And Wes?"

"Four years. But he fit in so well with our group that I can't fathom a time when he wasn't here. He's like the glue that keeps everything together."

"Sounds nice."

"It is, but meeting my guys is not why you came by."

"No."

"Then tell me. Everything's okay, isn't it?"

"Yes and no." He narrowed his eyes but waited for me to explain. "I called the circuit court because my friend Jessica from work said she thought they were closed on Saturday. Turns out they are. Appointments are encouraged, because they can be busy, I guess, so I asked about getting married and they had two times slots available. Tomorrow at eight thirty, or Friday at eleven."

Tristan opened his mouth to answer and then promptly shut it. He stared at me a moment. The information must have thrown him. He finally said, "I, um, wow. I'm rebuilding a transmission on Friday, and it's going to take all day. I don't know how I can slip out in the middle."

"Which is why I booked eight thirty tomorrow morning. I hope that's okay."

Tristan let go of my waist and stepped back. "Um, yeah." He leaned on the counter behind him and rubbed his head. "Tomorrow," he reiterated. "We're getting married tomorrow."

I nodded. "Yup. Unless… unless you want to call it off and plan something in the spring."

"I don't know."

Just then, the main door to the office opened behind me. I turned, expecting to see some guy or other coming in for an oil change or something, and nearly choked on my own saliva when it was Teresa, the baby momma. I gasped.

She sneered, "Oh, jeez. I didn't expect *you* to be here." She gave me a look of disdain and then turned her wrath on Tristan.

"I'll have you know, my daughter will not be coming to your house on Saturday if it's only to see two fags get hitched so they can justify their immorality."

"Ha!" I yipped in protest. Tristan held up his hand in my direction, so I kept my diatribe to myself.

"Then it's a good thing we decided to get married tomorrow," he responded without hesitation.

"What?" she asked, her surprise evident.

"Yeah," he said. "Grant and I talked it over, and we decided not to wait. Our love is so strong and immovable that we couldn't stand another moment apart."

I swallowed hard, struggling against my mounting anxiety.

"Oh, that's disgusting. I can't believe a court would allow it." She visibly shivered.

No matter how scared I was about jumping in to marry Tristan, Teresa always seemed to push me toward it because of how angry she made me by protesting the very rights I had as an American citizen. I pulled back my shoulders and stepped to Tristan's side, facing her as a team. "It is not disgusting," I huffed. "What we choose to do with our lives is none of your business."

"Oh, I think it is. You do this, Tristan, and you'll never see Claire again."

He made a guttural sound, like a growl, and stepped into her personal space. "No, you don't get to alter your protest. Last time, you said you wouldn't allow her over if I was just some bed-hopping homo who had a different man in my house every weekend. I'm not. I'm marrying Grant, and then I'm filing for full custody of Claire. Now take your homophobic, man-hating ass out of my shop."

From the expression on her face I thought she'd scream, but all she did was turn sharply and slam the door behind her after mumbling, "You'll regret this."

I muttered, "Then I guess we're getting married tomorrow."

He turned and placed his hands on my shoulders. "I'm sorry, Grant. I couldn't let her win."

I gave him an understanding half smile. "Which is why I blurted the very same thing Saturday. I get it. We're getting married. We'll make it work."

"Will we?" He didn't seem as sure as a second ago.

I nodded. "No matter how freaked out I am about the timing and the gravity of everything, I do care about you. I want a relationship with you. I want to wake up spooning every morning and make pancakes on the weekends. I want you to lick my nipples and make me beg you to make love to me every night."

He widened his eyes. "Every night?"

I took in a deep breath and exhaled. "Probably. Sex is supposed to be awesome, right? I'm guessing I'll want it a lot once I know what I've been missing."

He chuckled and pulled me into a hug, rubbing my back and squeezing me before letting go. "Gosh, I hope so. I care about you too. Why don't you go home, get a shower, have some dinner, and relax, and we'll talk about everything when I get there later. I need to finish a job I promised for a guy who's going on vacation tomorrow. I'll be by your place by nine. I promise."

"Okay. Tell your employees it was nice to meet them."

"I will. You have no idea how excited they were that you dropped by. Wes was jabbering incoherently about how fucking cute you are."

"If he was incoherent, then how could you tell he thought I was cute?" I pointed out.

Tristan ignored my cynicism. "I caught that part. The rest was scrambled."

"Is he gay?" I felt a mix of emotions when I asked. If he was, then had he and Tristan ever done things together? If he wasn't, then why would he say I was cute?

"No, but he's young and hip with the times. He knows I'm gay and he's been trying to set me up with some of his gay friends."

I stiffened and sputtered, "His friends? He better stop. He knows you're mine, right? We're getting married, and I will not take kindly to a guy who—"

He cut me off with his lips pressed to mine. The kiss was sweet and took all the rage out of my jealousy. He told me softly, "He knows." He kissed me again. "Go home. I'll see you later. Stop worrying, and forget being jealous. I'm yours. All yours."

I nodded. I knew he was right. His intent was clear, and I knew, logically, he meant every word he said. I left and drove home.

I OPENED the door and was overtaken by the scent of gardenias. It was such a powerfully sweet scent that I closed my eyes and took a deep breath through my nose to appreciate it fully before scanning the house for the source. The wonderful aroma came from bouquets of flowers—gardenias, lilies, and carnations—set all around the house. I found a vase in the kitchen, two in the living room, and three in the bedroom. I picked up a note left on my pillow.

It read:

> *I hope you're not allergic—I probably should have asked. I wanted to say I'm sorry for pushing. If I truly was a dom, then I would have gotten off on being in charge, maybe, but I'm not so I didn't. I want this to be an equal partnership. You and me, together. I don't want to force you to do anything, even something so seemingly innocent as removing your shirt. I'll try to understand if you want to keep it on, but I have to say, one more time, you are beautiful.*

I'll admit I got a tad choked up. Tristan did have a good heart, and neither one of us knew how to *be* in a relationship so we were bound to do things wrong. He'd forced me to do something I didn't want to do and scared me, but he hadn't hurt me, not really.

I bent over and sniffed the flowers next to my bed. They were lovely.

"That's why they kept asking me if I'd gone home," I said to myself as I realized what they'd meant. Tristan must have used the key I'd given him to come in earlier. He was such an awesome boyfriend. I sighed as the lyrics to "Dear Future Husband" sung their way through my head. He *was* treating me right, I had to admit.

My phone signaled a text so I grabbed my phone, thinking it was Tristan. It was Mel. *Are you busy? I miss you.*

I texted: *No. I just got home and guess what? Tristan put a zillion bouquets of flowers in my house. Okay, not a zillion. Six. It smells so wonderful in here I want to cry.*

That's nice.

I didn't like his tone. Flat. No inflection. True, it was a text, but I could hear him in my head. Instead of texting, I called. I didn't wait for a hello; I spoke right away when he picked up. "What's wrong?"

"Nothing," he mumbled.

"That's not a nothing voice. I know, because I know everything. Spill," I said sternly. If he was going to ruin my happy, then he had better fill in all the details. No ambiguity accepted. I placed my shoes next to my chair and undid my pants.

Mel hemmed and hawed but finally told me, "I talked to Cindy."

"You did? Was it about going on a date, or did you order macaroni and cheese this time?"

"Shut up! Yes, I asked her on a date. She paused a bit too long before answering, but she did agree to go. I'm not sure if she finds me attractive."

"I think you're attractive, especially since you have more facial hair than last fall. I think you look real manly."

"It's not the manly qualities I'm worried about. It's my *un*manly qualities—my high, feminine cheekbones and soft skin—that I'm worried about. What if she doesn't like my figure or my height? The mastectomy was a huge step. I can't change everything."

I felt bad. "I know the situation is messed up and not at all where you planned."

"I'm not sure how well I planned this, Grant. Originally I didn't want to date a girl until my outside reflected who I was on the inside. But then you moved, and I'm alone all the time. It was easier to think of dating as a *future* possibility while I had you to hang with. But then you met Tristan and things seem to be going well for you, and I feel like my life is going nowhere."

"I'm sorry." I didn't need to apologize for my new life, but I felt bad.

"Yeah, well, I want what you have. So I metaphorically grew a pair and asked her on a date. Now I'm freaking out about what might happen. When do I tell her? On the first date? The second? It's not like you with your fear of being naked!"

"Hey!" I squawked. "No fair! I told you, I went through two years of therapy for what Mikey Thompson did to me in sixth grade. His teasing still haunts my dreams!" I wasn't holding back while I fussed at Mel, but in doing so I heard a little voice reminding me I might need to fill Tristan in at some point. He'd pressed me into removing my shirt without understanding my suppressed trauma over it. If I was going to trust Tristan with my naked body, then I needed to trust him with my past hurts as well. I'd tell him soon.

He regretted his words right away. "I'm sorry. I know it wasn't fair. Your pain is just as legitimate as mine."

I held the phone between my shoulder and ear as I hung my pants up. I knew enough to know this was his lament. There was no answer for comments like that. They were simple facts. "Tell her when it feels right, but you shouldn't let it go past the second date, because it might seem deceitful. You have nothing to hide. You are an amazing person. You're so brave and strong, you have no idea. If Cindy is the right girl for you, then I'm sure she'll accept you just as you are. There isn't much else you can do."

"You're right." He sighed. "I'll do it. First I'll take her out and get a feel for the kind of person she is."

"Sounds good. Hold on, I need to change my shirt." I set the phone down on the bed, removed my white T-shirt, and tossed it in the hamper, closing the lid. As I reached for a fresh one, I hesitated. *What if I went the rest of the night without one until Tristan got here? I could show him I'm not afraid. Moreover, I could show myself I'm not afraid.*

"Hello," I heard Mel beckon from the other end.

I picked it up. "I'm sorry. I was just thinking about my shirt. But yeah, I agree. Feel her out and tell her the truth about everything before it goes very far. Honesty is best." My mother had told me many stories about her sister, who was a habitual liar, all of which ended badly. So as a kid I had never wanted to be like my aunt Crystal.

He said, "My honesty worked on you."

I smiled. "Exactly."

I changed my underwear and slipped on my pajama bottoms. I strolled into my kitchen shirtless and glanced at my front windows. *No one can see,* I rationalized, but I still went over and pulled the curtains closed. It was strange poking around my fridge only half-clothed, but if Tristan liked my body, I knew I needed to be comfortable in my own skin, half-naked. He would probably want me fully naked, and soon, but I was working up to that.

Mel and I chitchatted for a while. I put the phone on speaker while I ate leftover ham and macaroni and cheese. I liked to cook enough for several days, because then I didn't have to cook every night. Some people didn't like leftovers—my father had been one—but I found them convenient. By the end of the conversation, after I'd cleaned up dinner, Mel had agreed to text me how his first date went.

I was on the couch reading by the time I heard a knock at my door. It was 9:10 p.m., and the knock was probably Tristan, even though he had a key. I peeked through the tiny window in the door to make sure, since I was not going to answer the door shirtless unless it was Tristan. It was. "Hey," I said, opening the door and sweeping my hand toward the inside of the house. "I hope you know you can walk right in. I gave you a key for a reason."

He said, "I know. I gave it to Wes so he could bring the flowers over, and I forgot to get it back." His eyes widened. "You're shirtless! Wow, baby," he beamed, gripping each shoulder and studying my body. "You make my mouth water just looking at you."

I was glad he'd said it like that, because I was two seconds from crossing my arms over my nipples protectively. It was hard exposing my flesh, but his obvious pleasure made my discomfort worth it. Then my brain caught up to what he'd said. "Wait, you gave my key to your coworker?"

"My office manager, Wes. Yes. I had a few jobs I was working on at the same time and couldn't get away. He offered because he's a sappy romantic, and I appreciated it. The delivery guy brought the flowers to my shop and Wes zipped them over here."

"You work five minutes away," I protested. "You couldn't take ten minutes to do this yourself? You send a stranger into my house, into my bedroom, and you think I'll be okay with that because the flowers were awesome?"

He backed up. "Grant, I didn't mean to upset you. I told you I've been getting behind."

"Because you met me and I ruined your routine. I heard you." I was suddenly angry. The flowers had been so sweet and wonderful, until he admitted they hadn't been brought over and arranged in my house *by him!* A stranger brought them in and still had my key. I blurted, "What if he comes into my house when I'm not home and steals things? I can't file a claim if my house wasn't broken into, you know?" I didn't know if that was true, but it sounded true to me.

Tristan held his hands out in front of him. "Whoa, whoa, whoa, Wes would never do that. You don't need to get angry, Grant. I'll get the key back. I'll call him right now and tell him to bring it by if that's such a huge issue for you, but I think you're being ridiculous. Wes is very honest. Accusing him of something like that is out of line. Actually, I'm not calling him, because it would hurt his feelings. Besides, if you had answered my texts hours ago, I probably would have remembered to ask Wes for the key. Where have you been? Why weren't you answering your phone?"

I took out my phone. I hadn't noticed his texts asking if I was all right, if I liked the flowers, and one asking where I was because I hadn't responded about the flowers. Tristan looked upset, and I guess I couldn't blame him. I had exploded for no real reason.

I slouched. "I'm sorry. I'm not used to people having keys to my house, unless it's my mother. I guess I didn't like how you gave my key to someone I didn't know, the first week you had it."

"Next time, I'll ask. Okay?"

I nodded. Tristan held open his arms and I sank into his embrace. That is, until I caught a whiff of his manly stench. I pushed back out of his arms. "Um, no offense, but you reek."

"I know. I was hustling to get things done and sweating like a pig. Then I spilled engine degreaser on my shirt, and that stuff is nasty. I need to look into buying a different brand."

I felt guilty asking, but I had to. "Are you going home first to shower?"

"No, I have clothes." Tristan pointed to a bag next to the door. He must have dropped it upon entering, and I hadn't noticed.

"Oh. Then can you put your dirty clothes in a trash bag so the dirt and stuff doesn't get on my carpet?"

He rolled his head to the side. "Really? You think I'm going to get your carpet dirty? Grant, I wasn't rolling on the floor. We have lifts. I stand most of the time. You know what? Never mind. I'll strip down outside." He turned for the door before I had the chance to stop him. Tristan hopped out onto the porch and pushed his pants down in seconds.

"What are you doing?" I shrieked.

"I'm taking my clothes off out here so I don't get dirt in there." Then off came his shirt. I was glad no cars drove by while he was stripping, or he might have caused an accident. "I'll even toss them in the bed of my truck until tomorrow."

"But...," I started to say, but he rushed over to the truck parked next to my car.

He came back to me in underwear, and my heart palpitated. He was so sexy. He stepped past me into the house. "If you don't mind, I'll be taking a shower now." He stalked off.

Tristan was upset. He didn't get that I kept my house clean and that he was filthy. I never got that dirty. When I came home, my clothes looked almost like they did when I'd gotten dressed in the morning. I went over to the bathroom door and knocked. I heard the water running, but he didn't answer. "Tristan?" I turned the knob, but it was locked. "Shit," I cursed under my breath.

The water shut off while I waited by the door. He opened it abruptly and jumped at the sight of me standing there. "I didn't mean to make you mad," I said, head hung low, hoping he would take it as regret.

He strutted into the bedroom, towel around his waist, water droplets on his chest. "Yeah, well, I guess we're even. We seem to be good at pissing each other off." He left the bedroom, and I followed him through the house to the front door, where he grabbed his bag, and then back into my room. He placed the bag on my bed and dropped the towel. I looked away.

Tristan snorted, but I couldn't tell if it was from amusement or irritation.

"I didn't think you rolled on the floor, by the way. I didn't mean to make it sound that way." I kept my eyes averted as I spoke.

"I'm not mad about the clothes."

"You're not?" I asked, looking back. He was in his underwear, sitting on my bed.

"No. I'm hurt because you didn't say anything about the flowers. I went to all the trouble of sneaking them in here, and you didn't even text me to say thank you. Why? Because you were talking to your friend Mel, that's why!" His voice grew louder by the end of the sentence, and I shrank back a little.

"He had an issue. I was trying to be supportive."

"What about me? Didn't you think that I'd be waiting by my phone? I sent six bouquets, Grant, not one, but six. I thought maybe you hated them and I was stupid for even considering it."

"It's not stupid."

"Oh, no? Then I guess your conversation with your best friend was more important than your boyfriend, or soon-to-be husband." Tristan got off the bed and walked over to "his" side. He got in and pulled the sheets up, rolling onto his side away from me.

He was really upset about it. I quickly brushed my teeth and returned to bed. I scooted up behind him and stared at his back—it was like a gigantic, tan, muscular wall, intricately carved with black lines. I had briefly seen the tattoo of a dragon that covered most of his back, but I hadn't had a chance to study it until now. I traced my fingers over his scapula where the great beast's eyes were. Tristan wiggled. I wasn't sure if it was a wiggle to get away or an I-like-this wiggle, but I did it again.

I kissed where my fingers touched, his skin warm against my lips as I trailed kisses down part of the dragon's wing.

I scooted closer and lifted up on one elbow, kissing his neck, behind his ear, and his bald head. It felt weird kissing his scalp, but as I hadn't kissed anyone's hair except Mel's, I couldn't compare the feeling. I rested my hand on his shoulder and whispered, "I'm sorry."

He didn't say anything, but he touched my hand and then tried pulling my arm across his chest. My arms weren't long enough to comfortably drape over his shoulder, so I suggested, "Here, let me try spooning you this time."

I slid down behind him and pressed my body against his with my face tucked by his neck. Tristan quickly grabbed on to my arm as I slipped it around his waist. The position wasn't exactly uncomfortable, since we were only separated by a few inches in height, but he was bigger, and I felt like I was wrapping a stick figure around a sumo wrestler. That was a bad analogy, though, and I was glad he couldn't read my mind, because he wasn't fat—he was simply larger than me.

He whispered, "Press your dick against my ass."

Not exactly something anyone else had ever suggested. I immediately got self-conscious. I wasn't hard, but of course I was getting there thinking about what he wanted me to do. Would he feel me? I was not endowed. I realigned my body and pushed my hips forward, pressing myself against his ass.

Tristan grunted.

When he said nothing further, I was forced to ask, "Was that a good grunt, or a bad grunt? I couldn't tell. Can you even feel me?" I nudged forward again to emphasis my question.

He grunted again, closer to a moan. "I feel you, baby, and it's real good." He reached behind him with his long arms and grabbed my ass, pulling me tight against his rear. "You feel real good," he reiterated.

I was trying to relax and go with it, but he was squeezing my ass and I couldn't calm myself down.

Tristan let go and instructed, "Roll over."

I wasn't sure why. I thought he'd liked me nudging my groin against him. I did as asked, and Tristan rolled over with me. He spooned me like he had done before, pressing his seal club into my butt and wrapping his long arm over my chest. I felt his breath on my ear.

"Calm down, Grant. Just go to sleep."

"You're not mad?"

"It's the first time I've ever sent someone flowers. Your reaction was not what I'd hoped for, but I'm sure the next time, you'll at least say thank you."

One tear slipped from my eye. I'd been a dick. Not the first time, and probably not the last, but I hated the sound of his voice. I rubbed his arm and held it securely.

"Grant?" he whispered.

"Yeah?"

"Thank you for going shirtless."

I smiled. I knew everything would be okay.

Chapter Ten

Need, Want, And Fearing The Things
I've Never Done

I WOKE up and Tristan was gone. I panicked slightly but spied a note on my dresser.

> *Grant,*
> *I left because it's bad luck to see the bride before the wedding... or some shit like that. I'll meet you at the courthouse at 8:15. I'm not mad. I want to marry you.*
> *~T*
> *P.S. Sorry about the sheet. I had a wicked wet dream about you last night.*

I walked back to my bed and inspected the sheet. It was dry, but I could see the spot he referred to. I rather enjoyed knowing he dreamed about me so vividly, since I dreamed about him all the time. I pulled the sheets off after tossing the pillows aside and remade the bed. I couldn't leave it until after work.

I walked into the kitchen, and it hit me. "Holy shit, I'm getting married this morning." I tried my best to remain calm as I ate some cereal and made my lunch for work, but my nerves were jumping. I took a shower, only to stare at the cowlick in my hair afterward as I combed it. "Seriously?" I asked my hair. "Of all the days for you to decide to look like Alfalfa."

I was admittedly too young to have watched *Our Gang* when it was originally on television, but when I had lived with my mom she had often watched reruns of very old black-and-white shows like *Our Gang*, *The Andy Griffith Show*, and *The Munsters*. I thought they were funny, so I had never minded watching with Mom. Now, though, I didn't want to look like the kid with the single clump of hair standing straight up on the top of his head. I was getting married!

I did what I had to do to fix my hair and went to the closet.

I donned the shirt Tristan had picked out. It was white with thick blue pinstripes. A very different look for me, but it matched so well with the sports jacket I had also bought that I was very pleased. Moreover, my new shirt matched the navy blue shirt Tristan had picked out, which meant the pictures we took together after the ceremony would look nice.

Deep breath. I left my house, got in my car, and met Tristan at the courthouse.

THE CEREMONY took ten minutes, and the pictures took two. In no time, we were back in the parking lot standing next to my car. I stared at Tristan, and he stared back. It was obvious neither one of us knew what to say. I swallowed and took a stab first. "Um, I guess that's it." The whole thing seemed anticlimactic.

"Yeah," he responded slowly. I never thought one word could be drawn out so far, but it was as if he couldn't form any other words.

"Yeah," I agreed, tapping the tips of my fingers together and mentally registering the added weight of the rings on my left hand. It wasn't much, but enough to remind me of their presence without looking.

He must have caught my fidgeting, because he took my hands in his and said, "I'm glad we did this. I'm sure once we settle into the idea, this marriage won't sound so preposterous."

"Yeah, you're right." Was he? We had sort of done it to prove a point to his baby momma. That probably wasn't the worst reason in history to get married, but I'd bet it was up there.

"I've gotta get to work and change. How about we go out to dinner tonight. Your choice."

I thought it over. We hadn't gone to dinner except for the one time when I had spilled my drink on him. Dinner could be nice. "Okay," I agreed.

"I'll pick you up."

"Okay."

Tristan brushed my lips with his and caressed my cheek before sighing and running his hand over my hair. He paused and pulled my head down gently. "Um, what's this?" he asked, pulling the pin from my hair. "Is this a bobby pin?" He eyed it curiously.

"Yeah. My hair wouldn't cooperate this morning."

Tristan chuckled. "You're adorable." He kissed me again and then handed over the pin. "I'm going. I'll see you later." Tristan turned and walked to his truck, parked two spaces down. He grinned and waved at me from the driver's seat before driving away.

I got to work early, so I had a few nervous minutes to relive the simple vows in my head. We had promised to love and care for one another. We had promised to support one another and respect one another. I had pledged my life to Tristan Carr; I was his husband, and he was mine. I should probably inform my mother.

I needed Alka-Seltzer.

AT THE bank, I went right to my work window in my "cubicle away from home." I straightened everything, aligned my deposit slips, and made sure my pens were all facing down. My eyes caught sight of the rings on my hand, and for a moment I stared at the diamond. It sparkled. I turned my hand and tilted it so the light caught in the stone at several angles. Something inside caught, like my breath hitching, but not. It was that feeling when you want to sob, but your eyes haven't quite watered. My whole chest seized. I was married.

"Good morning, dear one," Mrs. Snyder said in a sultry voice.

I jumped and pulled my hand down to my side. As she explained her deposit and subsequent transfer, I used my thumb to slide my ring around backward, hiding the diamond inside my fist. "No problem," I said with a smile. I took her stack of money and checks and turned to enter them in.

"Is that a wedding ring on your hand?" she asked boldly.

I hadn't told Jessica. What if she overheard? She'd probably get angry and yell or make a scene. I said quietly, "Yes."

I felt her eyes raking over me, but I refused to glance at her. "Hmm. I suppose congratulations are in order."

Not what I'd expected. I smiled thinly, still worried what those around me might say if they heard our conversation. "Thank you."

"I don't remember seeing it on your hand last week."

I finished up the transaction and turned my attention fully her way. "No. It was recent."

Her grin was more seductive than I expected. "You realize, dear boy, that being married only makes you more appealing."

I drew in a long breath. "And on that note, here's the receipt for your deposit and transfer." I didn't need to fuel her interest any more than I was apparently already doing with my mere presence.

She chuckled deep in her cougar throat and walked away.

I breathed a sigh of relief and then turned around to find Jessica standing right there, glaring. "You're married? When were you going to tell me?"

"Um, now." She was upset, and I had a feeling it was because she saw us as friends and I had somehow betrayed her by not disclosing the information first thing. "I'm sorry, Jessica. It all happened really fast," I apologized. Whether or not it was my fault, I didn't want her to feel hurt. "I called the courthouse like you suggested, and there were only two times available. We got married this morning."

Jessica surveyed the lobby to make sure no one was waiting in line before commenting. "But is this what you want? Is this the dream wedding you planned your whole life? Is standing in front of a judge—"

"Clerk," I corrected.

"Whatever… the way you pictured it?"

"I haven't really pictured anything." Not exactly true, but I knew what I had dreamed about through the years was not the same as Jessica.

"Bullshit. I've been planning my wedding since I was five. I know what flowers I want and the kind of gown. Let me see your ring," she demanded. Reluctantly, I brought up my hand. She eyed it curiously and then figured out I had rotated the ring around to the inside of my hand. I rolled my eyes, huffed, and righted it. "Oh my God!" Jessica howled and grabbed my hand. "That's huge! How much money does Tristan have?"

I winced at her volume. "Shhh, I don't want to advertise my life in here."

She quieted. "I'm sorry." She held my hand and tilted the diamond in different directions like I had. "This is the prettiest ring I've ever seen. And you're going to stand there and tell me you've never dreamed about your wedding? A guy doesn't pick out a ring this ostentatious without thinking about it. If you didn't care about any of it, then you'd have been fine with just the one simple band. This ring screams 'romantic.'"

She had me there. As soon as I had seen it, I had known I wanted so much more than a court clerk officiating our wedding with as much emotion as the chief justice swearing in the president. I did want romance. I did want flowers. I knew I had looked nice—so had Tristan—but wouldn't a white tux have been more grand? "We're planning the spring wedding thing. I told you. This is just so it's official and he can file for full custody and show how stable his home life is compared to his ex." I kept repeating the same reason, but it sounded less and less convincing each time.

"I hope it's worth it."

I assured her, "It is. This is sudden, but fine. Really." Jessica walked back to her cubicle when a customer walked up. As she helped him I couldn't stop thinking about what she'd said. Was I really fine? I told myself I was. Everything else had happened so suddenly, but if I thought about it, then yes, I wanted more. I was a romantic. I wanted music and laughter. The clerk had been kind and had told us afterward he was glad for the ruling in June for marriage equality nationwide. I appreciated the sentiment, but I felt the emptiness of our marriage without our loved ones as witnesses. The two employees who witnessed our wedding were strangers. I wanted my mother there. I'd texted, but she had been on another bus trip—two in one week! She'd texted back her apology and left me feeling cold. I felt gypped. So much of the morning seemed imaginary. It was like getting married in secret, which it kind of was.

AT LUNCH, I called Mel. He was upset, but ultimately understood. "Did you tell your mother?" he asked.

I muttered, "Yes. She was on a bus trip—again. She couldn't be bothered to cancel it last minute. It's as if she's glad I'm not coming to her with every concern, instead of getting upset I'd forgotten to call. I admit I've been caught up in the whirlwind of it all, but I also feel disappointed at how it's gone down." I couldn't believe I hadn't thought about my mother more. I used to think about her all the time, but lately she hadn't been in my thoughts at all. I felt guilty.

"I can't say I'm surprised. You're not a kid, and I think she'd agree with me your clinginess was becoming an issue."

"I'm not clingy!" I paused and thought about it. Arguing was pointless. "Fine, maybe I am," I amended. I sighed over the phone. "You're right. I've avoided being an adult for far too long. How'd you get so smart?"

Mel chuckled. "By doing all the wrong things too many times. When do I get to meet Mr. Carr? Or is he changing it to Mr. Adams? You could hyphenate it too. Were you thinking of hyphenating?"

Too many questions at once—I nearly choked on my water. I coughed to make sure I could breathe and then answered, "I haven't thought about it. But… Grant Carr has a pleasant ring to it, don't you think?"

Mel agreed, "Yeah. If you did Adams-Carr, then people might mistakenly hear 'Adam's car' and be looking out the window for a Volkswagen or something."

I giggled. "That would be bad. I'll have to ask Tristan. This weekend is out, because his daughter visits every other weekend. I'm pretty sure Saturday is her visit."

"Are you nervous?"

"No, not really. I'm worried for Tristan because she's going to be upset. He told her last weekend she could come to the ceremony. Now it's done, and she's going to yell at him, I know it."

"You realize what this means, don't you?"

"What?"

"You're the stepdad. You have a kid, Grant, a teenaged kid. You need to make sure you always side with Tristan, or discuss things privately when you disagree. Maintaining a solid parental front is best when dealing with teenagers. My advice: never get in between Tristan and his daughter."

"Why?" I asked innocently, wondering how Mel had gotten so knowledgeable when he didn't have children.

"Because you'll alienate Tristan if you do, and give his daughter more power than she deserves as a child. She'll try to work you in order to get her way, thinking you're the weak one, but you should always talk things through with Tristan, especially if she tries manipulation. Never let her think she's in charge."

"Wise words from a single person," I said.

"Maybe—but I have two sisters, one brother, three half sisters, and two stepbrothers, don't forget. My gigantimous family has taught me a thing or two."

The truth dawned on me. "Oh, right. I'll listen to you from now on, Obi-Wan."

Mel laughed. "You better!"

"Listen, my break's over. I gotta go. I'll talk to Tristan and see if we can have you over for dinner next weekend or meet you at a restaurant."

"Okay, sounds good."

We both said good-bye, and I cleaned up my trash before heading back out to my station. Work picked up after lunch, so the rest of the day went by swiftly. One customer noticed my diamond ring and only said congratulations. It made me feel less nervous about wearing it facing front. I knew I shouldn't be embarrassed to show it off, but part of me was still tentative. I knew I'd feel more confident in time.

I LEFT my pinstriped shirt on, because I hadn't gotten it dirty, and leaving it on reminded me of our marriage that morning. Tristan arrived, and we were off to Olive Garden.

In the truck, he said, "I called Claire. She was upset at first, but after I explained why, she calmed down. I told her we'd promised to have something in the spring, and she was pleased."

"Yeah, I talked to Mel. I texted my mom and she was fine. Jessica was pissed she hadn't been there, so we definitely need to plan a spring wedding. I'd like to wear a white tux, if you don't mind."

He stopped the truck at a light and turned to regard me. He gave a slight grin. "A tux, eh?"

I nodded. I was afraid to tell him about my conversation with Jessica. I hadn't thought about being a romantic before, and now that I knew I was, I didn't want Tristan to think I regretted our haste.

He turned back to the road and drove on. "You know, this was only a legal thing. If I'd had a choice to do it differently, I would have showered you with romantic gestures. Flowers at work, dinner at the inner harbor, maybe even a trip to New York to see a show on Broadway, especially since I know you like that kind of stuff. I would have swept you off your feet."

I reached over the console and placed my hand on his thigh. "Really?" I asked, choked up at the mere mention.

Tristan took the wheel in his left hand and stretched his right arm around the back of my shoulders. "Of course, baby. My life's ambition now is to learn what makes you happy and do it. Every day."

"Oh, my gosh," I gushed, rubbing my cheek against his arm like a cat would. I disliked cats, yet I found myself acting like one. I probably would have purred too. "That means a lot to me, knowing you'd even consider it."

"Grant, that ring you picked out says quite a bit about you. I wish I had a picture of your face when I slid it on your finger. You may not realize it by my life now, but I've known a few flamboyant gays over the years. I've heard about fashion and trends and the way people dress to reflect who they are inside. Sometimes it's to cover up what they don't want others to see, whether that's dressing loudly to hide the fragile person on the inside or dressing conservatively to reflect a calm demeanor, or any combination of those types. With you, I had some time after you picked out that ring to look at it and think about what it meant to you. I think you dress conservatively because you're like that on the inside, but the pastel colors hint at your dramatic flair."

I snorted. "Dramatic flair? They're pastel dress shirts. I have nothing in sequins or neon."

"No, but you work in a bank. I think you wear what's appropriate there, and you're not so frivolous as to buy a shirt with sequins when you know you'd never wear it. I don't think you're flamboyant. I think you're conservative, but with a desire to stand out a bit more than the guy who wears a white button-down. You have six pink shirts, Grant."

"So? Straight guys wear pink."

"Straight guys don't pick out vintage-style engagement rings and sigh as though marrying a prince. You're romantic, slightly effeminate, shy, and a bit obsessive. And you're only just learning to stretch your wings to be yourself. Am I right?"

"Yes," I relented. Why bother refuting it when he'd pegged me in one sentence?

Tristan turned down another street and continued, "I also watched a few episodes of *Glee* on Netflix and listened to Meghan Trainor on YouTube, so now I understand your musical tastes."

"You did?" I groaned. I almost held my breath, anticipating ridicule, but he made no rude comments.

Tristan said, "You and Claire are going to be great friends, I can tell."

I had to make sure. "You don't think I'm weird or too childish?"

"No, baby. You like what you like. If the song 'Title' is any indication of your opinion of sex and dating, then I get why you jumped at marriage. As long as you let me hold you when you watch your shows, I'll be happy."

"Yeah. Kind of." I was glad he hadn't cited "Lips Are Movin."

"You're adorable."

His caring smile warmed me all over. I could have melted.

OUR FIRST dinner as a married couple went well. I didn't spill anything, and I didn't pull my hand away when the waitress stopped at our table. We talked, and I truly enjoyed his company. It didn't hurt that he smiled and rubbed his thumb over the back of my hand almost the entire time. When the waitress suggested dessert, we both declined.

WE RETURNED to Tristan's house after dinner, and the surrealistic feeling returned to my gut. This wasn't a date that ended with sleeping together—this was a night to consummate the marriage. Would we? He wanted to go slow, and I'd certainly freaked out enough to warrant gradual progression, but we were married now. Shouldn't we make love like other married couples?

I got out of the truck and followed Tristan up the steps. He stopped, turned, and asked, "Are you all right? You didn't say anything on the ride home. It's too fast, isn't it? You're having second thoughts."

I heaved a sigh, stepping up onto the landing with him and looking him in the eyes. He had lovely eyes, so expressive and pensive. I explained, "Maybe, but not really about the marriage as much as about tonight." I paused, because it was difficult to ask. "Are we...? Do you plan on having sex?" I stuffed my hands into my pockets and looked down at my shoe, scuffing it on the welcome mat.

Tristan chuckled.

I snapped my attention back up and squinted at him. I didn't understand what was so funny.

"You know, you're right," he said, descending the steps. He went over to the truck and hopped back in.

I opened my side. "Where are we going?"

"Your place," he said, turning the engine over.

The five-minute drive didn't give me much time to figure out why he thought my house was any better than his for doing the deed. I didn't know what I was doing either way. His place had a bigger bed. My place was cleaner. His place was cluttered and chaotic. My place smelled like vanilla and lavender.

He parked, and I got out and followed him up my own steps this time. He opened the door and went inside.

My couch was larger, and the pillows matched. I sighed.

Tristan came up behind me and squeezed my shoulders. He leaned in and whispered in my ear, "We're here because you're more relaxed when we are." He kissed my neck and turned me around. "I want you, Grant," he whispered against my lips, licking them before planting a kiss. "But you're still hung up on not being good enough, sexy enough, or appealing enough."

"No!" I protested. "I'm...." I had no real argument. He was right. I slumped forward and rested my forehead against his chin. "Why do you put up with me?"

"Because I find your insecurities endearing."

I laughed, but in that way people do when on the verge of crying over something ludicrous.

Tristan took my hand and led me toward the bedroom. "Come on, I have some ideas." He started unbuttoning his shirt and kicked off his shoes as soon as we entered. "Get undressed, but leave on whatever layers you need to feel comfortable."

I nodded, feeling stupid for needing to keep layers on. At least he was making a huge effort to respect my needs. I took off my shoes and set them in their spot. I removed my trousers and hung them up. My shirt went into my dry-cleaning sack. I took off my socks and put them in the hamper. *My undershirt.* I paused, contemplating what I should do. I took a deep breath. He'd seen my chest already. He hadn't run screaming, nor had he laughed. He'd liked it. *Tristan liked my chest.*

I removed the undershirt and tossed it into the hamper. Only my boxers remained. I turned around and found Tristan sprawled out on top of my comforter, fingers laced across his stomach and boxer briefs bulging. "You wore underwear," I mused, joining him on the bed. I reached out and caressed the back of his hand.

"I did. For you." Tristan took my hand and held it. We sat there gazing at one another for several minutes. I knew he wanted more, I could see the lust in his eyes as he studied me, but he waited... and waited. Then he tugged gently on my hand, beckoning me closer.

"Should I lie down?" I asked.

"Only if you want to." I did, after fluffing my pillow, and Tristan stretched out on his side next to me. "Give me your hand." I offered the left, but he took my right and held it to his lips. He kissed the back of my hand a few times, and then I felt his tongue slide over my knuckles before he kissed them. Tingles shot down my arm when he did it again. He opened his mouth and ran his tongue down the length of my index finger before play-biting it. I jumped, but it hadn't hurt.

"What are you doing?" I asked apprehensively.

He grinned lasciviously. "It's called foreplay. I'm stimulating you."

"By licking my hand?" It seemed odd, but I had felt things stirring when those tingles shot down my arm.

He chuckled wickedly. "Yes, Grant, by licking your hand." He turned my hand so my fingers faced him. He held my palm and then very slowly took my entire forefinger into his mouth. I gasped in surprise. I felt his tongue curling and swirling around it. Hot and wet, I felt the different textures of his tongue on my finger, especially when he sucked it in farther. The back of his tongue had larger bumps and ridges compared to the smooth tip. I knew I'd puke if I had anything that far back in my throat.

He started bobbing his head as he licked, which sent more tingles through me. He switched to my thumb and sucked on it fervently. I was breathing harder, so his tactic was working. I reached down with my other hand and grabbed myself through my boxers.

He stopped abruptly. "No," he instructed, shaking his head. "You don't get to touch it."

"But...," I pleaded. "You're killing me."

He chuckled again. He so enjoyed torturing me. "That's the goal. When you've had enough and you need to come, tell me what you want me to do." He returned to my hand and drew two fingers to the back of his throat, sucking wildly.

I gripped the sheet next to me. My cock was throbbing with need. I felt it pulsing, begging me with tiny involuntary movements. Little Adams Junior wanted what my fingers were experiencing. Little Adams Junior needed the same enthusiastic attention Tristan was giving my fingers. He opened wider and took in three fingers, and that's when I lost it.

I arched my back and desperately moaned, "Please suck me."

Tristan released my hand and reached for my waistband. I was already pushing my underwear down. He helped and then took ahold of my leaking cock. He didn't even pause for a second; he merely took me all the way to the back of his throat, to the root. I cried out and slapped the mattress, struggling to catch my breath as he moved his mouth up and down on my erection.

Instinctively, I grabbed the back of his head and rubbed his scalp as he ministered to my need. His tongue slid around my shaft as he bobbed his head. I felt him fondling my testicles, so I spread my legs and groaned. I was so close. His mouth was hot and wet, and I was going to fill it with my cum any minute, and he was going to take it. I thrust upward, feeling the tip of my dick jam hard against his throat. His muscles convulsed around me, and I thought he might choke and pull off, but I had no time to consider Tristan when my balls, right then, let loose and exploded. Wave after wave of tingling electricity radiated outward from my groin to every little nerve in every extremity. I shot and shot, dumping buckets into Tristan's throat. I felt suction and realized he was swallowing my juice.

As my body melted into a pile of bones and limp flesh, I finally opened my eyes and watched Tristan as he released me from his lips and continued to study my appendage as it shrank. "What are you doing?" I asked, much like I had before, only this time I couldn't muster the energy to panic.

Tristan inspected my tiny organ, flopping it from one side to the other. He said, "Just looking. I didn't expect you to have foreskin."

Suddenly, I was teleported back to seventh grade, where the whole gym class had laughed at me for being different. My stomach muscles quaked as I prepared for his ridicule.

He turned his head and eyed me uneasily. "Grant, what did I say?"

I turned away as the tears rolled down my cheeks. I didn't know why I was getting so emotional about it, except my whole body felt raw and exposed after orgasm. Tristan was there, pulling me into his arms and holding me securely to his chest.

"Shhh," he soothed. "It's okay. Whatever it is, just tell me so I don't say it again."

I sniffled and explained between sobs. "I've always hated... myself... for...." I sobbed and gulped air. "Being different. Kids... in school... laughed at... me." I knew if I didn't calm down, I was going to hyperventilate.

Tristan rubbed my back and hugged me again. "Oh, baby, no. They were wrong. I'm so sorry you went through that. I wasn't making fun of you—I like it."

Had I heard him correctly? I took another convulsive breath and eased out of his arms to look him in the eyes. If he was lying to save my feelings, I was 80 percent certain I would know. "Are you... serious?"

He smiled, the corners of his eyes wrinkling in that familiar way they did when he was happy. "Yes, I'm serious. I like your foreskin. It's hot."

I made a face. "Eww, no it's not."

"Yes, it is," he reassured me. "Do you realize all the fun we can have with that? I like to play, Grant."

"Play?"

"Yeah," he responded, in a way that told me I should understand what he meant, only I didn't. "I like to lick and taste, and... plaaay. One of these mornings, I'm going to take your foreskin in my mouth when you're asleep and flick my tongue inside the folds until you harden. Then I'm going to slide your skin over the head of my throbbing cock and use it to jack us off together."

I was no longer hyperventilating, I was stunned into not breathing at all—wide-eyed and speechless.

"Breathe, Grant."

I inhaled sharply and then let the air out long and slow. "You aren't joking."

"No."

"What about the stuff you said about being rough and not wanting to scare me?"

"That's all true, but as I get to know you, I'm adjusting my pleasures to fit yours. I know *how* to be gentle, but I haven't found the need to be until now. I'll be gentle with you, but I love playing. Sex is supposed to be fun. We're going to have fun."

I tucked my head under his chin and snuggled very close, thinking about what he said. With every little thing, I had assumed that he would react or think a certain way based on my past experiences. So far, he wasn't like anyone I'd ever met. If Tristan was willing to adjust for me, then maybe I needed to rethink the way I thought about things he said and did.

"So... you think it's okay that I'm not cut like you?" I asked in the tiny little voice of a child. I almost embarrassed myself with how I sounded, but I wasn't feeling very adultish at the moment. I felt small.

He rolled me onto my back and propped himself up on his elbow so he could look at me. "Let me tell you something. I don't know where you got the silly idea that you have to look like me, but you need to stop. There are several fun things to do with foreskin that guys like me miss out on. You will learn to love your penis just the way it is. I promise."

"Don't forget how small I am," I pointed out.

"Only compared to me. Most guys are small compared to me, but you have to be six inches."

"Five and a half."

"See? You're smack dab in the middle of average."

I huffed.

"Grant," he warned. "You're fine. Stop comparing and enjoy what you have. I do."

Tristan had a way of making me feel so good, even about inadequacies I had obsessed over for years. I asked, "Promise?"

"Promise. I fell for you just the way you are. I like that you're fastidious and peculiar. I like that you're *not* muscular, although I'm glad you joined my gym because everyone's body can stand some toning. And yes, I like that you're uncircumcised. You need to stop second-guessing me and realize I say what I think. No one makes me feel like you do."

As he said all those nice things, Tristan rubbed my stomach. It felt so nice, like he was trying to calm my nerves as he set me straight on what he thought. He was so handsome and patient. A random thought popped into my head, and I said, "I'm naked."

He blinked. "Um, yeah.... And?"

"And this is the longest I've ever lain around without clothes on. I'm only ever naked in the bathroom. But here I am, on my bed, next to you, naked. I'm not as anxious about it as I thought I'd be."

"Is there a reason you'd feel nervous? Because I've told you how I feel about your body."

As he continued mapping out my skin, I had to consider what I had promised myself about telling him. If I was to trust him with my body, I would have to trust him with my trauma. I started slowly. "When I was a kid, I made friends with another boy up the street. Behind his house there were acres of cornfields. Now there are housing developments, but back then it was a kid's dream to run and explore. My friend and I would make up games all the time based on TV shows."

I paused, and he said, "Uh-huh."

His attention encouraged me to continue. "In sixth grade, his sister was into watching *Smallville*. I don't know when it came on television originally or when it ended, but she had DVDs, and my friend watched them sometimes. He suggested we pretend. When I asked how, he explained this one scene where Clark was tied up to a post in a cornfield in his underwear. I didn't understand why he wanted me to do that, but I went along with it because I was stupid and naive, and he assured me it was only a game and he wouldn't tie my arms too tight. Well, he tied them really tight. And once I was helpless, he shoved my underwear down."

"Oh, Grant," Tristan whispered, kissing my shoulder.

"He left me there for a long time—I'm not sure how long—but when he came back, he wasn't alone. He brought four other boys, and they laughed at me. They called me a skinny faggot and threw tomatoes. Luckily, one of their mothers had followed them, wondering what they were up to taking her tomatoes from her window ledge. They all got in trouble, but it didn't change how they'd made me feel. After that day, I never let anyone see me naked." I wiped my eyes as Tristan pressed a kiss to my jaw.

"Your body is beautiful, baby. Simply beautiful. I don't care how long it takes for me to erase what that kid did, but I will make a point to never make fun of your body." Tristan smiled and then kissed me. "I want to help you relax and enjoy being with me."

"Oh, I do!" I asserted. "I've never felt so calm around anyone before. You make me feel good, and I don't just mean the blowjob."

He laughed, which made me happy, because it was getting very tense and heavy in the room. He said, "I'm glad. Do you want to try something else, or are you good for the night?"

I could tell he was sincere, especially when he ran his fingers through my hair and rubbed his foot against mine. Tristan wasn't suggesting anything, he was only wondering. "I think I'm good. This was a lot for me, especially recapping the sixth-grade nightmare. Besides, I'm starting to feel like people are watching through the window and judging me."

Tristan glanced over at the windows. "The curtains are drawn, Grant. No one can see."

I looked away. He still didn't get it. I had lain on the bed naked as long as I could, but the fact was that I still had a hard time looking at myself. Knowing his parts were almost twice the size of mine made me feel so inadequate.

"Grant?" His tone commanded I explain myself, even if his volume was hushed. "You're doing it again."

"I'm sorry," I whimpered. "I'm not used to being so exposed. I feel awkward being next to you. It was fine when I was distracted during sex, but now I feel so small and... vulnerable. You have no idea how perfect you are, and how hard it is for me not to compare myself."

I thought he'd say something, but he didn't. His eyes told me the gears were moving, but so far no steam rose from his ears. "Will you let me try something?"

"I guess."

He grinned. "All right. Trust me, okay? I'm not going to hurt you, and I promise not to bite anything."

"Okay."

Tristan rolled off the bed and went to my closet. "Do you have any ties you don't wear?"

I sat up on my elbows. "Um, no. What are you doing?"

"How about this one?"

He'd found the one Christmas tie I'd gotten at a white elephant party three years ago. I'd worn it to work at Christmas, but rarely more than once a year. I conceded, "Okay. Use that one, but what are you doing?"

Tristan came back to the bed swiftly, shedding his underwear in the process. "Lie back down," he said. "I'm going to blindfold you."

"I don't know what this has to do with anything."

"First, it's an exercise in trust. Second, if you can't see anything, you can't know what you're self-conscious of. I want you to close your eyes and let your body feel."

He did have a way of making me feel good, so even though I was unsure, I nodded and closed my eyes.

Tristan tied the tie around my eyes. "Think about what you feel."

"I feel cold. I feel the air around my body, and the heat of your leg next to my hip."

"Good." The bed shifted.

I felt the bed dip on both sides of me. His hands? His feet? I didn't think his knees were on either side, because I was certain I'd feel his groin as he straddled me. Something smooth ran down the center of my chest. It was warm, but thicker than his knuckles. His large hand cupped my left pec. I hoped he wouldn't refer to them as tits again, because I'd decided I didn't like that term. He grunted. The bed shifted and dipped by my head, and then I felt that soft warm object rub over my nipple. I flinched in surprise. At first I thought it was his palm, but the skin of his palm wasn't that soft. The bed dipped again, and he was back down by my hips. The smooth thing touched my dick this time. It ran down my length and back up.

I jerked, hips tilting, stomach tightening, but I did my best not to rip the tie off my face and jump from the bed.

"Shhh," he said in a soothing tone.

I felt that same part of him slide up and back again—only this time it wasn't just soft, it was wet. I asked, "Are you rubbing your dick on me?"

He snickered low and deep, and that smooth object, the one that oozed liquid as it slid across me, pulsed and moved lower across my ball sac and then down the inside of my thigh.

Knowing what it was, I shivered.

Tristan moved his big cock to my other thigh and ran it up my skin. He batted my once-again-hard dick left and then right with his club. I felt him nudge my tip with his, and his wetness dripped down my skin. He paused again, and I felt the bed shift, but after several seconds of nothing, I wondered what was going on. I suspected—but surely he wouldn't be jacking off while I was blindfolded?

"Tristan?"

I heard a breathy grunt.

I lifted the tie and peeked out. Tristan was on one knee, the other leg arched over my hips with his foot planted on the other side. His massive cock in hand, he stroked rapidly, eyes closed, chest heaving as he breathed erratically. I was about to ask if he needed help when his body jerked and white semen shot out, splatting my stomach. Another ribbon shot up my chest, and another short-shot and landed on my dick. Before I could react, I was covered in white ropes of his ejaculate.

Tristan moaned and tilted his head back, still holding his cock.

I felt gross, yet moderately turned on. "Are you done?" I asked, tie blindfold slipped up on my forehead.

Tristan opened his eyes and smirked at me. "Sorry. I was trying to get you to realize how fun it can be without seeing every little thing that happens, and then I got too worked up and needed to come. You made me so horny I couldn't stand it."

I sat up and removed the tie, tossing it on the nightstand. I was right up next to his body where he knelt. "I guess I can't blame you. Whatever that was, it was kind of erotic, particularly after I figured out what you were rubbing all over me. Your dick is quite soft for being large enough to beat baby seals to death."

"What?" he asked incredulously.

"Oh, um, I said that out loud?" I remarked, guiltily squinting my eyes.

"Yes. I know it's large, but don't you think that's appalling? I would never beat baby seals. Can you think of another analogy that doesn't involve killing animals?"

"Baton? Battering ram?"

"A little better. So you're not mad? I thought you'd be mad if I spunked all over you."

I shrugged. "No. It's gross, but it did turn me on." I looked down and wiped up a big glop that was sliding down my chest. I studied the opaque liquid as it ran down my finger, then sucked it off. It didn't really taste like anything. "Next time warn me, and I might let you shoot in my mouth."

Tristan growled and dove forward, pinning me to the bed. He ravished me with kisses as he rubbed his body all over mine. Our skin slipped and slid with his cum, and I could not contain myself. I giggled. And giggled some more. Tristan sucked on my neck and yet I still giggled.

"Tristan! Tristan! Stop, this is so gross. I need a shower."

He lifted his head and smiled down at me. "Okay. Shower *with* me this time?"

I hemmed and hawed, but in the end I relented. "I guess."

"Great!" he beamed, leaping off me and jetting for the bathroom.

We showered, but with minimal exploration. I think he was afraid to push me. He was so patient with me, knowing everything we'd done was a first. In fact, his patience made me yearn to try more things. I didn't, but I knew I would soon because of how safe he made me feel.

We dried each other off and then spooned under the covers. Falling asleep in his arms was the most comforting experience in the world.

Chapter Eleven

Housekeeping, Parenting, And Facing My Number One Biggest Fear

WE HAD toast and eggs before work. Tristan sat at my tiny table and sipped his coffee as I grinned at him, poking my eggs with my fork.

"Listen, tonight we need to sleep at my house. It's Claire's weekend, and Teresa usually drops her off at eight."

"Okay," I said. "It's not a big deal."

"It is. My place isn't as nice as here. It's bigger, but it's not as nice. I think it's something we need to talk about soon; I own my house and you rent. The logical thing to do is for you to move in with me."

I knew it was inevitable, but I hadn't thought it through. "Yeah, I guess. Or we could buy a place together?" I lifted both eyebrows and gave him my forlorn expression.

He grinned. He seemed to think everything I did or said was amusing. "Maybe, but if we sold my house and bought a different one, that would still take time. Logically, you should move in while we look for a house." He took the last bite of his eggs and waited.

I slumped in my chair and glanced around my house. "I just painted the kitchen," I complained.

"I can tell. Look, how about I let you do whatever you want to my place? Even if we sell it, it will still need a fresh coat of paint and some remodeling. If you do all that, who knows? Maybe you'll like it and we can stay."

"You're hoping I want to stay."

"I grew up in that house, Grant. My dad bought it when I was five. I have a lot of memories there—but if you still hate it after you redecorate, I'm willing to move. Like I said, you're the only one I'm willing to change my life for." Tristan downed his last sip of coffee and took his dishes to my sink. He rinsed them and put them in the dishwasher. I hated to tell him I never used it because I didn't dirty enough dishes.

I got up, took my dishes into the kitchen, and set them on the counter, then slipped my arms around his waist and leaned my head on his shoulder. He was always saying things that made me feel so special. "If you're willing to sell the house if I hate it, then I'm willing to help clean it out and repaint it. I'm not sure how much time I'll have, but I'll try."

Tristan rubbed my back. "What if I paid you for your time?"

I scrunched up the side of my face and pulled back far enough to give him my weird, what-are-you-talking-about look. "Paid me?"

"Yeah, hear me out. If I had someone else do it, I'd have to pay them. If you cut back your hours a little to make time to paint and stuff, then I'd be willing to pay you."

"It seems weird. We're married."

"True. But are you going to continue to work full time?"

"I guess."

"Then work for me for a few weeks to get the place spruced up. I know you hate being there."

"Hate is a strong word." Still, I had to admit he wasn't far off. The grime made me squirm when I was in there, especially after that first night. In the dark it wasn't so bad, but in the light of day I could see dust buildup and clutter everywhere. I had focused hard on Tristan and his lovely bare chest just to keep from screaming at him about the mess he had obviously never purged from 1939. I consented. "I'll do it. I'll clean your house. Although I might get professional cleaners to finish up and detail it after my part is done."

Tristan kissed my forehead. "Deal."

I added, "A clean house may also look good to a judge."

"You're amazing." He winked. "Now I gotta run. I'll be at work until probably seven thirty. I need to finish this transmission job and go through my mail from this week." He left me in the kitchen and sat down to put his shoes on. In no time, he kissed me good-bye and was out the door.

"This is married life, I guess," I mumbled to my tiny house. He was right. I rented, and this place was great for one person but not for a family. I had to accept that changes were coming.

I GOT off work at five and headed to Tristan's in order to make us dinner. I stopped by the shop to let him know where I'd be, and ended up talking to Wes for twenty minutes. He was a nice guy. Before cooking, I had to clean off the counter. I put on my big boy panties, stepped into his kitchen, and found a ball of old bloody bandages wadded up behind the sugar bowl. I threw up in my mouth as I tossed them in the trash. I put on rubber gloves after that, not knowing what else lurked in his kitchen.

I found a dead mouse in the first cabinet I opened, dried and shriveled like a mummy in an Egyptian exhibit. It wasn't in a trap, just lying next to some juice glasses with its eyes sunken in. Discarding its little body was another near-vomit moment for me.

I could not bring myself to use any of those dishes, even if I sanitized them. I couldn't. Not when I'd found dead mice resting in peace next to them. I found an empty cardboard box in the living room—because all hoarders have piles of empty cardboard boxes lying around—and stacked his dishes and glasses in them. Once all the cabinets were empty, I filled a bucket with hot water and grabbed a stepladder from the bathroom—an odd place to keep those—and started washing every nook and cranny. Under the dust and dirt, I found very fine mahogany cabinets. After the second time I washed them, because once was not enough, I considered how nice new dishes would look in them. Tristan could even replace several of the doors with glass fronts to show our dishes off.

I sighed and took in my vision. Maybe, just maybe, Tristan's place had potential.

I opened the refrigerator to find beer and pancakes. Not exactly the dinner of champions, and when confronted with a bottle of mustard and several dead flies lined up along the bottom, I opted to clean out the fridge before even attempting to make a list of items to buy at the store.

By the time Tristan left work and walked home, I was too tired to cook and we ordered pizza. Much to my delight, Tristan liked Hawaiian pizza just like me.

When 9:00 p.m. rolled around and Claire hadn't been dropped off, Tristan had to call Teresa. She told him she'd forgotten what time it was and would bring Claire by in the morning. He told me he didn't believe it for a second but hadn't fussed at her because at least she wasn't being belligerent about bringing Claire in the morning. I only hoped she wouldn't come in for coffee.

TRISTAN ASSURED me the sheets were clean, even though he'd confessed at my house he only changed them once a month. They smelled clean, so I believed him. When sunlight streamed through his dingy bedroom windows, I knew it wouldn't be long before his daughter would arrive and my new life as a stepdad would start. Would she respect me? Would she acknowledge me as a dad? What did stepdads do differently than regular dads?

I heard the floor creak but thought nothing of it until someone—Claire—pounced on the bed and crushed the two of us under her squealing body. "Daddy!"

Tristan only grunted, locking his arm across my chest as if he knew I'd try to flee.

"Oh my God!" Claire exclaimed, the bed still moving up and down as she bounced. At least she'd moved off of us and onto the side of the bed. "You're married and you're sleeping together. Oh my God—you're married! Ohmygod! Ohmygod! Ohmygod!" She kept bouncing to punctuate her exclamations, and I felt like our bed was on a ship rocking at sea.

I murmured to Tristan, "Please let me move. I promise not to bolt from the bed and lock myself in the bathroom."

He chuckled but released me. I rolled onto my back as he did the same, and I looked at my new daughter. Claire was on her knees beside Tristan, bouncing like a little child on Christmas morning, her smile taking over her face. "Hi, Claire," I said lamely, pulling the sheet up to cover my chest. She didn't need to see my body.

"Hi, Claire?" she asked, sounding irritated with my greeting. "Hi, Claire! Grant, I'm your daughter now. How great is that?" She bounced some more. "You can call me whatever you want—Daughter, Sweetheart, Honey, Princess—you know, whatever."

"How about 'Annoyingly Perky Child Who's Going to Make Me Vomit if She Keeps Bouncing on the Bed Like a Four-Year-Old'?" I said, completely serious.

She giggled but stopped bouncing. "Okay, but what can I call you? I call my dad 'Dad,' or 'Daddy.' I can't call you the same thing."

"You can call me Grant."

She waved her hand dismissively. "No. Everyone else calls you that. How about 'Papa'?"

I lifted my eyebrow. "That makes me sound really old."

"True," she said, still thinking. I thought she'd fuss or get mad with my directness, but she took it all in stride. "Maybe 'Dad' works fine. I'll think about it." She eyed both of us. "So what's on the agenda for today?"

Tristan answered, even though his eyes were still closed and he seemed seconds from drifting back to sleep. "Claire likes a list of things we're going to do. We normally hit the gym at nine and then go for brunch at Baugher's Restaurant."

I told him, "Then that's what you should do. I really want to clean some more. This place is gross, and if I'm going to live here for any length of time, I need order and cleanliness."

Tristan chuckled and leaned over to kiss my jaw. "I love you," he said, smiling.

My breath caught in my chest as I widened my eyes at him. He'd said it. Here. Casually, like they were words he used in every conversation.

He turned to Claire. "Claire, can you give us a moment? Maybe make me some coffee before we head to the gym?"

"Okay," she agreed enthusiastically, hopping off the bed and dashing out the door. She returned one second later, leaping back onto the bed and diving into my arms. She hugged me and then bounded back out the door, exclaiming, "I'm so happy!"

Tristan turned back to me and said, "I'm sorry. I shouldn't have said that. It slipped out. I've been trying not to overdo it, but with Claire here I was too relaxed and it slipped out. I'm sorry."

"You love me," I said in my shocked state. My brain was frozen, looping those words over and over in my head. Tristan had said he loved me in front of his daughter. He'd said it in the jewelry store too, and I'd believed him, but something about saying it in front of his daughter made my insides feel squidgy, like Silly Putty or Play-Doh.

He hunkered down next to me, pulled the sheet back to rub my bare chest, and reiterated, "I love you. I can tell it makes you uncomfortable to hear it. It seems too soon to say, but I do. I knew when I first laid eyes on you I was doomed. I knew when you spilled your drink into my lap

I was smitten. But when you jumped into my battle with Teresa and blurted we were getting married, Grant, I knew I'd lost my heart."

"You love me?" I asked again, not fully comprehending how he knew.

"Yes. It's the same feeling I get when I see Claire."

I pulled back and glared, which tipped him off about how odd that sounded.

"Hear me out. When I see Claire, I feel happy—genuinely happy—from my head to my feet. My whole body tingles, knowing I get to spend a couple of days with her, listening to her talk and hearing her laugh. I miss her during the week, but I've always worked so much that I told myself if she'd been here, I wouldn't have seen her anyway. Then I met you, and that tingling feeling happened every time I saw you. I'm happy hearing you laugh and listening to you talk. I was even happy when you fussed about the dead mouse in my cabinet."

He chuckled, and so did I. Only I had tears in my eyes, and my chuckle dislodged them so they rolled down my cheeks.

Tristan continued, "My niece, my sister's kid, once described the feeling as 'family tingles.' It's a sensation you only get with family, because you love them deep in your bones, and no matter what, you can't bear the separation for long. When I met you, you felt like family."

I was full-on crying then. I pushed myself into his chest and held him so tight I thought my arms would fall off when I let go. He held me and rubbed my back—he was always rubbing my back—and after a few minutes, I found my voice enough to respond. "I've never felt like that," I squeaked.

"It's okay. I don't expect you to say it back right away. I want it to be real, Grant. Don't say it until you feel it in your bones. Okay?"

"Okay."

"The kitchen looks great, but where are all the coffee mugs?" I heard Claire ask from the doorway.

"They're in the boxes by the wall. Take three out, and wash them before you use them. Grant's going to pick out new dishes this week."

"Okay."

I sniffled and leaned away. "I am?" I wiped my eyes and looked at him.

"I assumed so, since you chucked all mine."

He wasn't even angry about it. I gave him a half smile. "I guess I am."

TRISTAN GOT dressed, and soon the two of them were out the door on their way to the gym. My plan was to pick a spot and clean it to the best of my ability while I had a quiet house. I called my mom first and filled her in on our brief ceremony. She seemed to understand but said she'd appreciate dinner sometime soon in order to meet the guy who'd swept me off my feet. After I told her I'd call Monday, I plugged my phone into the charger and turned on Pandora. The *Glee* cast mix got me pumped for anything, even cleaning what could have been described as an indoor junkyard. The muffler under the coffee table had to go! I put on sweatpants and my Journey T-shirt and got to work.

FOUR AND a half hours later, Tristan and Claire came home. I was in the middle of singing the Warblers' rendition of "Hey, Soul Sister" when I spun around and spotted them in the doorway. Tristan had a huge smile on his face, and Claire was covering her mouth with her hand. I stopped singing two seconds before my body stopped wiggling as I locked eyes with them.

"You are too adorable for words," he commented with a smirk.

I thought Claire would comment on my moves, possibly make fun of me, but she didn't. Instead, she went immediately to the living room. "Oh, wow!" Claire exclaimed. "Look at what Grant's done to the living room, Dad. You can see the television console." Her sound of wonder made me feel really good.

They came over to where I was standing with my rubber gloves, dust cloth, and furniture polish. Tristan asked, "Where did you put everything? I'm pretty sure there were at least some salvageable items on the surface, even though the rest was trash."

I pointed over to my growing stack of boxes near the dining room table. "Over there. I have one box for car parts, one for receipts, and one for odds and ends that might be important but I didn't know what they were. The other boxes next to the dishes are for stuff that's going to Goodwill. And you'll have to move the engine off the table, because I can't lift it."

Tristan wrapped his arm across my shoulders and kissed my temple. "Okay. I'll get Jeff in here to help me on Monday. I wanted to rebuild it for the '68 Pontiac Firebird I've got sitting out back under a tarp, but I never got around to it. Such a shame. I sold my motorcycle to buy it."

Motorcycle? Jessica had mentioned a motorcycle. At least now I knew what had happened to it. "I'm not saying you have to get rid of the engine; I'm only suggesting that you move it out of the dining room. I'd like to set the table and serve you dinner sometime, and I can't do that if we don't have a dining room table."

"Gee, Dad, you've been married for two days and he's already trained," Claire said, catching me so off guard I twitched.

I turned, my face hardened, ready to rebuke her, but Tristan jumped to my defense. "Hey," he said sternly. "That's not very nice."

She blinked in surprise and threw some sass his way. "Jeez, Dad, chill. I just meant he makes a great wife."

I gaped and widened my eyes. "Ahh!"

Tristan straightened his stance and squared off. "Claire, Grant is my husband, not my wife. We're equal partners in this marriage. If he wants to make me dinner, I'm appreciative, but he's under no obligation, nor was he trained like some sort of servant."

She tossed her head. "That's not what I meant, Dad. Look at him." She gestured. "He's decked out in rubber gloves cleaning your house in just a couple of days. This place has been a dump for years! I'm just saying you've picked the right guy to cook and clean and take care of you. He's not a servant—more like a domestic engineer."

A small tremor rippled through me. Tristan's arm was still around my shoulders, his fingers gripping the top of my arm. I knew he felt my body when it shook. I could have protested; but instead of anger from shock, my brain decided to get all emotional over it. My chest tightened, and my eyes stung. True, housewives all over the world battled the same comparison, trying to assert that their job was so much more than a list of chores, but I didn't see myself the same way. I was a bank teller, and even that title was small compared to my list of duties at work. People shouldn't be defined by their job title, but in this case the term "domestic engineer" made me feel unimportant.

Tristan turned to me instead of reaming Claire. "Grant, you know that's not why I married you." He spoke very directly, probably so I wouldn't misunderstand him. "Claire is being rude, baby. Don't listen to her."

It was too late. Even the tiny notion that he married me to be his "housewife" whispered to my subconscious and convinced me it was true. He didn't love me. Tristan needed a housekeeper and a cook. My eyes locked with his at the same moment one tear escaped.

Tristan's expression dropped. "Oh, Grant," he said quietly. He turned immediately toward Claire and growled, "Go to your room!"

Her eyes went wide. "What?"

"Go. To. Your. Room. Now!"

She took three steps and whined, "But, Dad."

"Go!" he yelled, pointing emphatically at the stairs. I had seen the stairs but hadn't gone up them. I had wondered what was upstairs, since his bedroom was on the first floor. Apparently, Claire's room was upstairs.

"Okay, I'm going!" she grumbled, stomping up the steps. "Jeez, I don't see what the big deal is!"

As soon as she was up the steps, Tristan turned back to me. He reached out, but her words had felt like a slap. I turned away, but Tristan grabbed my upper arms.

"Look at me," he said.

I did, but I wanted to run to the bedroom and bawl. She had made me feel so small.

"I married you because I love you. Claire is a hormonal teenage girl who doesn't think before she speaks. You are *not* my maid, Grant. You're my husband. I appreciate your desire to clean my house, but if you think for one second that's why I married you, then I'm calling a maid service right now to clean the rest. I am not going to stand here and have you disrespected by my own daughter and made to feel like hired help in your own home."

"But you did offer to pay me," I peeped.

"Only so you could take off a few days and not feel taken advantage of. This is our house, Grant. Even if we decide to sell it so we can buy a house together, this is still *our* house. You're cleaning your own house because you're good at it and you like doing it. You *do* like cleaning, right?"

"Yes, but the way she worded it made me sound like—"

"Don't listen to Claire. She's an only child, and she lives with a psychopathic alcoholic. Teresa doesn't teach her how to filter anything." He took a deep breath and admitted, "I haven't taught her much either. I see her every other weekend, and we play. We work out at the gym, we eat at restaurants, we watch movies and go bowling. When have I ever taught her not to say things like that? I'll go talk to her."

I nodded slightly and bowed my head.

Tristan pulled me to his chest and hugged me before going upstairs to talk to his daughter.

I discarded the rubber gloves in the kitchen and walked into the bedroom to sit on the bed. A chilly breeze floated over my arms, and I noticed the window was open. "Why did Tristan open the window?" I stepped over to shut it and saw that the screen was on the ground in the bushes outside. "Great. This place is falling apart, and he expects me to live here."

As I turned back to the bed, something caught the corner of my eye. I shrieked as a wolf spider darted under the bed. As I ran from the room, I collided with Tristan.

"What is it?" he asked, alarmed by my reaction.

"Spider!" I cried, pointing emphatically and practically crawling up his body to escape the floor. He started laughing, and I glared. "It's not funny," I growled. "They are evil creatures, and I'm not sleeping in there with a spider on the loose."

He lost his silliness and led me to the couch. "Okay. Stay here and I'll go kill it." A minute later, he returned with a smashed spider. "See, here it is." He opened the paper towel he had used. "It's a big one."

My body quivered with the heebie-jeebies. I jumped up, ready to run if he brought it any closer. "I don't need to see it," I said, looking away.

He tossed the body in the trash and returned to the living room. "It's all taken care of, Grant." He sat and gently pulled me down next to him. "I talked to Claire. She's being stupid and doesn't see why I got mad, so she's cleaning her room and scrubbing the bathroom floor. I'm sorry she spoke to you like that. She didn't think anything of it. Again, I'm sorry. I didn't marry you because I needed a housewife, or a domestic engineer. I do make enough money that if you chose to stay home, you could, but that is your choice." He took my hand and gazed into my eyes.

"But I like counting other people's money," I said weakly.

He chuckled quietly. "Okay."

"I think my job is fun. Cleaning this place isn't fun. It's disgusting."

"You looked like you were having fun."

"That's because I had music playing, and I like to dance and sing. It doesn't mean the task was fun."

"Okay." Tristan closed his eyes briefly. "I'm sorry. Then maybe asking you to clean the whole house was too much. I guess we'll have to live apart longer than I'd like."

"No, I didn't say that. You can move in with me while we clean this place up."

His voice went up when he said, "But everything I own is in here, and I work fifteen feet away from the side door."

The frustrated tone rubbed me wrong. "Okay, but doesn't it make more sense? Why should I move in here when it barely passes as living space? I opened the closet door and almost got buried under twenty feet of crap," I argued. "This house should be condemned."

"It's not that bad," he rumbled.

"Not that bad?" I countered. "I found a dead mouse in your cabinets! Not in the cabinets under the sink where anything could crawl in and die, but the ones where your dinner plates and glasses are. The FDA would shut this place down!"

"It's not a bed-and-breakfast."

"No! Far from it. By the way you get flour all over the floor when you make breakfast, I can see why you have mice moving in." I jumped off the couch and headed to the bedroom.

"Where are you going?" Tristan asked as he followed me.

"Back home! This place gives me the creeps." I pushed my sweats down and sat after snatching my jeans off the floor. As I pulled them on, another wolf spider the size of Iceland scurried across my leg and over the comforter. I screamed bloody murder and fell to the floor as my legs got tangled in my pants leg. I shook and shivered in terror as I scrambled to get away from the hairy beast, but as I planted my hand to hoist myself off the floor, I crushed something large and squishy. I lifted my hand slowly and turned it over to find another wolf spider stuck to my palm, its gooey center oozing out.

The sound that came from my throat could have shattered glass. I stumbled forward, clawing my way to the shower. My jeans had slipped off by the time I reached the tub, but I didn't even bother removing my shirt as I climbed in and turned the water on full blast. Using the hottest water possible, I scrubbed every inch of my body, hoping to burn away the tickling sensation that remained on my skin, telling my brain something was crawling on me. Logically I knew it wasn't there, but I still felt it as I scrubbed and scrubbed.

Shaking like an aspen leaf, shivering like I had hypothermia, I pulled off my sodden T-shirt and removed my boxers. I washed again and then curled up in a ball under the spray.

"Grant," he said, outside the shower curtain but in the room with me, "I killed all of them. I checked under the bed and behind a few chairs. The spiders are gone. Grant?" he questioned when I didn't answer.

I heard the curtain move, but I couldn't look up. My fetal position felt much safer than unfurling.

Tristan gasped. "Oh, Grant." He turned off the water, but I refused to move. Spiders generally didn't like water. I wanted to stay where I was. He laid a towel over my shoulders and petted my hair. "Grant, they're gone. They're all gone. I checked."

"What if there are more in the other room?" I mumbled, my head still resting on my knees.

"There aren't. But just in case, I'll go look around if that makes you feel better." I didn't answer. His solution was a given as far as I was concerned. Tristan returned after a short while and confirmed, "No more spiders. I promise. I don't know where they came from or how they got in, but I killed all of them."

I looked up, wide-eyed. "H-how many were there?"

"Twelve. Big hairy things that even started creeping me out as I found another and then another." He shivered. "Yeah, they're gone. Once we get this place cleaned out really well, I'm sure we won't see things like that again. I'm sure it was a nest or something that got disturbed while you cleaned."

"T-twelve?" I felt the tremors rippling through my body.

"Yes. But they're gone. Come on, Grant, you can't stay in that tub all day." He reached for me, and I shrank away. "Grant, don't be ridiculous. They're gone. I understand spider phobias, but they're all dead. I don't know how many times I can say it. You need to trust me and get out of the tub. You can get dressed, and I'll take you home."

I shivered, half registering his proposal. Tristan was trying to help in the only way he knew how, and part of me appreciated that, but the other part knew there was nothing to be done until the quaking inside subsided. He didn't understand how deep my fears went.

Just as I touched the tub wall to steady myself while I attempted to stand, I heard Claire's voice. "Where's Grant? I want to tell him I'm sorry about what I said."

Tristan jumped away from the tub and angled the door so she couldn't see me as he blocked her path. "You could think of knocking before entering my room. You know I'm married now. We're going to have to lay down some rules."

I could imagine her rolling eyes by the sound she made. "Seriously? Since when do we have rules? Dad! You're the guy who said rules are for those who don't like to have fun."

He conceded. "Um, true." I could hear the embarrassment in his voice. Then he amended, "But for fifteen years, it's only been the two of us. Things are different now."

"Because of him," she huffed.

He stressed, "Yes, because of him. I love Grant, Claire. I will do whatever necessary for him to be happy. So if I have to set down a few rules for my spoiled teenage daughter, I will. Number one, no barging into the bedroom like you did this morning or just now."

"Because you might be having sex," she said matter-of-factly.

"No! Good God, Claire. Why would you even say that?" he asked, shocked out of his mind. I was alarmed by her statement as well, and mildly wondered if she'd come in hoping to find us.

She made another disgusted sound. "I don't know. Mom does it, so I figured you'd probably do the same."

"Claire," he said, concerned, drawing her away from the door and into the bedroom. I stood up and dried myself off. I removed my glasses, wiped off the water droplets, and set them back on my face. I wanted to hear what they were saying, so I leaned closer to the door. Tristan continued, "I would never have sex while you were in the house, or at the very least I'd lock the door. Has your mom…? Have you…?" He didn't finish his thought, but it was implied strongly enough.

She snorted. "All the time."

My heart actually hurt for her. She was a kid. It wasn't right for her to see things like that. But her next words made me gag on bile.

"When I was ten, I walked in on her with this guy she'd been seeing. I didn't know what they were doing, but he was mounting her from behind like the elephants I'd seen at the zoo. I stared for a few seconds, listening to her moan. At first I thought he was hurting her, but she kept saying, 'Yes!' When I finally asked, 'What are you doing to my mom?' they both yelled at me to get out. She rarely remembers to close the door, let alone lock it. I've seen all kinds of things."

Her admission was sobering, and I stopped shivering from spider-induced heebie-jeebies. I rubbed the excess water from my hair, wrapped one towel around my waist and another around my shoulders, and made a mental note to bring over a robe. I walked into the room and joined Tristan on the bed next to Claire just as she finished.

Tristan glanced at me but then hugged Claire from the side. "Oh, sweetness. I'm sorry. Why didn't you ever say anything?"

She lifted her shoulders. "I don't know. I didn't realize until seventh grade that kids didn't know about that stuff. I mean, we have Health, but it was never as graphic as what I'd seen. I was embarrassed to say anything, because I didn't want anyone at school calling me a slut if I corrected them. No one I knew was doing it anyway, so I let them think they knew stuff."

"You could have said something to me," he said. He reached over and squeezed my knee, letting me know my presence was welcomed.

"Dad, I didn't think you cared. I know we've always had fun on our weekends, but you never asked about my life with Mom. You never asked if I wanted to live with you. You never asked if I enjoyed living with Mom. I didn't know I had a choice."

"I'm sorry. I guess I haven't been a very good father."

"I survived."

"I do want you to live with us—that is, if you want to."

"I know. Mom told me. Actually, she yelled it. I'm sorry I told her you were gay. She's been really weird lately. She's angrier than usual. She got pissed and mentioned you were filing for full custody."

"Would you want that?" he asked.

Claire shrugged. "I don't know. I guess. Mom might drink too much, but she's always been strict about my grades, homework, and chores. I've come to appreciate it. I have a 3.9 GPA because of her. I want to get into college, Dad. I don't know if I can, living with you."

"Why?" he asked with an edge to his voice.

"Because you're the party guy. That's what Mom calls you. You're never serious. In fact, I think today is the first time you've ever yelled at me." She leaned forward and locked eyes with me. "I'm sorry, Grant. I didn't mean to imply that you were a maid."

"Thanks," I replied. Having just this little bit of history about them helped me see her and Tristan differently. This wasn't a change just for me, but for both of them too.

Tristan let out a heavy sigh and said, "I'm sorry too. I guess the years rolled by faster than I realized. I've been in a holding pattern since the day you were born. I didn't know how to be a father. I joined the military, served my country for four years, and then went to college. By then, your mom had a nice little routine living with her mom, and I felt as if I was intruding. We were never married, and I didn't want to get in the way, especially after I figured out I was gay. I let her raise you and played the weekend dad. Maybe I should have spoken up sooner."

"Dad, it's fine. Mom pushed me—hard. I'm actually glad for it. After she started drinking, I kept thinking I didn't want to be like her, so I worked even harder. If you want me to live with you, then you have to push me. Yell at me like you did about Grant. I'm not a little kid. I want more than what Mom has. I know how much you give her every month, because I've seen the checks, but I also see how much she spends on booze. If you're serious about being a family, then I'm willing to try."

"How did you get so wise?" he asked.

"I don't know."

It had been nice to be a part of the conversation, at least marginally, but I was done sitting around in towels. I was getting cold, and the creepy feeling that a spider was lurking under the bed, getting ready to scurry up my leg, prompted me to get dressed. "As nice as this talk has been, I'd really like to get dressed," I told them.

Tristan patted my knee and rose. "Yes, definitely. Claire, will you give us a minute?"

She stood up. "Sure." She looked at me and said, "Again, I'm sorry. I'll try to be more respectful next time… Dad." She winked, much like her father, and I instantly forgave her.

I nodded and gave her a grin.

Claire left the room and Tristan sat next to me again. "Are you sure you're all right? You freaked out pretty badly."

"I know." I bowed my head, embarrassed. "I've always been afraid of spiders. I used to have nightmares about them hiding under my pillow. I imagined spiders as big as buildings watching me as I walked down the street. I felt them crawling on my arm in the middle of class, only to scream and find out nothing was there. I went to a therapist when I was eleven because my fears were so bad."

"Did someone lock you in a basement with a bunch of spiders or something?"

"No. No one has ever been able to explain it. I'm just terrified of them. I think it's the legs—they scurry so fast. I don't know. My mother pointed out one time that centipedes have more legs and run fast, but for some reason they never bothered me like spiders."

He put his arm around me. "I'll make sure our house is spider free, okay?"

I nodded.

He eyes dropped to my chest, and another emotion washed over his face. Lust. Tristan licked his lips. "I see your nipple isn't swollen anymore. I never got the chance to use ice cubes on you."

I blushed. "No, but you could try that another time."

"Yeah?" He reached under the edge of my towel and rubbed my pec, squeezing it and thumbing my nipple. "Will you lie back and let me kiss you?"

I glanced at the door. "But Claire?"

"Just for a second. Please?"

I couldn't resist the desperate edge in his voice, especially when he said please. I reclined, and Tristan brought his mouth down on my nipple, licking and suckling me. I was slightly startled because he'd said "kiss," but from the way he'd enjoyed my nipples so far, I wasn't bothered that he actually meant "suck." In fact, it amused me. "You have a nipple fetish, don't you?"

Tristan laughed wickedly. He murmured, "Yes," as he continued licking me and flicking my erect nub with the tip of his tongue. He moved his hand over my stomach and rubbed circles over my lower belly. He untucked the towel, and I would have protested if he hadn't latched his mouth onto my neck at the same time. I rolled my head away from his attention to give him easier access. I whimpered when he moved the towel aside and fondled my dick. A couple of days ago I would not have been so relaxed, but the more time I spent with Tristan the more I yearned for his touch.

After a few seconds, he released my neck and looked me in the eyes. He panted as he whispered, "I want to fuck you so bad right now."

"But…."

"I know. Your ass isn't ready for me yet either, but I'm saying it's going to be soon. I want you more than anything."

I spread my legs absently as he dipped his hand down over my balls. I closed my eyes.

"That's it, baby. I like how you respond." He roved his fingers all over me but covered me up with my towel way before I was stimulated enough to shoot.

I questioned him with my eyes.

"Claire's in the house. We're not going to be Teresa."

I chuckled, but not from humor. It was more like a sad laugh, because we both knew kids shouldn't have to see what she'd seen when she was ten.

He kissed me and then hopped off the bed. "Get dressed, and I'll take you home if you want."

I shook my head. "No, I think I'm okay. But if you see any spiders, please kill them."

"I will."

Just as he opened the door, I jumped up and stopped him from leaving. "Tristan?"

"Yeah?"

I may not have been overly confident about my body, or ready to strut my stuff openly around the house, but I could not deny the pull he had on me. Maybe it was his confidence, or the feel of him pressed up against me every morning we'd woken up together, but I felt it deep in my belly. I stepped up close and whispered, "I want you too." I rose up on my tiptoes and kissed him.

Tristan pushed us into the room far enough to shut the door and wrapped his warm arms around my bare back. I swear, if Claire hadn't been there, I would have begged.

Chapter Twelve

Parents, Friends, And Getting Fucked Out Of My Mind

MONDAY MORNING I called my mother as promised. She asked us to come to dinner that night because of other commitments. Tristan was reluctant but agreed, knowing we'd have to do the same with his mom and siblings eventually. We got in my car and headed to my mom's after Tristan grabbed a shower after work.

"Couldn't we just tell your family by inviting them to the wedding in May?" I asked. We hadn't set a date yet for our spring wedding, but I used May as an example.

He sighed, "I thought that too. We could, but I feel guilty knowing your mother knows and mine doesn't. It all came together so fast I haven't had time to think about anything else."

"Claire told Teresa, do you think she told your mom?" I asked, wondering how close his family was compared to mine. I basically only had my mom and my Aunt Crystal, who lived in Wyoming.

Tristan watched me as I drove. I rather liked the feeling of his eyes on me. It made me lightheaded. "No, I don't think so. We visit my mom the first Sunday of every month. Claire didn't know about you then, and I don't think she's called her since or I would have heard about it."

"What about Teresa?"

"My mom doesn't like Teresa. They get along for Claire's sake, but she never liked her to begin with. I think my mom was glad to find out I was gay rather than hearing I'd proposed to Teresa."

"So she was okay with it—your sexuality, I mean?" I asked because it had been a tough thing for me to admit, even though my mother was as liberal as they come. I'd been thirteen, and disclosing personal information that significant had taken every ounce of courage I'd possessed. After I'd told her, and she'd cried loving tears all over my shoulder as she hugged me, I had locked my bedroom door and cried silently in my bed for twenty minutes. It had been the scariest moment of my young life at the time.

Tristan said, "Yeah. I think so. She was quiet, but she hugged me. She told me the next day that she still loved me and was glad she'd have at least one grandchild from me. She loves Claire. My brother acted the weirdest. We didn't talk for two years, but after running into each other at Buffalo Wild Wings he apologized for being a dick."

"And your sister?" I remembered Tristan mentioning a sister.

"She's fine. We've always been close, and she told me she suspected when I was in high school, before I'd gotten Teresa pregnant. I told her I wished she'd said something, but then we both knew I'd never trade Claire for figuring out my sexual orientation earlier."

"Do you ever think about having more children?" I wasn't sure where that had come from, but my curiosity had never learned tact in the past, so it didn't surprise me when the question escaped my lips now.

Tristan was quiet. Too quiet. Maybe he didn't like my question. Perhaps it was too presumptuous or invasive. As soon as we stopped at a red light, I dared to glance over at him. He had turned his body toward mine and was watching me with the biggest smirk I'd seen yet. After the entire rotation of the light, probably two minutes, I stepped lightly on the gas. He had yet to say anything. It was starting to freak me out. My hands started shaking. Maybe he noticed, because he reached over and took my right hand off the steering wheel.

All he said was, "You're adorable."

My mom's house was five minutes away, and he still hadn't told me what was so funny. "Forget I asked. I'm sorry. I don't know why I say things like that. It just slipped out." I took my hand back as I turned the corner, using both hands to steer.

"You don't need to be defensive, Grant. I'm not bothered. I remember your response at the bank when you saw Claire's picture. You said you liked kids and that you'd like to have some of your own one day."

"Oh," I uttered nervously.

"And my answer's yes, I would like other children. I simply hadn't thought about it logistically until now. I've been alone for years. So... does that mean... you want...." He left the question open-ended, but I understood. Then he added, "With me?"

Somehow I parked, mind whirling, thoughts exploding. I *had* always wanted children, and I couldn't restrain myself even if I should have. "Um, I, yes?"

"Is that a question?" He snickered and took my hand again. "Are you asking *me,* if you want children... with *me*?"

I'd done it again. Every time I got nervous and thought I'd say the wrong thing, I ended up wording it as a question. It wasn't really a question—I knew my answer. I didn't know *his* answer. "No," I moaned at my own ridiculousness. "I do want children." I heaved a sigh and finished my thought. "With you." I turned my attention back to him as he squeezed my hand.

Tristan had lost his smirk. His look was more... *emotional* than I'd anticipated. "You have no idea how good that makes me feel."

I could have cried, but I held it in since I was sitting in my mother's driveway and did not want to explain to her why I'd been crying. I think Tristan could see it in my eyes, because he lifted my hand to his lips and kissed it several times.

"I love you, baby," he whispered.

I felt the words forming for the first time. *Did I?* I wasn't completely sure, but this moment in the car was certainly emotionally fueled. His expression, his tenderness, the topic of conversation, all prompted me toward love. But as I considered it, I noticed my mother standing in an open doorway. I cleared my throat and took back my hand.

"My mom's waiting," I said, opening my car door.

We would have to continue the conversation another time. I couldn't think about it now. I had to explain to my mother why I'd gotten married to a man I hardly knew and face her ridicule and possible disapproval. I needed all the strength I could muster.

DINNER WITH my mom had gone very well, but it left me drained. I fell asleep as soon as my head hit the pillow.

"Grant," Tristan whispered in my ear. He rubbed his nose up the shell of my ear and whispered again, "Grant. You need to get up for work soon."

I opened my eyes and read my clock. "Shit," I mumbled. I couldn't understand why I was so lethargic. I had never had a problem getting up to go to work. I liked my work. I didn't remember the alarm going off, but it must have. Had I turned it off and remained in bed? If so, why would I do that? It seemed so unlike me.

Then Tristan trailed kisses down my neck, across my shoulder, and down my arm, and I realized why my normal behavior was changing. Tristan. His presence in my bed had coated my responsible, organized routine with a fuzzy sheen of dreamlike euphoria. We hadn't even made love properly, yet I could not pull myself away from him. It was like being hypnotized without needing to watch an object swinging in front of my eyes. His voice, his touch, his lips lulled me into a constant state of vulnerability on the verge of irresponsibility. I would gladly face getting fired for one more hour in his arms.

I reached behind me, but he wasn't under the covers. "Why are you…," I began to ask, turning to find him fully dressed and on top of my blankets.

As I lay on my back, he rested his arm across my chest. "I've been at work for three hours already," he explained. "You didn't stir when I left, so I thought I'd take ten minutes and check on you. I found your alarm going off and you dead to the world."

I groaned.

"Come on, last night wasn't that bad."

"Not bad? I think the Spanish Inquisition had less questions."

"I should be the one mentally exhausted, not you. She asked me more about myself than the naval recruiter. If I can handle it, you should be fine."

I rubbed his arm affectionately. "I'm worried she disapproves."

He gave me a look. "She doesn't. I'm pretty sure she liked me. But Grant, even if she doesn't, you couldn't have thought this would go smoothly. People are going to give us a hard time. We met and got married in four weeks, after only one real date. It will take time to prove to friends and family that we're serious."

What he said was true, but I didn't want to think that *my* friends and *my* family would be as skeptical as everyone else. "I guess," I pouted. "I don't want to go to work."

"Why not? I thought you said you loved your job."

"I do, but I just don't want to deal with people. My boss noticed my ring yesterday."

"And?" he asked as if he didn't see the problem.

"And she all but laughed at it." I lowered my eyes and studied the ring on my finger.

"Why?"

I felt that damn emotion surging again. Somehow, since meeting Tristan, I'd become the kind of guy to cry at every little thing. I couldn't understand it, but it was real. "She said it was a very girly ring." I didn't want to think about it, but I couldn't keep anything from Tristan.

"Is that why you were out of sorts last night, even before the conversation about kids?"

I nodded pathetically.

He touched my hand and turned the ring as if examining it. "It's not masculine, that's for sure."

"I don't need you siding with her," I whined, on the verge of tears.

"No. I'm agreeing that it's not manly, but that doesn't mean I like what she said. It's your ring, and she shouldn't make you feel bad for choosing it."

"Do you think I should get a different one? Maybe something simple?" I couldn't look him in the eyes as I asked, because I was afraid of his answer.

"No," he answered firmly, maneuvering so he was leaning on my chest and looking me straight in the eyes. "The look on your face when I slipped that ring on your finger in the jewelry store took my breath away. It was the closest I've ever been to a real-life fairy tale. I have a daughter, Grant. I've seen more chick flicks than I care to admit, and there's one thing they all have in common: the princess always wants to be swept off her feet by the prince."

Tristan brought my left hand up to his lips and kissed the back of it. "You are my princess, Grant, and I refuse to allow you to give in to anyone's preconceived notion of what is acceptable as a wedding ring. This one," he stressed, squeezing my hand, "made your eyes shine. And this one is the one you should have. You tell your boss to go screw herself."

I laughed even as I wanted to cry. "Thank you."

He scooted up my body and kissed me. "You're welcome. If you decide to play hooky from work, you could go to my place, or search online for a maid service to finish it."

"I think I'll give it another try. It's pretty gross, but I don't think a maid service sorts through personal belongings. They mainly clean. I'll go through your crap and make a pile out back for you to take to the dump."

He smiled. "Thank you. If you come across any eight-legged critters, I bought a can of bug spray that shoots twenty feet. You can kill them without getting close enough to get jumped on."

"You have no idea how comforting it is to hear you helping and not laughing." I'd heard my share of laughing for a while.

"I'll never laugh *at* you. Laughing with you is different, and I do find the things you do amusing, but I hope you know I don't mean it maliciously."

"I do," I admitted. "The way you look at me says you enjoy me… like *really* enjoy me."

Tristan slid his hands under my shoulders and kissed me again. He was lying completely on top of me, but the stupid blankets in between us prevented me from wrapping my legs around him. But I wanted to. I held the back of his head with one hand and caressed his neck with the other while he plundered my mouth. He grunted as he wiggled his hips and spread his knees apart. He was hard now, rocking against me. He released my mouth, but only so he could give me another hickey, this time on my throat. I think he liked marking me, and I was not about to complain when the slight stinging on my neck traveled as tiny tingles all the way down to my toes. I wanted more tingles.

"Mmm, more," I urged.

He chuckled deep in his throat and kissed his way down my neck, then moved the sheet and kissed down the center of my chest. I thought he'd keep going all the way down to the throbbing part that seriously wanted attention, but he stopped when his cell phone rang.

He fished it out. "Hello?" He listened and nodded. "Yeah. Okay. I will. Be there in a minute." He hung up and sighed. "I'm sorry, baby. I gotta go. Will said there were some bugs behind a cabinet or something. I need to figure out what he's talking about before anyone goes to lunch." He crawled off me and stood next to the bed. "I'll see you later. I'll grab some clothes after work and spend the night here, okay?"

I nodded.

He kissed me and left.

AFTER CALLING in sick to work, I cleaned out more of his shit, but I didn't come across any more spiders. Thank God. I ventured upstairs for the first time and found that Claire's room was the only clean one up there other than the bathroom. Three other bedrooms were piled to the ceiling with crap older than the Jurassic period. Or was it an age? I wasn't sure. Anyway, Tristan was almost ready to be on television for his hoarding skills, and I was not about to let that happen. I picked a room and sorted through it.

A few hours later, I heard him calling me from downstairs. "Grant? Are you here?"

"Upstairs, Tristan," I called back. I was on my hands and knees scrubbing a spot on the carpet with stain remover, and I was determined to get it out.

"Hey," he said from the doorway, leaning on the frame. "We can just replace the carpet once all this is cleared out, Grant. There's no need to expend all your energy when I can think of a few things that are way more fun."

I sat back on my legs and let out a long breath. It was tiring work. "Now you tell me," I complained, but with minimal irritation. "What are you doing here, anyway? I thought you had a brake job or a lube job or a… hand job?" I grinned, thinking myself wickedly funny. It was unlike me to make lewd jokes, but something about Tristan was bringing out my inner bad boy—something I hadn't realized was in me.

He grinned back, eyes gleaming. "Oh, really? I could take you up on that." He started unzipping his work pants, and I panicked.

"No, no! I was joking. I'm not doing that here, not now. This place is dusty and full of yuckiness. Tristan, don't." I stood up as he sauntered toward me, all sexy swagger and lust. I swear the man dripped sex, but it wasn't like I had anyone to compare him to. I backed up as he kept coming, until I hit the wall behind me. "Tristan," I implored.

He grabbed both my upper arms and kissed me hard, pressing me against the wall with his entire body. I probably should have protested, seeing how I didn't want to do anything like that in a room like this, but his kiss made me weak. Instead of pushing him away, I made involuntary cooing sounds, my body becoming more pliable as he continued kissing me.

My mind swirled as the room tilted. He made me dizzy. I was aware of his hands moving south, and I heard the zipper of my jeans, but Tristan was nibbling my ear as he did those things. His tongue in my ear made me shiver. When he reached into my pants and pulled out my cock, I felt like a heaving mass of goo leaning on the wall. I let my head fall back as he dropped to his knees and blew me.

I managed to remain standing, but after he finished swallowing my jizz I seriously felt like slipping bonelessly to the floor. "I can't believe you just did that."

He looked up at me with a wicked grin as he tucked my softening penis back inside my jeans. He zipped them up and stood. "I didn't intend to. You bring it out of me." He winked.

I glared, but there was no anger behind it. "I need a shower now."

"I could take one with you." Coy smile, caressing fingers. Tristan could probably coax me into doing anything.

I shook off the trance and stepped away. "No. I'm right in the middle of this. I really want to get more done in this room before I stop." I turned around in the middle of the room and gestured to all the piles of stuff around us. "What are you doing here, anyway? I thought you had lots of work to do."

He shrugged. "I do, but it was interrupted by an earwig infestation."

A chill ran through me. "Earwigs?"

"Yeah. Remember Will called me earlier when I was at your house?"

"Yes."

"He moved a box of old spark plugs and found a nest of earwigs. He was freaking out, so I went back to the shop. When I got there, Jeff had found more behind the trash can, and Wes about ran out the door when he opened the desk and found more in there. I don't know where they came from, but I had to call an exterminator."

"Eww." I made a sound and shuddered. "I think I really need that shower now. You just made my skin crawl."

"Mine too, actually. I've never seen so many bugs in one place. It was nasty."

I left the room and headed down the steps. I was itching my skin as if the bugs were crawling on me, which they weren't. Tristan followed close behind me. I pointed to the breakfast bar as I reached inside the back of my shirt to scratch. "A package came for you."

"Oooh, wonderful," he said, picking up the box. He opened the top and grinned at me.

I frowned. "Why do I get the feeling I don't want to know what's in that box?" I lathered up my hands at the sink so I could get rid of the smell of carpet cleaner.

He laughed. "Oh, but you will. Let's go take that shower, and I'll show you what I bought."

I dried my hands and scowled. "Really?"

Tristan smiled and waved me to follow him. "Come on, baby, indulge me." He winked, and I knew he'd seen right through my mock irritation. In fact, less and less irritated me. Being around him had worn down my will to fuss. Heck, I'd even washed my hands at the kitchen sink! I tossed the towel on the counter and ventured into the bedroom to find out what Tristan had ordered that was so mysterious.

I never thought showering together would be as unsatisfying as it was, but we really did only wash. Of course, I was harder than I'd ever been, because having Tristan's hands on me was extremely stimulating even if he merely soaped me up. Apparently his little surprise in the box was worth waiting for, and he hurriedly rinsed me off and ushered me to the bed.

Once we were lying naked, still covered in water droplets and side by side on his bed, Tristan revealed the contents of his package: a dildo.

"You've got to be kidding me." He was very pleased with himself, but I was not so thrilled.

"Oh, come on, this'll be fun."

I shook my head emphatically.

He lost his smile and gave me a serious look. "Grant, think about it. Look at the size of this dildo, and then look at me." He held the dildo up and then held his baby seal club at its base and tilted it away from his stomach. There was no comparison. The little toy he bought was tiny.

"Why didn't you get something bigger? Your cock is huge compared to that."

He tilted his head. "Grant, it's meant to help you adjust. First we try this, and then we try me. I'm not going to press inside you until you're loosened up. It'll hurt."

I took the dildo and looked it over. It really wasn't that small. As I held it, I realized it was about *my* size. Probably six inches, so a tad longer than me, and a little wider. I shifted my eyes over to Tristan's massive rod. I got it. There was no way he could push that huge thing into me without ripping my asshole to bloody shreds. He was being considerate. I gave it back and said, "Okay. We can do that."

He placed it on the bed and kissed me. He caressed my face and fingered through my hair. "You'll thank me. I promise. All you need to do is relax. I'll take care of you."

I knew he would, but there was a part of me inside that was disappointed. I didn't want silicone, I wanted flesh—his flesh—and I wanted my first time to mean something to the both of us. I licked my lips and took a deep breath as I spread my legs. "Do it," I said, closing my eyes.

Tristan took a bottle of lube and coated his fingers. He lay next to me, up against my side, and kissed my cheek as he slid his fingers down my crack. I felt them touching my hole, but I couldn't react. Tristan whispered, "I know this isn't what you want."

How did he know? How could he tell? I opened my eyes and gazed into his. He slipped one finger inside, and I flinched, but I kept my gaze locked. He kissed me some more as he slipped two fingers inside. It stung, but I fixed my mind on the feel of his tongue slipping and sliding around mine. I loved his kisses. I needed them. I bent my knee and pulled it back with one hand. Tristan used more lube and crammed three fingers in. It hurt, and I closed my eyes. The dildo felt about the same. It forced me open, but I told myself to relax, to let it happen, to enjoy it. This was for the best. I needed this.

I tilted my face away from Tristan's because I didn't want him to see my disappointment, my sadness, or my pain from the feeling I was being used. I knew Tristan didn't see it the same way, but I did. This wasn't what I wanted. Tristan pushed it in and pulled it out a few times but then withdrew the silicone penis entirely.

"You win."

I snapped my head back to face him. "What?"

He climbed between my legs and settled his weight on me. "You win," he reiterated. He kissed me on the mouth, and this time I gave in fully to my senses. When he had been fucking me with that *thing*, I couldn't let myself feel it. I didn't want to think about the sensations I felt, most of which had hurt. But now that he had tossed it aside, I gave myself over to everything I felt mounting on the inside. Tristan. I wanted Tristan.

I curled one leg around his hip and ran my foot up and down his body, ass, and leg. I moaned as he kissed my neck and reached between us to play with my balls. "Tristan," I begged. "I want you."

"Okay, baby. I know you do." He leaned back and grabbed the condom off the nightstand. After unrolling it down his cock, he repositioned himself. "Hold your legs back. This isn't going to be easy, Grant. You're not ready."

"I don't care," I said, feeling all my emotions flooding to the surface. I truly didn't. I wanted to feel *him* inside me, no matter the cost or pain.

"Okay," he said reluctantly, pressing the tip of his cockhead at my entrance. He paused and locked eyes with me. "Just breathe. Remember to breathe." He pressed harder, and suddenly the sting I had felt from the dildo resembled a tiny pinch compared to what went screaming through my body.

"Ahhh!" I cried.

"It's not in yet, baby. Do you want me to stop?"

"No. No," I panted. "Keep going."

He did, and the amount of pain radiating from my ass exceeded anything I'd ever experienced before. Tristan wasn't joking—he was hurting me.

He came back down over me, positioning my legs on his shoulders. I could barely take a breath. It was like every cell of my body was frozen, waiting for the pain to subside, but it wasn't. It was hot as the sun, splitting me in half like a blowtorch slicing through butter. I whimpered, sucking in a sudden breath as Tristan pushed in just a little bit more. Then, almost like he knew what I needed, Tristan gently took ahold of my chin and turned my face to his.

He kissed me gently and then whispered, "Relax. Everything will be okay." He rubbed his nose over mine as he slid in the opposite direction, pulling out a fraction before pushing back in.

I gasped and held my breath again as the pain intensified.

"Breathe, Grant," he urged, kissing my neck, my ear, and my jaw.

He pressed in again, but it hurt less. Tristan moved slowly but rhythmically, in and out; he filled me with himself, and as he slid his arms around my body to hold me tight, I found my breath. "Tristan," I rasped. I whimpered and cooed, running my hands up and down his back, the motion between us so powerfully vivid it was as if lightning jolted all my nerve endings from the inside out.

"So tight. You're so fucking tight, Grant. I'm not… going to… last." He grunted as he thrust.

I came in white-hot waves. The electricity dancing through my body exploded through my cock, spilling my emotion through cum, sweat, and tears. I held on to Tristan as he growled and jerked his hips, jutting hard into my ass one last time as he collapsed on me, panting.

After a few moments, as our breathing slowed to normal, Tristan pulled back and slipped from my body to remove the condom. He tossed it in the trash can and then collapsed on his back next to me, eyes closed.

My legs were difficult to unbend after being over his shoulders, but the soreness in my thighs and calves was nothing to the throb in my ass. My orgasm fading, the sharp agony of being penetrated returned with a vengeance. But as soon as I reconsidered what I had insisted he do, Tristan whispered those three words that made the pain worth it.

"I love you," he whispered.

I was already crying, tears streaming down my face from the raw emotion my orgasm produced, yet fresh tears warmed my cheeks as I curled into him. I pressed my sticky body to his, tucking my face next to his neck. Tristan hugged me and caressed my arm. Whether produced by postcoital euphoria or genuine emotion, I knew I had to say it in return.

"I love you too."

His arms tightened around me, and then moments later he was snoring quietly. I closed my eyes and continued to cry as I fell asleep in his arms.

I WOKE up sometime later on my side, with Tristan wrapped around me. We had shifted positions in our sleep, but he had not let go of me. His arms were around my back and mine were curled between my chest and his. His legs were tangled with mine. The sticky-wet mix of sweat and cum, slick between us, made me long for a shower, but I didn't want to move. Instead, I kissed his collarbone and then his throat.

Tristan stirred. "Mmm," he murmured.

I ran my tongue up his Adam's apple and then nipped with my teeth.

He let out a throaty chuckle and rolled over me. His smile was debauched, and he kissed me deeply, holding nothing back. One of his legs was between mine, and he nudged me with his knee. Tristan took ahold of my hands and held them above my head as he lifted up to gaze down at me. He licked his teeth and said, "Take a shower with me."

He jumped off the bed suddenly, but his smile was bright and mischievous. He waved me to follow. "Come on."

I got off the bed, but not quickly. My ass hurt. My body hurt. My legs wobbled as if I was using them for the first time after being in a hospital bed for a year. I glanced at the clock. It was 5:09 p.m. Where had the day gone?

From the look in his eyes, I thought we would do more in the shower, but all he did was wash me from head to foot. *Maybe he's not into shower sex?* He stroked soapy fingers over my asshole several times and even pushed one digit in, but it was obvious he wasn't trying to get me off. He was cleansing me of our lovemaking evidence, and some little part of me was sad. I liked the feeling of what we'd done, even if I hurt all over.

Tristan washed himself quickly, and I found the courage to lean in and lick his nipples. He'd done it to me several times, and I'd liked it; now I wanted to feel his nipples in my mouth. He groaned and grabbed my back as I nipped him. I kissed my way up to his neck and pressed my body tightly to his. "I want you," I whispered in his ear before sucking on the lobe. "I want you again."

I wasn't sure where the hunger came from, but it was taking over my good sense. Good sense said, "Rest awhile, maybe for days," but hunger had a louder voice, and that voice said, "Sex. Now. Fuck. Me. Please." I made sure he understood how badly I wanted him by dropping to my knees and taking his ample cock into my mouth. Well, only the first few inches—the dang thing was too large for me to swallow whole. I needed more practice.

Tristan groaned and held the back of my head as I bobbed, but after a moment he pulled back. "Stop," he said. "Let's go back to bed. I want to try something. I think it will help soothe the pain in your ass."

I stood up and gave him a look. "How did you know?"

He lifted an eyebrow and smirked. "Really? You're going to pretend that what I did left no residual effects? I heard you crying out, Grant. I thought I was ripping you in half."

"Then why didn't you stop?"

"I was only about halfway in. I didn't think I'd hurt you permanently, but I know that wasn't easy for you."

I kissed his chest and neck, needing to touch him. In fact, I wasn't sure how I'd ever pull myself away after this. "No, it hurt a lot." I looked him in the eyes. "But I still want you to do it again. I *need* you to do it again."

He kissed me and smiled. "Then I will," he announced, turning off the water. "Dry off and bring the towel so your splooge doesn't get all over the bed."

I followed him in, and Tristan asked me to get on the bed. "On your hands and knees this time."

"But I like watching you," I said, pouting.

"You'll like this," he said with a wink. He got behind me and rubbed my ass with both hands. "Try to relax, okay? I promise I'm not using a dildo or a butt plug, nothing artificial. Just my fingers and my...." He paused, long enough for me to get curious and crane my neck to look at him, and then he finished, wickedly adding, "tongue."

My eyes bugged out. "Tongue?" I asked as he dove in. Just like there was no comparison for what it felt like to be fucked for the first time by a dick the size of a medieval cudgel, there were also no words to express how it felt to have his hot, slick tongue probing my asshole. For one thing, I had never known how sensitive my sphincter was. I began babbling incoherently as my stomach turned to goo and my arms gave out. I fell forward, my face on the pillow and my ass in the air. I couldn't see him, because I had no strength to keep my eyes open, but I imagined his face was buried in my ass. I felt the scrape of teeth, which told me he was opening wide so he could press his tongue in as far as he could reach. He stretched my hole with his fingers or thumbs—I couldn't tell—but nothing hurt as he laved my hole, my crack, and even the skin from my balls all the way back up.

I thought I would melt into a puddle on the bed from the pleasure, and then suddenly he stopped. Cold lube ran down my crack. Tristan gasped and croaked, "I can't stand it, Grant. I need to fuck you." He was panting harder than I was.

I hardly had time to consider what he'd said before he pressed in. Yes, that was his cudgel sinking inside me, impossibly deep, painfully wide. My breath hitched as I held it, paralyzed by the sensation of being split in two.

Tristan groaned as he caressed my ass. "So tight."

I cried out as he pulled out and pushed back in. It felt deeper than the first time, and his pleasure rumbled down his chest and into my skin. Out. In. Deeper again. Something slapped against me, and I realized only after it happened again that it was his balls. That meant he was all the way in this time. Tristan was giving me all nine and a half inches, and I was taking it.

"That's it, baby," he encouraged. "Relax and enjoy it." He moved his hands all over my backside, back, and thighs. "You feel so good."

It definitely hurt, but my heart swelled, feeling proud of myself for being man enough to take something so large up the ass. My ass. He was also thrusting harder than the first time, and God, he was hitting something inside that sent other sensations through my body. Sensations that told me to jerk myself right the fuck now because I needed to come or die.

I lifted up on one hand and took care of my need. As I finished, Tristan yanked my hips backward and growled like a grizzly bear as he jutted forward one last time.

THE NEXT morning, I could barely walk.

I STOPPED by Tristan's shop on the way home from work. He'd said the exterminator had given the all clear as far as his earwig infestation was concerned, but Will wasn't coming in until Friday, just to make sure. His paranoia had to do with getting the little buggers inside his clothes while crawling under a car to retrieve something he'd dropped. Tristan couldn't blame him.

"Hey, Grant," Wes greeted me with a smile as soon as I walked through the door. "I'll go get him."

"Okay," I said, lifting the hinged counter and stepping into the office space where customers weren't allowed to go. I felt so naughty.

Tristan came bounding through the door with a joyful smile taking over his face. "Hey baby, what's up?" He kissed me and wrapped his arms around my lower back.

"I'm still in pain, so be gentle," I whispered. He loosened his hold. "Thanks. I came by to ask you if you want to go to dinner at Mel's house?"

He shrugged. "Sure. When?"

"Um, tonight?" I felt guilty, and I know it came across in my expression. First, we'd gone to my mother's at a moment's notice, and now Mel's. I knew it was a lot to ask.

Frustration flashed across his face, but it was quickly transformed into resignation. "Sure," he said. "If you want to, I'll go to dinner with anyone. Besides, I really want to meet your best friend."

"Thank you." I kissed him and smiled. "It would be great if you could finish up here and take a shower first. He lives over an hour away. I'd really like to leave as soon as possible."

Tristan's eye twitched, and he released me. His expression was back to frustration. "That's fine, but I hope you realize that every time we do this, I get further behind at work. I'm going to have to work this weekend to get caught up. I own the business, Grant; if I don't do the work, then it doesn't get done."

"But you have Wes, Jeff, and Will. Let them do it," I suggested.

It seemed logical, but his lips pressed into a tight line. "Grant, I pay the bills. I do the books. They don't. I don't expect you to understand this, since I barely know you, but this job is my life."

He might as well have slapped me. I backed up and said, "Okay. Then work. I'll call Mel and tell him we'll come over another night. I'm sorry I bothered you." I was back on the other side of the counter and out the door before he caught up to me. I wasn't moving very fast, so I wondered if he had to think about whether or not he should stop me from leaving. That kind of deliberation bothered me more than a little.

"Grant, wait!" he fussed, grabbing my arm as I attempted to slide into the front seat of my car.

"What?" I asked, none too politely.

"I didn't mean to say it so... so sternly. I *do* have a lot of work, but I'll wrap things up here and head home to take a shower. I'll meet you at your place as soon as I can."

"Thank you," I said blandly. I wasn't going to make him think he could be forgiven so easily. I hadn't appreciated his tone.

He let me go, and I went home to wait for Tristan to be ready.

He was at my house half an hour later.

MEL INVITED us in with a strained smile. I narrowed my eyes and realized the problem even before I asked the question. Cindy wasn't there. Mel shut the door and led us into the living room.

"It's nice to meet you, Tristan. May I get you a drink? I have beer, wine, Sprite, and water," Mel said, after Tristan and I had taken a seat on the sofa.

"Um, water is fine," Tristan said.

"I'll have water too. Let me help you," I offered, jumping up and heading into the kitchen with him on my heels.

"Grant, what are you doing? Why did you just leave Tristan alone in there? What's wrong?" Mel asked.

"Nothing's wrong with me. What's wrong with you? Where's Cindy?" I asked, stepping close so I could speak quietly enough to keep the conversation between us. "I thought you told me you invited her."

"I did, but she… she said she wasn't feeling well."

He was lying. He always glanced away when he was lying. "Mel?" I stressed.

He fessed up. "She said she had a date."

I touched his shoulder affectionately. "What?"

"She told me right before you got here she's been seeing someone else for a few weeks. Our date was casual, for her," he said, sniffling just a bit.

"Oh man, I'm sorry. Do you think she'll go out with you again?"

"I don't know." He got choked up and pinched his eyes. Mel wasn't as emotional as I tended to be, so this was quite a display for him. "I feel like this whole thing was a mistake. I'll probably be alone forever."

"No, no, that's not true." I pulled him into a hug, and that was when Tristan walked in. He narrowed his eyes. "What's going on in here?"

"Nothing," I said. "Mel just needed to get something off his chest for a second."

Mel pulled out of my hug and wiped his eyes. "I'm sorry, Tristan. I didn't mean to keep Grant in here this long. Let's just get the drinks and sit at the table, why don't we?" He took out some glasses and handed them out, grabbing a pitcher from the cabinet to fill up with water.

Tristan looked perturbed but held his tongue. He snagged my arm as I walked past, waiting until Mel was far enough ahead of us not to hear as he snapped, "Are you sure there's nothing going on between you?"

I pulled my arm out of his grasp and responded incredulously, "No!" I joined Mel in the dining room, not waiting for Tristan, who was being rude for no reason.

Tristan and I sat, and Mel brought out dinner. "Salmon," I enthused, patting the back of his hand. "You remembered how much I love it."

"Of course I did," Mel said, smiling brightly.

Tristan muttered, "I don't really like fish."

I looked over and glared at him. He was sitting opposite Mel, with me in between them and an empty chair opposite me. "Then don't eat it," I fussed. "There's salad and asparagus," I said, taking inventory of each dish. The last one made me pause. "And hash-brown casserole," I added, beaming back at my best friend. "I can't believe you remembered how much I like that."

"Of course I did," Mel said, patting my hand this time.

I thought I heard Tristan growl, but I ignored it. He was being unreasonable, and I wasn't going to let it spoil my evening.

As the dinner progressed, we started telling Tristan about all the times we had worked together, the customers we remembered, and even some of our excursions outside of work. It was so fun reminiscing, I found myself getting more and more worked up with each story. We even relived our vacation to Ireland. It was the most fun I'd had in a long while.

"Oh!" I exclaimed, jumping in my seat and waving my hand in the air. "Remember that time at your grandmother's house, when that lady—"

"The one with the goats?" Mel asked.

"Yes. When she came rushing over? She rapped on your grandmother's screen door so hard—"

"We thought a bear was chasing her," Mel laughed. "But it wasn't a bear."

"It was a hummingbird," I said. It had been a long time since we'd finished each other's sentences, and I was soaking up the joy of it.

"You were amazing that day," he gushed, his laughter turning serious momentarily.

"No, I wasn't," I denied, feeling self-conscious.

"No, you were." Then Mel directed his attention at Tristan as he told the rest of the story. "This wild old lady lived next door to my grandmother. She had six goats and treated them like children. One day, she came rushing to my grandmother's, rapping on the screen door like—"

"A bear was chasing her," Tristan offered dryly.

"Exactly. But it wasn't. She ushered us all to her house, where a hummingbird had gotten trapped. Somehow it had flown in the door when she came in from gardening. It kept circling the living room but wouldn't go out the window she had opened. She was so worried the little bird would break its neck on something. She asked us to help her catch it, but it was too fast for the butterfly net she was using. Then Grant gets this wild notion to grab it."

"So I did," I told Tristan. "I snatched it right out of the air."

Mel continued, "Only the bird was so tired and scared it just sat in his hand. It wouldn't fly away even when we walked outside."

"I figured," I explained, "that it was hungry. Hummingbirds need to eat every two hours, and if it had been flying around the house for a while, then it was probably exhausted."

"So I go and make some sugar water with Mrs. Peatree in her kitchen, and she produces this teeny-tiny teacup that had to have been made for a doll, and fills it with the sugar water. We hand the tiny cup to Grant, and he holds it to the tiny bird sprawled out on his open palm, and the thing drinks it!"

"Unbelievable," Tristan commented.

"That's what I said!" Mel exclaimed. "It was unreal how that bird sipped the sugar water from the tiny teacup, and then moments later it sat up in his hand, ruffled its teeny-tiny little wings, and took off. Just like that!"

I smiled at Mel. "It *was* pretty cool."

"Pretty cool? You are the bird whisperer, Grant. You have a gift."

I chuckled and rolled my eyes. I glanced at Tristan and said, "Mel exaggerates."

Tristan said smoothly, "Oh, I doubt that. I think he tells it exactly like it is. You seem to have a lot of adventures together."

I ignored his cold tone and turned my attention back to Mel as another story popped into my mind. "Oh my gosh! Remember your crazy friend Darla?"

Mel whistled and tilted his head back. "Oh, wow. I can't believe you're bringing this up."

"It's classic!" I looked back to Tristan to tell my story. "So Mel has this friend from college."

"Darla," Tristan said.

"Yes. She's a bit wild."

"A bit?" Mel asked.

"Shush, let me tell it. Anyway, Darla wanted to go dancing one night. We were all over at Mel's sister's house, because Mel was babysitting, and Darla said that when his sister got back we should go out dancing. Only she found this old Fisher-Price airplane—"

"Complete with little wooden people," Mel broke into my explanation with uncontrollable laughter. "I can't believe she took it onto the dance floor! Oh my gosh," he declared, wiping tears from his eyes.

I scoffed, "Ha! You spoiled the story."

"I'm sorry," he said, still laughing and crying.

"Crazy Darla took the toy airplane with us," I told Tristan. He was sitting very calmly, not getting into the hilarity at all, hands crossed on the table in front of him. I ignored it. I was having fun, and he was not going to ruin it for me. "She took it onto the dance floor," I laughed.

"People gave her the most incredulous stares as she pretended to fly it around, but she didn't care. She just kept dancing with it."

"Stop!" Mel urged, clutching his chest. "I need to catch my breath."

I laughed at him, but I did stop retelling the tale.

"Let me see that ring you keep waving around," Mel said, reaching for my hand. I gave it to him, hoping his reaction would be better than my boss's. "Holy cow! This thing is gorgeous. Grant," he looked up, his eyes shining bright. "Your man has incredible taste."

"Um, actually, Grant picked it out," Tristan corrected.

"You picked Grant," he told Tristan, "so the comment still stands. Grant, this is beautiful," he said, squeezing my hand.

"Thank you." I blushed.

THE REST of the evening continued in much the same manner. I told stories, Mel told stories, we laughed, and Tristan sat quietly listening. I wasn't sure what had gotten into him, but I wasn't going to let it spoil my evening.

Chapter Thirteen

Fights, Bites, And Realizing Relationships Take Work

WE DROVE home in silence. At least for me, the quiet was because my throat was sore from all the talking. Tristan, though, hadn't said much of anything. I didn't know what to expect when we pulled into my driveway. Would he stay? Would he go back to his house? We still hadn't worked out the details of living together. I didn't really like his house, because of the dust and clutter, but it was improving with every hour I spent cleaning it. Maybe soon I'd be comfortable.

"Are you staying?" I asked, walking toward the door.

Tristan hung back, hands in his pockets. "I don't know. I think maybe I'll head home. It's been a long day."

I opened my door. "Okay. Whatever makes you happy." I went in but left the door open. It gave him the option of stepping through, as opposed to slamming it shut as if to say, "Fine, then go the hell home. See if I care."

I was in the bedroom when I heard the door shut. I hung up my pants. I'd only worn them for a few hours, so I thought I could wear them to work in the morning.

"You could have warned me, you know," Tristan said from the doorway.

I turned to face him. If he was going to make a big deal about the way Mel and I carried on, then I wasn't going to run from it. He could be jealous all he wanted to, but I wasn't going to alter my behavior because he couldn't take it. Mel and I had history. "Why?" I spat. "Because you can't handle a few funny stories? We've been best friends a long time. I can't help that we're—"

"That Mel's transgender," he interrupted coolly.

I blinked. "I don't see what that has to do with… anything," I said, running out of words to complete my thought. I wasn't expecting this reaction.

He strolled into the room and leaned against the dresser. "You could have warned me. I spent most of the night trying not to stare. Didn't you wonder why I wasn't speaking?"

I shrugged. "I assumed it was from jealousy."

He chuckled, but I knew he wasn't amused. "Yes, well…." He let the thought go and kept his eyes on me as he formed another one. "I didn't want to interrupt your long overdue bonding to ask why he wanted to change genders."

I felt a chill run through me. "He's not changing it. He's always been male."

"On the inside, but not on the outside," he emphasized hotly. "I get it, Grant. But this isn't about Mel. This is about you."

"I can't believe you'd be so cold to him." I huffed and turned away, fiddling with my shirt buttons but having difficulty undoing them.

Tristan came over and turned me back around. "You don't get to turn away. I'm not done. I don't like how comfortable you are together. Are you sure he's not gay?"

I pulled my shoulders back. "Yes!"

He clenched his jaw. "Fine. And there's nothing going on between you?"

"No! How many times do I have to say it? Mel and I are close. I'm the only one he's trusted during his transition. Do you have any idea the shit he gets? Do you know what it's like to be born in a body that doesn't match your inner identity? He's struggled with it since he was five and realized he was a boy, while everyone around him told him he was a girl. Do you know what that's like? To be told you're wrong, how you feel is wrong, what you desire is wrong?"

Tristan looked down, rubbed his chin, and then stepped closer as he brought his gaze back to mine. "I was in the US Navy, Grant. Stationed on a submarine with one hundred and forty other guys, all straight. What do you think happened when one of them found out I was gay?"

I blinked, well aware of what his answer might be.

"They beat the crap out of me. Not enough to send me to the hospital, but enough to say 'touch one of us and you're dead.' So I know what it's like to be hated for what you were born as. I'm not trying to criticize Mel or how he feels."

Tristan turned away and walked out of the room, leaving me there to sputter. "But... I... you...." I didn't know what I was supposed to say. I felt guilty for talking about Mel the way I had, but in the heat of the argument, it had tumbled out. I ran after Tristan and found him sitting on my couch. I stopped short. "You didn't leave."

"No," he said. "I'm not angry about Mel." He looked at me with such weariness in his eyes. He looked exhausted. "I was hurt because I felt left out of most of the conversations tonight. I'm not used to feeling jealous, and the way you two spoke made me want to punch Mel's face in. I was worried about him being gay and stealing you away from me."

"Why? I told you we've been friends a long time." I walked over and took a seat on the couch next to him. "I'm not interested in Mel. I'm attracted to you. Very attracted. Insanely, wrapped-around-your-finger attracted."

He smiled and reached over to squeeze my knee. "I'm sorry."

"You're forgiven."

"Thank you. When I stormed out of your room I realized why your relationship bothered me so much. I reconsidered my feelings when I thought of my pal Marc."

"Marc?"

"Yeah. We were in the Navy together. We spoke much like you and Mel did. We finished each other's sentences, anticipated each other's needs—heck, we even read each other's minds on several occasions, much to the chagrin of the guys playing poker with us. So I get it. Mel is your Marc."

Suddenly I was the jealous one, and I wanted to meet this guy. "Are you... do you still talk to him like that?" I asked, my hands shaking.

He shook his head. "He died about five years ago. Shot in the thigh, and the bullet hit his femoral artery. He bled out in under three minutes."

I gasped and covered my mouth. "I'm so sorry."

He shrugged. "It happens, Grant. People die. I try to remember all the good times we had. If I only fixate on the negative, then I let bitterness take over and I chance losing all the laughter we shared." He took my hand and squeezed it.

I sniffled, and Tristan reached up and wiped away my tears. I never remembered crying as much as I had since I'd met him. He leaned in and kissed me. "I'm jealous because I want that same connection with you.

I want to know you so well I'll be able to finish your sentences and tell stories to our friends about the time you caught a hummingbird."

I chuckled through my tears.

"I'll call Mel tomorrow and apologize for being so grumpy at dinner, okay?"

I nodded. "I'm sorry too."

Tristan turned his body into mine and kissed me again. I felt his hand sliding up my inner thigh as he deepened the kiss. His fingers ran over the hairs of my bare leg, and it tickled. When he rubbed my dick through my boxers, I gasped and pulled back.

I shook my head and whined, "I can't. My ass really hurts, Tristan."

He chuckled, moving his hand to my knee. "Okay. Fair enough. But what if I offered to blow you?" He waggled his eyebrows.

My dick pulsed and I lifted one corner of my mouth. "Um, okay." It was hard refusing a blowjob.

TRISTAN UNDERSTOOD my dilemma. I wanted more sex, but my ass ached for days after Tuesday. He'd fucked me so damn good, but the aftereffects were difficult to ignore. I needed time to recuperate.

When I wasn't working at the bank, I was cleaning out his mess. As he'd suggested, I also cut back my hours in order to get the house cleaned. I brought most of my dishes over to his house so we could use them whenever we were there, but my clothes remained at my house because his bedroom was still untouched. The upstairs bedrooms had taken way too much of my time. By Saturday, Tristan was home with papers spread across the dining room table.

The upside: the engine was gone. The downside: more clutter.

He seemed very frustrated, more so than usual, so I stopped on my way back from taking out a bag full of trash. "Are you all right?" I asked, squeezing his shoulders and kissing his cheek as I leaned over him from behind his chair.

"I'm fine," he sighed. "This is more tedious than I thought it would be."

"What are you doing?" I asked, peering at the bank statements and copies of checks he had stacked in front of him. Bank statements were something I was familiar with.

"I'm looking for evidence of a cashed check." He picked up a piece of paper and handed it to me. "This bill was sent to collections, and I swear I paid it. I might be slightly behind, but I haven't forgotten to pay a bill since I took over this business. I'm normally very responsible." He huffed and leaned forward on the table, rubbing his head.

I read the paper and then looked at the papers and stacks of unopened mail on the table. "This is for fifty-three dollars, dated two years ago. Are you sure you paid it? It seems strange they would wait two years to try and collect it. Are you sure it isn't fake?" I had seen my share of scams trying to get personal information out of me.

"No. I remember that one. We had to return three different parts, and I never used them again after that. I know I paid it." He sounded certain.

I pointed to the unopened mail. "Then what is all this?"

"I haven't opened a bank statement in a few years."

"What?" I shrieked. Then I cleared my throat and asked again, in a more controlled tone, "What? How can you not open the bank statements? Don't you balance your checkbook every month?" The very thought made me nauseated.

He turned and looked at me. "Don't yell."

"Why would I yell?"

"Grant, you just pierced my ears with your first little shriek."

"I won't do it again."

Tristan took a deep breath and then said, "I've never balanced the checkbook."

My voice went up three octaves involuntarily. "What?" I immediately covered my mouth and whispered behind my hand, "I'm sorry." I took my hand away and asked, "But I don't understand how you can do that. What if checks don't clear or are cashed for the wrong amount? Or if they get lost and are sent to collections." I stopped talking when he glared. "Oh. Yeah. That's what happened."

He huffed loudly. "Yeah. It hasn't happened in ten years. I hate math."

I ran my palm over his bald head. I felt stubble for the first time. If he'd been so caught up in this issue that he forgot to shave, then it must be serious. Although I rather liked the feel of the hairs growing back. "Tristan, why don't you let me help you? I'm really good with numbers."

"Are you? I know you work in a bank, but I didn't want to assume you knew how to do everything money related." His reply seemed not to make sense, but I wasn't going to argue about it. He was stressed enough.

"Yes," I answered. "I'm good with all money-related issues. I have a degree in accounting from Loyola University."

"Then why aren't you the manager of the bank or running your own accounting firm?"

I chuckled. "Yeah, because all accountants start off opening their own businesses right out of college." He didn't react to my sarcasm, so I let it go and shrugged. There was no easy way to tell him I was lazy. "I didn't try because those jobs take more effort than I'd like to give. Being a teller is easy. I really liked working alongside Mel every day. Things have changed since I moved to this branch, so I guess I should consider using more of my skills. I always thought moving up would be too stressful."

"You mean you have all kinds of knowledge and you choose *not* to use it?"

I felt like a schlub for admitting it. "Yes. I haven't found a reason to."

Tristan looked back to his stack and gestured. "You think you can sort this out?"

How hard could it be? "Most definitely. Go make me some coffee and start cleaning out your bedroom. I'm tired of looking at those ships on the walls. The frames never stay straight."

Tristan stood up and offered me his seat. He kissed me before I sat down and then rubbed the back of my shoulders this time. "You're pretty awesome."

"I haven't fixed anything yet." I glanced around the table. "Um, where's your checkbook? I should probably cross-check these numbers and go back as far as you have records."

"You're going to yell about that too," he said, closing his eyes and sighing.

"Don't tell me you don't keep a checkbook. You have to. How do you know how much money you have in the bank?" He was right, I was close to speaking louder than I should, but I contained myself.

Tristan walked over to the counter in the kitchen and returned with a box. "These are my checkbooks. Number forty-three is the current one. I do keep a checkbook, but I keep a mental ledger on how much I have in the bank. I know roughly how much comes in, and the checking account is linked to a savings account in case of overdraft, although I've never been overdrawn. I don't write a check for money I don't have." He set the box in front of me.

I took the top one off the pile inside the box and opened it. All the figures were for even amounts. No change. I knew some amounts could be even, but not *all* of them. I had to question him. "Er, Tristan? Why are all the numbers even?"

He drew in a long breath, exhaled, and said, "I round everything up."

"What do you mean? You round to the nearest dollar and pay that amount?" I doubted that was what he meant, but the alternative might give me a stroke.

"No!" He shook his head. "I pay what I owe, but I round up the number I write in the checkbook because then I always have more money than I think."

"But you said you keep a mental ledger. You should know how much you have anyway." He ran his hand over his face. I could tell this was getting more frustrating for him the more questions I asked. I let it go. "Okay, I'll just take this one statement at a time. Bring me that trash can, and help me open the statements and make a pile according to the dates. I'll get this sorted, I promise."

It was a daunting task, especially when I opened a statement from 2006, but this was also what I was good at. Helping Tristan would make me feel good. Cleaning his house made me feel like a maid no matter how many times he assured me I wasn't, but straightening out his money situation made me feel important.

A COUPLE of hours later, Tristan had some mail to send out and stepped out the door. I watched him walk down the sidewalk from my seat at the table since it was next to the window, and found myself appreciating the sway in his gait much more than I ever remembered enjoying a guy's ass moving before. Tristan had a very fine posterior. I licked my lips and adjusted myself with a tiny tug to the front of my jeans. I'd been sitting at the table a long time; surely Tristan wouldn't mind a short break to let off tension.

He opened the mailbox and then yanked his hand back and held it to his chest, dropping the mail. He kept walking backward, into the road, while staring at the box. I got up and went to the door. "What's wrong?" I called to him. He was still staring at the mailbox and standing in the middle of the road. "Tristan? Stop standing in the road. You're going to get hit!"

He did as I suggested but gave the mailbox a wide berth. As soon as he was past it, he ran over to me, still clutching his hand. I could see he was bleeding.

"What happened?" I asked, reaching for him. There were little droplets of blood all over his hand.

"S-s-snake," he stuttered. "There's a s-snake in the mailbox." He pointed with his other hand.

"What?" I questioned. The notion was ridiculous. Snakes didn't slither up poles to hide in mailboxes. "Are you sure?"

He glared hard, angrier than I'd ever seen him, and hissed, "Yes! I know a snake when I see one, and this one bit me. I hate snakes. Look what the hell it did!" He thrust his hand at me. Yup, it looked like a snakebite to me. A bunch of tiny blood spots on the back of his hand and on the palm over the fleshy part by his pinky finger.

"I'll go see what kind it is. You got bit really good, and we shouldn't wait around if the thing is venomous. Most likely it isn't because of the bite pattern, but it's best to be sure." I took a step, and he grabbed my arm.

"What are you doing? You can't go look. It'll bite you too!"

"I'm not afraid of snakes. Spiders, yes—snakes, no." I patted his hand. "I'll be fine." I walked toward the mailbox and picked up a stick I found in the yard on the way as Tristan watched, wide-eyed.

The metal box was already open, and I could hear hissing coming from deep in the back of it. I extended my arm and used the stick as a gentle prod to get the snake to move. I didn't want to kill it; I only wanted it to reveal itself. A black head poked out. I used the stick like a rake and pulled the snake forward. It struck at the stick but also fell out of the box as it did so. It coiled up and struck again.

"It's a black rat snake," I called to Tristan. I mumbled to myself as I moved it with my stick. "In my experience, I've never seen one this angry before." My eye spied blood. "What the...?" Thankful I was wearing shoes, I positioned my foot over its head and gently lowered my toes until I was pinning the snake down under the tip of my shoe.

"What the hell are you doing?" Tristan asked frantically, joining me by the mailbox but not close enough to get struck again.

"I think it's injured. I've never seen this type of snake act so aggressive before. I'm not saying they're docile, but this seems out of the ordinary." It thrashed its body around, whipping its tail, but I had the head pinned to the ground. I grabbed the tail and found the problem. "What the fuck?" I questioned out loud. "There's a nail through it."

"What?"

"A nail. Someone drove a nail through this snake's tail. That's probably why it's pissed." I pulled the head of the nail, and its body thrashed even more. "Tristan, you're going to have to help me."

He shook his head emphatically. "No fucking way!"

"Come on, you have to. It's suffering."

"You know how you nearly had a heart attack when that spider crawled up your leg? That's me with snakes. My older brother used to torment me with snakes when we were kids. I hate them. I would rather take a shovel to that thing than help it live." Tristan was not kidding. I could see it by his wide eyes and shaking hands.

"Then is there anyone at the shop? Jeff, maybe?" I asked, hoping all of them were workaholics like Tristan.

Right on cue, Wes walked up. "Hey, what's going on?"

Tristan glanced at him. "Hey. What are you doing here? I thought you had the day off."

"I do. I left my cell phone on the filing cabinet. I stopped by to get it and saw Grant poking a stick in the mailbox. Is that a snake?" He was curious and obviously not scared as he stepped closer.

"Yeah," I said. "Would you mind helping me with it?"

"Sure. I know Tristan won't." He grinned at Tristan as if amused by his phobia and then came down on one knee next to me. "What do you want me to do?"

"Grab its tail right there and the body over here. Someone put a nail through it, and I want to take it out."

"Eww. Why would someone do that?" he asked, disgusted.

"I don't know, but it's pissed and bit Tristan."

Wes grinned and glanced at Tristan standing just a few feet away. "I bet that made your day."

"Fuck you," Tristan grumbled.

I thought they were funny, but I had other things on my mind. As soon as Wes took a firm hold of the snake, I worked the nail out. I knew it would not feel very nice, but it was the only way I knew to help it. True, most people loathed snakes and many aimed for them when driving, but I thought snakes had as much right to live as any creature. No animal deserved to be tortured. Once the nail was out, I moved to grab its head as I lifted my foot.

"Whoa, Grant! You're a badass," Wes said, stepping back and watching me.

I had the snake by the back of its head and down by its mangled tail. I snorted. "Thanks. I don't think anyone else would call me that."

Tristan said, still standing back, "I would."

I smiled. "You just like my ass."

Wes chortled. I thought maybe he'd be uncomfortable, being a straight guy, but he wasn't. His reaction was refreshing and new for me. I liked the comfortable feeling that I could be myself around Wes and make sexual innuendos without snide remarks. Wes was a really nice guy.

"What are you going to do with that thing?" Tristan asked.

I considered the unhappy snake in my hands. "First I'm going to rinse the wound in the sink, and then I guess I'll let it go."

Tristan stepped back. "Not in my house!"

"Okay, fine. I'll rinse it with the hose. Then I'll walk it down the street and let it go in the woods over there." I motioned with my head in my intended direction.

"Okay," Tristan agreed. "I guess that isn't too close."

Tristan's reaction was kind of adorable, and when he related his phobia toward snakes to mine over spiders, that helped me to understand it. Everyone had something they were afraid of, and even a big tough guy like Tristan wasn't impervious to everything. Now I knew his weakness. After tending to the snake, I let it go and helped Tristan clean the blood off his hand. I smeared Neosporin on it and covered the worst bite holes with a bandage.

Of course he also insisted that another part of his body needed attention in order to soothe his frazzled nerves, and even though I laughed, I did make sure all of him was comfortably content before I resumed sorting his financial statements.

IN THE wee hours of Saturday night, after dinner, showers and making love, we lay quietly together, cuddling. Tristan ran his hand up and down my back while I drew lazy circles in his chest hair. The bathroom light was on so we could see, but it wasn't glaring like his bedside lamp

normally did. I had told him I liked making love with the light on because
the expression on his face, as he moved in and out of me, was orgasmic.
He'd chuckled, and ever since, the light was on every time.

"Tristan, can I ask you a question?"

"Sure," he said, stroking my face and running his fingers through
my hair.

"Who do you think put the snake in your mailbox?"

"I don't know. Punk kids? I did some pretty stupid things as a
pubescent teenager. I remember my brother driving around with his punk
friends, bashing mailboxes with a baseball bat. Kids do stupid things."

"I never did. I remember shoveling snow for my elderly neighbors
and refusing to take payment in anything other than hot chocolate."

There was a grin to his voice. "That doesn't surprise me." His
heartbeat was strong and steady under my hand.

"Aside from possible hoodlums, do you have any enemies? Or
people who know you don't like snakes?"

He admitted, "Everyone knows I hate snakes."

"But is there someone who is sick enough to injure a snake in order
to make it angrier?"

He sighed. "I don't think I want to know."

I lifted my head off his shoulder and looked him in the eyes. "Then
you *can* think of someone." The expression on his face was tired, like he
knew but didn't want to know.

"Maybe Teresa. She called me this week. She said my lawyer
sent papers to her house. She's pissed about having to find someone to
represent her."

I scooted up his body a smidgen in order to satisfy a strong urge to
kiss his neck. "Didn't she have a lawyer before?" I rubbed his skin with
my nose and planted kisses from his collarbone up to his ear.

He sighed heavily with a slight groan, but most likely from my
kisses and not from the topic of discussion. "No. We've never used a
lawyer. Every agreement we've had up to now has been verbal. The
years rolled by, and everything has remained the same. Until I met you."

"Me?" I questioned, bringing my head up from his neck to look
him in the eyes again.

He tilted his head to give me a kiss and then said, "Yes, you. Meeting
you helped me see all the things I wanted in life but didn't have."

"Aww," I gushed, nuzzling his cheek and kissing him some more.

"I guess it could have been Teresa, but that's stooping pretty low."

I curled my arms around his head and caressed his stubble as I nibbled on his earlobe. It disturbed me that his ex would do something so mean, but at least it was a plausible explanation if punk kids weren't to blame.

Tristan groaned and gripped my back. "Baby, if you keep doing that, I'm going to want inside your ass again."

I snickered. Pondering the snake in the mailbox had run its course. My libido, however, had not been satisfied enough to find sleep. Plus, I figured, the more we did it, the less my ass would hurt each time. Right? The muscles had to adjust to him eventually. "What if that's my goal?" I asked before I bit him.

Tristan pinned me to the bed in one swift flip, shoving my legs apart with his knee. "You little minx," he said, kissing me soundly. "If more is what you want, then more is what you'll get."

SUNDAY NIGHT, after basically a repeat of Saturday, I listened to Tristan breathing quietly as he slept. He had worked hard cleaning out what I almost considered *our* bedroom now, and had loaded all the remaining trash from another bedroom upstairs into his truck to take to the dump on Monday. Only the stupid ship prints remained, but he promised to take them down once we picked out paint. As we cleaned the house, I came to suspect it had been just like everything else in his life. The junk just piled up over the years, and he hadn't found enough motivation to get rid of it. Apparently I was his motivation for everything.

I squeezed the arm that held me around the middle. I *did* love him. It hadn't taken as long as I had thought it would to realize it, and probably less time than it took other people, but in the five weeks I'd known Tristan, I couldn't deny this was the happiest I'd been in my life.

Tristan's mouth was by my ear, and I could feel his nose in my hair, nuzzling me every now and then as if even in sleep he was aware of my presence. I wanted to roll over and kiss his neck. I had come to long for the taste of his skin, so much so I dreaded work in the morning. Being away from him for hours at a time was torture.

I reached over and picked up my phone. 11:57 p.m. I hated when I couldn't sleep and ended up staring obsessively at the clock all night. It started ringing just as I set it back down. I jumped, grabbing for it frantically as if turning the ringer off would stop Tristan from waking up. I pushed every button, using both hands in my panic, and when it was silent, I turned to Tristan.

"I'm sorry. I forgot to put it on silent."

He groaned and rolled over, pulling the blanket up.

I couldn't tell if he was annoyed or simply trying to go back to sleep as soon as possible, since he had to work in seven hours. We'd only just turned the lights out an hour ago. I pressed the button on my phone to see who had called, but the fraction of the ringtone I'd heard already had given me a hunch.

Missed call: Mel Tersiguel

Curious. *Mel never calls me this late.*

I slipped quietly out of bed and went into the living room to call him back.

"Grant?" Mel asked, voice shaking over the phone.

"Yeah. What's wrong? You never call this late." I sat on the loveseat.

"I broke up with Cindy," he sobbed.

"Oh, no. Why?" I had a suspicion why, but I needed to hear it from Mel. My eyes dropped to the carpet I hated, and I pulled my feet up onto the cushion.

"We were on our second date. I thought it was going really well, because while we were sitting on the couch drinking wine, she kissed me."

"Okay. Then how…?"

"I took a deep breath and told her I had something serious to explain to her before anything went further. She said okay. So when I told her I was a transgender man, she got this funny look on her face and asked what I was talking about. I was confused for a second, and that's when she said she thought I was a butch lesbian."

"Oh, no," I muttered. I knew how much it hurt for him to hear those words.

"I calmly told her no, I identify as a man, so I'm undergoing a physical transition to reflect what's on the inside. After which, she said how surgery was unnecessary because she was bisexual and didn't care which parts I had. And then I told her how I felt, right before asking her to leave." Mel sobbed on the other end. "She slammed the door on her way out, and now I feel like I'm going to die."

A quiver ran through me. I hated the sound of his voice—he was never like this. His sobs reached through the phone and clamped around my throat until I was leaping off the loveseat and bolting for the door. I snagged my keys out of the little dish on the table by the door on the way out. "I'm coming. I'll be there as fast as I can. You'll be okay," I assured him as I ran to my car in my bare feet. I jumped in, started the car, and was on the road before I realized I was still in my underwear.

Oh, well. Mel needs me, I thought.

"Just keep talking, or don't, whatever you need. I'm listening. I won't hang up on you. If the line goes dead it's because I lost signal, so hang your phone up and I'll call you right back. I promise."

WE SAT up all night, talking some but mostly hugging. Mel was wrecked. He really liked Cindy, but it was the vulnerability of dating for the first time in years and its subsequent failure that had crushed Mel's spirit. Cindy was gone, and I wasn't sure he'd be able to pull himself back together. I worried for him. I think it was the first time I understood the term "heartbroken."

IN THE morning, I borrowed his clothes to wear to work. I was running late, and stopping at my house first would take another half hour to forty minutes to stop, change, and leave again. It was simply easier to use his clothes. My eyes burned from crying with Mel, my head pounded from lack of sleep, and my back ached from lying on a couch that wasn't made for human comfort. I made it to the bank on time, but Jessica noticed how bad I looked.

"Jeez, you look like shit. What happened? Did you and Tristan have a fight or something?" she asked, leaning closer to me up against her side of the cubicle wall. At least she was trying to be private with her inquiry.

I leaned in from the other side. "No. We're fine. It was my best friend. His girlfriend broke up with him, and he was a mess last night. I drove over to console him. Neither of us slept."

"Looks like it. And what's with the shirt? I've never seen you wear a polo shirt. Not that it's bad or anything, you look nice, but it's different."

"It's Mel's. I drove over in my underwear because I wasn't thinking, and wearing his stuff saved time this morning. His pants are too short, so don't laugh when you can see my socks."

She grinned. "Okay. You're a really great friend if you dropped everything to help him." She walked around the side of the cubicle and gave me a hug. "I wish I had friends like that."

I gazed into her pretty blue eyes and smiled warmly, genuinely feeling that tug of friendship wrapping around my heart as it had when I'd met Mel that first day. "You do. I'll be your friend," I declared.

She hugged me again, but two customers walked through the door and our sentimental moment was disrupted. I didn't mind, because for the first time in weeks, I felt like I belonged there. This bank was my home.

I sighed, waved the customer up to my window, and asked, "How may I help you today?"

SOMETIME IN the afternoon, Tristan walked through the door with a wad of something in his hand. He stood in line and kept his gaze down. When Jessica was free at the same time as me, he chose her window. I eyed him curiously, but I had a customer of my own to worry about twenty seconds after Tristan handed the money to Jessica. I kept glancing over, and just before he left, he glared at me. Hard. Bone-chilling. I shrank back and gasped, even though he was several feet away on the other side of the counter and couldn't possibly do anything to me.

"Could I have ten ones for this?" my customer asked, handing me back a ten.

I cleared my throat. "Of course."

During the next lull, Jessica came over to me and whispered, "What was up with Tristan? He looked like he was about to kill you. I thought you said you weren't fighting last night. What was his death stare about?"

I shook my head. "I don't know. I thought we were fine. Sex last night was mind-blowing—if anything, he should have been winking or licking his teeth at me." A blush touched her cheeks. I apologized, "Oh, sorry, I didn't mean to say that. It just came out."

Jessica shrugged but still didn't bring her eyes up to meet mine. "It's okay. You're the only gay friend I have, so hearing you say things like that is somewhat shocking, but kind of cute. I'm glad your spontaneous marriage is working out."

"Thanks. I think it's going good. I mean… there are some adjustments we have to make. Tristan's house is not what I would consider optimal living conditions, and obviously something's up with him today, but we're working on it."

She glanced over my shoulder. "Gotta go. Customer."

"Okay. We should pick a day we're both off and go have lunch or something," I suggested.

Her smile could have lit up the room. "I'd love that."

I grinned back, but I had a customer of my own so the rest of what could have been a great conversation had to wait for another time. *Whatever.* I felt pretty good about our friendship.

I THOUGHT about going straight home, but as I neared the shop I reconsidered. I hadn't talked to Tristan all day, and it felt strange. No texts. No messages. Not even a smile from him at the bank. I pulled in and parked in front of the office door.

The bell on the door sounded when I entered, and Wes stood up on the other side of the desk. "Hey, Grant," he greeted me, but with less enthusiasm than previously. He walked over to the counter and stuck out his hand. I shook it. "Is everything okay with you and Tristan? He's been seriously off today. He even threw a wrench across the floor when the bolt he was removing wouldn't budge."

Tristan was "off" here *and* at the bank? A cold shiver of dread ran down my back. I stuttered, "Um, I-I don't know. Maybe he's mad about something and h-hasn't told me." If he was throwing things at work, maybe I didn't want to know.

"Whatever it is, he's pissed." Wes's eyes were wide, and he wasn't smiling.

I heard a grunt from the doorway as Tristan walked in. He glared and possibly considered walking back out, but he didn't. I think Wes wanted to avoid standing in between us, so he ducked his head and quietly exited the room.

My stomach jittered, and I wasn't sure why. I'd only been afraid of Tristan that one time when he'd pinned me to the bed and attacked my nipples. I shivered, reliving it in my head. When the silence lingered and I could hear him breathing heavily, I nervously asked, "H-have you had a rough day?"

He brought his gaze up and locked his burning eyes on me. "What do you think?" he snapped.

My hands were shaking now, and I swallowed hard. He seemed so large and commanding that I felt like an ant looking up at his shoe as it was coming down on me. "I d-don't know," I stammered.

Tristan stormed to his side of the counter and thundered, "You don't know? Where the hell were you last night, Grant?" he demanded.

"I was…." I couldn't look at him like this. I felt guilty and trapped, even though I had a door behind me. I finished explaining, "…at Mel's."

His frown deepened. "In the middle of the fucking night?"

"He needed me."

He threw his hands up exaggeratedly. "Ah! That explains it. He needed you. What about me, Grant? When do I get to need you? How would you feel waking up in bed… *alone*… after blissfully falling asleep with your lover in your arms? Or maybe you'd blow it off as no big deal." He mimicked my voice. "Oh well, I guess Tristan just went off to work without saying good morning. Except… no, wait… it's four o'clock and no one goes to work that early," he finished, twisting his tone into a snarl.

I stepped back. If he flipped the hinged part of the counter to jump at me, I was fairly certain I could flee through the door behind me. "I'm sorry," I peeped.

"He's always going to come first, isn't he?"

I answered, "Cindy broke up with him, and he was crying on the phone. Mel never cries, so I thought the best thing I could do was drive to his house and comfort him. He's my best friend."

He snarled, "And I'm just your husband. I guess my title counts for less because I haven't been around for years. I can see where I rate on your priority scale." He was bitingly sarcastic as he turned around and paced the two feet between the counter and the office door. Then suddenly he whirled around and punched the door dead center, splintering the thin wood.

I jumped back and grabbed the door handle, readying my escape. "I love you, Tristan," I said quietly, knowing there was little I could say when I was indeed at fault for not telling him where I'd gone. "I didn't mean to—"

"Do you? Do you really love me? You could have left a note!" he roared.

I trembled.

"You could have…." His voice broke, and tears rolled down his cheeks. "You could have told me where you'd gone." He gasped as a sob escaped his throat. He bent over the counter and rested his head in his hands. "I knew…," he confessed through tears. "I knew you went to him. I knew when you left the bed with your phone that you were talking to him in the living room. I knew when I heard your car leave just after midnight that you drove over an hour in the middle of the night to see him." He looked up, red eyed, and my chest seized. "Are you always going to put him first? Or will there be a day when I finally mean enough to you that you'd ask me to go with you?" He bowed his face again and buried it in his hands.

I sort of expected anger, because I knew he had it in him, but this total breakdown threw me. I released the door handle and stepped closer. I reached out, but hesitated to touch him. I whispered, "I'm sorry. I wasn't thinking."

He looked up, all strength draining from his voice, as he said, "No, you weren't. You just took the call and left me without considering my feelings at all. Maybe you were right when you said we should live apart while fixing up my house. You don't feel like a part of my life yet." Tristan stood up and backed toward the office door. His eyes fell to the floor. "Maybe getting married was a bad idea."

"No!" I said sharply, reaching out as he turned and left, sucking all the air from the room with him and leaving me trembling.

Chapter Fourteen

Headaches, Heartaches, And Saying You're Sorry For Things You Didn't Know You Did Until You Did Them

TEARS STREAMED down my face as I drove home. This was not something small that would blow over in a day or two. The situation between me and Tristan existed because I'd forgotten about his feelings completely. He was right. I was a dick. I think had it been anyone else, or any other circumstance, I would have gotten defensive and possibly yelled back. But I truly loved Tristan. Last night, before I'd gotten up and left him, we had been closer than ever. He'd made love to me so deeply, so tenderly, it felt as though we inhabited the same skin. Before, I had cried afterward on several occasions, but last night Tristan had cried quietly as he came inside me, gazing into my eyes, arms wrapped around my body and lips searching for mine.

I never imagined love feeling like my heart exploding until he mentioned living apart.

When I arrived home, I parked and bent over the steering wheel, giving way as heaving sobs racked my body. "I can't," I cried. "I can't live without him." Was I having a panic attack or something? My reaction was way over the top for as little as Tristan had said.

I didn't know what to do, but I had to do something. I needed to calm down and look at this logically. As I went in my little house, I wiped my eyes and thought about how I could prove I loved Tristan. Needing help, I grabbed the phone and called Jessica, blowing my nose while it was ringing. I could have called Mel, but he'd have felt guilty for being the reason for the argument.

"Hello," Jessica answered.

"I screwed up," I blurted, diving right into the mess without the buildup. "I left Tristan in the middle of the night to comfort Mel after he broke up with Cindy, and now Tristan's pissed. He doesn't believe that I love him, or that I'll ever feel like a part of his life to the point of putting him first in anything." I inhaled sharply and pleaded, "What do I do? Tell me what to do."

"Wow, Grant! That was an earful."

"Sorry. I'm really upset. I've never been in love before, but I know I am now because it feels like my heart's falling to pieces. He was crying!" The very thought made me feel like crying too. "Jessica?" I whined.

"Okay, give me a second. You say you left in the middle of the night?"

"Yes. Mel was really upset."

"Tristan's jealous," she stated.

"No, he's pissed because I didn't tell him. He woke up alone this morning and—"

"You didn't tell him? That was dumb."

"I know that now."

"Grant, you left in your underwear, I remember you said that. You leave without saying good-bye or telling him why. You show up the next day wearing *Mel's* clothes. Why wouldn't Tristan be jealous? You just blew him off to hang out with another guy."

Tristan had been jealous before, but I was sure he'd gotten over it after our talk. I rationalized, "But he's my best friend."

"And Tristan is your husband," she reasoned. "Priorities change when you get married, Grant. Whatever you did when you were single is trumped by what you *should* do now. If you're treating Tristan like he's in second place, then he's got every right to be jealous."

"But he knows I don't feel the same about Mel."

"Really? You just left in the middle of the night, Grant. Not many people do that for a friend unless they have feelings for the other person. If you do love Tristan, then you need to show him he takes first place in your priorities as well as in your heart. Have you moved your crap into his house yet?"

"No."

"Then do it. Forget about the dirt and the dust and the zillions of wolf spiders."

"You had to mention the wolf spiders," I mumbled as a shiver ran down my back.

"Forget all the reasons that keep you in that rental house. Tomorrow, while he's at work, you move into Tristan's house and tell your landlord you're done. When is your lease up?"

"At the end of the week. It's month to month since my mom knows the landlord."

"Good. Get out. Keeping that other house only makes it easier to leave him."

"I don't want to leave him!"

"Does he know that?" she asked firmly.

I had to consider that question and mull it over. *Did he?* I certainly hadn't given him solid reasons to.

"Another thing… and don't get mad."

"What?"

"You need to tell Mel he's got to find other friends to cry to. I know he's your best friend, but it doesn't seem logical or practical to depend on you when you live—what, fifty miles away? You can't be his only friend."

"I'm not. I don't *think* I am." Now that she questioned it, I wasn't completely sure. But her argument made sense. Mel needed a friend like I had in Jessica. Someone local. The realization was like hot pokers jabbing me in the chest, but I had to consider whom I should spend my time with from now on. Moving to Westminster had put distance between Mel and me. When we had worked together and had spoken regularly on the phone after work, our conversations had lasted hours and came practically every day. After moving, we hadn't seen each for a long time, and the calls came less frequently. This last week I might have spoken to him twice.

Come to think of it, I hadn't called or texted my mother in a long time either. When was the last time? It had to have been at least a week. I couldn't remember. I'd met Tristan, and other things had stopped, other *people* had become less important.

"Grant?" Jessica called to me. "Are you still there?"

"Um, yeah," I answered hazily. "You're right. Everything you said. I think I've been fighting to keep my life the same after I moved here, and I just realized it's not. I have a different life now, and I have to put Tristan first."

"That's what I said."

"I know. You're right. Thank you." I looked at the ring on my finger. Tristan had said it was a ring a princess would wear as a gift from a prince. Tristan was my prince, but here I'd gone and done things that might make him feel unneeded and useless. I had to show him he mattered to me. "Will you work for me tomorrow?"

"Yeah."

"Thank you. I need to move my stuff to Tristan's."

"Good for you." I could hear her smiling over the phone.

I HAD hoped he'd call, but he didn't. I had hoped he'd sneak into my bedroom in the middle of the night, but he hadn't. I touched the cold pillow next to me as I sat up in bed. I woke up alone, just as I'd fallen asleep, and I felt miserable.

True, we weren't broken up, it was only an argument, but the reasons for it went deeper than the superficial reason, and I knew I needed to change or the separation and loneliness could become permanent.

After calling work to let them know I wasn't feeling well and I'd gotten Jessica to work for me, I set to packing up my stuff. I didn't have empty boxes, and I owned one suitcase. I packed as many of my dress shirts in it as I could and then shoved everything else into garbage bags. I got a queasy niggle in my stomach with every article of clothing I crammed into a vanilla-scented garbage bag, but I reminded myself I could get them dry-cleaned. I could wash every stitch of clothing I packed if they smelled like plastic or vanilla when I took them out.

I packed up my sheets, even though my bed was smaller, my extra blankets, my seven pairs of shoes, my two fuzzy blankets, my afghan, and what remained of my dishes. Some of my stuff sat on the backseat, because I wasn't about to fill an entire plastic bag with one pillow. I crammed everything into my car until I couldn't see out the windows and then walked around the inside of the house to take inventory of what was left for a second trip.

"Wow," I marveled. "I don't own that much. I often tell people I don't, but it's really true."

The bedroom was empty. I even took the paint sample papers off the wall and the soap out of the bathtub. I closed the door. The only items remaining were the empty vases from the flowers, my coffee pot, and whatever was left in my fridge.

My challenge now was getting to his house, parking, and unloading without Tristan noticing. I took the long route to his house, coming to it from the other end of the street. I parked on the opposite side of the house from his shop. Making multiple trips from my car into the house through the front door without being seen would be a challenge, but I thought I would try. It wasn't like moving in would make him angry or anything, but I wanted it to be a surprise. A gesture of goodwill that I hoped would make him happy.

Before unloading my car, I had to make sure there was a place to put my stuff, so I snuck into the house and headed to the bedroom. We had cleaned out some things, but not enough. I stepped into the room and sucked in a breath when I glimpsed the bare walls. Tristan had removed those terrible ship pictures. I had been trying to remain calm, cool, and collected, but his effort to make me happy in that small way, even while he was upset with me, made my emotions surge. I wanted to cry happy tears, but I knew I needed to concentrate. Crying would slow me down. I needed to get this move-in done in a hurry.

I rearranged two of his dresser drawers so I had room for my socks and underwear, and made room in his closet. He only had a few coats hanging in there, so I thought I would relocate them after I'd hung up my stuff. I needed the bedroom closet for my work clothes. Once space was made for me, I slipped out the door and brought in my suitcase first. I wanted my shirts hung up before they wrinkled too badly. On the second trip, I brought in my garbage bag of dress pants and hung them up.

I'd just grabbed my bag of shoes and shut the trunk when I heard a noise behind me. I turned and nearly jumped out of my skin. "Wes! What are you doing? You nearly scared me to death."

He shrugged. "Sorry. I saw your car, so I wanted to come and say hi."

"How? The office window faces the other direction, and isn't the house in the way? How could you see?" I refused to think I wasn't as stealthy as I'd planned.

"I came out back to feed the cat."

"Cat?" I hated cats. No, actually, I didn't hate them. That was unfair. I was allergic to cats, so therefore I generally stayed away from them.

"Yeah. There's a black-and-white cat that hangs around the shop. I started feeding her a few months ago, and when she kept coming back I named her Oreo. I went out back to feed her just now, and I saw your car."

"Oh. How's Tristan?" I had to ask, even if it wasn't related to the cat.

He shrugged again. "Not great. He's really quiet."

"I upset him, didn't I?" I felt horrible.

"Yeah. I don't know what you did, because I wasn't listening to the argument yesterday, but he was really upset." Wes was a caring sort of guy, I could tell. He had a soft smile and kind brown eyes. I hadn't learned much about what he liked or if he had a girlfriend, but the idea that he cared enough about getting to know me because he was Tristan's friend made me feel warm inside. I wanted to get to know him, but I hadn't exactly gotten off to a great start with my new friendships.

Could I tell him? Would it matter? I sighed. "Yeah, I did something stupid. I'm hoping that he'll be pleased to find me moved in when he gets home tonight. I haven't brought all my stuff over yet because his house isn't exactly clean, but I think it's important to do it now."

"You need help?" Wes asked.

"Don't you have to work? Won't you be missed?"

"It's my lunch break."

It occurred to me that Tristan often ate lunch at home. "Lunch? Is Tristan heading home for lunch?"

He shook his head. "He needed a part, and the place we normally use didn't have it. He found one in Frederick, so he left to go get it. I offered, but he said the drive would help him clear his head. He'll be gone for at least an hour and a half."

I breathed a sigh of relief. "Then yes, I'd love for you to help me. Grab the pillows and my comforter and help me find a place for all my blankets. Then maybe we can go back to my house and grab the vases I left. I want it to be obvious I live *here* now. Once everything is moved in, maybe we'll have time to break down my bed and move it into one of the spare bedrooms I cleaned out. I've always wanted a guest room."

He smiled. "You got it! I'll do anything for you if it makes Tristan happy."

"That's the idea. I only hope I'm right."

WITH WES'S help, moving my stuff in didn't take very long. As I had realized at home—er, the rental house—I didn't own much. By late afternoon I was officially living at Tristan's. His kitchen was full of my things, and I hadn't seen a mouse since cleaning the dead one out. Maybe it had been a fluke. Maybe mice were not living in his house. I would have to stock up the fridge if he expected me to cook dinner, because beer and pancakes weren't real food, but that could be done later, maybe together. I liked food shopping, yet by the looks of it Tristan did not. Perhaps I could persuade him with sexual favors.

It was late, maybe 8:30 p.m., when I got a call from Tristan. It wasn't the call, per se, that threw me, but the time. Was he calling to say he'd be home late? And why wouldn't he have called before now? Or why hadn't he just come home? And why did I always have to second-guess everything instead of just answering the call no matter the time? I was an idiot.

"Hello?"

"Grant, this is Jeff."

"Jeff? Why are you…?" I let it hang when a feeling of dread washed over me.

"Calling from Tristan's phone, I know. Listen. Tristan is fine. Really. He's fine, but he's in the hospital."

"What?" I shrieked, piercing my own ears. "How? Why? When did he—"

"Grant! Listen, please. He… hit his head… in the shop. It was bleeding. He needed some stitches, and I suggested he get checked for a concussion."

"I'm fine," I heard Tristan growl in the background. "Give me my fucking phone."

Jeff said, "He's not very happy. Anyway, they said he'd probably be here another couple of hours for observation, so if you want to head over, I'll text you the room number. Go in through the emergency entrance of Carroll Hospital Center."

My heart was racing out of control. I was glad I didn't have a history of heart conditions in my family, or I would have worried about having a heart attack. "O-okay. I'll be there!"

"Grant," he whispered. "Just so you know, because he won't say, Tristan misses you and he needs you to be here."

I heard Tristan again. "I told you not to say anything!"

"Yeah. Grant, he needs you."

I was grabbing my keys even before he hung up the phone.

I ARRIVED at the hospital twenty minutes later, and Jeff met me out at the front desk. "He doesn't want to talk about it," he told me as we waited for the nurse to open the security doors. "Don't ask him to. Just take whatever he's saying, and wait until you get him home to ask for details. He fell and hit his head. Leave it at that."

I followed him through the doors and down the hall. "Why do I get the feeling there's more to this that you're not saying?"

Jeff answered, "Because there is. We'll talk about it when you get him home. Promise me."

"I promise," I said, wanting to break that promise even before I learned why I made it. I didn't like feeling forced to comply with something I didn't have all the facts on.

Jeff stopped in front of room 3 and pulled back the curtain for me. My heart just about stopped, seeing Tristan on a hospital bed in a hospital gown, head wrapped in bandages. A soft cry escaped my throat, and Tristan opened his eyes.

He sighed. "I told you not to tell him," Tristan said, glaring at Jeff.

Jeff replied, "And I told you I'm not listening to you when you say stupid things." Jeff turned his eyes to me. "Grant, I'm going to leave you here. I'm tired, and I haven't eaten all day. Stay with Tristan, and let me know when they release him."

"Okay, I will," I said. Jeff patted Tristan's leg and then left me alone with him. I stepped closer and took his hand. "What happened?"

"I hit my head," he said, looking away.

"Is that all? Then why are they keeping you here? You look fine."

He still wouldn't look me in the eyes, but at least he hadn't pulled his hand away. "My blood pressure won't come down. I told them I'm stressed and that it would come down once I got home to my own bed, but the doctor said it has to come down before I leave."

I looked at the monitor. It read 157 systolic over 109 diastolic. I didn't know much about blood pressure, but I was pretty sure that bottom number needed to be under eighty. "That's really high."

"Yeah. I told them I'm stressed about being *here*, but they said being in a hospital shouldn't make it spike that high. They wanted to know about my family history. The thing is, I don't know my family history, and I wasn't about to call my mom to ask her about it while I was in here."

"But what if it's vital?" I asked.

"It's not. I know why I'm stressed. I know why I'm in here."

Suddenly I was seeing my name printed in neon on the monitors. It was my fault. I started weeping quietly. "I'm so sorry. I didn't mean to do all this."

Tristan immediately brought his eyes to meet mine. "No, baby, it's not your fault." He reached for my face. "Come here," he said, touching my cheek and bringing me close enough to kiss. "This isn't about you. Yes, I admit I was angry, really angry, but not like this." He squeezed my neck and jaw and kissed me harder. After several kisses that left my toes numb, he let go of my face and leaned back on the pillow. "It's about Teresa. I'll talk to you about it when I get home. Not here."

He stressed the point much as Jeff had. "Okay. Home. Fine," I agreed.

As if he couldn't find anything else to say, Tristan said, "Thanks for coming."

I gave him a smile that strained to hold my tears at bay. I never wanted to see him like this again. It hurt my heart. "Thanks for not making me leave."

Tristan scooted over as far as he could on the bed. "Come here." He patted the bed beside him and opened his arms.

Climbing into a bed made for one was a challenge, but lucky for me I was small. I laid one leg over his and my body against his chest. I closed my eyes as I snuggled close. After a short time, I heard the monitor beep and the blood-pressure cuff inflate. Tristan didn't move, so neither did I.

Another few minutes, and a doctor entered the room. "Well, Mr. Carr, I can certainly see what, or who, makes your blood pressure go down."

"This is Grant."

"Ah! The husband. It's nice to meet you," he commented cordially. The doctor walked closer to the monitor. "This number is much better. If in another twenty minutes it remains this low, we'll release you."

"Thank you," Tristan said, still holding me firmly to him. Even if I had wanted to get up, Tristan wasn't allowing it.

The doctor pointed to me. "I recommend more of that, and less falling on your head."

Tristan chuckled. "I'll see what I can do." He gave me a squeeze.

"Remain calm, and I'll inform the nurse of your release and my instructions for aftercare. Make sure you aren't alone for the next few days, and if you experience vomiting or blurred vision, call your primary care physician."

"I will."

He stuck out his hand. "May I never see you again, Mr. Carr." He grinned. "Good to meet you, Grant." He walked out and closed the curtain behind him.

I texted Jeff as soon as we left the hospital. Tristan was quiet on the way home, and I couldn't discern whether it was from the stress of being in the emergency room for hours, from the head wound, from whatever was going on with Teresa, or from our previous argument. I pulled into the driveway, and Tristan got out before I even walked around to his side of the car. Yes, he was very self-sufficient.

I allowed him to walk through the door first, and then nearly ran into him as he stopped short just beyond the threshold. He turned sharply and said, "You moved in."

I shrugged and answered humbly, "I'm not sure how you can tell."

"That's your lamp and your afghan," he pointed out. "And the pillow with the fringe you play with every time you sit on the couch."

"I don't know how you know that when you haven't sat on the couch with me that many times. But yeah, those are mine. I didn't realize how little I had until I brought it over here. Wes helped me set up my old bed in one of the spare bedrooms. I want to buy a new couch, and I think the carpet needs to go, but—"

Tristan grabbed my face in both hands and kissed me. It took seconds for him to deepen the kiss. He moved his hands and held me securely around the back of my head while squeezing my ass with his other hand. After kissing me for a few minutes and pulling me snugly to his groin, he said, "I know it's late and we're both tired, but I need you, baby." Tristan's voice was ragged and desperate as he kissed my neck and jaw. "I need you now."

I hopped into his arms, wrapping my legs around his waist. It was a strange maneuver, I'll admit, making me feel like a teenage girl hopping into the embrace of the captain of the football team. Tristan, however, grunted hungrily; holding me up by my ass, he headed straight for the bedroom. He dove onto the bed, pinning me underneath him as he ravaged my neck. He adeptly unbuttoned my shirt while continuing to kiss me, rocking not so subtly against my crotch.

"I missed you," he rasped, his voice heavy with lust. "Can't sleep without you." He opened my shirt, lifted my white T-shirt, and tongued my nipples. He sucked on one and then bit it—hard.

I cried out, "Ahh!"

"I'm sorry," he said, laving the spot he'd bitten and blowing on it alternately. I had to admit, I liked when he did that, although the pain I could do without.

I rubbed his smooth, bald head, and after a time Tristan stopping playing with my nipples long enough to remove both shirts. Then he nibbled on my nipples again, which made me giggle because I thought his nipple addiction was cute.

He reached down and undid my belt one-handedly after groping me through my pants. Maybe it was to make sure I was interested. Maybe it was to stimulate me. Maybe he liked feeling me harden through my clothes, as he was often in the habit of groping me like that.

"Are you sure you're allowed to have sex with a concussion?" I asked as he removed my pants and underwear.

He nodded. "As long as you don't shove me up against the wall."

I snorted with laughter. "Yeah. I can really see me doing that."

He licked from my balls to the tip of my cock, smiled, and said, "I think over time I'll be able to stir up the bad boy inside of you."

I gasped as he licked me again. "Oh yeah?" I questioned, barely able to speak when his tongue was on my dick, yet knowing what he said was truer than he realized, since I'd already come to that conclusion myself. Tristan was making me more daring and less obsessive. Or more obsessive over things he'd enjoy, and less over every little item out of order. Case in point: I was aware of how sweaty I'd been earlier in the day, and I considered suggesting a shower since he had to be sweaty from work and stuff, but then he licked me again and lapped the precome from my slit, and my brain shut off. Giving in to my baser desires had allowed me to let go of anal-retentive ones.

Tristan confirmed, "Oh, yeah. I can see you wearing a leather harness and smacking my ass with a riding crop." I would have laughed, but he grinned again and held my cock to his face so he could nuzzle it. The sensation took my breath away. I felt the stubble on his cheeks. It prickled my sensitive skin, yet his movements drove me crazy. He was rubbing my erection all over his face, his cheeks, his lips, under his chin, and back again. I pulled on the sheet, twisting it in my fist. He wasn't kidding when he'd said he liked to play. He was "playing" now, and I was seconds from begging. Yet Tristan, cool as he could be, just kept talking. "I even have a box of toys I plan to use on you, but only when you're ready."

I gasped again, unable to respond verbally as he took me entirely in and down to the root. I fisted the sheets with both hands. *Toys?* Oh God, I couldn't think about what that meant while he sucked my dick.

Tristan worked on me, but only briefly, pulling off and letting my cock flop back down as he sat up and removed his shirt. "Will you sit on me?"

"Sit?" I asked, because his intent wasn't registering through my lust-induced fog.

"Yeah," he said, removing his pants. "I think you're probably right about sex with a concussion, so if I'm lying down, relatively immobile, it might be better for me. My head does kinda hurt." Once naked, Tristan lay on his back with his head on the pillow. "I want you to sit on my dick."

I felt the heat of an inexplicable embarrassment flush over my face. "Oh," I said, eyeing his cock as he held it up off his stomach. "O-oh, o-okay," I stuttered nervously. This would be different for me. So far, we'd only tried a few standard positions. I rather liked missionary position, as it allowed me to kiss him, hold him, and watch his face. I was relatively passive. Tristan did the work, and I held on. Sitting on his cock would take me to a different place, a more assertive place, a place where I had to maintain the rhythm and motion. Plus, his cock was massive! I'd taken him in fully, but not without difficulty. The last time had been much easier than the first, but the thought of impaling myself on him scared me a little.

"Grant," he said with a certain intonation that told me he saw the trepidation in my eyes. "You'll be fine. Grab the lube and take it slow. It's not like you have to sit down and impale yourself in one swift motion."

I breathed a snort of relief as he read my mind.

"Tease me. Take in just a little and pull off. Do whatever you want, and however much you feel comfortable with. I'm going to pop just watching you."

I blushed and turned away. It was hard to believe that he saw me so provocatively. My body was so bland and undefined, yet every time we'd been naked together, Tristan had been so... *enthusiastic*. His eyes had glazed over with such lust-filled hunger that I practically came considering what he might do. Maybe it was because it was him, and because it was me, and we both wanted each other so badly, we looked past the imperfections. Although I would say *he* had no imperfections. His enraptured gaze on me surely made me reconsider my self-image. Maybe my naked body wasn't as unappealing as I had previously thought.

"Okay," I agreed. I grabbed a condom and the lube and coated everything liberally. Straddling his waist, I reached behind me and guided him to my clenched hole. I pushed down against him, but there was no way his wide head was going to breach my entrance. I tried again and then admitted, "I can't. It's not going to go in. You're too big."

He rubbed my thighs and grinned. "No, I'm not. I've been inside you a number of times, Grant. It'll fit, but you need to relax first. You're too tense; I can see it in your scrunched-up face as you're trying to put it in. Relax. Why don't you lean forward, and I'll help you? Then you can sit back and go with whatever rhythm you want. Okay?"

I nodded nervously. I did what he wanted and focused my energy on relaxing my asshole. *Relax. Relax. Relax.* Tristan propped himself up on one elbow, bent his knees, and reached under me to position his cockhead against my hole. He tilted his hips, lifting them off the bed as he pressed in before lying flat once more. Pressure. Burn. Stretch. Pain. More pain as he slid in deeper. "Ah!" I cried out, my breath fluttering as I gasped.

"Relax, Grant. Let it happen. Shhh," he soothed, caressing my thighs. "Let your weight down slowly. I'm all the way in, so all you need to do is move when you're ready."

It hurt, true, but not as badly as I was bracing myself for. I needed to relax, and I'll admit it was a difficult thing to remember every time I glimpsed his size. Yet… he said he was in. I let my hips down and my thigh muscles go slack, and I realized I *was* sitting on his cock—fully—and it wasn't bad. It was my fear of being ripped in half by his massive tree trunk that had me tensing up. I laughed at myself for being so silly.

I lifted myself and eased back down, gasping slightly from the stinging friction. Up again and back down. "Ohhh," I groaned raggedly, reveling in the wave of pleasure that rippled through my body. I hopped again, more aggressively, and gasped. "Mmm," I moaned. The rhythm wasn't as easy to set as I'd hoped, but the more I moved my hips up and down, the easier it was to find a gratifying cadence. In fact, I found myself wanting more, needing deeper penetration, and yearning to come. My thighs burned, yet for the first time in my life I ignored my own pain in lieu of the sensations that radiated from my ass outward through my extremities.

"Tristan," I rasped. "I need…." I swallowed hard, reaching for my cock and eagerly jerking it.

Tristan grunted as I spilled myself all over his stomach. When I was finished, he lifted me off the bed, repositioned our still-locked bodies, and thrust savagely into me several more times until he came. He pulled out when he was done and flopped on top of me, panting and mewling—contented as ever. He kissed my skin wherever his lips could reach without moving his body as he held me tight.

"That was fucking amazing," he remarked.

Understatement of the year! I only chuckled breathily.

LATER, AFTER we showered and brushed our teeth and I removed my contacts, Tristan and I lay on the bed facing each other—he said it hurt his head to lie flat on his back, and spooning only allowed him to nuzzle the back of my head. This time he wanted to watch me. It was a different feeling, lying on our sides inches apart, yet only touching where he held my hands and our knees bumped. I think it was the perspective. His nose was inches from mine on the pillow, so our eyes really had nowhere else to look but directly into each other's. It was more exposing than when we cuddled or spooned, or even gazing into one another's eyes during orgasm.

With the slight light from the bathroom, I couldn't exactly see the color of his eyes, but I knew how beautifully blue they were. Tristan was a very handsome man, and he was mine. The very idea made me swell with pride. I squeezed his hands and whispered, "I love you."

He smiled and whispered back, "I love you too."

"How does your head feel?"

"It's fine. Lying still like this is good. Sex earlier, while lying on my back, was not so good. My head hurt more and more, especially when I flipped you on your back. I probably should have rested first."

"Why didn't you say? We could have stopped." I felt bad thinking I'd caused him more pain.

He snorted. "Grant, unless a fire starts in the bed while we're doing it, I'm not stopping in the middle of sex just because my head hurts. If I did, the ache in my balls would surpass anything in my head. I'll be fine."

I grinned. He had a point. I'm not sure I would feel very good stopping in the middle either. I pulled his hand up to my lips and kissed his fingers. His gaze softened, and the look he gave me was probably the most intimate I'd seen—so open and tender. I wanted him to look at me

like that forever, but my mind had other ideas. One thought popped out
that might kill the mood, yet it was one I really wanted to talk about.

"So what happened with Teresa?" I asked. My question was not
exactly romantic, and it wasn't the best timing, but it seemed right to
open up here like this, when there was nothing between us.

Tristan's mouth twitched. He lifted his fingers and touched my chin.
He sighed heavily, and I hoped I hadn't killed our beautiful moment.
"I'm not sure you really want to know."

"I do. I want to know what happens to you, and about the people
who affect you." It was the God's honest truth. I had realized it in those
moments right after our disagreement, and I was determined never to
repeat that sort of indifference to his feelings. If it mattered to him, then
it needed to matter to me.

He tenderly touched my cheek. "I didn't fall at work."

"Okay. I kind of got that, the way Jeff talked to me before I went in
to see you, but I don't see what that has to do with Teresa."

I was glad for the bathroom light seeping into the room, because I
could make out his facial expressions. I could see the strain in his eyes.
He didn't want to tell me. When he dropped his hand from my face, it
seemed even more serious. What could be that bad? So he didn't fall?
I could only think of one other way to get a head injury. "Tristan? Did
somebody hit you?" I didn't want to think of anyone beating him in the
head on purpose, but if he didn't fall, what other option was there?

He closed his eyes as if gathering his thoughts. "Yes. Someone
hit me."

I tightened my grip on his other hand. "Oh my gosh! Who? How?
With what?"

He paused again. It was hard for him to say, and the longer he took,
the more tension swirled in my stomach.

He explained slowly, "I was in the shop. Everyone had gone home,
but I still had a few things to take care of. I told you I've been behind. I
was angry with you, and I didn't want to go home to an empty house. I
stayed to work more because working is something I'm good at. I was in
the bay, standing under an Impala on the lift, when I heard a noise behind
me. I thought it was that damn cat Wes has been feeding, so I ignored
it. I heard it again, but before I turned around someone struck me on the
back of the head. I went down on one knee, but I turned fast enough to
see someone dressed in black run out the side door."

I gasped but couldn't form words, thinking this sounded like a murder mystery novel. Only the intended victim caught a glimpse of his "killer."

Tristan kept going. "I wasn't on the ground long when Jeff ran in. He said he heard a screech and bolted for the shop. Ironically, his car had run out of gas a half mile from the shop, so he was walking back for a gas can."

"He didn't call you first?"

"He said he did, but Wes turns the shop phone over to the answering machine after hours and my cell phone was on the desk on vibrate because I wasn't in the mood to take calls."

"Oh," I lamented, knowing that part had been my fault.

"Grant, don't. I'm over it. I was pissed at you enough to want to avoid you for the day, but then I got hit on the back of my head with what felt like a tire iron or a crowbar, and all I wanted was for you to be there."

I felt the need to point out a flaw in his reasoning. "But you told Jeff not to call me."

"I know. By the time I was at the emergency room, I felt stupid calling you. I'm a grown man. I didn't need you to hold my hand."

"But your blood pressure went down when I got there. Remember? The doctor even said you needed more snuggling with me and less falling on your head."

He grinned and touched my face again. "You're right. I *did* need you to hold my hand, but I was too stubborn to admit it. As soon as you came in, it felt like a wave of tranquility rushed over my body. Yeah, I fussed at Jeff, but that's because I'm pigheaded. I don't like admitting I'm wrong or that I need people."

"It's a good thing Jeff got to you so quickly."

He nodded, head still resting on the pillow. "Yeah. But the worst part is that Jeff thought he recognized the sound of the car. He thinks he knows who snuck up on me."

"How could he by a car's sound?"

"Because the car has this stupid fan belt that sticks all the time. It makes a very distinctive squeal."

"Who's was it?" I asked, not wanting to jump to the conclusion that brought all the parts of the conversation together.

"Teresa's."

"Why?" was the only word I could form as the rest of my body debated on whether to get sick in the bed or run for the toilet to puke bile.

He confessed, "I don't know. I need to talk to her, but I'm not sure how. If I go to the police with Jeff as an *ear*-witness, then it could go really wrong for her. I have to think about Claire. Whoever it was, if I were to describe what I saw to the authorities, it was someone about five foot one, thin, with good aim, but not the muscle power of a grown man. I was hit hard, but I think if Jeff had done the same I would have blacked out. He said I was cut deep, but my skull wasn't dented."

I really did want to puke, but mostly I wanted to be as close to him as I could. I pressed my body forward and tucked my head under his chin as I curled my arms between my chest and his. I felt a tear escape and run over the bridge of my nose. "Can we talk about the rest later? I don't like where this is leading. It makes me scared for you."

Tristan had moved his arm under my neck when I scooted closer, so he could hold me securely. "I know, baby. Don't worry. I'm pretty tough. I'll figure it out."

The longer we lay there, bodies entwined, the more I thought about the what-ifs. What if he'd been seriously hurt, and our last conversation was about living apart for a while? What if I never got another chance to tell him I loved him? Or worse, what if he had died and our spontaneous marriage ended a week after it started? Overthinking had always been an issue for me, and I managed to work myself up into a good hard cry. I wasn't sobbing, but my face was wet as was his skin where I touched it—all from my tears.

"I love you, Tristan. I don't want to lose you," I whispered, sniffling.

"I love you too. Go to sleep. We'll talk about it more tomorrow."

Chapter Fifteen

Clues, Capers, And Fifteen-Year-Old Detectives

TRISTAN HUNG up the phone and groaned loudly. "Ah! That girl! She wants to know why I asked her to look for a crowbar in the shed."

I lifted my eyebrow. "What teenage girl wouldn't? Your explanation didn't make any sense. Then, when you changed the whole story because she had too many questions, even I would have a hard time believing you."

"I just don't want to be wrong and trap Claire in the middle of it." He sat on the breakfast bar, tapping his hands on the clean counter.

"You already have. When you called and asked her where her mom was last night, you involved her. When she told you she didn't know, she became a witness to the fact that Teresa wasn't home around the time you were struck."

He laid his head on his arms and groaned again, forlornly. "Why is this happening?"

I set the stirring spoon down from the chili I was making us for dinner and stepped over to pet his head—not exactly in the way I would pet a hairy head, but more like giving it a good rub. I liked the smoothness, and I avoided the bandaged area. One good thing about being bald was they hadn't needed to shave part of his scalp in the hospital. I leaned down and kissed his head before returning to the stove.

"How does your ass feel?" he asked. I shot him a look, wondering where his question had come from, and found his attention fully on me where I stood at the stove, head propped on his hand.

I said, "You snagged that question out of left field."

He shrugged. "I know. I was wondering because you've been walking gingerly."

I blushed and smirked. "It aches. I'm glad I had a short shift today. I bent down to pick up a pen and—man oh man—I swear I could still feel you inside."

"Hmm," he mused, gazing at me rather lustfully. "I like the sound of that."

"You would. I, on the other hand, was not too thrilled when we had a meeting at the bank and I had to sit down."

Tristan laughed. He stood up and rounded the counter, but as he was about to wrap his arms around me, the phone rang. He answered, "Hello?"

I couldn't really hear the person on the other end, but it sounded like a girl. He was standing fairly close as he talked. "You did? Hey, do you mind if I put the phone on speaker? I don't want to leave Grant out of this. Thanks." He set the phone on the counter next to me, and I could hear music in the background.

"Dad?" Claire said.

"I'm here. So's Grant."

"Hello, Grant. I can't wait to see the house. Dad said you've done so much work."

I answered, "I have. I still need to replace the carpet. Will you help me pick out some furniture? I want to get a new couch, but your dad works too much."

Tristan was about to protest, but I winked at him and he seemed to understand my intent.

"I'd love to!" she cried happily. "Do you want to do it this weekend?"

"Yes. I was thinking it would be fun to do after we went to the gym. Tristan and I haven't worked out at the gym in a while. We could get lunch after, and you and I could go look at couches."

"Oh my God. That would be awesome," she squealed.

Tristan cleared his throat. "Um, not to break up this daddy-daughter bonding time, but I want to know what you found out."

Daddy-daughter? My heart fluttered. Tristan could say the sweetest things.

Claire answered, "Okay, fine. I took a bunch of pictures and a video. The place was gross. I had to shower after I got out of there just to get the creepy-crawly sensation off my skin. That shed was infested with earwigs. Blech!" She made a disgusted sound.

I shot my eyebrow up. "Earwigs?" I whispered to Tristan.

I could tell he was thinking the same as me. Teresa could have been the one to stick the earwigs in his shop.

"Can you send them to me? I need to look them over," Tristan said.

"I already did. I sent them to Dropbox because my video files were too large."

"Okay, cool. I'll open them after I get off the phone. And Claire?"

"Yeah?" she asked.

"Don't do anything else, okay? And don't say anything to your mother," Tristan stressed.

"Dad, I haven't talked to her about anything but 'what's for dinner' in eight months. We used to be close in sixth and seventh grades, but she seems to have less and less time for me. I never asked you before, because I thought you liked living alone—but, Dad, if you wouldn't mind, I kind of want to spend more time with you. And I want to get to know Grant."

My breath hitched, and I brought my hand up to cover my mouth. Tristan reached for me, and I fell against his chest. He rubbed my back and kissed my temple before telling Claire, "I want to spend more time with you too. I've never wanted anything more."

I heard her voice crack as she said, "Thanks, Dad." She sniffled and then said, "I guess I'll let you go. Let me know if you want more pictures. Mom isn't home from work for another twenty minutes. If you see that piece of equipment you're looking for, let me know."

"I will." Tristan picked up his phone and ended the call before going over to his computer. He brought the laptop to the breakfast bar and opened it. "Part of me hopes I'll see something, and yet I'm afraid to."

I turned the stove to simmer and then took a seat next to him. I was anxious but curious.

Tristan opened Dropbox and clicked through the pictures of a typical shed filled with flowerpots, bags of soil, tools, and a lawnmower. He stopped on one and zoomed in. "Does that look like paint to you, or blood?"

I swallowed, my shoulder muscles twitching inexplicably. "Um," I hesitated as I studied the picture of several hand tools lined up against the shed's wall. The crowbar he zoomed in on sat in the center of the picture. *Tristan had surmised the perpetrator used a crowbar.* It did have red on it. "It does look curiously like blood, but why wouldn't she clean it off?"

He breathed out heavily. "I don't know. But if it was Teresa, then she's the same person who put a nail through the tail of that snake. She's not in her right mind."

He clicked the video, and we watched as Claire scanned the small space.

"Oh my God, Dad. This is gross," she noted, holding her phone out as she walked in a circle. I couldn't see her, but her voice came through clearly. "I come in here all the time for the lawnmower, but I've never actually stood in here and looked around. It's nasty. There are earwigs crawling all over the shelves and the floor, spiderwebs attached to everything, and even a huge jar of wolf spiders. Eww! I mean, look at this thing," she instructed as she zoomed in. As soon as I caught a glimpse of one hairy leg, I turned away. "These things are huge, Dad. See?"

Tristan whistled and sat back. "I don't believe this."

I turned back, only to cringe at the sight of a wolf spider close up on the computer screen. He had paused it right when Claire had zoomed in. I turned away again. "Eww."

"Sorry. There, I exited Dropbox. I've seen enough, Grant. I think I need to call the cops, or at least file a formal report in case she denies everything."

"But what about Claire?" I asked.

He paused. The struggle in his expression told me he battled over doing the right thing. But what *was* the right thing? Going to the cops would mean putting Claire's mother in jail. "You're right. Okay, maybe I talk to Teresa and record the conversation."

"Are you going to her house, or asking her to come here? I don't want you alone with Teresa, but I'm not keen on seeing her again."

Tristan closed the computer. I could tell this was difficult for him, as he rubbed his head and paused before answering. His jaw was tight, and his voice was strained. "I guess... I guess I'll ask her to come here. You don't have to stay if she makes you uncomfortable. We used to be on good terms, and she often popped in unexpectedly. Coming here would be natural. I rarely go there."

"Then when?"

"I guess now," he lamented. He ran a weary hand over his face and rubbed his eyes. "I'm afraid if I wait, she'll only come up with something else to torment me." He took out his cell phone and started pressing buttons.

"You're calling her now?" I asked, shocked.

He nodded. "The twenty minutes Claire mentioned means she's already on her way. If I can catch her in the car, then she might stop by for five minutes." He paused and then cocked his head in a way that told me she'd picked up. "Hey," Tristan said in a different tone of voice. He shifted in his seat and sat up. "I was wondering if you'd mind stopping by for five minutes?" He paused again. "No. I wanted to talk to you while Grant was out." I bugged my eyes out and he waved his hand at me. "Yeah. I wanted to ask you some things about Claire, and if I can catch you before the weekend, I'd appreciate it. I really want things to work out. Okay…. Yeah. Okay. Thank you. Bye."

He hung up and I fussed, "Why did you lie?" Not that I didn't lie on occasion myself, but I wasn't in the habit of blatant fabrications.

"I didn't," he explained. "You're going to move your car to the other side of the shop and hide out in the office until I text you."

"What? I'm not leaving you alone."

"Yes, you are."

"No, I'm not. She's psychotic, and possibly sociopathic. She could do anything!" I grabbed his hand and squeezed it. "I don't want to leave."

"All right," he relented. "Then move your car to where she can't see it, and hide out in our room. Only this time, don't rush out like a bristled badger, spewing things like, 'we're getting married,' or 'we're adopting children.' I need her to think we're alone." Tristan paused and studied me. I could only imagine my expression after he'd mentioned kids and called it "our room." A tinge of color painted his cheeks, the first I'd seen on him. He had to be reading my mind again. He smiled softly. "Give it time, Grant. I'm not opposed to adopting kids, but I'd rather be married to you longer than two weeks. How about we revisit the idea in a couple of years?"

I melted into Tristan as he spread his legs on the chair and opened his arms for me. His embrace was reassuring yet fleeting as he pulled back and instructed me to move my car before Teresa showed up. I was safely in our room, hiding in the closet behind my shirts, when I heard him open the door.

"Hello, Teresa," he said.

He closed the door, and Teresa asked, "So why do you want to talk to me? Am I right? Did you and your gay lover break up? Are you finished lying to our daughter about living your life with another man?"

I could imagine him growling in frustration, even if I couldn't hear it. "Teresa, stop. I don't understand why you're doing these things, but I know it's you." He'd warned me about his intent to jump right into her attacks, even though I thought he should work up to the subject. Tristan had said Teresa could be difficult, and he'd learned to be direct.

"I don't know what you're talking about," she countered defensively.

"Teresa," Tristan broached. "I know about the spiders and the snake, and I know you were the one who hit me."

"What?" she screeched. "You're sick, Tristan. I don't know why you had me come here." I heard the door rattle, and she shook it. Then her voice betrayed her panic. "Why'd you lock the door? You can't prove anything! What are you going to do, kill me? You'd go to jail and never see Claire again. I can't believe you're going to do that to her!"

"Teresa, don't be ridiculous. I'm not going to kill you. I want to know why you're trying to kill me?"

She laughed hysterically. "Kill you? That's funny. As if a few spiders could harm anyone."

"Then you admit you put them in my house?"

More laughter drifted through the house into the bedroom closet, but it was sad laughter, defeated laughter. "Of course I did. I figured that little pansy of yours would run screaming after something—spiders, earwigs, snakes. I was planning on ants next and then bees, but finding an active hive in late October has been difficult. So, tell me, did he leave you?"

I clenched my fists to keep from bursting from my hiding spot. I'd never been so insulted. Spider phobias were universal, not strictly male or *gay* male issues. She made me so angry with the stupid statements she tossed around.

"No, Teresa. Grant is my husband. He's always going to *be* my husband. In fact, we were just talking about adopting kids."

I warmed with joy. It moved me how often we thought alike.

"Ah!" she scoffed. "I've never heard of something so sick."

"Teresa, stop it. Some babies have zero parents. So you're telling me you'd rather those kids grow up orphans than find a family with two dads?"

"Yes," she sneered.

As I waited and listened, the smell of my fabric softener filled my nostrils and calmed my nerves. I really did like cleanliness. The more Tristan and I had purged his crap and organized his clutter, the more I settled into living in his house—our house. I would have to tell him we could stay here when all the trauma with Teresa was over.

Tristan retorted, "Then I guess we're done here. You're sick, Teresa. I can't believe you'd fill my shop with earwigs, let alone hit me in the head with a crowbar. You need professional help. What if you had actually succeeded in killing me? Did you really think you'd get away with it? What would happen to Claire when her mother was sent to prison?"

"I'm not going to prison, and you're the one who needs help, Tristan. Homosexuality isn't natural," she snarled.

"Yes, it is. For me, it's as natural as breathing. So you can stop attacking me, or I'll press charges."

"You have no proof!" she barked.

"Yes, I do. I took pictures of everything in the shed, and several videos. Jeff even heard your car peel out of here on Tuesday. I've sent everything to my lawyer, and he's waiting to hear from me about pressing charges."

Tristan was lying with that one, but I knew it was to show he wasn't joking, and probably to keep her from rushing home to destroy the evidence.

"No one will believe you," she insisted with less conviction.

"Yes, they will. I'll have the cops send a car to your house so fast you won't have time to get rid of the spiders or throw away the net you used to capture that snake. I'll have it all documented." Tristan's smooth, calculating tone made me shiver. He sounded so in control, so dominating, even though he kept his voice as level as normal.

"What do you want?" she asked, her voice now the exact opposite of his in its timidity.

"I want *you* to talk to a doctor, preferably a psychologist. You need to talk about your obsession with hurting me, and the anger you have toward your father and men in general. You also need to stop drinking. Lastly, I want Claire full-time."

"Please don't take Claire from me, please?" she begged. Her desperation was so strong and unexpected that I came out of the closet and peered into the living room. Teresa was on her knees at Tristan's feet, tugging on the bottom of his shirt. "Please don't take her," she pleaded, dropping her hands to the floor in front of her. She sobbed into the carpet until Tristan bent down and lifted her face.

"Teresa, I'm not trying to keep her from you, I merely want her to live with me full-time. You've had her with you for fifteen years. Claire will be out of high school in three, and then she'll go to college. Don't you think it's about time I get to see her every day? You've had her most of her life." His voice was calm and reasonable, where mine would have been fiery. After all she'd put him through, Tristan still seemed to forgive her.

"She's all I have," Teresa confessed.

"Then maybe we can do every other week, or every other month? I'm not the same person I was, Teresa. After I met Grant, I knew I wanted a family. I'm sorry it wasn't with you, but I love him. I'm willing to share Claire's time, if you're willing to get mental help. What you did was wrong, Teresa. I could have you locked up for assault."

I wasn't completely sure if what he said was true, but it sounded reasonable to me. He had strong evidence against her. He glanced up and locked eyes with me but made no move to reveal my presence. From her angle on the floor in front of him, she wouldn't see me unless she turned her head.

"Why don't you?" she beseeched.

"Because I love my daughter. No matter how angry you make me, I've never once shown Claire the kind of evil person you are. She suspects, but that's on you. I understand how you feel from your father leaving the way he did, but it was years ago. Your resentment has festered into something unspeakably awful. His actions may have been wrong, but so are yours. I'm not telling Claire her mother's a lunatic. You get help, you change, and then we'll figure out a visitation schedule."

"But what about the lawyer and the papers you drew up? What about all the legal stuff you did?" I felt sorry for her, because her voice was so tiny—like Oliver Twist asking for more gruel.

"I can ask him to shred them. We never needed a legal agreement before, Teresa. I think we can work this out between us again. Don't you?"

Teresa nodded.

Tristan helped her off the floor and squeezed her shoulders. "No more snakes, right, Teresa? No bees, no spiders, no creepy-crawlies to scare the bejeebers out of Grant and me?"

She nodded slowly.

Tristan nodded again and then opened the door for her.

After she'd gone, I stepped into the living room and joined Tristan by the window. We watched her car go down the road.

"You believe her?" I asked, because I didn't. "You trust that she's going to comply without any other freaky attack or infestation? It can't be that easy."

"I do believe her. This is the first time I've brought up her father and she didn't flip out on me. I think she knows she has issues that need sorting, and that I'm not trying to take Claire forever."

"Aren't you?" I looped my arms around his waist.

"Yes… and no. I want her full-time, but I also know she's going to leave for college in a few years, so living with us is only temporary. I'm pretty sure Teresa understood that too."

"I don't know. She looked broken to me. I think she's desperate to keep Claire all to herself."

"We'll see. If Claire is here Friday night as usual, I'll ask her if Teresa talked about any of this. If she's really willing to allow Claire to live here without a court order, then she has to talk to Claire about it." He was always so logical. I loved that about him.

"She wouldn't hurt Claire, would she?"

"No." Tristan turned, taking me with him into the kitchen. "In the meantime," he said, "I think it's time to have some chili. What do you say?"

I smiled and grabbed some bowls from our nice shiny cabinets.

CLAIRE ARRIVED on Friday night without Teresa making excuses about forgetting the time. She dropped her bag on the chair and hugged her dad before walking over to me. She held her arms open. "Can I get a hug from you, Papa Number Two?"

I snickered and hugged her tightly to me. Her floral perfume filled my nostrils and her squishy feminine parts pressed against my chest. I had hugged women before, but this was very different. She was a kid, but not. I had a teenage daughter now! The notion made me emotional and sentimental, so I tightened my grip around her tiny body.

When she pulled back, I was not the only one weeping. "I guess I like having two dads." She sniffled and grinned through her tears. "And I'm glad I'm not the only one emotional about it."

I laughed. I wiped my tears and grabbed for a tissue from the box on the counter. I pointed an accusing finger at Tristan. "Don't you say a word."

He smirked and held his hands in the air but remained silent.

Claire walked over to her bag and pulled out a jar full of ants.

I gasped and stepped back. "What are you doing?" I asked, fearful she'd drop it on the floor and I'd have ants all over my kitchen in seconds.

"I brought this for Dad. I found it in the shed." She handed the jar to Tristan, who turned it over to inspect it. "Why do you think Mom had a jar full of ants? I can see if the jar had been open, then they might have crawled inside on their own, but that jar was shut. It even has air holes smaller than the ants. Don't you think that's weird?" She glanced at me, and I shrugged.

Tristan said, "I don't know. I can only hope it was some strange experiment and not a project meant to hurt the ants or anyone else."

Hurt the ants? I would hurt the ants myself if the jar somehow opened… in my house, near my food. "Can we take them outside, then? Because I have a new bottle of Raid Ant Killer under the sink just for occasions like this."

Tristan chuckled but took them outside. Claire and I looked at each other, and when he didn't come back right away, I offered her a cupcake. She said, "Ooh, these are really good. Did you make them?"

"Yes."

"Wow. I'm impressed. How'd you learn to bake so good?" She licked the icing off her lips and then took another bite. "What is this on the inside?"

"Boston cream pie filling."

"It's really good," she complimented, with her cheeks filled with cake like a happy little hamster.

I told her, "I watched some videos online. I like to eat, but I don't like paying to eat out every time I want something special. I learned to bake because I love cupcakes. They're my guilty pleasure, and I eat way too many of them."

"What's your guilty pleasure?" Tristan asked as he walked back in without the jar.

"Cupcakes," I said, rolling my eyes at him because I knew he was trying to get me to say something else. "What happened to the ants?" I asked, securing the lid on the cupcakes.

"I returned them to the woods. I had to walk all the way to the tree line so the ants would make their way in there. It's dark, so I had a hard time weaving my way around the car parts. I think I need to clean up my yard." He sat next to Claire. "Do I get a cupcake?"

"You think?" I reopened the container so he could pick one.

"Dad, do you think something's wrong with Mom?"

We exchanged glances. "Why do you ask?"

"Because she's been acting weird for weeks. Ever since I told her about you being gay, Mom's been… off. She used to only drink on the weekends, but after I told her about you she started drinking during the week too."

"She did?" I asked, beating Tristan to the question. He glanced at me and then Claire.

"How do you know that, honey?" he asked, and I knew he felt bad for her.

Claire took another cupcake out and removed the paper as she explained, "I used to measure the level in the bottles. I knew if she drank a certain amount, she'd need me to wake her up in the morning. I knew Jack affected her one way, and vodka another. It seemed like a game when I was little, but as I got older it was just sad."

He reached over and rubbed her back. "I'm sorry," he said. I loved how affectionate he was with me as well as his daughter. Tristan was such a wonderful man. "Why didn't you ever tell me?"

She lifted one shoulder. "We covered this already, Dad. I never knew you cared so much. It's not like I thought you didn't want me or love me, but I felt the distance between us like an invisible wall. But that weekend when you told me you were gay, it was as if someone put a blowtorch to the wall and melted it away. It felt like the very first time you told me something personal. I guess I felt closer to you, and at the same time, Mom felt further away. I already knew she wasn't the best mother, but my mom was better than my friend Deana's. Not everyone has great parents, so I was happy that she cooked for me and did my laundry. But lately...." Claire looked down, and Tristan kissed the side of her head.

"Lately things have changed." He voiced her thoughts.

She nodded. "Yeah. I also talked to Grandma."

"Oh?" Tristan's voice went up.

"She called looking for Mom, but we ended up talking about Grandpa. She told me Mom blamed him for everything, and that's why she's so mean to you."

"Your mom and I have always had issues."

"I know, but I used to think it was my fault somehow."

Tristan looked as though she'd stabbed him in the heart. "No! Sweetheart. It was never your fault."

"Oh, I know," she stated matter-of-factly. "Grandma was very open about it this time. I'm not sure why, but I think when I mentioned the possibility of living with you, she changed her mind about avoiding things. She told me you'd asked Mom to marry you, but she turned you down."

"I did."

"Grandma said Mom hates men because of Grandpa. She said you never stood a chance. I wish you would've told me that years ago. I felt like you didn't want me, or Mom, but that wasn't true."

"No. I'm sorry, sweetness. I never wanted you to get stuck in the middle of it. My whole life has slipped by and only now have I realized what makes me happy. I want a family," Tristan said. Every so often he lifted his eyes to mine as he talked to his daughter. "I want you and Grant. Teresa isn't going to make it easy, but… would you want to live here… with us?"

Claire gazed at her father, moved her attention to me, and then back. She sighed. "Do I have to answer right now?"

"No. Of course not." His strained smile gave away his disappointment.

Claire must have seen it too, because she explained, "I've been thinking about it for a while now, because I've always lived with Mom. The last couple of weeks have been different. She's clingy, and I worry about her drinking. Seeing you every day will be different too. Besides, I'll have to take a different bus and leave earlier. Mom's house is close to the school, and yours is all the way out here. I wouldn't ride with Kirsty anymore." Her reasons were logical and she seemed so grown up about the whole thing.

Tristan patted her on the back. "I understand. Those are all good reasons to consider."

Claire took another bite of cupcake while I gave Tristan a sympathetic half smile. I didn't think I could make him feel better, but I hoped he'd know I was here when he needed a hug later. Claire asked for a glass of milk to go with her cupcake, so I got her one. She drank half of it and set the glass down, pausing before she continued, "It's not like I haven't thought about it a hundred times. I love you. I really like Grant. Danny lives closer to you. I think I'd like living here, but…."

"But what?" he encouraged.

She glanced at me and then asked Tristan, "But would you guys be having sex all the time?"

I choked and quickly snatched a glass out of the cabinet for a drink of my own. Her question caught me completely off guard.

Tristan was more in control than I was and only needed to clear his throat nervously. "So, um, Claire—" He coughed. "—why would you ask me that? I thought we'd already covered this."

She was unfazed. In fact, her expression was so casual I wasn't sure she was thinking about our previous conversation at all. "Um, I don't know." She lowered her eyes to her plate. "Danny was saying how some guys only want to have sex all the time, and he was worried about hooking up with a guy who wouldn't care about taking things slow." She picked at her cupcake wrapper. "He said the first time's supposed to hurt, and he's worried about penetration. He's never had sex either, so we were talking about our fears and—" She glanced up with a wide-eyed expression as she finished. "—and I cannot believe I just said all that. Oh my God." She glanced at me and back to Tristan, and then buried her face in her hands. "Please, please, please, forget I said that." Claire groaned. "I just want to die."

Tristan's shock drained away, and then he chuckled.

"It isn't funny," she grumbled quietly into her crossed arms on the counter.

"Yes, it is."

I piped in, "No, I agree with Claire. This isn't funny. Those are valid fears."

"No, I think it is. Claire, sweetness," he stressed, rubbing her back until she lifted her head to look at him. "As much as I think it's healthy for a parent to talk to their kid about sex, I also don't want you getting your information from your mother, or from other virginal teenagers. I'd rather you talk to me than Danny. Although maybe I need to talk to the both of you, since it sounds like he needs someone to talk to as well. I'd rather inform you myself than have you make a huge mistake. I'm not talking to you about the specific things Grant and I do together. It's unnecessary. We're an adult, married couple, and what we do behind closed doors is no one's business but ours. As far as having sex all the time while you're here, I told you I wouldn't. Grant makes too much noise." She gasped, and I jumped in shock. Tristan kept going, but with a smirk on his face. "If we were to have sex in the middle of the night, he'd wake up the entire neighborhood with his wailing and moaning and begging and—"

"Please, stop. Stop now!" I cried.

Claire cupped her ears and started humming loudly. "La, la, la. I can't hear you."

Tristan laughed heartily and sat back in his chair.

Claire put her hands down. "That wasn't funny, Dad!"

"Yes, it was," he laughed.

"No, it wasn't," I added.

Claire got out of the seat and made haste to the steps. "See if I help you look for crap at Mom's house again. I think you need to do it yourself!" She stomped up the steps. "And if I hear Grant moaning while I'm living here, I'm going to shoot myself. Thanks for the cupcakes, Grant."

"You're welcome," I called back to her.

"And Dad, you need to fill out a paper for me to change buses," she added from the top of the steps.

"Okay, sweetness," Tristan answered. He was laughing so hard he had tears running down his face.

I declared, "I don't know what that was, but if you meant to scare her, I think you succeeded."

He wiped his eyes. "No… and yes. I wanted her to know I'd talk about sex, but it wasn't a good idea to ask about you and me."

I snorted. "Yeah! And now *I* don't even want to talk about you and me."

He laughed but held out his hand. "Come here." I took it, and he pulled me into his arms. "You heard her, didn't you? She's agreed to live here." He kissed me. "That means I might need to buy a ball gag for you when we have sex, to keep you from screaming."

I swatted at his chest and blushed. "Stop!"

He lowered one hand to my ass and squeezed. "You love it." He winked and kissed me again.

Chapter Sixteen

Hopes, Dreams, And Financial Planning

CLAIRE DIDN'T move in right away. It took her another week and a half to decide she was ready to move more of her clothes into Tristan's house and change her habit of riding the bus to her mom's after school. Like me, she didn't own that much besides clothes, but her shoe collection was enough to make me jealous.

I had needed that week to prepare for her arrival. I'd only been around Claire for two weekends. They had been good ones, but living permanently with a teenaged girl in the house was something to work myself up to. Moving in with Tristan had changed my routine already. I was no longer living alone, and I was also not living with my controlling, albeit well-intended, mother. I was living with another man and sharing his bed, his space, and his time. When Claire moved in, it meant sharing even more of my space, with someone who potentially wouldn't like it.

With Tristan, we'd fallen into sync quite easily. I got up with him, adjusting to an earlier schedule without difficulty. Tristan even set his alarm thirty minutes before his previous routine to allow for morning sex, which I was not complaining about. In fact, for the week and a half it took Claire to move in, we had sex three times a day on most days. I think it was a challenge to see where we could do it, and how many times, before our freedom became limited. We're talking the kitchen counter, the dining room table, in the shower of course, up against the front door, over the back of our new sofa, on our new recliner, on top of the washer during the spin cycle—which actually made me nauseated—and on the stairs. I'd thought that would be uncomfortable, but Tristan insisted we try a variation of the reverse cowgirl, and I actually enjoyed it. And we also had sex on our new carpet.

We had had an enormous amount of sex in the two weeks I'd lived there, and since we'd only just been married, Tristan compared it to being on a honeymoon. I had no problem with him fucking me however and wherever he wanted. Since those first tentative times after we'd been married, I had learned how to relax and take him in. In fact, I craved it.

WE DECIDED to throw a dinner party for our one-month wedding anniversary coming up on Sunday, November 15. It was up to me to call or e-mail the last minute invites to our friends. I'd worked a long shift on Wednesday so I could take off Thursday, Friday, and Saturday to put another coat of paint on the hallway upstairs and finish the living room. I also wanted to be there when Claire got off the bus, and to finish up the work I'd been doing on Tristan's accounts. I had too many things going on at once, but I worked more efficiently when I overextended myself.

Tristan's records were atrocious. I had no idea how he'd escaped an audit by the IRS, but at least I was certain he was safe now. If the IRS did show up, his bank records and receipts were organized and easy to follow.

I was in the middle of altering his most recent checkbook on Friday afternoon when he came in the door. I glanced up. "Hey. It's not lunch yet. What are you doing here?"

"I wanted to see if you were done with the checkbook. I need to pay a guy, and I never write a check without looking at my balance." He strolled up to our dining room table, the place everyone keeps their financial statements, and peered over my shoulder at my piles. We'd made great progress cleaning out the clutter and unnecessary relics, but cleaning had also gotten in the way of finishing his finances.

I pushed an eyebrow up and quirked my lips. "Really? Your checkbook isn't accurate. I understand why you've never bounced a check, but I cannot for the life of me understand why you have to check the balance. You have plenty of money." In fact, I had unexpectedly married a rich man.

"It's a habit. So which one is it? I see six in front of you."

"They're the only ones I could find. Your issues go back further than six years, but I can't balance books I don't have. I started halfway through 2008 and went from there, assuming the bank statements are correct." I'd never had an incorrect statement, but that didn't mean everyone was as lucky.

"Then where's the one I'm using now?"

I picked it up and handed it to him over my shoulder. I squeezed my eyes shut and waited for the exclamations.

"Grant, you erased the totals. How am I supposed to know what's in there?" His voice wasn't as hostile as I had expected.

I explained. "I told you I had to start over. I've been working through the last six years' worth of statements. I think it took me the best part of a day to get them in order after we'd opened all of them."

"When did you have time to do that? I know you cut your hours back, but I've also seen how busy you are with cleaning around here, especially after the carpet got installed."

"I took a stack to work on Wednesday. It's all bank stuff, so no one really pays attention to whose statements they are. I could always say I'm researching an account for a customer." It *had* been relatively easy to bring in envelopes to open. I wasn't doing anything with them, nor was I using the bank computer system. All I did was open some envelopes and paperclip the statements in order.

Tristan pinched the bridge of his nose. He was very quiet, but I noticed his fist was clenched and his jaw was tight. Why was he getting angry? I hadn't done anything but try to help him.

"Why did you take my personal statements to the bank? Why would you do that?" he asked quietly.

"Because I thought I'd have time at lunch to organize them. It turns out I had time at lunch *and* half of my shift. It was easy." I had been very pleased with myself for being so productive.

Tristan dropped his hand, so I could see his eyes burning as he looked at me. "Why did you take my personal stuff to a *public* setting?" His voice was louder than the first time.

I gulped. "Because I was trying to be efficient. I got a lot done."

Tristan turned around and covered his face with one hand. I got the impression he was regrouping. For some reason, taking his papers to work upset him; while I wasn't sure why, I knew the best thing to do was apologize. This wasn't the same as driving to Mel's that night, but I wanted to avoid a fight with him at all costs. I rose from my chair and warily placed my hand on his back.

When I spoke, I made sure my voice sounded contrite and nowhere near smug. "Tristan, I'm sorry. I should have asked before taking your private statements to work. I didn't realize it would make you angry." I moved my hand in small, soothing circles on his back. "I won't do it again."

Tristan rubbed his face and didn't respond right away. Perhaps he was thinking over his reaction. When he finally looked at me, his expression was tight but not as hot. He said directly, "I don't like people knowing my business. It was a challenge to even allow *you* to look over my stuff." He swallowed, closed his eyes again, and took a few deep breaths before resuming his explanation. "I've always been a private person, Grant. I never liked answering questions about having a daughter, being gay, who I'm dating, why I was single, running my dad's business, or…." He paused. "How much money I make. I always thought that everything in my life was my business. Getting angry with you just now, as well as the other time about your friend, is all because I've never had to share my responsibilities, my decisions, or my time with anyone. It's all been part of a routine I've done for years. You came along, and I guess I'm still adjusting. I'm still learning to trust you." As he spoke, the tension softened into regret. His expression turned downcast as he waited for my response.

I took another step closer, resting my other hand on his chest. I didn't smile at him, because I thought it wasn't a "smiling" moment. He could misconstrue my intent. Instead I looked into his eyes and hoped he'd discover openness, honesty, and devotion. I said, "I think we're both learning those things." Our eyes remained locked, yet danced in the way eyes do when trying to figure out which eye to focus on, because you could never stare at both eyes simultaneously. I always seemed to look at one and then the other.

Tristan reached up and cupped my neck before kissing me. One lingering press of lips that told me he appreciated how open I was in admitting we were works in progress. He lifted the corner of his mouth and asked, "So you've straightened most of my clusterfuck?"

I snorted—he did seem to like that phrase—and stepped back to the table to answer. "Yeah, I guess so. Your bookkeeping leaves much to be desired, but I think you did what you did to save money. Right?"

"Yeah."

I picked up one bank statement and pointed to a figure. "These transfers are made once a month to this account, but I can't seem to find statements for that account number."

"It's a savings account."

"So you've transferred one thousand dollars a month into this account for six years? That's gotta be a lot of money by now, unless you spent it." I could do math in my head, so I knew he'd transferred at least $72,000 in those six years.

Tristan took the statement from my hand and looked it over. "Is this my current balance?"

I glanced at the statement date. "Yes, in 2011."

"Oh. Then what is it now?" He set the paper back on the table and looked at the scattered piles.

"I'm still working on that," I explained. "But if the most current statement from September 2015 is close, then you have about $45,000 in your business checking account. In my opinion, that's way too much. With that kind of cash, you should have it in a savings account, a money market account, or invest some of it. Why keep it lying around in your checking account?"

"That much, eh? I'm surprised."

"I guess so. When I started, I thought you merely rounded up to the nearest dollar when you subtracted, but you round up to the nearest ten. Every deduction is subtracted for more than the amount. At first I thought you couldn't do basic math. But then I found your payroll account, and it's accurate to the penny, which means you do keep at least one account correct."

"Of course I do. I have monthly transfers set up to that account too, but I change the amount whenever I give out raises. I basically know what I have coming in and going out."

"After the time I've spent on this project, I have a good idea what you have too. You have a lot, Tristan. If the thousand-dollar transfers are some small indication, then you have at least $72,000 sitting in a bank somewhere." I wished I had that much dough. I barely had $5,000 to my name. It was sickening how fast money spent after the government took their share. I had wanted to put money away and save for a house, but the more I worked the more I seemed to spend my cash on dinners out, vacation trips to other countries, and clothes for work. I wanted what Tristan had. I sighed. "That's insane." I looked over the stacks as if they were lost dreams of mine that were just out of reach. I'd never have what he had. Tristan took my hand, and I gave him an inquiring look. "What?"

"*We*, Grant, *we* have a lot of money, but it isn't $72,000."

"Huh?"

"I transfer money into a savings account, and then half of it gets split between a retirement account, investments, and bonds. Part of the reason I got angry when you said you took my statements to work is because I don't want the general public knowing what I do with my money. Allowing you to look at my statements was a stretch for me. I'm rather controlling, if you haven't noticed. That's why Wes doesn't pay the bills, and I do."

"I can understand that." I really could. A person's finances should be private.

"What I'm saying, Grant, is that I'm *trying* to let you in. I *want* to let you in. I've already asked my lawyer to rewrite my will to include you as my primary beneficiary. I've started changing my investments to include you, and all I need for the bank stuff is your signature for bank records."

I was blown away. "Really? You're serious?"

"Yes, I am." He cupped my shoulder and squeezed it. "I told you, I love you. Getting angry comes naturally, and I've even taken anger management classes for it. But I promise, I want you to be involved in my life, even on the financial level. I'm learning to let go and allow you to do things your way. Erasing my totals caught me off guard, and I got angry, but not *at* you. I was angry that I couldn't see my balance when I wanted to. I've always gotten what I wanted, when I wanted it. With you, I'm learning to be flexible, although my learning curve is more like a gradual incline."

I snorted and rolled my eyes at his math analogy. "You're so silly."

He winked and kissed me. "I'll just write the check and not worry about it." Tristan walked over to the door and paused before leaving. "Remind me when I get back to show you my ledger with all my accounts and passwords. I think I need to hire you as my accountant."

"Okay." I had an accounting degree, but I'd never considered using it in my job when my position at the bank had never utilized it.

He closed the door and then opened it to add, "One more thing. I started working for my dad as soon as I got out of the Navy. He didn't die until four years after that, and while he was alive, he taught me how to pay the bills and told me to save my money. So… I haven't been transferring a thousand dollars every month for six years—it's been ten." He winked again and closed the door.

Tristan had been saving money and investing it for ten years? I cupped my forehead as a wave of dizziness hit me. I turned and looked around his outdated house with laminate countertops and wallpaper borders. Tristan had the money to turn this place into whatever I wanted. He trusted me with his finances and had called me an equal partner in this marriage.

No, I decided for good, *we're not selling this house. I'm going to spend some money, get new countertops, and hire someone to remodel the bathroom so I can have one of those huge tiled walk-in showers I've always dreamed about.* He could afford it!

I knew Tristan wanted to stay here indefinitely. The house was next to his auto shop and had been in his family for years. I couldn't make him sell it. I only wanted a nice, clean, and organized house to live in, and this one was halfway there. As soon as Claire got off the bus, we were going to visit The Home Depot and pick out new countertops and sink fixtures. My new life was going to be perfect!

"Do I look okay?" I asked nervously, looking over my appearance in the full-length mirror I'd had Tristan attach to the back of the bedroom door.

Not only was this party for our one-month anniversary, but it was also a housewarming for all the redecorating I'd done. I'd cleaned and painted the whole damn house. It looked great, but I was exhausted. I still needed to screw the plate covers back over the outlets in several rooms, and the countertops wouldn't be replaced for another two weeks, but the house looked great! Claire had helped tidy things up on Saturday, but Tristan had reminded me none of it would have happened without my initiative.

"You look amazing," Tristan answered, coming up behind me. He rubbed my arms up and down soothingly as he gazed at me in the mirror, but I was still too nervous.

"Are you sure? I know you bought me those T-shirts to help me loosen up, and I feel guilty I've only worn the Journey one. Maybe I should change." I pulled away from him, but Tristan yanked me back in front of the mirror before I had taken two steps.

"Don't," he warned. "I like this striped shirt. You wore it on our wedding day, and it reminds me of the way you looked when I said 'I do.' I even bought this to go with it."

I turned around, and Tristan handed me a box. Inside was a boutonniere with a blue ribbon that matched the stripes in my shirt. "Oh, Tristan!" I lifted it out and set the box on the bed.

"You didn't have flowers on our wedding day, but I know you like them. I thought a white rose would look nice for today, and I'll try to remember flowers on every anniversary."

I flung my arms around his neck and bear-hugged him. "Thank you, thank you."

He caressed my cheek when I'd stepped back. "Anything for my princess." He winked.

I lifted my eyebrow. "Really? You're going to call me 'princess' now?"

Tristan kissed me sweetly. "Yes, because a princess is someone to be cherished, and cared for, and protected. I planned to do all those things after watching you nearly swoon when I placed this ring on your finger." He lifted my hand and kissed my knuckles right next to my diamond ring.

I couldn't refute it. I'd had plenty of princess moments, and picking out this ring didn't exactly build up my masculinity.

Tristan took the boutonniere from my fingers and pinned it to my shirt. He turned me around to face the mirror one more time. "Wear this shirt, and stop worrying about everything. The party will be fun. You've made enough food for an army, and Claire decorated every inch of everything we own. Whoever shows up will be blown away."

Tristan had suggested we make it an "open house" event, since our invitations had gone out only a couple of days prior. It made sense, but that meant I needed to plan for a huge crowd just in case. I'd made cupcakes, of course, and six different appetizers. Claire had helped me wrap bacon around scallops the day before. Even her friend Danny, whom I'd come to adore the first time he visited my house, had helped prepare hors d'oeuvres in bite-sized baking molds.

"You think so?" I asked, shifting my eyes to meet his in the mirror. I love how he looked at me. His eyes always held so much affection.

Tristan nodded and then bent forward to kiss my ear and neck, his hands sliding over my hips. "And after everyone is gone," he whispered all sultry-like, "I'll bring you back in here, undress you, and make all the tension from the night disappear as I slide my throbbing cock deep inside your ass." He ran his tongue up the shell of my ear and tugged my ass back into his groin. "How does that sound?"

I closed my eyes and swallowed, leaning back against his hard chest. Claire had been in the house for five days, and in that time Tristan and I had been very careful how we'd spoken to one another. The sexual innuendo had ceased because I wasn't good at veiling it, I blushed way too easily, and

I couldn't control my reactions. Tristan had also been true to his promise of not making love when she was in the house. We'd only had sex after she'd gotten on the bus or before she'd gotten home. For him to do this now, with Claire in the living room, and a horde of hungry guests arriving any minute, should have made me angry or frustrated. It should have, but this proved just how much I'd changed in the past few weeks. Tristan was talking dirty to me, my body reacted instantly, and I was powerless to pull away.

I licked my lips and whispered, "Would you take me from behind?"

He chuckled low in the back of his throat and reached both hands around to the front of my trousers, first groping me and then undoing my belt. "Would you like that?"

His husky tone spurred me on. "Yes," I answered breathily, my eyes remaining shut. "Would you lick my asshole first?"

Tristan undid my pants and slipped his hand inside my boxers. He took ahold of my cock and stroked it as he spoke quietly in my ear. "Only if you begged me to." I felt the cool air hit my skin as he pushed my clothing out of the way. I was glad I had locked the bedroom door. He fondled my balls with one hand and slid my foreskin forward, covering my tip instead of sliding it back.

Tristan was playing with me.

I admitted, "I would beg, Tristan." He suckled on my earlobe, and my knees nearly buckled. I reached back, over my shoulders, and looped my arms around his neck to be sure that wouldn't happen. I whimpered. "I'd plead for you to lick me. I'd offer to do anything as long as you used your tongue on my asshole." His stroking was slow and firm on the base of my cock, and I ached with need. I pushed my ass back against his crotch and wiggled it teasingly. Tristan groaned. He moved his fingers to the tip again, tugging on my foreskin and dipping his forefinger inside the folds. He circled that teasing finger around my throbbing head, and I squeezed the back of his neck as I started panting, the tingles mounting in my groin. "Mmm, Tristan," I rasped.

He chuckled. "Would you let me use nipple clamps on you?" he asked, nibbling on my neck.

My mind swirled. *Nipple clamps?* They sounded painful. What was the purpose? I stuttered, "I-I d-don't know. Would they h-hurt?"

"A little," he said. "But sometimes a great pleasure can be derived from a little pain." Tristan changed his tactics. Instead of stroking and using the natural movement of my foreskin to run his palm up and down, he gently pinched the tip of my skin and tugged on it. Tiny tugs, yet enough to stimulate the head of my cock because the foreskin hugged me all the way around my ridge, creating friction with each movement. He was using my own body to stimulate me.

I really had come to appreciate how I'd been born, no matter how many times I'd been teased for it in the past. Tristan made me feel so good about my body—foreskin and all. His thumb rubbed over my slit, teasing me one more time, and then he took my foreskin between his thumb and forefinger and pulled more aggressively.

"T-Tristan... I'm...." I tried holding my breath. I knew Claire wasn't far away on the other side of the door. I was going to shoot any second, and I had no idea how I was going to keep from moaning. Tristan was right about that too; I liked verbalizing my pleasure.

However, Tristan also liked to *shock* me into silence. Sometimes he'd kiss me just as I came, so my moaning would be muted in his throat. Sometimes he would switch positions unexpectedly and make my breath hitch right as I shot. Or, like now, he covered my mouth with his large hand and shushed me. "Shhh, just let it happen. Come in my hand. I won't let your spunk get on your nice pants."

Without a word or a sound, I sucked in a long breath through my nose as I bit my lip and convulsed, stomach muscles tightening and spurts of semen emptying onto Tristan's hand.

"Hey, Dad?" Claire called from the other side of the door, causing me to jump in his arms. "Dad? I think a truck pulled into the driveway." She knocked, yet my brain was so completely fogged by Tristan's unexpected handjob I couldn't even react. He had completely ruined me with those tiny little movements.

He called back, "I'll be right there, sweetness." He whispered in my ear, "Don't move." He released my mouth and carefully turned me around. He went down on his knees and licked me thoroughly before tucking me back into my pants. I helped retuck my shirt since only one of his hands was clean and dry. Tristan stood and smirked at me. "Sorry about that. I know how you feel about sex in the house when Claire's here, but I couldn't help myself. I really like this shirt."

I swallowed and sighed. I could hardly regain my breath, but I had just enough strength to retort, "No sex while Claire's home is *your* rule."

Tristan broke out in a full-on belly laugh. "Oh how I love you, princess." He winked, and I giggled.

"Dad?" Claire called again. "Are you coming out, or are you doing what you said you'd never do and I shouldn't ask you about?"

His expression changed quickly. He asked me, "Do I look okay? I don't have cum on my face, do I?"

I snorted. "No."

He opened the door immediately and addressed his daughter, holding his messy hand out of her view. "No, Claire. Grant was nervous about our first party, and I was calming his nerves. How do you like his flower?"

"It's called a boutonniere, Dad. It looks really nice. Did *you* pick it out?"

"He did," I said.

"I'm impressed. It matches Grant's shirt perfectly. Anyway," Claire said, pointing behind her, "Kirsty and Danny are here. And a girl named Jessica. I just wanted to know if you needed me to do anything to help, or if I can play that dance game you bought for me with my friends?"

I told her, "Go talk with your friends. I'll grab the game from the closet and set it up. I need to talk to Tristan for one more second, okay?"

"Okay," she answered politely, closing the bedroom door before she left us.

Tristan gave me an inquisitive look. I took ahold of Tristan's arm and brought his gooey hand back around from behind his back. "What are you...?" he started to ask.

I swirled my index finger in the spunk and scooped up a generous glob. I gazed into his eyes as I dipped that same finger into my mouth and sucked the juices off. Tristan groaned as his eyes turned fierce. "You enjoy playing with fire, don't you?"

I giggled wickedly. "Yes, I think I do." I bounced over to the door and opened it, turning back to grin at him. "Can you make sure there's a fresh hand towel in our bathroom in case anyone uses it?"

He chuckled. "You're evil. And yes I will."

"Thank you," I said, smiling happily. I left him to get cleaned up and met Jessica in the living room. I greeted her with a big hug. This open house party was going to be amazing.

SOMETIME LATER, I heard another knock on the door as I opened the oven. "Tristan, can you answer the door? I'm warming another batch of cheese puffs and spinach bites." I placed the tray in the oven and shut it. I sniffed my fingers and detected cheddar cheese and garlic.

"Sure, I'll get it, but why do you do that?" Tristan asked, as he headed slowly toward the door.

"Do what?"

"Smell your fingers. I've noticed you do it all the time, especially when you cook."

Claire added, "And when you use the orange ginger soap in Dad's bathroom."

I shrugged. "I have a thing for smells, what can I say? We all have vices, right, Tristan?"

He chuckled and then reached for the doorknob. I knew he knew exactly what I meant. He hadn't gotten the full explanation of why I liked soap scents so much, but I wasn't sure my reasons still held. I wasn't the same person he'd met in September.

Danny strolled into the kitchen. "Do you have any more lemons? Kirsty said you're all out, and she wanted one for her iced tea."

"Oh, yeah, let me cut up more." I went to the fridge and took out two more lemons. "I didn't think we'd go through so many lemon wedges."

Danny leaned on the other side of the breakfast bar as watched me. "Yeah, the girls thought it was fancy to put the lemon wedges in their drinks, so you ran out pretty fast."

"Hey, Grant," Tristan called from the open doorway. "I think you need to answer this."

I glanced over in midslice. "Really?"

"Yeah," he said, giving me a wink and a tilt of his head.

I exhaled and handed the knife to Danny. "Can you finish this for me?"

"Sure."

Danny came around to my side of the counter, and I went to see what was so pressing at the door that Tristan needed *me* to answer it. He stepped aside, and I pulled the door wide. The person standing on the other side of the threshold was... "Mel?"

He grinned and gestured to the girl at his left. "Grant, this is Cindy. Cindy, this is my best friend, Grant."

I could not have been happier in my life about throwing a party.

Chapter Seventeen

Psychos, Rednecks, And My
Not So Traditional Happy Ending

THE PARTY went on for a few hours. Tristan's mom and brother stopped by and raved about how wonderful the place looked. His mother told me how happy she was that Tristan had finally found the right person to spend his life with and wanted to make sure I knew she considered me family. I could have cried.

My mom stopped by and really got along well with Tristan's mom. She invited her to play mah-jongg one Sunday and asked if she'd like to go to lunch. I hadn't seen my mother so congenial in a long while. It made me feel good. All of our friends seemed happy and contented, talking, eating, and laughing.

Claire and her friends put on her favorite dance video game, and to my surprise, Wes, Will, and Jessica joined in. They took turns, as the living room floor only had so much room for people to line up and mimic the dance moves on the TV screen, but it was fun for everyone to watch.

I was sad when the guests started to leave.

"I had so much fun, Grant," Jessica said, standing by the door getting ready to leave. "You'll have to throw another party soon."

"I agree," Wes said, coming up behind Jessica. "I had a great time." He grinned at Jessica, and she blushed.

"Wait," I said, narrowing my eyes as their subtle nervousness gave away more than they realized. "Are you…? Is this…?"

Jessica blushed again and looked down.

"No way!" I said.

Wes smirked. "I told you I had a great time. Now if you don't mind, I'd like to walk this lovely lady to her car." He placed his hands on her arms, and she giggled.

I opened the door for them, and we all jumped when we found Teresa standing on the other side of the door, her arm held tightly in the grasp of a scuzzy-looking man I'd never seen before.

"I need to see Tristan," the man declared.

"Let me go, you dirty old man," Teresa hissed as she struggled against his grip.

"Shut up, woman," he said with a hard jerk. I could see he had one of her arms twisted around behind her back and the other firmly held at her elbow. She was furious, but for reasons unknown, she remained relatively quiet.

"Tristan," I called.

Tristan appeared by my side right away. "Bob! What's going on?"

"You know this guy?" I asked.

Wes answered, "Bob Crane's been a customer back long before I started working for Tristan."

"Oh."

Bob answered, "I was driving past your house when I saw this woman pouring something on your truck. I pulled over and managed to grab her before she ran away. I didn't see her smash the taillights, but there's a crowbar on the ground by the driver's side. I'm sure she done it. I would have called the cops, but she's a feisty bitch."

Teresa thrashed but couldn't pull out of his grip.

A crowbar?

"My truck's around back, Bob." Tristan glanced out the door over their heads and then called to the guests in the living room, who had turned the music off and were gathering around us near the door. "Who drives a 2014 blue Dodge Dakota?"

"That's my dad's truck," Danny said, stepping forward. "What happened to it?" His voice wavered, and his face paled.

The unkempt man who held Teresa's arms answered, "This woman poured a two-liter Coca-Cola all over the hood and smashed the taillights."

"What?" Danny cried.

"Mom!" Claire exclaimed. "I can't believe you would do that to Danny's truck. His dad trusted him with it this weekend for the first time since he got his license."

"I didn't know it was his," Teresa snarled. "I thought it was Tristan's."

"Oh my God," Tristan groaned, clutching his forehead and stepping back from the door.

Wes commented, "His is a 2009. The headlights are different."

I was sure there were other differences if Danny's dad's truck was so much newer, but the real problem was that Tristan could no longer keep Teresa's bizarre criminal activities from Claire. We were all here. We were all witnesses.

Claire stepped closer to her mother. Tristan tried to stop her, but she pulled out of his grasp. "Why would you do that, Mom?" Her voice was calm, much too calm for the situation. "Why would you pour Coke on Dad's truck? That would ruin the paint."

I heard Danny crying and noticed Kirsty attempting to console him with a hug. I felt awful for him.

"He ruined my life," she said, her voice cracking as if she might cry at any moment. "All I ever wanted was a family, and Tristan left me. He joined the Navy and never looked back. He abandoned us. He abandoned you!"

"Teresa…." Tristan started to speak, but Claire cut him off.

"Dad never abandoned us, Mom. You pushed him away. Grandma told me how much Dad wanted to be in my life, but you wouldn't let him."

"My mother never said that!" she barked, her sadness suddenly disappearing. "Tristan was selfish. Tristan should have done what was right and married me, but instead he left. I begged him to stay." She started weeping.

"Teresa, stop. You knew I signed up right out of high school. You told me you only wanted one night. I had no idea you'd get pregnant."

"Lies!" Teresa spat, turning off the tears like throwing a switch. She pulled forward, but Bob held her firm. "You left me to raise her on my own. I had to be the one to feed and clothe her! I was the one to push her to succeed in school while you played weekend dad."

I knew Claire had heard something similar from Tristan, but she'd also heard how much he regretted leaving her with her mother for so many years. Claire would have to believe one or the other, and no amount of arguing through an open door in November would do anything to tip the balance either way. I believed Claire was smart enough to see how insane her mother's behavior was, and also smart enough to have seen her father's sincerity of late.

"Grandma didn't lie, Mom," Claire said, her voice still eerily calm and unemotional. "I talked to her last Monday when she called looking for you. I told her I was moving in with Dad. She questioned why, and then we got into an hour-long discussion of things you should have told me sooner." Claire moved her attention to Tristan and then back to her mom.

Teresa hissed through gritted teeth, "My mother is a weak woman who forgave my bastard father too many times!"

Claire leveled her eyes at her mother and continued very calmly. "Stop. Just stop. No matter what Grandpa did, it doesn't give you the right to be so cruel to Dad or hateful to anyone else—my best friend Danny included. One man's mistakes shouldn't ruin it for everyone else."

"Yes, it does!" Teresa spat.

"No, it doesn't," Claire countered. "I didn't want to believe Grandma. But now, especially after living with Dad for a few days, I can see how much he loves me. So if Dad says he wanted to see me when I was younger, I'll believe him. If he tells me sleeping with you was a mistake because he always knew he was gay, I'll believe him. And if this man says you poured Coke on that truck, I'll believe him. Because I know you lie."

"Claire, honey, it isn't true. Please believe me," she begged, changing her tone of voice yet again. She strained feebly against Bob Crane's hold. "Your father was always working. Had I known he wanted to see you, you know I would have allowed it. Please, sweetness."

"Don't call me that," Claire snarled. "You don't get to use *his* nickname for me."

"I'm sorry. Please, don't be angry."

"I'm not angry. I'm accepting. *This* is the person you really are. So get out. I never want to see you again." She turned away and pushed through the crowd of people by the door.

Tristan spoke up. "We could have worked this out, Teresa. I told you we would work this out, but you just committed a crime in front of a witness. You vandalized that truck!"

"I thought it was yours!" she yelled. She lost her meekness and flipped her switch back to raging bitch as soon as Claire walked away.

"It doesn't matter. I have to call the cops. Danny's dad has to be told about this. You can't hide anymore."

Just then, Teresa collapsed to the ground, sobbing uncontrollably. I wasn't sure it was for real, since she'd changed her tune several times during the conversation, but everyone else stepped back. Perhaps they weren't sure what she would do. Tristan grabbed the phone off the counter and called the police.

In no time at all, a county sheriff pulled into the driveway and took statements from everyone as soon as he'd put Teresa into the back of his vehicle. The whole situation dampened the party spirit, and most guests left silently. Claire, Danny, and Kirsty were huddled on the couch as Tristan shut the door after thanking Bob Crane for his citizen's arrest.

Tristan took my hand and walked me with him into the living room. We sat on the new loveseat, which sat catty-corner to the full couch. "Claire? Do you want to talk about this any more tonight?"

She lifted her head off Danny's shoulder and shook it slowly before setting it back down. She was a wreck. Her mascara was smudged and clumped all along the rims of her eyes, and her lips held a sad frown. I squeezed Tristan's hand, knowing he had to feel terrible for her.

"I spoke to your father, Danny. This wasn't your fault, and I made sure he knew his truck would get repainted. Okay?"

Danny nodded.

"Can I use your phone to call my mom?" Kirsty asked. "My phone died while I was videoing Danny dancing, using FaceTime so our friend Christina could watch. It used too much battery."

"Sure," I answered, jumping up to retrieve the mobile phone right away. These kids shouldn't have to see things like this, and yet shielding them from the realities of life would only do harm at some point. Claire needed to understand her mom was not right in the head. Better to find out like this than to be caught in the middle of something worse.

Kirsty called her mom and got picked up a short time later.

After Danny's father came to get him, it was only the three of us again, sitting in the living room in silence. After some time, Claire got off the couch and sat next to Tristan. She pressed her body into his chest and cried against it as he held her. I handed her a tissue, and after she blew her nose, she got up and sat next to me. When she hugged me with as much love as she'd hugged her father, I felt deeply honored.

TERESA WAS soon admitted into a Psychotic Disorders Unit at Sheppard Pratt Health System for a two-week evaluation, and Claire went to see a counselor. Tristan thought it best to let a professional handle the effects on Claire, since he had no idea how deep her pain and resentment went, and I wholeheartedly agreed. After Teresa was released, she packed up her stuff and moved without saying another word. Tristan hoped she'd return one day for Claire's sake, and I hoped it would not be anytime soon. Claire needed to regain stability. To be abandoned like that would leave lasting scars on her heart.

THANKSGIVING CAME and went, but with some good memories. Claire was not in a social mood, but Tristan's mother had invited my mother over so we could all celebrate together. Tristan's family was amazing! I could not think of another time where I had felt so completely loved and accepted. They truly made me feel like a part of the family. And Claire sat next to *me* at dinner.

BY DECEMBER, my life had settled into a quiet routine. I worked ten to three, three days a week for the bank, and the rest of my time was spent working for Tristan. He laughed and joked about my work schedule, because he said it resembled the bankers' hours of the 1960s. I didn't care, because it was what I wanted. He really did need help with his finances, and the more I took care of them, the more time he had to spend with me in the evenings after work. I needed my easy bankers' hours so I could be home with my family.

I helped Claire do her math homework after school, and thereby gained brownie points when she got an A on three quizzes in a row. I'd never known I could be a tutor, but the following week she brought home two other friends in need of math help. I'd never been so flattered.

Mel and Cindy had gotten engaged on Christmas Day. As I had assured Mel, his soul mate had been out there. Her name was Cindy. After the breakup, Cindy had gone home and researched what it meant to be transgender and then returned to Mel's apartment two weeks later. She had argued with him about how he hadn't given her a chance, and told him she was mainly upset from feeling cast aside. She had gone on their second date to tell him she'd broken up with her girlfriend in the hope of something deeper with him. She'd felt a connection on the first date. Once she apologized for assuming he'd been a lesbian and confessed her attraction to him, Mel had forgiven her and asked for a second chance. The day before my party, they had gone out on their fifth date.

DECEMBER 30 was my last day at the bank for a whole month. Tristan had given me a trip around the country as a Christmas gift, and we left for Boston to start our trip on New Year's Day. Claire was super stoked to spend a month with Tristan's mom. Apparently, both of them enjoyed time together, and Teresa had kept their visits to a minimum. I felt bad for them, but Claire and Mrs. Carr seemed pleased to make up for lost time while Tristan and I were gallivanting around the country. I couldn't wait to leave, and yet I knew I would miss my new family and my friends at the bank.

I came back from the vault with my stack of change to find Jessica tapping her fingers on the half wall dividing our cubicles. Something was up.

"Are you okay? You seem preoccupied." I deposited my money in my drawer and locked it up while I waited for her response. It was a Wednesday, and abnormally slow, so I hoped she would talk about whatever was bothering her because it would at least give us something to do.

"I'm... worried," she said, keeping her eyes lowered.

"Why? Did Wes do something stupid?" I asked. I reached over and straightened my pile of deposit slips. They always seemed to get askew, even without being touched.

Her eyes shot up. "You knew?"

"About you and Wes? Yes," I snorted. "Wes tells Tristan everything, and Tristan tells *me* everything. Why would you think you could date Wes and keep any of it a secret?" Ever since my party, the two of them had acted differently. It had only taken two days after our party for Wes to ask Tristan if he could ask out my close friend.

She crossed her arms on the dividing wall and rested her chin on them. "I don't know what to do. Wes asked me to go away for the weekend. Since the shop is closed, he said he made plans to visit San Diego. I've never been to San Diego, so I said something about how fun that would be, and then he asked me to go." She lifted her eyebrows, beseeching me. "Should I go?"

Bank teller, math tutor, accountant, and now relationship advisor? I couldn't understand how I'd acquired so many new hats. I sat on my stool and drummed my fingers on the counter. "Um, I guess that depends on how you feel about him?"

"I like him. He's funny, and sweet, and I don't think he's only out to get me in bed."

The way she phrased that made me think.... "So you haven't...?"

"No. He works a lot, and so do I. We've only been out a few times. He's never pressured me to do anything, and I appreciate that, but what if he gets frisky while we're away? What if he tries something and I can't just go home?"

I had never been in that kind of position. Every time I'd gone out with a guy, I had hoped for sex. Wished for it. Longed for it. I think it was due to my underlying doubt that I'd ever lose my virginity, and therefore I kind of wanted to get it over with on every single date. The rub was that I'd never even made it to first base on all those dates until I met Tristan. He'd taken it slow, but I was always sitting on idle, ready to thrust my sex drive into motion as soon as he gave the signal. With Jessica, it seemed she wanted to wait.

"You're not a virgin, are you?" I asked, keeping my voice very low. We'd gotten to the point in our friendship where I felt comfortable enough to ask such an invasive question and know she wouldn't slap me.

Her head jerked up. "No!" she fussed, making a little sound in the back of her throat. "I've had boyfriends, but this is the first one I really, really like. What if we have sex and it ruins everything?"

She had a valid point. I knew that happened from time to time. "I guess you have to just see. If it helps, I like Wes. I think he's a great guy. I don't think he'd treat you poorly."

She plopped her elbow on the half wall and rested her cheek on her hand. "Me neither. He's been the perfect gentleman on every date. It took him weeks to even kiss me."

Kiss? I could use a kiss right now. I'd only kissed Tristan twice this morning, and my lips knew it. I cleared my throat and tried to focus on my friend. "The way I see it, you just need to go for it. You have my number. You have Tristan's number. Call either of us if you have a problem. Even if we're in Montana, we'll come get you if you need us." I secretly hoped that would never happen, because I could imagine Tristan getting pissed if she actually called.

Jessica reached over the wall, and I clasped her hand. "You're a great friend, Grant. I think I will. I'll call Wes right now and tell him I'm in. San Diego, here I come!"

She walked away, and I turned to survey my station. Everything was in its place. I had pens and deposit slips. My monitor was wiped free of dust. My keyboard was also wiped clean, even between the keys. I opened my drawer and checked on my money. One roll of coins was facing different than the rest, so I flipped it. I sighed. All was in order. I could face the day!

Mrs. Snyder walked through the door and grinned at me. *Why was she always throwing attention* my *way?* Jessica had called her a cougar. It wasn't like I didn't know what that meant, but I hadn't seen any cougarish activities. She was more flirtatious than most, but I was 95 percent certain she knew I was gay. Why would an older woman flirt with a young gay man? It seemed preposterous.

My phone vibrated, and I took it out to read my text. I knew it was wrong, but Tristan had promised to only text during the day if it was important, especially since my hours were so short.

It was from my mom. *Enjoy your trip, dear. Don't forget to text me once a week so I know you're alive.*

Thanks, Mom. I will. I love you.

I love you too. Give Tristan a kiss from me. I'm off to Zumba! :)

I snickered. My mom was a funny one. *I will. TTYL*

I pocketed my phone just as Mrs. Snyder sauntered up to my window and placed her stack in front of me. She didn't even look to see if another teller was free. How bold. "Good morning, my dear boy. How are we today?"

I gave her a kind smile. I wasn't going to allow her to fluster me. "I'm well. How about yourself?" Instead of waiting until she answered to get on with her transactions, I picked up her stack and sorted it while she spoke.

"I'm—" She paused. "—frustrated." I knew her eyes were on me, but I refused to look up as I counted.

"Oh, really? Why?" Blithe tone, steady facial expression—I was not going to give away any trepidation. Why should I? I was happy, very happy. It was my last day before a month's vacation, I was going on a trip around the country with my man, my best friend was getting married next year, my stepdaughter enjoyed my company and had started calling me Dad Number Two, and now my newest close friend was dating one of my husband's best friends. I didn't see how my life could get any better.

Mrs. Snyder made a little noise. Maybe it was a sigh, maybe not, but her eyes turned downcast. "You see," she explained in a pouty tone, "I'm normally very good at getting what I want. I see something… sweet, and I take it. In September I spied something very sweet, saccharine sweet, and I tried my hardest to snatch it up, but to no avail."

I punched in the numbers and glanced over to her to let her know I was listening. "Uh-huh. That must have been frustrating. What was it you wanted?"

When she didn't answer, I stopped what I was doing and glanced at her. She licked her lips and whispered, "A fine-looking young man."

I cleared my throat. "Um, oh, really?" I stammered. "A-anyone I know?" That damn shrill voice of mine just couldn't lay low for two seconds.

She gave me the most lascivious smirk I've seen in my life. "Yes. You know him… intimately."

My skin rushed cold. Was she really doing this here? In front of everyone? I looked for Jessica, but she wasn't around. She must have gone to the bathroom right when I needed her to bail me out. Tracy had her door closed. Lucinda must have been in the vault. How could I have been left alone with this woman?

Someone coughed behind her, and we both glanced over.

"Tristan?" I hadn't even seen him walk in.

Mrs. Snyder addressed him. "Mr. Carr. How nice to see you."

"Mrs. Snyder," he greeted her back, nodding slightly. He stepped up next to her in front of my window. "I don't mean to interrupt, but I stopped by to give these to Grant." Tristan produced a bouquet of flowers from behind his back.

I gasped and covered my mouth momentarily. "Oh, Tristan! What are these for?" I reached for the bundle as Mrs. Snyder stepped aside after catching daisy petals up her nose.

"Our anniversary."

I was confused. "Anniversary? It's not the fifteenth."

"No," he said. "But one hundred and three days ago, today, I met you. Right here." His deep blue eyes sparkled as he gazed at me.

I was about to cry when Mrs. Snyder interrupted our moment. "I think that's my cue." She reached for her receipt and slipped it into her purse. She regarded Tristan with a certain air of acknowledgment. "Grant told me he got married. I had no idea it was to you." She held out her hand, and he took it. "Congratulations, Mr. Carr. You've certainly landed a very special catch."

His eye twitched. "Why, thank you. I know I'm a very lucky man."

"Indeed. Grant's a very... *sweet*... boy." She redirected her attention to me, and I nearly choked on my own saliva, remembering her previous comment. Luckily, she placed her eyes back on Tristan a second later. "I wish you nothing but happiness. Now, if you'll excuse me." She released his hand and strolled proudly to the front door.

As soon as the door shut, I let out a little squeal.

"What's wrong?" Tristan asked.

Jessica appeared next to me and explained, "That woman's been trying to get him into bed. I swear it!" She held up her hand.

Tristan shook his head. "Is this normal customer behavior?"

"Yes!" I declared. "Some customers even ask me to marry them. The nerve." I rolled my eyes and we all shared a good laugh.

When I had moved to Westminster less than four months ago, I had worried about how much my life would change. Now, I knew change was a good thing.

WADE KELLY lives and writes in conservative, small-town America on the East Coast where it's not easy to live free and open in one's beliefs. Wade writes passionately about controversial issues and strives to make a difference by making people think. Wade does not have a background in writing or philosophy, but still draws from personal experience to ponder contentious subjects on paper. There is a lot of pain in the world and people need hope. When not writing, she is thinking about writing, and more than likely scribbling ideas on sticky notes in the car while playing taxi driver for her three children. She likes snakes, can't spell, and has a tendency to make people cry.

Website: www.writerwadekelly.com
Blog: writerwadekelly.blogspot.com
Twitter: @WriterWadeKelly
E-mail: writerwadekelly@gmail.com

NAMES
CAN NEVER
HURT
ME

WADE KELLY

What if sexuality wasn't a definable thing and labels merely got in the way?

Nick Jones can't remember a time when he wasn't part of the in crowd. Everywhere he goes, he stands out as the best looking guy in the room, and women practically fall into bed with him. Then, after kissing Corey on a dare led to much more and on many occasions, Nick's "screw anything" reputation escalated, but he didn't care.

When Nick meets RC at the restaurant where he works, it throws his whole life out of whack. RC lives up to his dubbed nickname "Scruffy Dude." He seems Nick's complete opposite, but Nick can't get him out of his head.

Because of peer-pressure and his fears about defining his sexuality, Nick struggles with stepping out of his comfort zone and caring about someone different than himself. If he's lucky, somewhere between arrogance and ignorance, Nick might find out what it means to be an adult, but if he's wrong, he could lose everything.

www.dreamspinnerpress.com

MY
ROOMMATE'S
A JOCK?

Well, Crap!

Wade Kelly

The JOCK Series: Book One

It's easy to become cynical when life never goes your way.

Cole Reid has been a social recluse since he was fifteen, when he was outed by his high school baseball team. Since then, his obsessive-compulsive behavior and sarcastic nature have driven away most of the population, and everyone else hates him because he's gay. As he sees it, he's bound to repulse any prospective friends, let alone boyfriends, so why bother?

By the time Cole enters college, he's become an anal-retentive loner—but it's not a problem until his roommate graduates and the housing department assigns Ellis Montgomery to move in with Cole. Ellis is messy, gorgeous, straight, and worst of all, a jock!

During a school year filled with frat buddies, camping expeditions, and meddling parents, Cole and Ellis develop a friendship that turns Cole's glass-half-empty outlook on its head. There must be more to Ellis than a fun-loving jock—and maybe Cole's reawakening libido has rekindled his hope for more than camaraderie.

www.dreamspinnerpress.com

No!
JOCKS DON'T
DATE GUYS

Wade Kelly

The JOCK Series: Book Two

What is a sexy soccer stud supposed to do when "following family tradition" falls 180 degrees opposite his closeted ideal?

From birth, Chris Jackson has been schooled on how to land a cheerleader. After all, his father married one, and his father's father before him. Heck, even his older brother married a stereotypical cheerleader the summer before Chris went off to college. For two years, Chris dodges invasive questions about relationships by blaming his lack of female companionship on grueling practices and heavy course loads. But his lack of interest in girls should've given his family a clue. It isn't until Chris mentions meeting a boy that his father's synapses short-circuit.

Alonzo Martin is anything but a buxom blond. From his black hair, combat boots, and trench coat to his nail polish and guyliner, the mysterious introvert isn't easily persuaded to date. Alonzo's insecurities keep Chris at arm's length, but Alonzo's painful past might meet its match in the charismatic jock's winning smile and sense of humor.

When opposites attract, only cheerleaders and gummy bears can help overcome fear and family tradition.

www.dreamspinnerpress.com

Unconditional Love: Book One

A six-year downward spiral into a world of lies and deception leads to the end of one man's life when self-discovery crosses the line between being the perfect son or following his heart.

Jimmy Miller never intended to lead a double life starting the day he fell in love with Darian, but his parents' divorce, fighting in school, and constantly keeping secrets for his closeted best friend and protector, Matt, force his hand. Jimmy finds the demands too great to withstand and ends it all prematurely, leaving behind an angry best friend and a shattered lover.

Matt and Darian cling to one another in the aftermath of their loss, forging a new friendship immediately tested by the truths of their relationships with Jimmy that are hidden in the pages of Jimmy's journals. Will Matt and Darian discover what truly happened to their friend? And will this tragedy birth something beautiful between them as they learn the balance between life, family, and friendship when love is simply not enough?

www.dreamspinnerpress.com

Unconditional Love: Book Two

Matt Dixon, a young firefighter, is the golden child of his family, and he never dreamed that coming out would challenge more than the way his church sees him.

For years, Matt has led a double life hoping to avoid ridicule. When a self-righteous pastor's statements provoke him to defend his recently deceased best friend's honor and subsequently out himself, he suffers the brutal aftermath of his revelation. Everyone in his life, including his family and his new lover, Darian, must deal with the ramifications as Matt struggles to come to terms with guilt, shame, and his very belief in God.

Darian Weston lost his fiancé when Jamie took his life, and his feelings for Matt added guilt to his burden of grief. Confused and lonely, Darian clings to Matt despite his inner strife. But small-town realities keep intruding, and if Matt and Darian hope to make a life together, they must first take a stand for what they believe in, even if they fear the cost.

www.dreamspinnerpress.com

www.ingramcontent.com/pod-product-compliance
Lightning Source LLC
Chambersburg PA
CBHW051531260626
47170CB00003B/876